MACHINE ROW

C. J. YEE

BOOK TWO IN THE  MERIDIAN SERIES

Machine Row

Copyright © 2025 C. J. Yee

This is a work of fiction. Names, characters, institutions, places, and events are a product of the author's imagination, or are used fictitiously. Any resemblance to actual persons, living or deceased, organizations, events, or locales is entirely coincidental.

Artwork and Maps by C. J. Yee

Published in the United States of America.

First Edition

Paperback ISBN: 979-8-9937155-1-3
Hardcover ISBN: 979-8-9937155-2-0

For Courtney, and for my grandfathers.

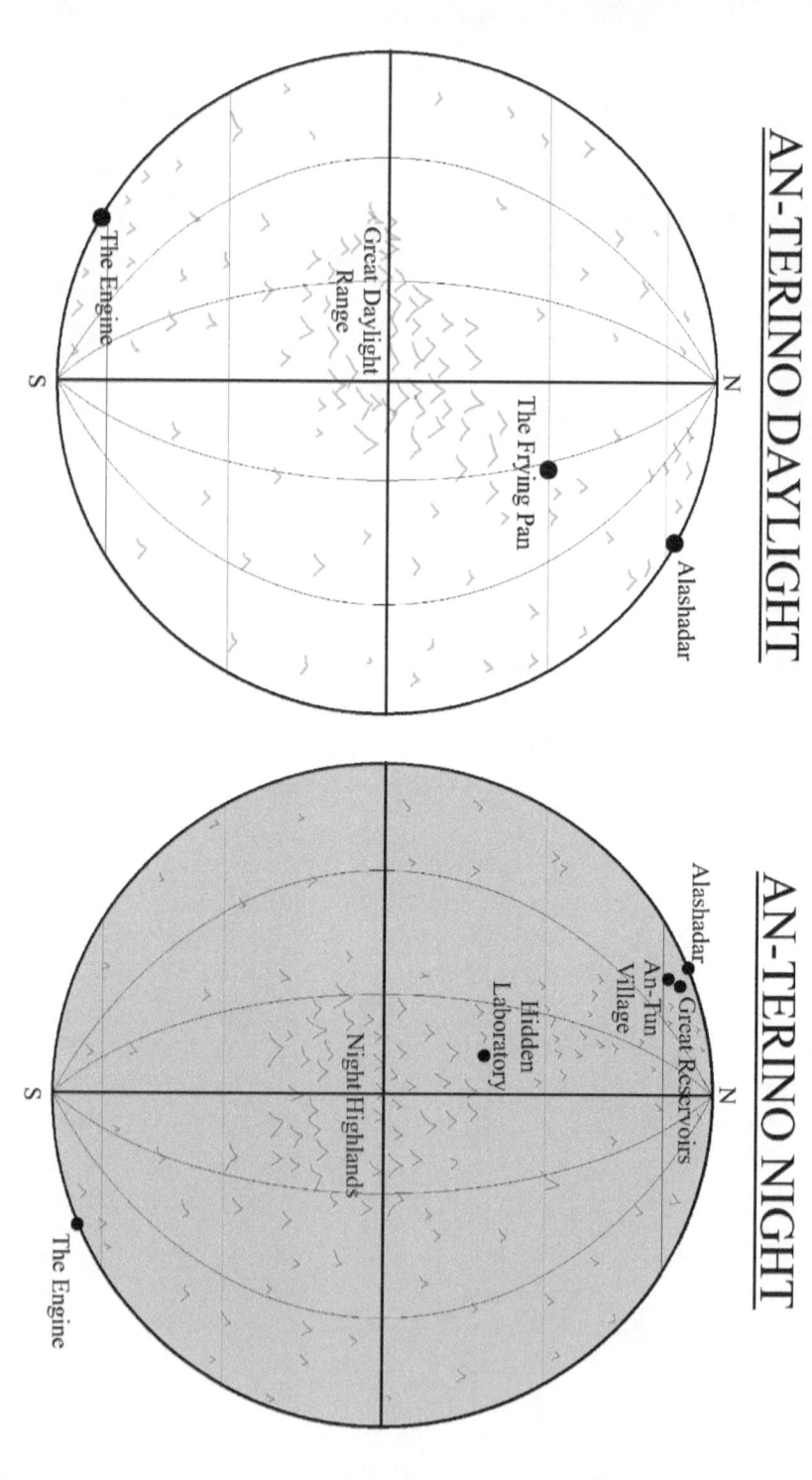

AN-TERINO DAYLIGHT

The Engine

Great Daylight Range

The Frying Pan

Alashadar

S

N

AN-TERINO NIGHT

Alashadar
Great Reservoirs
An-Tun Village
Hidden Laboratory

Night Highlands

The Engine

S

N

10 km

NewCen

To the Rifts

To the ROTO fields

Machine Row
Station

Niko's
Friends

Machine Row

The Dockyards

Niko's
Quarters

The Salvage
Yards

An-Mara Quarter

ALASHADAR

Oldcity

Middletown

The Estates

TABLE OF CONTENTS

THE EVENTS OF *BOOK ONE: MERIDIAN*

Five years ago, Niko Ryen and her friends were living their lives in peace on the Green Coast, an idyllic small town on the planet of Arhanda. It was all upended with the arrival of Ajane Solase and the revelation of Niko's attunement to psychic potential. A subsequent flight from the Green Coast brought them into the clutches of the An-Mara, who fixated on Niko's brother Riesen, claiming him to be the 'Child of the Nel-Mara'.

After being reunited with some of their hometown friends in Amalkyne, the group was once again split apart — Riesen sent to the tropical paradise of Sol City, while Niko and the others were whisked away to the northern shores of Nevaly. A group of Niko's friends was sent on a doomed mission to a bridge, while the rest of her company was attacked at Nevaly by Var Ashal-Han and the An-Mara.

After the fog of war lifted, her friends miraculously returned battered and broken, only to learn they had to leave Arhanda for good, as it was destroyed by the An-Mara with the use of the Engines.

Niko, shattered by the losses of her family and close friends — as well as her mentor Ajane — is now on her way to the desolate world of An-Terino…

PROLOGUE

Leviathan

THE endless ocean that engulfed the waterworld of Mareia spread across the horizon like a blanket. The blue-grey sky would normally be reflected off the water in such empyreal fashion, but today it was ruffled with massive, bubbling lumps.

Waves.

Ugly things, if you asked Logan. It was difficult to become accustomed to such anomalies on what used to be an exceedingly pristine surface. Much different than the image that was imprinted onto her mind from when she was younger.

Also different today: the heat was lamentably tolerable. In years past, it would have been dreadfully hot outside the luxurious confines of the resorts, but today, Logan almost *wished* for that heat. She had been looking for an excuse to hurry things along, and any excuse would do, really. But as it stood, she hadn't been so lucky; she would be out here for the entire duration of the power-up process, and that would take hours.

Unfortunate.

Sighing, she walked back along the deck a hundred meters above the waterline, her traditional royal gown getting tangled in her steps. She always hated this attire. Why couldn't she wear what the

1

men wore?! Their outfits, even the ceremonial ones, were *much* more comfortable and *much* more practical.

So unfair, she thought to herself. Her foul mood today did her no favors. She just wanted to be done with this whole thing.

"Your Highness?"

Logan hated that title, too.

"Yes, yes," she replied, waving her hand imperiously. She'd only been half-listening. "Tell them we will be inside at the commencement of the second stage."

"Very well," Alin replied. Bowing, the Valanse excused herself, then hurried off down the stairs to the narrow landing pad below.

"Oh, and Alin!" Logan called after her. "Tell my sister that she can join me at the front when she arrives."

Alin nodded, then continued down to relay Logan's requests.

The better part of two hours later, Logan still waited. She had been killing time staring up the sides of the largest manmade structure ever built by the Meridians, excluding the Harvesters, of course, which were technically much, much larger.

Leviathan, as it was called, spanned far into the distance in both directions, stretching for thousands of kilometers north to south. In the vertical direction, its gentle slope rose to such heights that not even half of the thing was visible before it disappeared into the rainclouds.

Rainclouds. Another oddity.

It seemed strange that there should even be any clouds *at all* on Mareia. When Logan was young, she had visited this place several times and had always appreciated it for its crystal-clear skies and mirror-like waters.

Serenity.

That was the word that had always come to mind when visiting this wondrous planet. Her father had even let her name one of the floating leisure palaces '*Serenity*' when she was young. He promised that one day, she would have the opportunity to govern this entire place and come here whenever she wished.

Of course, those promises fell flat three years ago, when he had allowed Shatter Industries to begin construction on Leviathan, the project designed to solve the Empire's water crisis. Within the year, the monstrosity was completed. Logan protested to her father for the entire year, but he would hear none of it. He only gave her lecture after lecture on the importance of compromise, something he claimed was the glue that held the Empire together.

She was never convinced, though. Compromise was such a convenient ideal in principle, but in reality, most issues were far more complex. Logan was beginning to learn that the more she attempted compromise, the more she became hated by both sides. Sometimes it seemed much easier to stick to one side. That way, she'd only be hated by half...

She had argued this point to her father, but he would just retort that 'easiest' and 'correct' were two different things entirely.

Maybe, but whatever.

To appease her father — and the rest of the Empire, for that matter — adding a massive generator to Leviathan was her attempt at compromise. It was so rudimentary, so simple and almost primitive, but it would still generate a fair amount more energy than zero, which was its current output. Hopefully enough to present a strong case against the implementation of mining practices on Trevi Nali.

Merely thinking of that possibility set her blood boiling.

Mining...!? On Trevi Nali...!? The thought was preposterous.

The fact that there even *was* a debate about it was absurd. That world was *sacred* — untouched from such destructive practices for tens of thousands of years. It was the crown jewel of the Meridian Empire, the most beautiful world in all of the sector, and suddenly people wanted to start tearing the place apart?! The foolishness of it was inconceivable. Unimaginable. *Laughable.* Yet the percentage of the population that favored the desecration was terrifyingly significant.

If she was able to get this project up and running, however, it should deliver enough energy to satisfy the increased demand the Empire faced. She didn't care what she had to do; she would *not* be letting Shatter turn Trevi Nali into a quarry like they had on Samarind or Ossion.

The plan was simple: capture all the water running down the giant slope and use gravity to turn giant turbines that generate an electric current. She was almost embarrassed for drafting up a plan so basic, so ancient — she couldn't believe it *wasn't* included in the original plans. She wasn't even a blasted engineer! How did *they* not think of it when she did?!

Logan huffed in irritation.

Sometimes, she felt like she had to do everything. Not only did she design projects such as this on occasion, but she also had to play at politics, often providing her father counsel on matters ranging from extrasolar policy to cultural tension to intragovernmental dealings. He was supposed to be the damned *Emperor* of the Meridian Empire, and she was only a mere princess, the youngest heir and third in line behind her two sisters. She would never rule, so why was *she* the one constantly picking up the slack of the entire Empire? It was ridiculous.

Still, she would happily do her part when she felt strongly enough about an issue, and preserving the pristine natural beauty of her homeworld was one such issue. Hence, the *compromise* she was spearheading.

A slight breeze tickled her skin as a wisp of thin, brown hair fluttered across her face. She subconsciously brushed it away and looked to the sky, disenchanted. Ever since they built the gargantuan mountain, clouds often blurred the atmosphere, diminishing the once ethereal panoramas. Hazy skies were common around the globe, and towering waves now roiled from one side of the planet to the other. Storms that formed in the summer regions dragged across the ocean with infernal fury, and every time one of those hurricanes popped up, the Engines had to be adjusted to help dissipate the thing.

A colossal waste of energy, if you asked Logan. This was all the doing of Shatter — the same group that was pushing for mining rights on Trevi Nali — so she shouldn't have been too surprised at the ignorance of it all.

To be fair, there was no way they could've known what the side effects of Leviathan's construction would be. What they attempted had never been done, at least not since the time of the Nel-Mara. There were so many micro-contingencies that couldn't have been calculated by the models. Not their models, at least. What they really needed were Nel-Mara computing machines, but alas, those no longer existed. They, along with most other Nel-Mara technologies, were only memories that would probably never return.

If only Kezane were still here... she pined to herself, a lump catching in the back of her throat.

He had been very important to her, almost like an older brother — too young to be a father figure, but too old to be an academy mate. Although he was an insanely gifted Valanse commander, he was not above spending time training her and nurturing her intellect when she was young. Maybe it was the perk of being best friends with his youngest sister.

If he were here today, he would surely smack some reason into those Shatter idiots for charging ahead with Leviathan without proper consultation. His genius was undeniable, but his strongest quality was his undaunted candor.

Perhaps that was the reason they got rid of him...

No one would ever admit as much, but she was convinced that his disappearance had something to do with the feud he was having with Silvane.

She had *never* trusted that man, and couldn't understand why everyone revered his opinion so much. He always struck her as weaselly and conniving, and it disgusted her that her father acquiesced to him so often. It didn't matter how high of a Valanse position that man held, or how charismatic he was — her father was the *Emperor*, and he should act like it.

The amount of power Silvane wielded did not sit well with Logan, and worse, when she disclosed her reservations about him to her confidants, they only told her it was because she was jealous that he showered *Morgan* with all his attention and not *her*.

Hah! Morgan...

The gall of those people!

As if she would *ever* be jealous of Morgan — it was more like the other way around. If her sister had spent more time learning the ways of governance and less time gallivanting around in the limelight, then their father might trust her for counsel more often than he did.

Ugh...! Logan's frustration toward her sister nearly boiled to the surface.

She had to admit, she never got along with Morgan as well as she would have liked. Morgan was nice when it suited Morgan, but she was such a mean girl otherwise. Just the fact that she refused to come today was a slap in the face, a passive aggressive attempt to tell Logan that she didn't matter.

At least Ingan was here today, though...

Looking down from her perch, Logan spotted her eldest sister making her way up the sides of Leviathan, flanked by an entourage of Valanses, Public Forum moguls, and an assemblage of very conspicuous Imperial Aegides.

Ingan was the oldest of the three sisters, now on her twenty-fifth year around Sol One, and heir apparent to the Meridian Empire. Although tall and elegant like Morgan, Ingan differed from the younger sisters in that she was much more sturdily built. She wore her blonde hair short, and her regal green eyes sat behind a shrewd face typical of a leader, a spitting image of their father. Maybe it was the wider age gap between them, but Logan got along *much* better with Ingan than she did with Morgan.

"Thank you for having us, sister," Ingan greeted, stepping forward with an open expression after climbing the long row of stairs. The two Ostreodase heirs embraced properly with their forearms, adhering to public decorum. "I look forward to this demonstration!"

"Thank you for coming," Logan replied, turning her voice low so only Ingan could hear. "But seriously, I just want this to be over so I can get out of this place."

Ingan laughed, but the sound was drowned out by a low, rumbling noise.

It was beginning.

Logan gripped the rail and clenched her jaw as she looked out over the expanse below. She was determined to keep her inner anxiety from working its way to the exterior, especially now that so many dignitaries were present to monitor the project's launch. She'd been coached on imperial stature her entire life, but she often let her guise slip. Moreso than her sisters, unfortunately, which only served to irritate her further.

Before long, the rumbling started to shake the ground... or structure, rather. Movement on the manmade massif drew everyone's attention skyward, to where Leviathan met the clouds.

The water had started to flow.

Good, it was about time.

"Thank you all for coming," Logan announced, addressing the gathered onlookers with chin held high.

To her annoyance, not many people reacted. All attention still seemed to be upon her sister, which was fair, since Ingan *was* the future Empress...

"Thank you all," she repeated, this time enhancing her volume via Ut. She hated having to use the thing to speak on such a small platform, but whatever means were necessary to accomplish the task... "We will be heading inside for this second stage. Please follow me!"

She whirled around and strode into the facility, maintaining her smile, however fake it was, all the while holding her head high in the manner that had been drilled into her over many years. Propriety dictated that she should've ushered her sister in first, but Ingan wouldn't care. Besides, this was *her* day.

After traversing a long corridor with all the elites in tow, she emerged into the belly of Leviathan, her breath catching at the awesome sight. She'd been inside the facility countless times over the last few months, but the sheer scale of it never failed to impress her. Even the air pressure seemed to shift upon the entry, the pores of her skin caressed by an unseen awareness of the unnatural ambiance that surrounded her.

The cavernous interior was so large that she couldn't see to the other side. Not even close. Column supports, catwalks, and buildings created a web of activity that faded into the horizon, bringing to life what almost looked like an underground city, though there were no actual residents. Only the handful of engineers and machine operators that kept this place functional actually lived here.

The low rumbling turned to a thunder that drowned out all else as they meandered further past the threshold, the water falling on such a scale the likes of which had never been seen before. Even the largest waterfalls on Trevi Nali *paled* in comparison. The structure around them creaked and groaned, but that was to be expected.

Several kilometers in the distance, at the base of a great void where the water fell in wide columns, huge cylindrical structures were intermittently distributed as far as the eye could see in both directions.

The capture mechanisms.

There were gasps, oohs, and aahs from the audience as they watched the water cascade thousands of meters through the air. Pride surged through Logan — this was *her* doing, her brainchild, crude as it was. The crowd's admiration over her accomplishment even went a small way to easing her poor mood from earlier.

7

"If you direct your attention to the capture mechanisms in the center, the process is just beginning." Logan had to turn up her volume even higher to be heard above the thunderous roar of the torrential waterfalls, even from several kilometers away. "Each mechanism should generate over a hundred Terawatt-hours per year on average, and since the entire facility contains more than four thousand of these mechanisms, it is more than enough to subsidize the excess demand we face."

There was chatter as the dignitaries turned to discuss the feat among each other, and Logan braced for the onslaught of questions. Even though she was well-prepared to answer anything she'd be presented with today, anxiety coursed through her veins. She *hated* this sort of thing... *hated* having to answer questions from people with very little technical expertise.

"And how can we expect something so... *primeval*... to generate that much power?"

There it was. Of course it would be Glace Castore. He was far from her favorite Valanse, but she still didn't expect a question *that* dumb. She was half-tempted to delve into all the technical math in her response, just to spite him.

"Well..." she began. "It's a relatively simple calculation that our machine models can compute. We use the data from buoys all over Mareia, as well as from rainfall sensors on Leviathan itself, then plug it all in, and we get our power output values. As far as how it works... Well, the water turns the electromagnets in the capture mechanisms, and that rotating magnetic field will produce electric current through the conductor."

Someone who asked such a stupid question probably wouldn't have understood even the simplest of explanations Logan had to offer.

Ugh. Valanses were supposed to know this kind of thing!

Luckily, someone else spoke up quickly, not allowing Glace the time for any follow-ups.

"I notice the water is moving so quickly at the base," an older woman stated. Logan knew her — Verane Anstrile was her name. She was a Public Forum Luminary, one of the elites, but Logan liked her well enough.

"Yes, using minimal resources, we created a vacuum for the water to fall into," she answered. "The velocity at which the water impacts the mechanism contributes significantly to the power

8

generated. This is also why there is no mist surrounding the falls. Nothing is wasted."

"I see. What an ingenious setup!"

Logan nodded professionally, maintaining the same serene countenance she had while addressing Glace. But inside, she brimmed with pride. As primitive and simple as it was, she did have to admit it *was* rather ingenious.

"I am curious…" started another critic. Logan did not know this person. She would need to look into them after everything was completed here. "Why are we reliant on this method when we have the means to build another Harvester?"

"A great question," Logan lied, expertly masking her irritation. "But it is simple — the cost and energy of building another Harvester would far exceed the output on the short-term. Harvesters are a long-term solution with payoffs not being achieved for roughly a century, sometimes much longer. Since the timetable of our current expansion is on the order of tens of years, we must opt for a method of quicker returns."

All of this was well known if these people had done even a semblance of research. Had they never bothered to learn how opposite particles were harvested? How the majority of their *whole civilization* was powered?! Did they just accept every convenience of their comfortable lives without a second thought for how any of it worked?

Public formalities like these were so exhausting, but she had to take a deep breath and remind herself that it was nothing more than a Memory-op, an inconsequential part of the larger mandate. Logan had been used to it, after all, being raised an Ostreodase.

"And this generator does not affect drinking water production in any way?" another attendee asked.

"No," Logan replied. "All the water finds its way through to the treatment machines."

Hadn't she already made it clear that no water was wasted? Logan was becoming very annoyed, indeed, but her regal visage never wavered. She simply smiled majestically, keeping her posture upright in true imperial fashion.

"Excellent," Ingan announced, redirecting attention away from the question phase. "I am curious to get a better look at the capture mechanisms. May we venture nearer?"

"Of course," Logan replied. "If everyone would follow me, we can board the trams, which run along the rails that lead right to the generators themselves."

Once she allowed the dignitaries the chance to inspect the mechanisms up close, that would pretty much be the end of the tour. Then she could retire for the day.

Good riddance.

The group followed as she made her way toward the trams, when she was alerted through her Ut by her pilot.

Logan!

That short warning was all she received. A sharp jolt rocked the platform, the ground heaving beneath her as it attempted to buck her off her feet. She stumbled forward, unable to prevent from slamming her wrists into the ground.

The jarring pain was short-lived, as a short moment of calm ensued, allowing Logan to embarrassingly pluck herself from the floor. She looked around, noticing many around her had also fallen to the ground.

What in all the worlds? The ground continued to ripple underfoot, but not nearly with the same ferocity as that initial shock.

Murmurs droned throughout the platform as the guests recovered themselves to their feet, some of them looking toward her with questioning eyes, others toward Ingan for direction. Slightly annoying… but there were bigger problems to worry about. Much bigger.

The air around her suddenly groaned with a hideous yowl as a tremor rattled Leviathan around her in a rising crescendo. It was reminiscent of a groundquake, but such a phenomenon would obviously be impossible in a place like this. After a few seconds, a squall of water burst from the hallway they had walked in from, flooding the deck they stood on with the power of a river.

What the…?!

Logan gaped at the unfolding incident, eyes wide with shock.

This was not good.

She planted her feet and crouched to avoid being swept away. It couldn't have been a rogue wave, could it?

No way. There was *no way* a rogue wave would be big enough to reach where they were…

Right?

As Logan contemplated the situation, her eyes were drawn skyward to a sight that defied all logic. Far in the distance, among a deafening rumble, enormous chunks of the ceiling appeared to be falling in slow motion, along with many of the crosscutting walkways. It was as if an invisible wrecking ball had been set upon the structure, erasing huge swaths in its path.

How??

How was this happening?

The height of Leviathan was so great that it took many seconds for the colossal pieces to land, but when they did, they impacted directly onto the capture mechanisms with fiery force. The entire facility pitched and tossed as a mountain of debris was thrown into the air with such vigor that Logan instinctively turned to gather everyone outside. The generators were several kilometers in the distance, but the shower of destruction would reach them soon...

"Everyone outside, now!" she shouted. She didn't need the sound enhancer to get the point across this time.

Ingan was already on it, though, shepherding people back through the hallway, which was ankle deep with water. At least it wasn't flowing as it had been a minute ago...

"Logan, get out of here!"

"I am!" she snapped back at her sister.

What did Ingan expect her to do? Abandon people on her own project? Not a chance.

Logan had Verane Anstrile's arm draped over her shoulders, assisting her as quickly as possible toward the exit. The woman had surely broken her ankle from the fall, as it protruded at an angle that caused Logan to wince. It looked quite painful, but the medical machines would take care of it shortly. Once they got out of this place...

Moving in any direction was becoming increasingly difficult, and the shaking became more and more violent with every passing moment. The hallway was now a moving target, one that she dearly hoped she was on course for.

She bit her tongue as a tumultuous surge heaved her to the right. She somehow managed to keep her feet, but then overcompensated to the left, the wobble nearly sending her tumbling head over heels. It was all she could do to maintain balance, even with Valanse training.

Her entire reality began shaking with such convulsions that it became difficult to see anything. She didn't bother looking behind her, but she knew she only had seconds before the oncoming cloud of doom enveloped them.

"Logan!" Ingan screamed, still waiting.

A good leader, Logan admired of her sister. But she shouldn't be sticking around on her account...

"Go! I got this!"

Ingan's eyes widened for a split second, then everything went black as a massive force hit Logan in the back, just after she shielded Verane with her body.

———————

Logan's ears rang, an ever-persistent whistle buzzing through her skull as consciousness slowly returned. She blinked, but her vision was imprinted with glaring lines, making it next to impossible to see anything with detail. She couldn't even tell if it was dark or light around her.

She blinked again.

At first, the only thing that registered was the oppressive thickness of smoke and dust, but soon, it all started to come back to her.

The ceiling tumbling down in slow motion... The massive explosion when it finally crashed into the generators... Hobbling away for her life with Verane Anstrile's arm slung over her shoulders...

Verane!

She pushed her weight upright through protesting pain and felt through the nothingness around her, hoping to find the woman nearby.

"Verane?!"

"I'm here." Her response sounded miserable — muffled, soft groans laced with barely concealed agony. "I can't see."

"I can't, either," Logan replied, calmly as possible. "I think we're inside still."

A hiss of pain and defeat followed. "I think my leg is broken."

Logan felt around until she grasped hands with the woman in solidarity. She would have tried to pull her free, but there was nowhere to go. They were buried, it seemed — a disconcerting feeling, to say the least — but Logan refused to panic. She was above that.

"Ingan!" she called, remembering that her sister had been right there beside her, only a few meters away before the wall of debris had slammed into them. "Ingan!"

No reply.

"Ingan!!" She shouted louder this time.

Still nothing.

Help! She reached out in local broadcast through her Ut, desperate that someone would respond, and to her fortunes, someone did.

Logan? Where are you!? It was Bayors, one of her Imperial Aegides.

In the hallway, I think, she replied. *That's the last thing I remember. It's collapsed around us.*

After a short pause, he responded. *Standby.*

Moments later, perhaps a minute, muted noises overshadowed the incessant ringing in her ears.

Then, light.

It crept slowly into the frame, along with the distinct fragrance of fresh ocean air, until finally, a jagged hole was punched through about eye level.

Hands and arms appeared first, fumbling and clawing at the debris, followed by the urgent voices of Logan's companions.

Thank the Mara!

"Bayors!" she shouted.

"Your Highness," he replied.

"Take Verane Anstrile," she commanded, gathering her wits about her. "Her leg seems to be broken."

"Of course."

Logan helped Verane to her feet and gently handed the injured woman off after a path was cleared.

"Thank you, your Highness," Verane strained through gritted teeth. The poor thing was in obvious pain.

Logan nodded to her as she was escorted off, then turned to the other two.

"I can't find Ingan. Come help me."

Alin and Bayors shared a concerned glance, but didn't question the orders as they scrambled over the rubble, calling Ingan's name.

Logan crawled further into the now-dark interior of the facility when she kicked something that did not feel like wreckage. She peered through squinted eyes, discerning what was clearly a human arm among the shadows.

"Ingan!"

Logan frantically shifted a few large shards of tangled metal to the side, revealing her unresponsive sister. She focused on Ingan's form and scanned through her Ut for any vitals, thanking every star in the sky when she heard the steady pulse of a heartbeat.

"She's here!" Logan called to the others, who both hurried over at once. "She's alive."

"By the Mara!" Alin gasped.

Logan returned the grim expression with tight lips. "We need to get her out of here, now."

Alin and Bayors both answered with sharp nods.

Ingan's face still looked beautiful, but the side of her head was slicked with blood, and both eyes were singed black through her eyelids. Her legs were completely mutilated, and one of her arms appeared to be dislocated, turned around at some awkward angle. She *was* breathing, though, and she *did* have a pulse, and that's what mattered. The medical machines should be able to do the rest. They had to.

"We can't move her like this," Alin said. "I'll call for a backboard."

Logan nodded, forcing herself to her feet through reeling dizziness. Leviathan continued to sway, but it seemed the worst of it was over. She staggered into the light, realizing she hadn't even given her own well-being any thought.

She surveyed herself up and down, but aside from her tattered imperial gown, the headache raging within, and an elbow that shot with pain, she seemed to be intact. No gaping wounds. No fractured bones. No internal injuries.

A quick Ut scan corroborated that assessment, so Logan took a brief moment to herself and gulped deeply. That could have been a lot worse.

But...

How...? What even happened...?

There was *no way* these events could have transpired in the manner they did. She had double checked, triple checked, *quadruple* checked every element of the design! It was so simple. *How* could this have happened?

Logan racked her brain for several long seconds, barely noticing when three Valanses rushed past her carrying a backboard. She glanced inside the hallway, which was torn asunder from the blast, and cringed as her sister — the future Empress of the Meridian Empire — was loaded onto the gurney, unconscious and broken.

What have I done?

Logan laced her hands on top of her head in shame and looked in the other direction, horrified at the scatter of casualties strewn across the platform. She sprinted over to an unrecognizable dignitary who lay face down, twisted into a position that did not seem consistent with life. She reached through her Ut to scan for vital signs...

There were none.

"Help!" she shouted to Alin, who was shuffling past as they carried Ingan to the transport. "I'm not getting any vitals."

Alin scurried over, assessing the man before meeting Logan's eyes, curtly shaking her head. They called for another backboard and worked together to load the deceased man onto the cart, and both of them leaned back on a rail in defeat when they were finished.

"How many?" Logan asked quietly.

"At least four, that we know of."

Logan bowed her head.

Four people. Dead. All because she didn't do her research thoroughly enough. And the toll was likely to climb, especially with all the engineers inside the facility at the time of the disaster...

She was lost for words. Never in a million years did she think something like this was possible. This contingency wasn't in *any* of the models. Her own gut instincts told her this *shouldn't* have occurred!

But it did. And *she* was responsible.

She shut off all doubts in her mind, though, refusing to allow any uncertainty to seep through to her indomitable exterior. She simply gathered her composure and set to work, cooperating with others to save lives, even if some of them gave her sideways glances and dirty looks.

"What happened?" one woman wailed, her grief carrying on the ocean breeze. She was another of the Public Forum Luminaries, but Logan didn't remember her name. The lady lay prostrate on the floor, hugging a man who was sprawled on the ground, unmoving.

"Rogue wave," Glace responded bitterly. "How *her Highness* didn't account for the possibility of a rogue wave, I have no idea…"

So it *was* a rogue wave. How big must it have been to cause such destruction, though? The models had confirmed that even a wave thrice as large as the biggest *ever* recorded on Mareia shouldn't have been enough to disrupt operations — not even localized ones. Leviathan was as big as the horizon itself! This made no sense at all.

There was sure to be an investigation that would tell the whole story, but her father was going to be beside himself with anger over this series of events. Even though he doted on Logan quite ardently — her being the youngest daughter and all — she was not immune from accountability when it came to the pride of the Empire. The consequences were likely going to be… extreme.

As it was, there was so much resistance to this project in the first place, and if Glace's accusatory words were any indication, the public would surely *hate* her for this.

And as well they should, since so many resources were diverted to the project. Her miscalculations had turned it all into one massive pile of waste. Literally.

She didn't know how much of the station had been destroyed, but it didn't look good. Smoke billowed as far as she could see in either direction, rising from colossal fissures that split the ceiling open — chimneys as gargantuan as Leviathan itself, remnants of the chain reaction that wrought so much devastation.

Logan sucked the air in, refusing to think about the power games Shatter would create from this catastrophe. She was more concerned with the poor souls who suffered, but she knew the political animals wouldn't care about them. They would only use this suffering to accelerate their own agenda. This was bad on all fronts.

Very bad.

After stabilizing two more victims, but losing another, the weariness finally set in. The marathon of triage had worn her down, but not quite as much as the weight of responsibility had. Chewing her lip, Logan walked over to the transport where medical staff were attending to Ingan. Her sister looked peaceful, her skin majestically smooth, as usual, regardless of her condition.

"How is she?" Logan asked one of the medics.

"She is stable," he replied. "But she requires several hours on the machines before she will regain consciousness."

"Thank you." At least she was stable.

"She will possibly lose her sight entirely, and her legs may lose much of their original function."

Logan pressed her lips tight and gnashed her teeth. If Ingan was permanently maimed, she would never forgive herself. Not only was she the future leader of the Meridian Empire, but that was her sister, and she loved her dearly.

"You would do well to stay away right now," the medic replied coldly, shutting the door to the transport in her face.

Normally, she would be so offended at the slight. To think that anyone would dare disrespect one of the Ostreodase heirs like that would ordinarily be unthinkable... But right now, she knew she deserved it.

All manner of panicked thoughts raced through her mind, from what she could've done differently in the design, to how she could've evacuated people to safety more quickly. She knew hindsight was always flawless, but nothing would soothe her self-criticism right now. Not even the extemporaneous consideration that this could have been sabotage.

But *could* it have been?

It seemed so improbable — *beyond* improbable — that such destruction should ensue from a simple miscalculation of rogue wave possibilities. The station was in such a complete state of wreckage...

How could a single wave have done this? How could a hundred waves have even done this?

Logan sighed. Sabotage was just as unlikely, she supposed. And besides, it didn't really matter. Ultimately, Logan was responsible — for this project, for this travesty, for *everything*.

She turned away and sauntered numbly off to the side, bracing her sagging weight against the rail with both hands as she stared out over the vastness before her, the light wind lofting her hair in loose threads. Far below, the ocean rolled on innocently, as if it hadn't just wreaked havoc upon Leviathan. Upon her project. Upon her life.

_____

PART ONE

Alashadar

CHAPTER ONE

1

Welcome to the Bleakness

THEY told her that this place was somewhere people went to get lost. After living and toiling here for over a year, Niko had no more doubts about those claims — time and desolation had trodden her into utter insignificance. If it weren't for her own desire to live, it would've made zero difference if she just faded into Oblivion, taking with her all hopes and dreams she may have once had. She supposed Kira-Tharn would not have stood for that, so toil it was.

Today was Niko's twenty-first birthday, but nobody cared. Not the men beside her excavating the tunnels and Rifts. Not the An-Mara she lived with in squalor. Certainly not the powers that be on this Mara-forsaken world. Niko herself barely cared. Birthday celebrations were a thing of the past, just one more backwater tradition that she had no choice but to leave behind.

Arhanda was no more, and neither were birthdays, apparently.

That's why it was so weird that Ravenna had contacted her today, of all days. 'Come over tonight,' she had said. 'Oh yeah, and Cryo says we need some nutrient mix, so stop by the market please.'

Typical Ravenna, blunt and straight to the point. She was never one for pleasantries, even when she hadn't spoken with her friend in months. Not that it mattered — Niko didn't take it personally. Her sixteen-year-old self might have, but that sensitive version of her was long gone.

"Watch the line!" Armond-Dei yelled to the workers from atop the Rift that Niko was perched within. "It is your pay that will be docked if it is damaged in any way."

What an ass, Niko thought. Armond-Dei was a washed up An-Mara sellout, a foreman that seemed to relish in ordering underlings about. He did have a point, though — it looked like Maro Del-Fiiz was getting awfully close to the line as he was dragging the gear into position.

Niko watched with an open mouth as Kira-Tharn stormed over to the crane he was operating. "Watch it!" she hissed. Leave it to her to take matters into her own hands.

Maro looked offended, holding up his hands as if to question what the blazes the woman was on about. He simply shook his head and continued, paying her cautions no mind.

Niko held her breath, half-expecting an accident to unfold. The line sat very exposed on the dark reddish dirt as the crane's load inched ever closer.

Two meters. One meter. Half a meter...

She closed one eye, but to her relief, the gear swung wide — maybe only by centimeters — leaving the precious line that drew water up from the reservoir below unscathed.

She exhaled in silent gratitude, carefully lifting her helmet and removing her mask. She instinctively took a deep breath, accidentally gulping in scorching hot air. She immediately realized her mistake, hurriedly wiping away the sweat and grime that were plastered to her face before resecuring the seal.

After all this time, she still hadn't gotten used to wearing all this gear in such sweltering heat. She had once thought Sol City was hot, but that was a refrigerator compared to this oven. Even venturing this far away from the Twilight was brutal. Dangerous even. She couldn't imagine what conditions would be like further into the Daylight. The things she did to make ends meet...

This whole currency thing was such a weird way of life to her. She had been raised in a Meridian system — whatever was needed was always provided. It was plain and simple. Now, it seemed like the hardest work was often rewarded with the least compensation, while those corrupt gangsters that ruled over the city hoarded all the wealth. Hopefully she'd have enough Terion credit to be able to pick up the nutrient mix like Ravenna asked her to.

"I shall throttle the one called Maro Del-Fiiz if he insists on putting all our positions in jeopardy," Kira-Tharn huffed.

"Do it," Niko managed to whisper, her throat now hoarse from inhaling the unthinkably hot, dry air.

"Our shift is almost over, and yet he insists on taking such risks," Kira-Tharn continued.

Niko hadn't often seen Kira-Tharn in such a fuss. What was her deal? Niko just nodded back at her as she reached for the time via her Ut. It *had* to be almost quitting time...

Idiot, she scolded herself. Of course there was no Ut — it had been years since she had the damn thing, but she still found herself reaching for it often.

"That one needs a swift education in the manners of proper behavior," Kira-Tharn ranted.

Blazes, was she still going on about Maro Del-Fiiz? Sure, it had been a close call with the line, but all turned out okay. Kira-Tharn hadn't been in a particularly bad mood today, so what was her big issue now?

"And I shall be the one to deliver that education if no one else will."

"Give it a rest," Niko sighed. The old Niko would've never talked back to Kira-Tharn like that, but she was far too confident for her own good these days. Or she just didn't care. After all, they did live together now, and had for over half a year.

Kira-Tharn turned to glower at Niko, although it was so hard to see through her mask because of all the dirt caked onto the visor.

"I'm just saying..." Niko started.

"If he cuts the line, then I shall take your pay cut, Niko Ryen." Kira-Tharn leveled the threat at Niko in a way that left zero doubt that she would follow through.

Niko didn't bother to respond. She didn't know what was going on with Kira-Tharn right now. Maro must have really struck a nerve...

"What time is it?" she asked, changing the subject for her own peace of mind. Back on Arhanda, she could've made a rough guess as to what time it was, but here on An-Terino there were no rotating nights and days. Only regions of permanent Night, permanent Daylight, and permanent Twilight.

"Our shift is completed," Kira-Tharn responded.

They would have to finish connecting the gear to the line of course, but after that, they'd be free to go. Niko was very glad to be done with the day. The work was exceptionally brutal today, and her stupid mistake of breathing in the Daylight air made everything feel so much worse.

"Thank the Mara," Niko half-heartedly exclaimed.

"You should not use such expressions," Kira-Tharn cautioned her.

"Sorry," Niko winced. "I forget."

"You have been living among the An-Mara for six months now, Niko Ryen," she continued. "That is more than simply forgetting."

Niko threw up her arms in exasperation. She would say sorry again, but Kira-Tharn would probably get mad at her for that, too. It was best just to shut up and focus on connecting the gear to the line.

"If you insist on work of that quality, nobody may leave tonight," Armond-Dei yelled down to the laborers. "If I have to come down there and perform your tasks for you, it will not go well for any of you!"

Niko was tempted to yell at him to do just that — come down there and actually work. That lazy, lazy man was truly awful at times. He seemed like he was going to be nice when she had first become employed here, but after only a few days on the job, she had come to despise the guy.

She sensed Kira-Tharn tense up, as if she could feel the bristling of hairs on her friend's neck. She knew Kira-Tharn hated him, also. Actually, pretty much every single Rift worker in the company hated him, but there was nothing anyone could do. He was the foreman and they all had to follow his word if they wished to remain employed. There was no justice in this place. No fairness at all. This world was devoid of it.

After a few minutes of struggling to connect the gear to the line, they were finished. Even Armond-Dei seemed satisfied, because he simply turned around, stepped onto his buggy, and drove off to the rail station. The rest of the workers would have to walk, of course.

Recently, the long walk back was the worst part of the entire day. Not only was she exhausted from an entire day of manual labor, but they had progressed the line so far along the Rift that it was now about five kilometers back to base camp. And this was all decked out in full protective gear under the oppressive heat of Daylight!

Niko settled next to Kira-Tharn as they both silently trudged back. Her feet dragged through the dirt one laborious step after another, each made more difficult as she looked toward the hazy orange glow of the sol — Bucon, it was called. How had her life come to this?

'Welcome to the bleakness'. That's what one of the transit clerks had told her when she first arrived, and prophetically, that was her existence now.

At one point, she desperately wished she could've gotten off this blazes Hole of a planet, but it was not to be so. Pretty much as soon as they arrived last year, it became clear that there was no way to book passage to the Capital system unless they had an insane amount of Terion credit. At the time, the entire group had a grand total of zero, so they were all conscripted into working grueling shifts just to scrape by, let alone secure transport off-world. Ever since, Niko had more or less given up looking for a way off.

Originally, she was living with Cryo, Ravenna, and Kyler in Machine Row, but those three had begun to spend inordinate hours working on very technical machine work, something she knew very little about. As the days went by, they had become so bogged down in their work that Niko started to drift away. Instead, she found herself spending more and more time with the An-Mara of all people, and now lived among them.

The good ones, though. Not the ones who destroyed her world.

Meanwhile, Jack and Callum, bless their hearts, had infiltrated a small contingent of Meridians here — an organization called Shatter — in order to find a way off-planet. She had grown so close with Jack on the long voyage to An-Terino, yet she now cursed him — and herself, she supposed — for never making a move to progress past anything other than friends. Circumstances had now separated them for close to a year, so she didn't know when, or if, she'd ever have the chance to tell him how she felt.

She lamented her misfortunes to herself. Her bad romantic luck would continue forever, it seemed. She thought it laughable that she was now *twenty-one* years old and had never been in a single relationship in her life. She'd never even kissed anyone.

How embarrassing, she mourned silently.

Kira-Tharn shot her a look that was unmistakable, even through her bulky, dirtied mask. She knew Kira-Tharn was well aware of what — or *who* — she was thinking about. Niko must have been making the *face*. Every time she thought of Jack, her chest became constricted and her hands grew clammy, and as Kira-Tharn claimed, she bit the inside of her lower lip. How Kira-Tharn even noticed *any* of that was a mystery… She should've just left her mask dirty so her face wouldn't be visible.

"You have only yourself to hold responsible for your own happiness," Kira-Tharn lectured her. "If you fancy a male, then it lies upon you to take action. Regretting inaction is not the way of the An-Mara."

Niko sighed. She knew Kira-Tharn was right, but it still did little to ease her regrets. She averted the judging gaze of her friend, instead focusing on not collapsing under the weight of all her protective gear.

"And do *you* have a male you fancy?" Niko asked flippantly.

"That is none of your concern," Kira-Tharn replied.

Of course it wasn't.

"Yeah, and so neither is it of yours," Niko retorted. Why was she so irritable today? It being her birthday surely had something to do with it. Last year, when she turned twenty, she had also been in a very strange mood.

"I only offer you advice," Kira-Tharn responded.

"Yeah, well I can't do anything about it now, can I?" Niko started to raise her voice.

"Is the one called Jack Sehs dead?" Kira-Tharn asked.

"Well… no."

"Then you very much can do something about it."

"There's no way for me to reach him!" Niko protested.

Kira-Tharn just glared back at her.

"I'm serious! I have no way to contact him! We've been over this!" Niko doubled down.

"You know who he is working with, do you not?" Kira-Tharn asked.

"Umm, well… yes," Niko admitted.

"And you know in what district he is located?"

"Maybe." Her eyes were now facing the ground in embarrassment.

"Then there is a way, Niko Ryen. You are just being obstinate."

Niko fumed, but she couldn't put words together to defend herself. Kira-Tharn had won this argument, but Niko refused to let her have that satisfaction.

She admitted there *was* a possible way to contact Jack, but it would require her to travel all the way to the other side of Alashadar, and she wasn't about to do that. Besides, what if Jack needed to maintain his cover? She blushed at the thought of her bursting in on one of his clandestine operations and professing her feelings to him. Now that would be a sure-fire way to *lose* a man forever... Not to mention, it might jeopardize their one chance to get off this hellhole of a planet.

"Just... nevermind. You don't get it."

"I *do* get it," Kira-Tharn pushed. "Better than you know. You are the one refusing to understand."

Niko just shook her head and continued on in silence. She was over this argument. How stupid was this? They were arguing over a *guy*...

No, not even that. They were arguing over Niko's *failed love life*...

After walking the remainder of the thirty-minute trek without speaking, the two roommates finally arrived at the base camp, and it wasn't a pretty sight to behold. Dusty hoses and ducts ran chaotically between makeshift tents that were arranged haphazardly. Discarded debris littered the ground and trash bins overflowed from careless use, or a lack thereof altogether.

Niko stopped caring about what the place looked like long ago. It wasn't worth taking the time to clean because every few weeks, the camp would shift as they progressed the Rift further and further. What was leftover unfortunately became part of an endless trail of rubbish as far as the eye could see, which, fittingly, wasn't very far because of the perpetual haze of this place.

Niko and Kira-Tharn wordlessly tramped through the base camp, then piled into the back of a transport truck that would take them about ten more kilometers to the rail depot. During this bumpy ride through excavated dirt, Niko let her mind wander to her friends from Arhanda. She hadn't heard from them in months — so what was it that Ravenna wanted today? It couldn't be that they wanted to celebrate her birthday... right? That would be a foolish notion. It was more likely that they needed something from her — an errand of some sorts, or maybe even some correspondence with the An-Mara, whom she was now very well-acquainted with.

Niko sat in the back of the truck without saying a single word to Kira-Tharn for the better part of twenty minutes when they finally arrived at the rail depot. Dozens of transport trucks all arrived simultaneously, with dozens more departing, taking new shifts of workers to the many parallel Rifts that fed Alashadar its water. The truck came to a rough halt, and the passengers jumped out quickly as a new set of workhands jumped in without missing a beat.

"I would be one to convey an apology, Kira-Tharn."

Niko turned around and Maro Del-Fiiz stood behind them with his head bowed. Niko didn't even think his stunt a few minutes ago was that big of a deal. Why was Kira-Tharn so upset about it? And why was he being so apologetic? The An-Mara never ceased to confuse the blazes out of her.

"It was not my intention to cause alarm at the site," he continued. "I was confident that I had the matter well under control."

Kira-Tharn didn't respond — she only nodded her head slightly. Niko waited for a split second for Kira-Tharn to continue walking with her, but she remained stopped, glaring at Maro.

Niko rolled her eyes and walked on, hoping that Kira-Tharn would join her and leave the poor guy alone. It really wasn't that big of a deal...

She entered the locker room, but Kira-Tharn never joined her. She probably stayed to lambast Maro, and Niko wasn't about to wait around to watch the unfortunate wretch deal with the wrath of Kira-Tharn.

Sweat and mud were caked to her face as she peeled off her mask, and heaps of dirt shook off onto the ground as she removed the several layers' worth of heavy Daylight protection. As filthy as she was, Niko opted to not take a shower there. She'd do it later; she just wanted to get home right now. Kira-Tharn was a grown woman and could find her own way back. They would almost certainly continue their argument later, but that was a worry for future Niko.

She quickly got dressed and made her way into the bustling rail depot, which was mostly filled with An-Mara, as they tended to be the poorer, more desperate class that took the jobs on the Rifts. It was important work and paid decently, but it was demanding labor. Every day, the rail that Niko rode would pass through the agricultural fields, and every day she would question whether or not to take a job there instead. That wasn't easy work, either, but those laborers at least had better hours than the Rift workers.

Niko mindlessly slogged over to a train that was loading, plugged her Terion badge into the console to allow her on board, and slumped into a seat that was farthest from anyone else. She laid her head back and allowed herself the bliss of comfort as she closed her eyes for a few minutes.

She would've loved to have napped the whole way back, but she sat up sharply when they slowed down for the stop at the fields, ready to pick up the agricultural laborers also on their way home from work. Niko looked out the window to see inclined hills forming the waves on an endless sea of black plants that stretched all the way to the horizon.

She really *should* find work here instead... Anything seemed better than toiling her life away at the Rifts day in and day out. The weather would be cooler, the work less brutal on her body, and the commute a little shorter. Plus, the field workers always seemed just a little happier than the Rift workers did.

I will *talk to Kira-Tharn about it*, she vowed. She was very serious about doing it if Kira-Tharn would join her, but that was another discussion future Niko would have to deal with. Something to worry about later.

As the train came to a complete stop, the doors opened up and field workers piled in by the dozen. Niko scooted over to make room for a girl with orange hair that she'd seen before. She was a petite young woman about her own age, but Niko always felt bad for her — she had heavy, disfiguring scars that marred her entire face. Whatever caused that must've been horribly painful.

Niko nodded to her, offering a contrite but genuine smile. She never opened conversation, though, so Niko never knew her name or her story, as curious as she was. Nobody really talked to each other on the trains, other than their own company they kept, so it wouldn't have been proper to talk to her now.

Only a few minutes after the train left the station, Twilight had almost completely set in. The atmosphere faded from a light, hazy orange to a darker reddish-purple, and soon, the glow of the city settled onto the horizon. The track turned around a low mountain, and towering buildings came into view far ahead in the distance.

Alashadar.

It was a *massive* metropolis that dwarfed even Sol City, but Niko always thought it to be a bit dreadful the way it was enveloped in perpetual Twilight. It stretched for kilometers and kilometers along the narrow strip of sol-set that banded the planet. For people who loved nightlife, it was a playground and a haven. But for those who preferred daylight and the outdoors, it was a hellish nightmare, an eternal purgatory that offered no more than the tiniest sliver of dark red sol-light from the setting Bucon.

As the rail sped forward at a blistering pace, the buildings resolved into towering structures that dominated the skyline as far as she could see in both directions, the only depression being that of the Machine Row district. There, smoke still poured from a few factories that gave the district its name, but in recent months, construction had been turning it into a tech manufacturing center, driven primarily by an influx of Meridians.

Niko hadn't actually been there in months, other than to the main rail hub, of course. Truth be told, she was a little nervous to go visit today, with all the Meridian activity about. She rarely saw her friends from Arhanda anymore, though, and it would be nice to see them, even if she had to make the long trek over from the An-Mara quarter. Machine Row was no NewCen, but it was a far cry nicer than the slums she was used to living in.

The train finally slowed down as it entered the central terminal, doors opening to reveal the busiest station in the whole city. Thousands of people bustled about, some loading onto several other rails that ran parallel to the city's orientation, others loading onto the trains that took laborers out to their respective workplaces radially. Though most of the major rails were at ground level, escalators and elevators rose a hundred meters into the air, connecting the terminal to adjacent trams and towers.

Alashadar was a vertical city, most of the skyscrapers packed densely along one major artery. The outlying areas, including the An-Mara quarter where she lived, were much flatter and far less luxurious, although they were just as densely packed, if not more.

As everyone filed off the train, Niko mindlessly followed, then blended into the steady stream of people bound for the An-Mara quarter. She'd been ground down to nothing more than a drone, a single cog in a vast machine. Her daily routine had become automatic:

Wake up.

Eat breakfast.

Walk from living quarters to the rail station.

Ride the train into the heart of Alashadar.

Trek to the Rifts.

Work until lunch.

Eat lunch.

Work some more until quitting time.
Trek back to Alashadar.
Transfer to the train to the An-Mara quarter.
Walk back to living quarters.
Clean up.
Eat dinner.
Sleep.
Repeat.

Every single day was the exact same now for over six months, with no end in sight. She really did need a change. She had decided on the train ride back that she was serious about switching to the agricultural fields. She would speak with Kira-Tharn tonight about it. For now, though, she needed to hurry home and clean herself up before going over to visit her friends. Aside from being happy to see them, she was very eager to hear if they'd made any more progress on getting off this Mara-forsaken rock.

CHAPTER TWO

2

The Shatter Yard

AS ugly as Niko's tiny living quarters looked from the outside, they were somehow worse on the inside. Unwashed dishes lined what little countertop space was available, and some even found their way onto the floors, which had been un-mopped for the entire time Niko had been living here. Had this place been on Arhanda, critters of filth would have abounded, but alas, life was sparse on this planet, the incomplete terraforming from eons ago too big an obstacle for native species to evolve and flourish.

Probably for the best.

Niko looked around ashamedly. She'd always been a clean freak when she was younger, someone who paid close attention to detail. At one point, she'd even been a conscientious gardener and had once aspired to turn her Green Coast home into a second Nevaly.

Now she couldn't care less about those details. Neither she nor Kira-Tharn had the time, energy, or interest to beautify their home. The only thing that mattered was having enough food for meals and a pillow to sleep on. Water for a shower was a bonus, a luxury they could barely afford. Nevermind that it was almost always cold water...

Niko's hair was now wrapped in a towel to dry — she let it

grow long during the voyage to An-Terino and had now become comfortable with it being at least mid-back length. It was annoying to deal with, but she did like how it looked. Not that it really mattered — she always had to keep it up while she was at work anyway. But still, it was a pleasure she allowed for herself. One of the few.

As her hair dried, she considered doing a small amount of long-overdue tidying, but just the sight of the clutter was too overwhelming. She wouldn't even know where to start! Besides, her stomach grumbled in hunger, and even though she assumed they were going to have dinner tonight, she was so starving after working all day that she had to refuel with something small for now. She unwrapped a small protein packet to eat, throwing the wrapper onto the ground.

Maybe she should empty the trash first...

After reluctantly scooping up a few piles of garbage that had been haphazardly scattered onto the dirty floors, she walked to empty their trash bin into the community pile outside. She wondered when Kira-Tharn would get in; it was strange that she still wasn't back. Niko started to worry because it was so unlike her, but she also knew Kira-Tharn was quite capable of taking care of herself. She must have been going to the markets or something.

Niko realized she forgot to tell Kira-Tharn that *she* would be the one going shopping tonight — she had to go anyway since Ravenna had asked her to. Now, in case Kira-Tharn did go to the markets, it didn't make sense for her to get anything else besides what Ravenna wanted. They sure didn't have any extra Terion credit to waste...

Oh well.

She dumped the trash onto the pile and was a little disappointed it hadn't been cleared out to the incinerators yet. It should've been taken out days ago. What was going on?? The whole block smelled so bad that Niko nearly had to pull her Garments over her nose. Still, she was much too tired to spend time tracking down the services to make it happen. She'd rather just deal with the smell.

"I do wish that the refuse services would complete their duties."

Niko whirled around to find Riiz Alke-Tani carrying his own trash bin to the pile. He was surely just as annoyed as Niko about the situation.

"Yep," Niko agreed. "Lazy chums."

"I do believe I may pay a visit to their offices in Machine Row and request immediate relief," he said. "Would you care to accompany me?"

Niko shook her head. "I can't today. I'm visiting Cryo, Ravenna, and Kyler in a few minutes."

"Very well," he said. "Please do wish them greetings from me."

"Of course." Niko nodded respectfully, then retreated back into her quarters. Riiz was a better person than she was. She could have very well stopped by the refuse service's offices on her way to her friends' place — she just didn't want to.

After returning inside, she replaced the empty trash bin into its corner by the kitchen, satisfied that their place was just a little bit cleaner than before. However, the smell of the community refuse pile wafted into the room when she opened the door, etching its stink onto every surface.

Whatever.

She finished her 'cleaning' by wiping her hair towel over the kitchen counter, then threw a jacket on before heading out into the night. The hazy purple-orange glow in the sky didn't really scream *night* by any meaning of the word, but her timepiece read 20:04. Hence, nighttime.

Niko felt ridiculous without a Ut. Having to look at the time on a clunky band around her wrist felt so *primitive*, but she supposed it was better than nothing. She was so used to time being tied to the sol's position in the sky, but here on An-Terino, the position of the sol only indicated how far you were away from the Terminator. The lighting never wavered in this place, so it was nearly impossible to tell the time without looking at her timepiece.

She walked through the An-Mara ghetto to the nearest rail station, which was a couple kilometers away. After a long day at the Rifts, she just wanted off her feet. At least she'd grown accustomed to walking many kilometers daily, so it wasn't exactly *painful*. Just inconvenient.

The sights and sounds in the neighborhood were enjoyable enough for Niko, though. A mother cooking a meal on a ramshackle fourth floor balcony. The clanging of hammers as two men were rebuilding a door across the street. A girl about her own age gathering water from the well on the next block. She didn't know any of them by name, but their faces were familiar. They all currently existed in the same unfortunate walk of life that she did, and she therefore felt a strong kinship with them.

A few years ago, the An-Mara had been such a mystery at best, with Niko feeling confusion, fear, and even hostility toward them after what happened to her home. But after getting to know the contingent of them here on An-Terino — especially after *living* among them — Niko had developed a great respect for their culture. True, the group living on this planet were the more progressive of the bunch, but even the social restrictions on laughing and entertainment weren't as bad as she once thought. It was just a part of the way they lived their lives, and they were humans just like anybody else.

When she first made the decision to live here, her friends told her that this ghetto was dangerous. Shantytowns always had a bad reputation, but she actually felt *safer* here than she did whenever she went into the heart of the city. Alashadar was a lawless place, one not safe for people to just walk around by themselves. Especially not young women.

Even in Machine Row, where she was headed now, she felt way out of her element. At least her friends lived on the outskirts, away from the nightlife and the crime that came with it. She'd be quick about this whole trip, and if her friends gave her any grief about it, she would have words for them — it was their own fault she was out here walking by herself, anyway.

With a huff, she continued on through the impoverished streets of the An-Mara slums.

Upon reaching the rail station forty-five minutes later, Niko clicked her Terion badge into the console and boarded the train that was due to depart next. The ride was short, only about five minutes, but soon after it departed, she realized that she forgot to visit the market by the An-Mara quarter before getting on the train.

How stupid!

She sighed to herself, but there was nothing she could do now. She'd just have to visit one of the markets in Machine Row. It was for situations like this that she wished Kira-Tharn was with her. That lady was so confident and unapologetic in everything she did; she never got worked over in a haggle the way Niko seemed to. That's why she was responsible for buying their groceries most of the time, while Niko got to do dishes and empty trash bins.

If she felt like it.

After a short ride, the train dumped her at the Machine Row station, where she exited and looked around. Where *was* the nearest market? To her left was a cluster of factories, and to her right was the busy commercial center of the district, even if it was a little bit further away from her friends' place.

She headed right. Surely there would be a marketplace in this direction before long. She hurriedly passed along a dark, quiet part of the street, trying her best to stay in the lamplight. A few men walked past her, and suddenly she felt very vulnerable. She smiled nervously at them, and was all too happy when none of them paid her any mind. As soon as she was out of sight of the rail station, she broke into a light jog, just so she didn't have to spend any more time in this place than was necessary. Her antics drew a few stares from passersby, but she didn't care. The fatigue in her legs held stronger protest than any strangers' side-eyes, anyway.

After about a minute of jogging through the dark neighborhood, she saw the telltale glow from large-scale neon lights in the distance. To her relief, the sights and sounds indicated a busy marketplace, so she resumed her walking pace, even if it was a little more brisk than normal. Before she stepped into the illuminated part of the street, however, her eyes were drawn to a cluster of boxes that lay in an empty yard behind a very tall fence to her left.

She stopped and looked closely, because she'd seen that emblem before. Sure enough, upon further inspection, she saw that it was the Meridian Crescent.

What was in these boxes? And why were they just lying about outside? Some even had the lids halfway opened. She stepped forward a few paces and saw another logo on the side.

Shatter Industries.

She knew of that company. It was one of the larger players here on An-Terino. It wasn't the company that she worked for, but they did control some of the Rifts, as well as most of the high-tech factories that were popping up here in Machine Row. She knew they were in league with the Meridians, but it was still strange they would associate with a *company*.

From what she'd learned over the past few years, Meridian civilization was based off a form of socialism, a system where goods were provided and shared. This was all she'd ever known growing up on Arhanda, so it seemed natural to her. The one caveat was that there were no private businesses that hoarded goods and currency the way that companies like Shatter did.

Her curious nature got the better of her and she looked for a way past the fence that separated her from the boxes. She followed around a corner to look for any breaks when she came upon a locked gate halfway down a dark alleyway. She walked forward slowly, just to investigate.

Should I be doing this? she wondered, almost pausing.

The fact that she even had to ask herself probably told her that no, she should *not* be doing this.

Just one look inside the boxes, she promised herself.

She tiptoed to the gate and pressed against it. A heavy, chain lock wrapped around the two fences that joined together at the gate. There was no way it would budge, but perhaps...

Yes! she congratulated herself as she slipped through the narrow crack, underneath the lock. *Finally, a benefit to being small...*

Though she had filled out a little bit in the last couple years, she was still quite slim and was able to fit through this gate, which was clearly meant to keep people out. She brushed the rust off her hands and snooped across the empty lot toward the building, where some open boxes were perched. As she got close, she stood over them.

Nothing.

Maybe the other ones in the front had something in them?

She turned to walk around to the front, but stopped dead in her tracks when she heard voices. She silenced her breathing and tensed her muscles as she crept to the corner of the building in the back, where some discarded wood provided a hiding place. Once there, she peered through an opening and saw two men with rifles patrol by. They were wearing Shatter uniforms.

Afraid to move even a centimeter, she put a hand over her mouth, as if that would make her breathing any quieter.

"That reminds me, have you gone in to place your bet yet?" one of the men asked.

"Of course I have," the other one responded. "Have you *not*?"

"I don't know who I'm pulling for!"

"Brother, come on."

"I mean obviously the safe bet is Delmatic, but I'm really tempted to go with Jon Wilhe."

"Wilhe's a Ripper, for sure. But are you really willing to put down Terion against Delmatic?"

"I don't know, I need to think about it."

"Deadline is coming up…"

"I know! I'll put it in tomorrow."

"You better! The race is in two days, my man."

"Three, actually. But I got this. I'll put it in tomorrow for sure."

"Well, as long as your guy doesn't *die* this time, I'll consider it a win for you."

"Yeah, yeah. Laugh it up…"

As if an invitation was given, the other guard started cackling so hard he wheezed. Niko didn't exactly think it was funny. As dangerous as Trackripping was, it wasn't funny in the slightest when racers got hurt.

"You know, I think I'm gonna choose Wilhe. There's no way he crashes, and if he wins, that's a *huge* odds payout. Plus, you can eat your words when he beats Delmatic."

"No chance."

"I don't know… It's possible. I've seen him on NewCen before and he rips."

"Oh I know he does! I admitted as much. There's just no way he beats Delmatic."

One of the two men's Uts suddenly made a loud, beeping noise, and Niko jumped. She clenched her teeth and pressed her palms to the ground, praying that she didn't make any sound. She was trespassing on the grounds of a Meridian warehouse wearing An-Mara Garments, and the two armed Shatter guards were stopped only a meter away from her. Not a great situation to be in…

How could she have been so stupid to think this was a good idea? And why did they have to stop right in front of her?!

Go! she commanded, as if the guards would heed her wishes. *Walk! Leave! Begone!*

"This Mara-accursed posting will be the death of me," the man whose Ut beeped complained. "They yank us around, expecting us to do this and that and everything."

"And?.. What do they want now?"

The men were *still* standing in the same spot, much to Niko's chagrin. She held her breath as she continued to will them to move on.

"They want us back at the docks for another shipment."

"*Another* one? We just finished unloading *this* one!"

"I know! It's unbelievable. Bunch of Minedyne stuff, also. I don't know why they are transferring that stuff here. They should've let it all burn with that other dump of a world."

Niko's breath caught.

Minedyne.

And were they talking about *Arhanda*? Slight anger coursed through her veins, but she stayed as silent as a field mouse avoiding a nightraptor on the hunt.

One of the men glared at the other. "You know we aren't supposed to be talking about that out here. Only behind closed doors."

"Oh, give it a rest. We're in an abandoned warehouse out in the middle of nowhere. As if there would be Terion Sight anywhere outside of NewCen or Machine Row. Maybe the nicer part of Oldcity, but this place is a load of scrap that nobody cares about."

"I guess so... But still. We should be careful."

"Grow a spine, brother," the one man chided the other. "Anyway, what I was going to say... the worst part is that I heard Andersane is being transferred here."

"Seriously? That hardass? When does he get in?"

"Not sure. Hopefully not anytime soon. Let's get back to the docks and see what they want, though..."

Not moving a muscle was torturous for Niko. She wanted to explode. Andersane?! Coming here?! And what was the connection to Minedyne?

She always made it a point to not spend much time dwelling on the events of her past, but this shoved everything that happened a few years ago back into her face, front and center. Her skin heated and she could feel sweat begin to condense on her forehead. It was as if every thought she felt when her home was destroyed was rolled up into a tiny ball and forced down her throat now, finding a way to lump up in her chest.

She coughed.

Actually coughed.

Time slowed down to a near stop, and Niko didn't even have time to second guess her actions as she raced across the yard for that hole in the gate. Fortunately, the Shatter soldiers had ambled back around the corner, giving her just enough time to pull herself clumsily through the gate before she heard the shouts of the men after her.

Run! She told herself.

And she ran.

"STOP!" one of the men bellowed.

She didn't stop.

"What do we do?! Shoot?"

"Of course!! Don't let her get away!" The answer came roaring back, just as she raced around the corner.

Soon thereafter, the ricochet of bullets sounded on the wall to her left.

––––––––––––

CHAPTER THREE

3

The Girl With the Scars

NIKO'S heart pounded, the adrenaline spurring her to sprint as fast as she ever had in her life. The fact that she'd worked a ten-hour day in the Rifts — and probably walked more than ten kilometers on top of that — was of no consequence. She felt as light as air darting into the adjacent street and toward the lights, and to what she prayed was a bustling crowd she could seek refuge among.

The shouts of the men behind her — and their death-seeking bullets — were gone, but only for the time being. She probably only had but a few seconds until they managed to open the gate...

Stupid, stupid, stupid, stupid, she thought to herself, instantly regretting her curiosity. Why couldn't she have just ignored that Shatter yard altogether?

Her regrets never slowed her down, though, as she continued to barrel down the street with reckless abandon. The people around her gasped and stared, especially the ones that were forced to jump out of the way before they were trampled by her onslaught. Normally Niko would be profusely apologetic if she did something so small as accidentally stepping in front of someone at the rail station, but right now, there was no force on An-Terino that would keep her from getting to safety.

She continued to sprint as if her life depended on it, as it may well have, but before she fully had time to process her surroundings, her run was slowed to a walk as the crowd thickened around her.

A crowd.

Good, she exhaled.

This was possibly the safety net she had been hoping for, but fear still pumped through her body, its icy grip wrapped around the entirety of her heart. Her hands quivered while she tiptoed through the masses, craning her neck as she occasionally attempted to look behind her. Unfortunately, her breathing was far too heavy to truly fit in, and worse, if the men happened upon her now, she was locked in place, too many people surrounding her to escape quickly enough.

Think, Niko. Think!

Was there a way she could blend in to where she wouldn't be found? Her An-Mara Garments were not exactly inconspicuous, but at least there were enough people around to provide a small distraction for a short while.

What she really needed was to get to Cryo and Ravenna, but their place was back in that same direction where the Shatter guards would be coming from…

Blazes!

She had no way to contact them, either. She was on her own, unfortunate as it may be. This was *really* a time where a Ut would come in handy…

"Fresh Cinto!" a short, round man shouted to her left, practically blowing out her eardrum.

Niko jumped back as she pushed him away. Cinto was *not* what she needed right now. Not ever, actually.

She shook her head angrily as she moved on, slowly becoming more attuned to the goings on around her — the shoving of the hundreds of people in a hurry to gather their spoils, the deafening buzz of relentless haggling between vendors and customers, the blindingly bright neon signs that served as advertisements. She realized the only way out of this mess she'd gotten herself into was forward. She *needed* to blend in.

One deep breath.

Two.

Three.

When the Shatter guards would inevitably come searching the marketplace for her, a terrified, panicked girl would be exactly who they were looking for. She *needed* to ease her heart rate. She *needed* to be calm.

Another deep breath.

Two.

Three.

Blazes, this was useless. Her heart was still pounding out of her chest.

"You there!" boomed a large woman to her right, holding fine looking clothes out in front of her. "Finest dresswear in Machine Row! I'm sure my wares would look lovely on you."

Niko jumped in fright before politely declining, moving on without looking back.

It was likely the guards found a way out of their warehouse yard by now, so she didn't dare stand up on her toes to look for them anymore. That would only draw attention.

She looked around for something, anything, that might help when suddenly, an idea came to her.

She was at the market now... Why shouldn't she pretend to be shopping for goods? After all, that would be the best way to blend in.

But wait... wasn't she supposed to be buying something anyway?

You're an idiot, she lambasted herself. She didn't need to *pretend* to shop around! In her panic, she'd forgotten that she came here to *actually* shop — Ravenna had tasked her with getting nutrient mix, so that's what she would do.

With the smallest inkling of relief at her excuse for being there, she continued to move with the throng of people around her, as if the crowd were a living entity that she was forced to drift with. She frantically looked to her left and right, desperate to find any stalls where nutrient mix was being sold. If she could acquire some now, she would have the perfect alibi in case the Shatter soldiers happened upon her.

Just an innocent citizen of An-Terino, going about my daily business.

Where would a nutrient stall even be, though? She was in a section where herbs were being sold, but she didn't see any nutrient mixes. She almost jumped up on top of a curb to scan the stands around her, but a rational second thought advised her that she still shouldn't dare draw any attention to herself. She tried listening to the vendors who were broadcasting their goods, but the chaotic din of the marketplace made it way too difficult to discern one call from another.

It was hopeless. This trading hub was *far* busier than the one in the An-Mara quarter that she and Kira-Tharn would go to. How did these people ever get what they wanted?! This must be an outing that would take *hours*.

She moved with the flow of the crowd for another minute, then was graced with a stroke of luck. Over the scattered noise of everything, she heard a distinct voice call out the words that she was desperate to hear.

"Nutrient mixes! Nutrient mixes!"

Thank the Mara.

Niko forced her way through the multitudes of people, clawing against the tide that threatened to sweep her along. Eventually, she found herself face to face with the vendor — a tall, broad-shouldered man that wore a harsh expression. Hopefully his bargaining skills were less intimidating than his appearance…

"Looking for nutrient mix?" he said.

He towered over Niko, and his appraising glare made her feel extremely uneasy. She'd never been good at haggling, but she had no choice but to engage. She *needed* that mix. Right now.

"Mmhmm." She gave her best effort to appear confident, but only ended up nodding meekly back.

"Two thousand Terion for one bag," he said, shuffling a few bags effortlessly between his thick hands. "Thirty-five hundred for two."

Two thousand?? Niko had never paid more than one thousand for a bag *twice* that size at any market she'd ever been to! What the blazes?…

"Uhhh…" she hesitated. "I think… how about…"

"Two thousand," he interrupted firmly. "Take it or leave it."

He must've picked up on her lack of confidence. She hated this. Most of these people had years and years of experience living like this, but the whole buying and selling thing was still so new to her. Maybe if she had time to collect her wits, she might've not been so skittish…

"I uhh…" Niko started. "How about one thousand?"

"Did you not just hear me, girl?" The vendor leaned forward menacingly. "*Two* thousand."

What an ass! Niko thought contemptuously.

"Fifteen hundred?" she pushed. Fifteen hundred was still an awful deal, but better than two thousand.

He stepped back, folding his massive arms across his chest. "Two thousand."

"Oh, there you are!" a strange voice suddenly called.

Niko froze, the blood draining from her face. Had she been caught??

Except, no... this voice was from a woman.

In a state of panic mixed with desperation, Niko whirled around to face a girl about her own age, one she had seen before.

It was the girl from the train.

The one with ragged orange hair and a face that looked as if it had been run through a meat grinder. Impossibly deep scars were carved into canyons that ran diagonally across both sides of her face. Her left eye was completely gone, as was her left ear. Ugly, thick scar tissue tugged at the corner of her mouth, pulling it into an awkward sort of grin. The poor thing...

"What are you doing? I told you to get the nutrient mix for nothing less than three hundred for the bag," the girl said.

Niko looked around, but she stood facing directly in front of her.

Is she talking to me? What in the blazes was happening?

"We will take two bags for six hundred, please." The girl with the scars turned toward the vendor confidently and held his stare.

"Two thous..." the man started, but was cut off immediately.

"If you say two thousand one more time, I will go to every nutrient vendor on the Row and have them set up shop in your stead," she warned. "And before you doubt me, let me tell you that yes, I do know several merchants who would be more than willing to follow through."

The poise in her voice contrasted starkly to her diminutive appearance. She was about the same exact size as Niko, but the way she spoke made her seem even bigger than this giant of a nutrient vendor.

The man stared back at her, his eyes narrowed to assess her threat.

"You're bluffing," he said.

"Am I?" She cocked her head assuredly to the side. "Let's see, there's Ragon Wilther, and Paul Lorise, and... oh, I almost forgot...

Mera Darline."

He continued to peer at the girl for several long seconds, but finally relented.

"Five hundred per bag," he grumbled.

"Three-fifty."

"Four."

"Three-fifty."

She didn't budge a centimeter, and Niko was absolutely shocked when she walked away with two bags for seven hundred Terion.

The girl then turned to Niko. "I didn't even ask... You are okay with seven hundred Terion, yes?"

Niko, still speechless, nodded and transferred the credits as she took the bags.

"Thank you," she managed to croak after they had walked away from the stall.

"It is nothing." The young woman casually waved her hand as both of them were enveloped into the crowd once more.

"Why, though?" Niko asked. "Why'd you help me?"

"You looked like you needed it. Men like that prey on what they think to be poor, helpless girls. You need to be ruthless and firm if you want to survive out here."

Niko looked down, ashamed that she was about to be taken advantage of so easily. She would have seriously paid the entire two thousand Terion for a single bag if he had pushed one more time.

"That's her!!"

The marketplace was loud, but the words cut through the bustle with clarity, this time from a deep male voice.

Blazes!!

She had stayed in one spot far too long, and now there was nowhere to go. Niko's eyes went as wide as saucers as she frantically searched through the annals of her mind for any options of escape.

The two Shatter guards had spotted her, though, and now shoved their way through the crowd, powerful as they were. They had almost reached her in mere seconds when the girl with the scars slapped her shoulder and broke into a laugh.

"You are too much!" she gushed, draping an arm over Niko as she turned away with her.

Before she spent too much time confused about what the *blazes* this girl was doing, Niko was instantly reminded of a time several years ago when Ravenna had put on an act to save her. This *had* to be what this girl was doing. Bless her heart.

"Stop!!" the men shouted.

Gasps and screams echoed through the market as the men drew their weapons. The girl stepped forward and stood up to her full height, which was barely as tall as Niko.

"What do you think you're doing?!" she demanded of the guards. "What is the meaning of this?"

"*She* was just trespassing on prohibited territory five minutes ago!" the more aggressive of the men said, pointing a finger at Niko. "She will be coming with us."

"Have you been hitting the Cinto?" The girl stared at the men incredulously. "My friends and I have been shopping here for over an hour!"

The men stared back at her, then looked back and forth at each other.

The girl laughed condescendingly. "It seems you have the wrong person."

The aggressive Shatter guard stepped closer, the moisture from his breath visible against the space with a sour sheen.

"I'm pretty sure we have the correct person," he challenged. "We would have a word with h…"

"Here," the girl interrupted. "If you don't believe us, look at the stuff we bought…"

Without invitation, she set her bags on the floor and rummaged through her haul, pulling out several stalks of produce and a couple blacksquashes before exasperatedly dumping the rest of the contents onto the floor.

Niko couldn't believe the amount of stuff this woman had bought! It was mostly food, but the guards appeared embarrassed when a clump of new underwear tumbled onto the pavement. They averted their gaze, as if realizing they'd maybe made a mistake. After more clothes were thrown onto the pile, the guards looked at each other confusedly, then scanned out toward the crowd.

Were they actually buying it?? The way the girl continued to act like she and Niko were the oldest of friends certainly helped. This all seemed like a brilliant ploy to get rid of them, but how did she even know they were after Niko?

"Forgive me," the girl said to them. "We got a *lot* of clothes. We've been out here forever…"

She finished dumping every last thing she'd bought onto the ground, which had grown into a considerable heap. How did the woman have so much Terion credit?! Did the fields pay that well?? Niko really should quit her job at the Rifts and start working there...

"Here, I suppose you can show them yours, too," the girl sighed theatrically.

Niko obliged and set her bags down, showing the guards the packs of nutrient mix she'd just purchased.

"You too, Amon," the girl said, gesturing toward a man that had just arrived. He looked dangerous, as if he were ready to dispatch these men that threatened this woman, had she given the request.

He looked back at her in question, then set his bags on the floor and opened them, revealing even more food.

"Our mistake," the Shatter guards finally admitted. They took one long look at Niko before walking on, rifles still in hand. "Pardon us."

After a few seconds, they disappeared into the crowd, which had resumed its normal bustle, but not before Niko heard one of them make a snide comment about the girl's face.

What a jerk.

After they were gone, Niko let out the deepest sigh of relief. She couldn't believe she had gotten out of that!

But who was this stranger, and why did she come to Niko's aid?! Niko was immensely grateful, but had no clue what she did to deserve this goodwill.

"I would convey much gratitude," Niko announced in her best An-Mara voice, hoping that she hadn't let her façade slip during the interaction so far. As much as this girl had done for her, she'd only just met her, and she was rightfully skeptical to trust a stranger enough to let her in on any secrets. "I am the one called Niko Ryen."

Her name was fine to give out at least, since that's what was attached to her Terion credit, after all...

The girl stared at Niko for a moment, clearly judging her. Both women were about the same size, petite and fairly short, but this girl's gaze made Niko feel *tiny*. It was not hard to see why the nutrient vendor had cowered in defeat so quickly...

"You are not An-Mara," she finally said, playfully cocking her head to the side.

Niko's face went red with alarm. The one thing that Callum

Sehs had made her promise was that she would never reveal her true identity as Arhandan. Of course, he didn't elaborate much on the reason why. Something about how they were all liabilities to the Meridians? Whatever. The failure of her masquerade was enough for Niko to panic now.

"I... I'm..." she stammered. "I'm..."

"Not to worry," the girl quickly interrupted. "Many come here to hide... You have nothing to be ashamed of."

"I... well... I..."

Niko sighed in defeat, realizing she'd been caught. This woman was *way* too astute. Besides, she owed her now — she had just bailed Niko out of a tight spot. *Two* tight spots, if she included the deal on the nutrient mix. The least she could do was be honest with her...

"I'm Niko." She introduced herself for real this time, bleeding with guilt. "Niko Ryen."

"Anda," the girl replied. Niko had her accent and mannerisms pegged as Meridian, but she didn't look the part. To be fair, her face was so disfigured that it would be hard to tell what she looked like before. "And this is Amon."

Something about this Anda was so enthralling that Niko had forgotten about the man standing right there. She looked over at him respectfully, noticing the tanned, weathered skin and short brown hair. Definitely a Meridian. Niko couldn't say how old he was, though — probably at least thirty, she reckoned. She was so bad at guessing ages...

"Nice to meet you," Niko said, nodding to both of them, still wincing on the inside after being caught in the deception. "Sorry I tried to lie about who I was."

Anda shook her head. "It's quite alright. Like I said, many people come here to hide. Your secret is safe with me."

"Thanks," Niko said sheepishly.

"It is nothing," Anda replied, pausing. "Do you live around here?"

Niko shook her head and lowered her voice. "The An-Mara quarter." She saw Anda's quizzical look and quickly added, "I'm visiting friends here tonight, though."

"Ah, I see," the girl hummed. "Do they live nearby?"

"Mmm, kind of," Niko responded, gesturing back toward the dark thoroughfare from whence she had been chased. "I gotta go back down that street before turning off the main Row."

"Those Shatter goons are on the other side of the market right now," Amon growled, pointing discreetly to the left. This was the first she'd heard him speak. "If you leave right now, you should be able to avoid them altogether."

"Thanks," Niko said, nodding deeply.

She was grateful beyond words. They had just saved her skin! She would have hugged them, but she didn't want to overdo it in front of people she just met. The gratitude was heartfelt, though.

"Fare well, Niko. Good luck."

Anda offered her the same deep nod in return, as did Amon, before the two parties split ways.

Niko turned around to head in the direction that Amon suggested, but stopped before taking two paces.

"Wait!" she called after Anda.

Anda stopped and turned around, but didn't say anything. She just fixated intently upon Niko, waiting patiently for her to say her piece. Even though she only had one functioning eye, its light blue gaze was intense and lively, radiating clear acumen.

"I've seen you before. On the train." Niko paused, unsure if she should ask the question. Before she thought too long about it, she blurted it out. "Are they hiring at the fields at all?"

Anda shrugged. "Why do you ask?"

"I kind of want... to *transition* out of the Rifts."

"Hmmm," Anda deliberated. "The fields don't pay as well as the Rifts for newcomers."

How did she have so much Terion credit, then? She did mention the word '*newcomers*', though. Maybe veterans were paid way more?

"Well, it's just... I just want out."

"Suit yourself," Anda said. "If you're set on that decision, they are always looking for more hands in the fields."

"Okay, good to know," said Niko. "Thanks."

"Of course," Anda replied. "You better get going, though, before those thugs cycle back around. I hope to meet again, Niko Ryen. Maybe on the train?"

With that, she flashed Niko a smile, though it looked unsightly and awkward against all the scar tissue. She then whirled around gracefully and glided away after Amon, disappearing into the teeming crowds of the marketplace.

Niko didn't know what made her think of it, but something

about that girl reminded her of Ajane Solase. She had to be Meridian — the way she conducted herself so confidently, not to mention her smooth accent. Whatever circumstances had taken Anda from wherever she hailed to scraping out a living on the desolate frontier of An-Terino, maimed and disfigured, must be a long story.

Niko departed the marketplace in a brisk jaunt, the background buzz steadily decreasing while the glow of the neon lights faded into deep Twilight once again. She became so lost in thought that she didn't even notice walking back past the Shatter yard.

Ajane…

That lady had given everything, and Niko had never properly grieved for her. Sure, she had moments where she'd break into silent tears in the days and weeks after leaving Arhanda, but after a while she just became numb. She no longer had any Memories — no Ut even — and some faces had faded to the point where they were only blurs now.

She clenched her teeth in frustration, feeling guilty that she was alive when they were not. Maybe it was good she was going to see her friends from Arhanda tonight, after all, if for no other reason than to keep her grounded.

CHAPTER FOUR

4

The Minedyne Connection

HER friends lived in a corner unit on the bottom floor of a large, square building about a kilometer off the Row. True, it was much nicer than Niko's flat, but she felt the place had no heart, no soul. The neighborhood wasn't even a *neighborhood*. It was on the dark side of the city, and there were hardly any people out and about. Just the occasional passerby, and anyone she did see only kept to themselves. Not that it was a bad thing... It just wasn't a place that she really cared to live. It felt so... *depressing*.

Cryo, at least, seemed sad when she moved out over six months ago, but Ravenna and Kyler had seemed indifferent. She knew that was only their personalities manifesting, and that they actually did care about her. At least that's what she told herself.

She had to make the move, though, for the sake of her own sanity. As it was, she barely held on by a thread anyway.

"Seven hundred Terion?!" Kyler eyed Niko distrustfully.

"Yeah," she responded nonchalantly.

She didn't dare tell them about her close call with the Shatter guards, or the girl that had saved her afterward. That would've only served to bring up too many questions, as well as a thorough scolding from Ravenna. She already knew she messed up — the terror of running from the guards had served as enough of a lesson. Besides, she had to live with plenty of scoldings from Kira-Tharn; getting one from Ravenna now would've been too much nonsense to deal with.

"How?? I didn't figure you to be the haggler..." Kyler prodded.

Niko just shrugged. She learned long ago that it was just best to ignore his digs.

"How've you been feeling?" she asked Ravenna, changing the subject.

"Good," Ravenna replied. "Almost back to a hundred percent."

"The good An-Mara doctors said you'd never be one hundred percent..." Kyler reminded her.

"Still good enough to beat your ass." Ravenna didn't even blink an eye. What she said wasn't untrue.

"Breathing getting better?" Niko asked.

Ravenna nodded. "Yeah. I just can't take super deep breaths without coughing."

"That's annoying. How long is that supposed to go on for?"

"No clue. It doesn't really make much of a difference anyway. There's nothing physical to do outside here. I just sit here and don't ever exercise."

"True," Niko admitted. She doubted she'd be getting any physical activity in, either, if she wasn't forced to work outside all day. It was either too hot or too cold out, and the only temperate zone on the planet was covered in a disgusting city, muggy from thick, dirty atmosphere. "I guess that's good for your recovery, at least."

"Hmph," Ravenna grunted. "Maybe."

Niko nearly jumped as the door behind her opened, but it was only Cryo, along with a man she'd never seen before. He looked older than any of her other friends, but younger than middle aged. Maybe somewhere around Kira-Tharn's age? He had short, dark hair and brown eyes that screamed stereotypical Meridian.

"Niko!" Cryo offered her a side-hug, which she returned with both arms. He was never very physical with hugs, but she didn't care. She missed him. "How've you been?"

"I've been okay," she said. It wasn't exactly a lie. She wasn't great — nobody in this Mara-forsaken place was *great* — but she also wasn't bad. She was just... *okay*. "You?"

"Not bad," he replied. "We've been making some good

progress."

"Oh yeah?"

"Yeah, we've been doing a lot of work on our predictive models. Kyler swears those are our best way in. We've also been working on a new machine. Let's eat and we can fill you in over dinner."

"Nice. Yeah, I'm starving."

"Oh, by the way… this is Ce-Ellum." Cryo must've noticed her gaze lingering on the new stranger. "He actually lives with us now."

He lives *with them*?!

Niko knew she shouldn't feel jealous or anything — she moved away to a different part of the city of her own volition, after all — but the fact that her friends took in this new guy made her feel… *replaced.*

"Nice to meet you. I'm Niko."

"Ce-Ellum," the man responded politely. "Nice to meet you, as well."

He also had a Meridian accent, as it seemed most people on this planet did. The An-Mara were actually the minority here, even though they were the first to settle here long ago. But if he was Meridian, why was it that he had an An-Mara name?

Strange.

"So, how'd you guys meet?" Niko asked. She wanted to find a way to ask her friends if they should be discussing any of their machine tinkering stuff in front of this guy, but she didn't want to be rude.

"Ce and I ran into each other at the Salvage Yards a couple different times," Kyler said. "Eventually we got to chatting and it turns out we were both using that stuff to make machines."

"You're a machine guru also?" Niko asked. She only hoped he wasn't as big of an ass as Kyler was.

"I dabble," he chuckled. "I've been here for years working with a number of people, but Kyler, Cryo, and Ven were the first I've met actually trying to crack into Terion."

Niko's eyes narrowed involuntarily. The only other person Niko had ever heard call Ravenna 'Ven' was Cryo. Who did this guy think he was?!

But wait… did he just say he knew of the plan to tinker into Terion!?

Niko's eyes darted around furtively to her friends, but only

Cryo seemed to notice.

"It's all good," he laughed. "He's with us."

'How can you be so sure?' she wanted to blurt out. Her initial impressions of this Ce-Ellum guy weren't great, but maybe that was just a continuation of her feeling weird all day. Besides, she had to admit that Cryo was a pretty decent judge of character. After all, he'd been right about Ajane all those years ago.

"Your secret is safe with me," Ce-Ellum beamed back at her. If she didn't know any better, the tone of his voice sounded like he was trying hard to win her over. Too hard. She must've been too exhausted to hide the look of distrust stamped all over her face.

She looked to Kyler and Ravenna, who weren't even listening to the conversation anymore. Clearly, they felt comfortable enough around this guy, so Niko just smiled courteously back at him.

"Well, that's good. Otherwise we'd have to kill you." She attempted the joke, but it fell flat, as many of hers tended to do. She really was spending too much time with the damned An-Mara...

Ce-Ellum laughed at least. "Noted."

"So, how long ago did you move in?" she asked, much too tired to laugh herself. "I used to live here, but I moved out about six months ago."

"Yes, I've heard a lot about you. I'm not sure if we ever crossed paths, though," he said doubtfully. "I moved in about three months ago, and I first started working with everyone about six months ago. You and I must have just missed each other."

"Yeah. Must have." So she really *was* replaced.

"So, you live with the An-Mara now?" he asked.

"Yep."

"How's that?"

"It's..." Niko hesitated. "It's okay. They're not so bad once you get to know them."

"I guess so, although the whole not laughing thing seems so crazy," Ce-Ellum remarked. He added, "I spent a lot of time around them when I was younger. I even got an An-Mara name."

So that explained it.

"Oh cool. I don't have to follow every one of their customs, although I don't really have much time for laughing these days anyway."

Blazes, that came out way more pathetic than intended...

She would be most thankful if she could make it through one

interaction today without coming across as weak, incompetent, or pitiful. Ce-Ellum only looked back at her blankly, though, so it was hard to tell what he thought of her. The man was difficult to read in general, but she'd give him the benefit of the doubt since her friends seemed to like him well enough.

"Are you trying to get off An-Ter…"

"Oh yeah, Ce!" Kyler interrupted her. "You have to check out the lines I told you I was working on today. I kind of see what's turning it into a loop, but I think we can refactor it and use that to our advantage. Here, let me show you…"

He dragged Ce-Ellum out of the room before the man even had a chance to say anything at all. She wasn't exactly sad to end the small-talk, but Niko shook her head nonetheless. She would never understand machine tinkerers…

She turned back to Cryo and Ravenna, who were tidying up in the living room.

Good for them, she thought. She knew tidying was something *she* should've been doing in her own living quarters — maybe this would give her the inspiration she needed to clean up the trash heap she was living in.

"Did you guys need me to help make dinner at all?" she offered. Not that she would be able to make anything good. Meals back home with Kira-Tharn almost always involved eating mix straight out of the bags. Maybe some broth or soup if they were feeling fancy. Neither of them had the time or energy to ever prepare anything complex, let alone cook a meal.

"Nah, we got this one!" responded Cryo. "Enjoy your night here."

"Oh yeah, that reminds me," Ravenna added. "Happy Birthday, Niko."

As bleak as she'd been feeling all day, her pulse quickened ever so slightly at the excitement of feeling special.

Wow, they really did remember…

———————

The dinner was excellent by An-Terino standards. Cryo had cooked the nutrient mix together with some blacksquashes, and somehow they'd gotten ahold of some Cinto that he lightly sprinkled onto the dish. She was surprised they even had any — it wasn't the type of herb she expected any of them to have possession of, even though it was largely impotent in low quantities like they used tonight. Tasteful even, she had to admit.

Cleaning up, on the other hand, was not so pleasant. The evening had now devolved into discord, a classic Green Coast arguing session, one she'd become so accustomed to over the years. One would think that all the tragedy they endured together would have brought them closer to the point where they never argued, but it was not so. Maybe it was being cooped up on that damn ship for nearly four years — or being stranded in this dystopian deathtrap — but whatever it was, everyone seemed so cantankerous all too often. Especially Kyler.

No shock there...

"A laugh!" Kyler tormented Niko. "Isn't that against the code? Or whatever it's called..."

"The Time," she corrected. "And it wasn't a laugh. I was *slightly* amused at how lame you're being."

"Don't you even hear yourself?!" he howled. "You're defending yourself about *laughing*?!"

"No, I'm defending myself from you being an idiot," she retorted.

"Me?! *Me* being an idiot?" he strained. "I think you're the one who's being..."

"I was just asking about your progress and you immediately start lighting into me about spending more time with the An-Mara than you guys." Niko had become heated, and she definitely didn't care if she interrupted Kyler at this point.

"Is it not the truth?"

"I..." Niko stumbled for words. She supposed it was the truth, but that was beside the point. "You know I'm doing what I can."

Kyler snorted.

"You can't imagine the work I have to do every day!" she protested. "You wouldn't last thirty minutes in the Rifts! You sit in your room all comfortable and get paid nicely from whatever... *company*... you're doing machine work for these days."

"And if it weren't for the work I'm doing — that *all* of us are doing besides *you* — we'd have no way off this rock," he accused.

"Oh yeah? And how's that coming?"

"Pretty good, actually."

"Oh really?! Last I checked we've been here for over a *year*!"

"So what are *you* doing to help, then?!"

"I... I..."

She sighed. Her words weren't forming the sentence she wanted. She really should take this down a notch. Why was she so snappy tonight?

"I'm sorry," she apologized, seizing the rare opportunity from a short lull where Kyler didn't immediately bark on the offensive. "But dude, can't you just hack in and get the Terion we need to get off this dump?"

"Holy blazes!" he exclaimed. "You're right! Why didn't I think of that?!"

Niko held her head up proudly, only to be shamed immediately after. She should've known he was being snarky.

"You dimwit!" he snarled. "Of course that's always been the goal! What do you think I've been doing this whole time?"

"Then where's our Terion?" she demanded.

"It's not that easy! Do you have any idea what kind of security that place has??"

"Enlighten me."

"Well, on top of the near-infinity level encryption and the ridiculously layered key access, there are tripwires at every API endpoint... And then physical access to their servers is out of the question — Terion has the largest armed security force on the entire damn planet. You don't just walk in there and siphon credit."

"I thought you were a wiz with this stuff?" she prodded.

"This isn't some fantasy where you just plug a magic twig into the machine and it gives you whatever you want..."

"I know that!" Niko snapped back.

"You don't know the first thing about it!" he yelled, his voice squeaking like it sometimes did when he got too frustrated. "Anytime someone volunteered to teach you *anything*, you refused to learn! You wouldn't even understand the *basics* of what I do."

"I know more than you think I do, Kyler," she pushed.

"Oh yeah?" he jeered. "Explain to me how a logic gate works. That should be easy for you since it's the simplest fundamental in digital technology..."

Blazes, Niko thought. She knew a *little* bit about gates, but she had to give a legitimate answer if she wanted to maintain any semblance of respect.

"Okay, well, those are like the AND/OR statements that you program into your machines," she guessed.

"Yeah, but the question was how do they work?" he demanded, staring at her very intently.

"I don't know. You just program a statement: IF one thing AND/OR another thing, THEN a result?"

"How. Do. They. Work?" he enunciated. "Tell me how I'm supposed to program them. And what about the other five fundamental gates? Do you even know what those are?"

"Of course I know what those are!" she snapped back. It wasn't entirely a lie, although she didn't remember what all of them were called, nor all their precise functions. "You just plug the inputs in and they each process that data differently."

"That would be the explanation where you plug the magic twig into the machine and it miraculously gives you what you want."

"I don't know! I mean I'm not about to *build* a transistor just to demonstrate that I know everything inside and out," she relented. She thought she did a good job answering his stupid questions, but of course he was still being a jerk about it…

"I'm actually shocked you even know what a transistor is," he drawled sarcastically.

She squinted her eyes and made a face at him. "I didn't claim to know as much as you! I only claimed to know more than you *thought* I did."

"And I *thought* you know pretty much next to nothing," he sneered. "Which you so eloquently demonstrated."

"You're an ass," Niko charged.

"Well! You're a little…"

"Both of you, shut up!" Cryo interrupted exasperatedly, cutting Kyler's return insult short. "Give it a rest, dude. You don't need to prove that you know more about machines than Niko does. Just the same as she doesn't need to prove that she has more psychic potential than you do."

Psychic potential. Those were words she hadn't heard in a long time. She'd left that part of her behind, and had no desire to further her education in that realm.

Kyler's face turned pink, but at least he didn't levy any further insults. Niko had really worked him up, and it was only Cryo's incredible calming effect that kept him in check.

Cryo turned back toward Niko. "We've been trying to build a machine that will be able to tinker into Terion, but it's been really challenging with only a few of us working on it."

"I was mainly kidding," she muttered. "I know it's been hard."

Kyler scoffed unintelligibly, but refrained from continuing the quarrel. Ce-Ellum and Ravenna just sat leaned back in their chairs, enjoying the show like they had skylight box seats to a NewCen entertainment show. Niko grew slightly red in the face for feuding with Kyler so intensely in front of this man she'd only just met.

"Kyler does have a point though," Cryo said, aiming a soft glance toward Niko. "You really should learn how this stuff works. We're trying to convert our machine construction from processing binary inputs to quinary ones using wave interference patterns. Then there's another idea we've had to process probabilities in order to factor more quickly. You're so blazes smart that you could be a lot of help to us here."

Niko sighed. She didn't think she was *that* smart... Most of what he said went over her head. "I just... I feel like it would all be so overwhelming," she said honestly. "I'm so far behind at this point that I feel like I'd never learn. Plus I have my job."

"I hate to break it to you, but your job is barely paying the bills," Ravenna leveled bluntly. "You're breaking your back daily, and for what? Just to barely squeak by?"

"I know," Niko admitted. "I'm actually looking in to getting a job in the fields tomorrow. I met Anda tonight and she was saying... nevermind."

She cut herself off before having to spill how she met this Anda girl, or the two Shatter guards, but it was too late.

"Who?" Ravenna asked.

"Nobody," Niko lied.

Ravenna only looked back at her with that trademark no-nonsense glare.

"Just a girl I met at the market on the way here," she relented.

"You're being weird."

Ravenna knew she was hiding something. How??

All eyes were now on Niko. The way she squirmed, hugging her elbows while her eyes drifted all over the place, must've given the game away, and her friends weren't going to let her off the hook now.

Oh, blazes, she bemoaned to herself. "I'm not being weird!"

"You literally are," Kyler accused. "So who's this Anda you're being all weird about?"

Blazes!... "Nobody! Just someone who helped me haggle for the nutrient mix. That's all."

It wasn't a lie... It just wasn't the entire truth.

Kyler jumped up and pointed a finger at Niko as if he'd just won some huge victory. "I knew it! No wonder you got the two bags for seven hundred Terion! I knew that couldn't have been you!"

Niko just rolled her eyes and emphasized a rude gesture back at him.

"What else aren't you telling us, Niko?" Ravenna was glaring daggers at her. She really wasn't going to let this go.

"Nothing!" Niko threw her hands up. Now *that* was a lie.

All three of her friends, plus Ce-Ellum, were now staring at her, waiting for her to spill the full truth. How the blazes could they all know she had stuff she didn't want to tell them?! She *hated* that she was so blazes obvious about it.

"Fine!" she exhaled. "She helped me out of a bind."

"A bind?" Cryo asked concernedly.

"Nothing huge." Niko did her best to downplay the situation. "Just some Shatter guards wanted a word with me, and I didn't wanna talk to them."

"Shatter?" Ravenna blurted, her brows furrowing. "Why?"

Niko looked down at the ground sheepishly. "Well, I *may* have snuck into one of their yards."

"For the love of the Mara, why?!" Ravenna cried, arms now crossed over her chest. This is the lecture Niko did *not* want to deal with. "Why would you do something so stupid?"

"I saw some Meridian logos on their boxes," Niko responded with a shrug. "I just thought that was fishy."

Low murmurs went around the room between the friends before Ce-Ellum joined the conversation.

"Meridian? You're sure? You saw the Crescent?" For emphasis, he held up his thumb and forefinger in the shape of a 'C' with the other three fingers squeezed into a ball. The likeness to the logo was uncanny.

Niko nodded and her friends looked around at each other.

"So it's true," Cryo remarked.

"I guess so?" Ravenna shrugged.

"I hate to be the one who said 'I told you so', but I told you so," Kyler added, as they all rolled their eyes at him.

"Well this complicates things," Ravenna said.

"Yes and no," Ce-Ellum said. "It depends what they're after, but if they're trying to influence Terion this soon…"

"Oooh, you're right," Cryo chimed in.

Ce-Ellum nodded his head and smiled at Cryo.

What the blazes are they all talking about? Niko was beyond confused.

"This will definitely split their attention," added Ravenna.

"Hmmm yeah. There was that chatter of those shipments coming in from off-world," Kyler said.

"Oh yeah, about the shipments…" Niko started, as all eyes swung back her way.

"What do *you* know about it?" Ravenna demanded sharply.

"I just… I *overheard* the guards talking and they mentioned there were boxes coming into the docks from *Minedyne*."

At first, her friends didn't say a word. They simply reeled in disbelief. It would've sounded outlandish to her, as well, had she not heard it with her own ears.

"*Minedyne*?" Kyler asked incredulously. "Are you sure you heard that right? I thought they were long gone. You know… with… Arhanda." His voice trailed off. It was still such a sensitive topic with Kyler. He, more than any of the others, took the loss of their home very hard. Maybe even harder than Niko. "There's been no mention of *Minedyne* on any of the transmissions. I don't know if you heard it right."

"I heard what I heard," Niko said defensively. Kyler could doubt her publicly if he wanted, but she knew what was said, clear as the Celean Sea.

"Well, if it is Minedyne, then we have some investigating to do," Ravenna declared. "This just got confusing as blazes."

"You all know this company, I presume?" Ce-Ellum asked. "Minedyne?"

Everyone nodded.

"It was a company the fake Meridians set up on our planet," Ravenna said.

Niko was still amused at how they all just called the Meridians from Arhanda the 'fake Meridians' now. Very fitting.

"Yeah, they mainly did a lot of mining on the South Continent,"

Cryo added.

"When we were cooped up with all the An-Mara on our ship, they told us that once the Meridians found out Arhanda was rich in the rare metals, they 'tore our planet apart for their Empire'."

Kyler made it sound so dramatic, but that *was* what the An-Mara told them, more or less.

"The Lanthanides?" Ce-Ellum asked.

Ravenna narrowed her eyes at him. "What does that mean?" she asked honestly. Niko admired how naturally she could admit when she didn't know something. "I've never heard that term before."

"Meridian word for a particular group of elements," Ce-Ellum said. "They're very useful for many materials."

"Oh," she replied. "Well, they were definitely mining something. And shipping much of it out."

"Is that what they're importing here, then?" Kyler asked.

"I have no idea," Cryo said. "Maybe Niko got a look in the crates?"

"I only saw the Meridian boxes and Shatter boxes, and they were empty," she replied, shaking her head. "The guards only *spoke* about Minedyne shipments. I didn't actually see them."

"Did they say when they were coming in?"

"I think it was tonight," she responded. "One of them got a call when I was right there, and they said they were needed back at the docks for another shipment. A Minedyne shipment. That's all I heard."

"Well, who's up for an outing to the Dockyards?" Kyler said, standing up.

"Kyler, you were just berating Niko for not knowing about machines," Ravenna said dryly. "You know very well tapping into their comms is something you *can* do."

"Yeah, but a field trip is much more fun."

"I think we need to get ahold of Callum and Jack before doing anything," Cryo suggested. "I'm sure they're aware of this."

"Have you heard from them recently?" Niko eagerly asked. Butterflies pulled at her stomach just from hearing Jack's name spoken aloud, even though she *was* still upset with him for disappearing for so long.

Cryo shook his head. "Not in about three months."

"Oh." Niko hoped they were okay. Alashadar was so sketchy...

It wasn't a great place to conduct whatever underground business they were involved in. Especially Oldcity, where she'd last heard Callum and Jack were spending their time.

"But I do know how to reach them," Cryo assured her. "And now we have a reason to. If the Meridians are in league with Shatter…"

"Looks like they are," Ce-Ellum interrupted. "And if any random girl can sneak into their yard and see evidence of their collusion, then they must not really care who finds out at this point."

Umm, excuse me!? Niko was beyond irked that he just referred to her as some '*random girl*'.

It was unbelievable — this man just comes into their lives, replaces her in the friend group, then proceeds to insult her?! Whether he meant to or not was beside the point. For blazes' sakes, it was supposed to be *her* birthday dinner tonight!

She couldn't put her finger on it, but there was something about this guy she *just* didn't trust. He seemed… off, and it was unfortunate no one else could see it. But, as much as she hated to admit it, he did have a point about the Shatter guards.

"One of them did get a little concerned when he heard the other one talking about it so loudly," she said.

"Maybe you did stumble onto something then…" Ravenna regarded Niko carefully, her violet eyes swirling with deep thought.

Maybe I did. That would make a lot of sense as to why those Shatter guards were so desperate to chase her down in that market earlier.

She stifled a shudder that threatened to shake her entire body. She did *not* want her friends to learn just how dicey that encounter had been.

"Hmm, I'm thinking Niko had the best presence of mind out of all of us to go snooping around that yard…" Kyler joked. At least he wasn't acting so derisively anymore. "I'm telling you, I haven't seen *any* chatter about that stuff. If they *are* in league, it's all very hush hush."

"Well, for now, we shouldn't do anything brash," Cryo decided. "I'm gonna reach out to Callum and Jack and see what they have on their end. Until then, let's all just lay low." He looked over at Niko, the corner of his mouth tugged into amusement.

"You don't have to tell me twice," she said, putting her hands up in submission. "I learned my lesson, no more Shatter yards."

"Oh speaking of," Kyler announced, looking at his portable monitor screen, "I'm seeing a wanted notice for an An-Mara girl that matches Niko's description…"

The blood froze in Niko's veins.

"Seriously?!" Ravenna snatched the screen away from Kyler and pored over it intently. "You're right. This is unfortunate."

She handed the screen to Cryo, who scrunched his brows in thought. "Well, that's not good."

No, Niko pleaded to herself. She thought this saga was over. Anda had seen to it that they'd moved on from her, but Niko now felt foolish that she didn't stop to think that they would put out a wanted alert broadcast.

"This just shows exactly how sensitive that information is," Cryo said, "and reinforces that we should lay super low right now."

"Yep," Ravenna agreed, turning to Niko. "I'm sorry, girl, but your Garments have gotta go. You're gonna have to wear some of my clothes for when you head out."

"Actually, can you stay the night with us?" Cryo asked. "I don't think you should be out and about at all, honestly."

Niko shook her head. "I need to get back. Kira-Tharn would freak if I never came home."

"Well, if you absolutely have to go, then you better get going soon," he cautioned. "They're expecting someone in the Row. And *'last sighted heading toward NewCen'*, according to the latest updates. If you leave now, they might not be looking in the direction of the An-Mara quarter."

That seemed strange, considering they were searching for an An-Mara girl, but she wasn't about to question it.

"Okay." She nodded her head and let Ravenna lead her to the back rooms, where she changed into some of her friend's clothes.

Niko thanked her, but sighed to herself when she looked in the mirror. She hated wearing the tight-fitting clothes that Ravenna always wore. She much preferred looser attire, which was one of the reasons she loved the Garments so much. Oh well, whatever kept her out of the clutches of any Shatter search parties…

"This should all blow over tonight or tomorrow," Ce-Ellum said as she walked back out into the living room. "This is always what happens. Literally every night. They search for one perpetrator, whatever the person did, then they either catch him or they don't. Mostly, people get away and just disappear into Alashadar. They don't have the resources to be able to hunt down every single person that's wronged them. Not yet, at least."

I guess that's reassuring. Niko was grateful that he attempted to make her feel better, but she still didn't trust him.

"My thoughts exactly," Ravenna said, probably noting the panic still written all over Niko's expressions. "I think you'll be fine. But it doesn't hurt to be smart for a few days."

"Yeah, no An-Mara Garments for you," Kyler chided. "And maybe even laugh or something. Throw 'em off your scent."

If only she could laugh.

"Well, thanks for coming over," Ravenna said. "We need to do this more often. Not the arguing part, though." She leveled a sharp look at Kyler, who only spread his hands innocently.

"We're gonna watch the race in three days if you wanna come over for that?" Cryo invited, tagging onto Ravenna's suggestion.

"Sure," Niko nervously accepted. "But are you sure they won't be looking for me anymore?"

"Just don't wear the An-Mara Garments for a day or two and you'll be fine," Ce-Ellum promised with a grin. The guy seemed like he was really trying hard to make her accept him. Did he catch on to her wariness of him?

"Okay, yeah I won't."

"Good," Ravenna declared. "We'll see you in three days."

Niko thought she might even have fun. She'd never been interested in racing of any kind back on Arhanda, but she did have to admit that Trackripping on An-Terino was oddly captivating. Maybe it was the high stakes? Or the speed. Or the way the tracks were seamlessly entwined into the surroundings. It was a very entertaining pastime.

"Will do."

"We'll see you then." The way Ravenna said it made it clear that she needed to leave. Now.

"Sorry we're kicking you out so soon," Cryo grimaced. "And on your birthday."

"It's okay. It's my own fault for getting into this."

"Nah," he reassured her. "It's actually super important we found out what we did."

"If you say so."

"Trust me, I mean it."

"Okay, well, see you guys later."

Niko turned and waved awkwardly to her friends. She stepped over to the door, but stopped just short of exiting.

"Oh! And one other thing I heard..." she started. "The guards I overheard mentioned *Andersane* was coming here..."

There was a short silence as all heads in the room turned toward Ravenna.

"So he did make it out," she whispered, without so much as even twitching a muscle. Niko could feel the burning heat from Ravenna's gaze as she stared into the distance.

"Andersane?!" Kyler half-shouted after the pause. "That chum's coming here?! And here I'd hoped he was dead back on Arhanda..."

"That's what I heard," Niko said. "The guards didn't seem to like him much, either."

"No one likes him," Ravenna muttered. Niko hadn't forgotten that Ravenna had wanted to *kill* that man for years and years.

"Let's worry about all this later," Cryo said, steering the conversation back on track. "We do need to get you out of here now, Niko, before they start swinging their search to this side of the Row."

"Yep," Ravenna concurred. "See you later."

Niko would've normally felt offended for being kicked out so unceremoniously, but rationality told her they were right. She needed to get out of there.

"Okay, thank you guys," she said graciously, but without hugging any of her friends. "See you in three days?"

"Yep," Kyler confirmed. "On race day!"

He slammed the door shut as soon as she stepped out.

Rude.

CHAPTER FIVE

5

Discussions

THANKFULLY, the trip back had been uneventful. No Shatter
search parties. No guards. No insufferable friends to hassle her every
step of the way. She was only accompanied by her own thoughts
swirling around in her head, though they were plenty enough.

Niko was on edge, and rightfully so. She didn't understand
what in all the blazes had possessed her to sneak into that Shatter
yard earlier in the night, but it had caused her more than enough
trouble. On her way back to the An-Mara quarter, she crept around
corners awkwardly, rushed quickly through crowds with her head
down, and even pretended to sleep with her arms draped over her
face on the train, all to avoid any potential run-ins with Shatter.

The one good thing that came from that inadvertent intrusion
upon Shatter business was that her friends seemed to find what she
had to tell them important. But why? What did Ce-Ellum mean about
them influencing Terion so soon? And Ravenna said something
about that splitting their attention? Niko rubbed at her temples. She
didn't know what any of it meant, nor did she know how it could
possibly help them in their quest to find their way out of this
forsaken wasteland.

Now safely back in the An-Mara quarter, she finally allowed

herself some room to breathe. Strangely, this place felt more like home than anywhere else she hung her head ever since she'd been ripped away from the Green Coast a lifetime ago. The sights, sounds, and smells of this place were somewhat odd, but in a homely sort of way — when the refuse service was working properly, at least. She couldn't describe the feeling, not even to herself, but this place *was* home.

Home as it may have been, though, her feet screamed at her to lie down, the pressure of each step pulsating with ultimate fatigue, even borderline pain. Still, this discomfort was nothing out of the ordinary. She had developed into little more than a robot who could handle it without complaints, a mindless laborer programmed from many months spent working in the Rifts. Pushing through this wall wasn't anything she couldn't do.

If anything, her mood was *lighter* tonight — at least now that she'd made it back to her neighborhood — because she had just been thinking of how tomorrow she would quit her job in the Rifts to work in the agricultural fields instead. After she had the discussion with Kira-Tharn, of course.

I am *going to talk to her*, she promised herself.

She also needed to smooth things over after their senseless disagreement a few hours ago when their shift ended. Why had they been so mad at each other? Sure, she'd been annoyed when Kira-Tharn hassled her about Jack, but truth be told, she appreciated when anyone would talk about him. Hearing his name alone usually brought her cozy spirits, even though she still wasn't completely forgiving him for his long absence.

And about that... when she finally saw him again, she would give him a piece of her mind, oh yes she would. How he had the nerve to up and leave her alone in this place... It was inexcusable.

She was going to scream out loud if she thought of it any further, so she forced Jack out of her mind for the time being, again thinking of Kira-Tharn and why they'd been so upset with each other. It didn't make sense. They hadn't even walked with each other back from the Rifts, as they did every single day for months now! Niko racked and racked her brain, when the answer finally came in the form of a man emerging from the doorway to her living quarters.

Maro Del-Fiiz, the poor guy.

Kira-Tharn had been so unreasonably cranky about his stunt from earlier. Sure, Niko felt nervous at that reckless maneuver also, but the Rift line was fine, perfectly intact! Besides, he was one of the nicest people they worked with, and he definitely didn't deserve the angst that Kira-Tharn directed at him.

He was surely over at their place apologizing in person right now, bless his heart. He really didn't need to. His eyes widened ever so slightly as he saw Niko, then he put his head down and scurried away. He looked... *embarrassed.* Niko muttered a curse under her breath.

I swear... if she was just being a blazes bully and yelling at the poor man again, I promise I'm gonna...

Heated anew, Niko threw the front door open.

"Did you blast Maro Del-Fiiz agai..."

Niko was more than ready to duel wits with Kira-Tharn, but she abruptly cut herself off almost as soon as the tongue lashing had commenced. Instead, she only stood there speechless, ogling for several long seconds at her roommate, who was barely half-dressed and still in the process of putting her sleepclothes back on.

Kira-Tharn met Niko's gaze with a fiery attitude that she knew all too well.

"Do not even *think* about saying one more word, Niko Ryen," she threatened. "I have completed revolutions around Sol One twenty-nine times. I am plenty old enough to make decisions for myself."

Niko didn't say anything at first; she only let her lips accidentally curve into the smallest of smiles. It was something she hadn't done in months, and it unfortunately came at a time when Kira-Tharn would have none of it. She cocked her head dangerously to the side, letting Niko know that she was *not* about to mince words with someone so ignorant in the ways of the Time.

"I didn't say anything!" Niko protested, arms spread wide, still not quite hiding the small hint of a smile well enough.

Kira-Tharn didn't respond. She only continued to finish getting dressed in silence, shoving past Niko to scoop up Garments that had been tossed aside.

There was a strange, celestial glow about her aura, one Niko had never noticed from her friend before. She looked great — even almost *happy* — though that was not an emotion one would assign to an An-Mara. Outwardly, though, Kira-Tharn fumed, muttering something under her breath that Niko couldn't decipher.

"Does the Time allow for this?!" Niko blurted out, against her better judgment. It was half-joke, but also half-curiosity that got the better of her. "Is this *proper*?"

She didn't know what possessed her to tease Kira-Tharn in this moment; she'd already been told to shut up, and ignoring those warnings was more than unwise.

"Do not lecture me in the ways of the Time, Niko Ryen," Kira-Tharn lashed out. "I was educated long before you were even in existence. Have you forgotten everything I have taught you? Must I re-teach you that the Time is an..."

"Yes, yes, I've learned the Time a hundred lessons over," Niko said in exasperation. "Not like I had anything else going on during the Fleetnesses..."

Kira-Tharn stood and glared back at Niko. She needed to really watch what she said — this was not a time to be humorous, or even sarcastic.

"I'm sorry, I didn't mean to make fu..."

"You may think our ways a mockery, living among our quarter without even wearing the proper Garments," Kira-Tharn scolded as her eyes raked judgingly over the outfit Ravenna had provided her, "but I, for one, will adhere to the Time until we become Tel-Mara again."

"Blazes! I'm not trying to make a mockery of your ways!" Niko pleaded. "I had to change clo..."

"Then why do you speak at all?"

"I... I..."

Before Niko could begin her sentence, Kira-Tharn stormed off and slammed the door shut to her room.

What the actual blazes??

Niko was vexed beyond words at this point. It's not like she cared about what Kira-Tharn did, or who she fraternized with. If anything, she was *proud* of Kira-Tharn! At least one of them was having success in their romantic life...

But how would that even work between two An-Mara? They weren't allowed to laugh... They weren't allowed to smile... None of them ever even came to watch Trackripping races! Were they allowed to indulge in any social pleasures at all?

Thinking about what happened, Niko's face turned bright red. She wished she could speak with Kira-Tharn like normal friends would, but she was instructed in no uncertain terms to never say another word about it.

She shook her head and dragged herself miserably to her room. Why must she be at odds with everyone tonight?! She made enemies with Shatter, argued with Kyler, felt immediate aversion to this new Ce-Ellum guy... Now she found a way to antagonize Kira-Tharn, on top of everything else. Normally, she would look to herself as the common denominator, but she really felt that Kira-Tharn's blowup was *not* her fault. Not in the slightest.

She finally found some relief when she kicked off the boots she got from Ravenna, which were much less comfortable than the Garment footwear she'd grown accustomed to. She surely developed blisters on the bottoms of her feet, but that was something she paid little mind to right now.

She quickly performed her bedtime routine in frustration, finally collapsing onto her bed and forcing her eyes closed. Strangely enough, she wasn't as sleepy as she thought she would be, but she needed to try, if she was to wake up in six hours.

Thinking of her decision to switch jobs summoned a fresh wave of anxiety, due in no small part to her current quarrel with Kira-Tharn.

So much for talking to her about quitting the Rifts tomorrow...

Kira-Tharn didn't say a word to Niko the next morning. In fact, she didn't even make eye contact. The two roommates only passed each other for less than a minute before Kira-Tharn left early for the Rifts.

How long is she gonna ignore me for?

Niko thought it was so unfair that she was being punished for this. They were supposed to be *friends*, and friends should support each other. Niko would've absolutely supported her one hundred percent when it came to a relationship with Maro! As far as An-Mara went, she completely approved of Maro. He was nice, hard-working, and he wasn't bad to look at, either.

Niko was completely dumbfounded at the pigheadedness and... well, there wasn't another accurate word that Niko could think of to describe how Kira-Tharn was acting. 'Childish' came closest. She just shook her head and put it all out of her mind, instead turning her focus to the current task at hand, which was to go into the Terrovian Aquatics company office and speak with Armond-Dei about quitting her job in the Rifts. That was a prospect equally as unpleasant, if not more so, than dealing with a pouty Kira-Tharn. The man was a chum of the highest order.

Niko had decided to sleep in an extra thirty minutes, so she didn't even have time to take a shower. Did it really matter, though? She knew she smelled awful, but she skipped out on washing all the time these days. Feeling clean and smelling nice was a luxury from a previous lifetime.

She simply rushed through the necessities of her morning routine, such as grabbing a small bite to eat and halfheartedly brushing her teeth, then swept outside in a flurry, nearly crashing into Riiz Alke-Tani as she did.

"Sorry!" she squeaked.

"It is quite alright, Niko Ryen," he drawled as he looked around to Niko's right and left. "Is the one called Kira-Tharn inside still? I must speak with her."

Niko couldn't stop from involuntarily rolling her eyes. "No. She left super early this morning." She didn't dare elaborate on their latest spat. "I can pass on a message if you'd like?"

"It is not something you need burden yourself with, but thank you for the offer. It has to do with the ones called Callum and Jack Sehs."

Niko immediately perked up. "Have you heard from them?"

"I have," Riiz nodded.

"Where are they?! Are they okay? What've they been doing?" The questions flew out of her mouth without restraint. Most An-Mara were so limited in their responses, but Riiz was different. He was one of the more talkative ones, and he'd answer her questions if he could.

"They are doing well, I presume," he responded. "The one called Jack Sehs asked me to pass along his salutations to you."

Salutations!?... she thought incredulously, a hint of disgust lining her eyes. Of course he would say something like that... Niko was going to wring the guy's neck when next she saw him. *Pfft, salutations...*

She nearly huffed in audible scorn.

"Well, thank you. Tell him he gets my *salutations* also when next you see him." She didn't intend her snark to be directed toward

Riiz — he was only the messenger, after all — but she most certainly hoped he would deliver her message with the intended tone.

"Of course," Riiz responded. "And if you so wish, I suppose you may pass along my message to the one called Kira-Tharn. The ones called Callum and Jack Sehs did not tell me where they were, but they did say they had narrowed down the search for the one called Kezane Pfase. He has been sighted in Oldcity as recently as one month ago, but is rumored to have moved out and is now living on the Night side of the planet."

Of course this was big news for Riiz. He had been searching non-stop for this Kezane guy ever since they arrived here over a year ago, and to no avail. Kira-Tharn had been searching also, as many An-Mara had been, but like Niko, she'd become tired in recent days. Much too tired to search for someone who didn't want to be found. After all, An-Terino was a huge place, and if he'd now moved into the Night side... well, good luck finding anyone out there.

"How would one even survive in the Night?" she asked.

Riiz shrugged. "It is the one called Kezane Pfase we speak of. Before the one called Riesen Ryen, he was conjectured to be the Child of the Nel-Mara, and has had years to hone his skills. He is impossibly advanced in his capabilities."

"I still don't understand why we need to find this guy," Niko mumbled.

"He is the one who has come back from the precipice," Riiz began. Niko had already heard this spiel from him, verbatim, time and time again. "He carries with him the secrets of the Machine and is our best chance at defeating it."

Niko didn't know if she bought the whole Machine thing, at least to the extent that people exaggerated it. It seemed too far-fetched. Too fantastical. She'd heard many chimeric tales over the last few years, but this one may have taken the cake. The thought of an artificial intelligence overrunning the galaxy seemed absurd. Besides, even if it was real, it wasn't something Niko would ever *want* to believe — it would be too terrifying to be real.

But everyone seemed to believe it — all the An-Mara and many Meridians — so Niko didn't waste too much time questioning it any longer. The one thing that made even less sense, though, was their belief that one person would make such a difference. This Kezane guy, and then Riesen blazes Ryen, the Child of the Nel-Mara...

It was preposterous, if you asked her. What would a single

person be able to accomplish that an entire civilization couldn't? That's not how things worked in real life. It seemed like such a colossal waste of time and effort to be searching for this guy, especially if he didn't want to be found.

"And what exactly is it you expect him to do for you once you find him?" Niko asked.

"He knows of its operational function. If Meridian society will not accept him, then he may work with the An-Mara to protect our sector."

It still didn't make sense to Niko. It seemed like such a long shot. Surely there were more practical ways of dealing with such a threat.

"So are Jack and Callum going out into the Night to search for him or something?"

"Not currently." Riiz shook his head. "Perhaps later. They have their own troubles brewing. Meridian presence is... *troubling* of late."

He must've been referring to whatever had her friends worked up last night.

"We were talking about that at dinner," she admitted.

"I have been in communication with the ones called Cryo Siriar, Ravenna Night, Kyler Pierson, and Ce-Ellum, and we have all been made aware of the increased Meridian imports in recent days," he said.

"You've been in contact with them?" Niko said, surprised.

"I have been working with them for some time. They have been designing a new machine program that they have tasked me with creating an application programming interface for."

"Oh, wow, I didn't know that," she said. Niko didn't even know that Riiz was a machine tinkerer at all, although it made sense, considering his extensive knowledge in the sciences. "They mentioned they were working on something new."

"Yes. The Infinity Machine."

"The *what* machine?!"

"The Infinity Machine. Some of the operations are very different from binary languages, yet the intended function is for it to work in tandem with standard machines. I do admit it has been a struggle retraining my brain to think in terms of quinary code, let alone superposition and probabilities of particle values. It is all a brilliant concept, but rather difficult to implement in practice."

"I don't really understand much of *any* of it," Niko regretfully confessed. "They've been trying to get me to learn, but I feel like it would be too late at this point."

"It is never too late to learn anything, Niko Ryen," Riiz assured her. "They have asked me to reach out and teach you before, but I always maintained that would be overstepping my bounds. Now that you are made aware of this undertaking, I can attempt to teach you the basics, if you would assent?"

"Umm…" Niko had always been way too intimidated to learn machine tinkering, but she also didn't have much of an excuse anymore, now that she was quitting her job in the Rifts. "Sure, I guess? I just… I don't know a lot. I don't even know where I'd begin."

"That is not a concern," he said. "We will commence with instruction on the simple basics. Would you care for a lesson now? Or do you have current business to attend to?"

"I have to go into the Rifts today. I'm actually quitting, though. I'm getting a new job in the fields."

Riiz eyes widened. "That is momentous news. Your discussion with the one called Kira-Tharn went well, I take it?"

Niko grunted. "I didn't get a chance to tell her. She was extra cranky last night."

"I see," he replied, giving Niko a knowing look. "If I may give you some advice: talk to her. It may seem like she does not wish to speak with you, but I believe she does. You must force the issue."

"Thanks, you're probably right," she lied. Sticking her hand into a flaming hot Rift-borer seemed more pleasant than forcing the issue with Kira-Tharn.

Riiz nodded. "Well, you would do well to be on your way. I wish you best of happenings in your endeavors for new employment today. Would tonight at 20:00 be satisfactory for brief instruction in the ways of machine tinkering?"

"Sounds good," she replied blankly.

She turned to walk away, but remembered one more question that she meant to ask a few minutes ago.

"Oh yeah… you said you know Ce-Ellum?" she asked.

"I do. What is it you wish to know?"

"What's your take on him? I got… weird vibes from him."

"He seems acceptable to me," Riiz responded, shrugging.

"I don't know, I get the strange feeling that he's hiding

something. Like I almost think he might be in league with the crime bosses in Alashadar. It just seems too convenient that as soon as we have a plan to tinker into Terion, he shows up out of nowhere."

"I did ask myself all these questions, and I still have many," Riiz admitted. "However, I have come to know confidence in the one called Ce-Ellum in the sense that I do not think he will compromise our work."

"Hmm, okay." Maybe she *was* crazy? Cryo, Kyler, Ravenna, and now Riiz all seemed to think he was okay...

"Did you have any specific interactions that made you exceptionally suspicious?" Riiz asked, now peering at her through narrowed eyes. He undoubtedly trusted her gut instincts by now — he knew very well of her psychic potential. What he had no clue of, though, was that she refused to tap into it anymore, and hadn't in years.

"Nothing too specific," she said. "I guess it seemed like he was trying way too hard to get me to like him. And then he kept steering the conversations, and he and Kyler even disappeared forever, even though the whole gathering was supposed to be for my birthday!"

"Such an odd custom," he remarked, clearly referring to the birthday celebration.

"No more so than not laughing," she shot back quickly.

Riiz was unfazed — it would take a lot more than that to offend the man. His demeanor was so patient compared to the fiery disposition of Kira-Tharn, which was refreshing to Niko.

"I would clarify that it only seems odd because it is an archaic tradition that promotes self-centeredness," he reasoned.

Self-centeredness!? For a *birthday* celebration? The An-Mara really needed to lighten up...

"We see it as promoting the individual, not necessarily selfishness," she countered.

"It seems to me that if its objective was to promote the individual, is not the mother more deserving of that promotion than the one who was born?"

Niko couldn't argue there. Why *did* they celebrate the person whose birthday it was, and not the mother? She shrugged and nodded her head, conceding the point to Riiz.

"But your assertions of the one called Ce-Ellum are not to be taken lightly," he said, refocusing the previous conversation. "That said, I have known him for several months and I do strongly believe that his intentions align with our own, at least for temporary arrangements."

"Okay," she replied skeptically.

She still didn't trust the man. Not completely. She'd keep her eye on him, but what else could she do?

"Fare well, Niko Ryen." Riiz bade her goodbye, then turned to walk back to his own living quarters across the commons.

"See you, Riiz. And thank you for sorting out the business with the refuse service! It smells a *lot* better out here," she called back to him.

He offered her a nod, then continued on his way, as she split off to make her own unpleasant trek to the Rifts. Niko was going to be late now, but she realized she didn't really care all that much. She was quitting anyway, a good parting note from Armond-Dei be damned. His word didn't really matter in the grand scheme of things. As long as she'd be hired in the fields, nothing he had to say carried any weight anymore.

The thought soothed her just enough to spur her on toward her impending meeting with fate. She'd deal with Armond-Dei first, then find hire in the fields, then, grace permitting, deal with Kira-Tharn last, if she found the time. A discussion for future Niko to deal with.

CHAPTER SIX

6

Black Plants

TWO days had now passed since that regrettable outing had nearly landed Niko in the clutches of Shatter. Fortunate as she was to avoid that unpleasant business, she had learned that an ill-fated An-Mara girl named Fellen-Sor had been scooped up off the streets that night and violently interrogated by those thugs. She shuddered at the realization that it could have been her.

...That it *should* have been her.

The guilt she felt was none that she'd ever experienced before in her life. It was an awful feeling, one she could very well do without, and one that threatened to wash away all rational thought on her part.

Case in point: she had *almost* gone and turned herself in, but Kira-Tharn, of all people, restrained her.

By some twist of fate, the woman had happened upon her leaving the flat in the late hours of night, and she was forced to recount the entire series of events, for which she received a thorough scolding of the break-in to the Shatter yard. Unwanted as it was, the verbal thrashing was probably well deserved — and at least her friend was speaking to her again...

Kira-Tharn had talked her off the cliff, insisting that it was

Shatter's fault, and Shatter's fault alone, that Fellen-Sor suffered abuse. Kira-Tharn made it clear to Niko that she, under no circumstances, was to turn herself in to Shatter. Niko knew the reasoning was sound, but she still couldn't shake the truth that had she *not* decided to go snooping around, this innocent girl wouldn't have been harmed.

She wanted so badly to go apologize to the girl — as if a mere apology would even come close to being sufficient amends — but she knew she couldn't. Kira-Tharn forbade it. Niko wasn't to let anyone know that *she* had been that girl in the Shatter yard.

Fortunately, the whole thing seemed to blow over, just as Ce-Ellum had told her would happen. There were no more door-to-door searches for An-Mara girls, no more wanted alerts from Shatter, and no more patrols visible in the area. Even Kyler had reached out to confirm that she was in the clear.

How did Ce-Ellum know exactly what was going to happen, though? He *must* have had personal experience dealing with these authorities while being on the wrong side of the law...

Very suspicious, indeed.

It was exactly the information she imagined an underworld gangster would know of. She swore to herself that she'd keep a vigilant eye on him; if her friends weren't going to watch their own backs, then she would just have to do it for them. And if he *ever* made a move to screw them out of their project they were working on...

Niko nearly growled as she shoved thoughts of that inscrutable rogue out of her mind, stooping down to pull another sizeable blacksquash off the vine.

Blazes, this was harder work than she'd expected!

She'd anticipated the work to be leisurely compared to that of the Rifts, but Anda had warned her it would be tough. Her back ached in places she didn't even know muscles existed, and her quadriceps burned as badly as if they were squeezed by a pressure melter.

Why there weren't automated machines to do this work, Niko had no clue. It probably had to do something with the available energy budget on the planet. More and more, it seemed like the lights were being shut off in the An-Mara quarter. Corporations like Shatter or Terrovian Aquatics, her old company, were hoarding an ever-increasing amount of the energy resources, often siphoning power from the poorer areas. Even the massive entertainment moguls in Alashadar were beginning to spar with the rising industrial giants based in Machine Row.

Niko blinked through stinging sweat and looked around wearily to her left, then to the right.

Blazes, she cursed to herself.

She still had three more rows of vines to get through before she was done for the day, and she already felt as if she couldn't pluck off a single blacksquash more, let alone toss it into the bin.

"I told you," Anda said, looking rather smug standing over her own collection, which was infuriatingly full. The girl was almost the exact same size as Niko, maybe even less muscular, but yet she cranked at this.

"You did." Niko wiped her forearm cloth over her face, which was completely slicked with sweat. "This is brutal."

It *was* brutal, yet something about it still seemed less oppressive than the Rifts. The fact alone that she didn't have to wear layer after layer of heavy protective equipment made the work far more tolerable. All she needed to wear in the fields were light long-sleeves and a wide-brimmed hat. Of course, even at this low angle, Bucon's radiation was far more intense than the sol on Arhanda ever was.

"Once you invest in a rolling stool, it will be way easier," Anda told her, pausing as she peered thoughtfully at Niko. "You know what... use mine for the rest of the day. I'll manage without. I've been doing this for years."

She stood up and pushed the contraption over to Niko. It was a small, padded stool with three large rubber balls arranged into a tripod, and looked specialized for this sort of harvesting work in the dirt.

"You sure? I think I'll be fine," said Niko. "We're almost done today, anyway."

"I'm quite certain," Anda replied. "Take it."

"Alright, well thanks," Niko accepted graciously. "Please take it back if your legs start hurting."

Anda waved her hand, shooing Niko away, as she set about harvesting more blacksquashes with rapid ease, even without the use of the stool.

Exhaustion overruled any notions Niko had of being polite, so she didn't push further in offering the seat back. She only sat down and leaned forward, twisting and snapping another squash from the vine, this time a little more easily.

"Wow. This really does make a big difference!" she noted, exclaiming her feelings aloud.

"Let's stop by the market after we're done," Anda suggested. "You can probably get your own for about fifteen hundred Terion. Maybe less."

"Well, you know how great of a haggler I am…" Niko grumbled.

"Hah! Even more reason to go. It will be proper practice for you." Anda looked sideways at Niko. "You'll go?"

"Okay, fine." She would prefer if Anda would do the haggling for her — the girl was amazing, as she'd witnessed firsthand the other day — but Niko knew she *should* practice. "I'll go."

"Good."

The two girls worked for several more minutes in silence, both of them focused on one blacksquash after another.

Twist. Snap. Bin. Next…

Twist. Snap. Bin. Next…

Twist. Snap. Bin. Next…

Eventually, they came upon the final row, the red-brown dirt illuminated by the dimmed rays of Bucon, its hazy orange glow still shining at that same low angle it had the entire shift. Nevertheless, Niko envisioned it to be a sol-set, a symbol she had once known as the end of the day.

She looked to her timepiece.

17:00.

Niko had only been working here for two days, but she was pleasantly surprised at how quickly the time went by. The late sleep-ins were nice, and 17:00 seemed like it arrived much quicker than it had when she worked in the Rifts. Of course, she wasn't contracted by the hour, but by the number of rows that were harvested. They worked in teams of ten, and each team needed to gather a particular quota of blacksquashes for the day. So far, it seemed to line up with about a seven-hour workday, which was much, much better than the standard ten-hour shifts — or longer, on many days — from her previous job.

She tried to get Kira-Tharn to switch with her, but the stubborn woman refused. She had used the excuse that the Terion credit was better in the Rifts, but Niko suspected the real reason she declined was because she wanted to spend more time with Maro Del-Fiiz.

Which Niko was totally fine with!…

She still hadn't spoken to Kira-Tharn about him; she wished her friend would understand that she was *happy* for her. There was nothing to be ashamed of, for blazes' sakes! Niko could only shake her head at the mystery that was Kira-Tharn.

"Almost done…" Niko grunted, the smell of dirt overwhelming the senses as she hefted another blacksquash into the bin. Tenderly, she stood up off the stool to stretch her legs. Oh, how she would be sore tomorrow…

Her face was smothered by sticky sweat, so she attempted to wipe it off as best she could, using the break to also redo her bun. Her hair was a blazes mess, absolutely disgusting from not showering in three days. She'd been so exhausted from the other night that she hadn't mustered enough energy to even bother. She promised herself that she would tonight, though. It was either that, or she cut her hair.

And since she rather liked her longer hair, a wash it was.

"Almost done," echoed Anda.

Niko looked down the final row of blacksquashes, their darkened, bulbous bodies silhouetted against the orange horizon. The plants were undoubtedly ugly compared to their counterparts on Arhanda, but Niko found them interesting, nonetheless. It still felt so odd that all the vegetation on this planet was black. She remembered Riiz telling her many months ago that the plants were engineered to optimize the energy intake from the sol-light of Bucon, whose peak emission was in the infrared range. Since the vegetation reflected light between the main absorption wavelengths, they appear black, he said, since those wavelengths were beyond what humans perceive as any colors.

Niko figured this was probably information that would go in one ear and out the other for most people, but she always harbored a fascination for stars; she was familiar with this stuff.

"Where was Amon today?" she asked, striking up conversation to distract herself from the physical toil.

"They needed him in the office," Anda replied.

"Oh," Niko responded. She didn't know what Amon's relation to Anda was exactly, but she didn't feel comfortable asking just yet. Anda was still a relatively new acquaintance. "Must be nice."

Anda snorted. "Must be nice, indeed."

"Do you ever get to work in there?"

"Sometimes, but not usually," Anda replied. "It's mostly company business in there."

"Oh," Niko replied. "They haven't promoted you, even after you've been working here for *years*?"

Anda shook her head. "Oh, I've been *promoted* well enough, but not to the point where I get to manage logistics."

Niko remembered when she first met Anda a few days ago, she'd been floored by the amount of premium quality goods that the woman was able to procure during her shopping spree in the markets. How could she have afforded all that by being a lowly blacksquash harvester? Could Amon be paying for her, perhaps?

"Is that what Amon does?" Niko asked. "Manage logistics?"

"Sometimes." Anda shrugged, shifting uncomfortably.

Niko wondered if perhaps those two were *together*. It would make sense from the standpoint of splitting finances, but Amon seemed far too *old* for Anda. It was none of her business, though, she supposed. If she was making Anda uncomfortable, then maybe she should change the subject.

"So, where do you live?" she asked.

"The light side of the city, between NewCen and Machine Row, on the other side of the market we met at a few days ago."

"Is it nice there?"

"About as nice as curling up inside a metal dumpster for the night."

"I know the feeling…" Niko rolled her eyes thinking of her own living situation.

"What brought you to live among the An-Mara?" Anda asked, her head tilted curiously.

Niko froze momentarily, unsure if she should go against Callum's wishes by telling this stranger of her origin and the plight of her people. Anda wasn't really a stranger, though, was she? As odd as it was, seeing as how she'd only met this girl a few days ago, Niko considered Anda to be about as close a friend as she had — at least one her own age.

"I…" she hesitated. "They saved my friends and me, and then took us in."

In the end, she decided it best not to divulge too much information. She wasn't so much worried about the trustworthiness of Anda as she was unwilling to dredge up the unpleasant ghosts from her past — of how the An-Mara had quite literally destroyed her homeworld.

Anda seemed accepting of her limited explanation, nodding with what Niko thought to be a tight-lipped, sympathetic smile. It was difficult to tell if that's what was intended because the girl's mouth was so mangled.

Niko could obviously care less about her new friend's outward appearance, and often forgot about Anda's disfigurement herself. She actually found it disgusting that wherever they went, people always made some sort of deal about it. Some pitied her, offering to hold doors open or offer her discounts. Others averted their eyes, as if they were embarrassed to be there in front of her. And then there were the worst kind of people — those who made jokes or snickered behind her back, which Niko abhorred to admit accounted for the largest percentage of all. The girl had no control over what her face looked like. Besides, if Niko had to be honest, she thought Anda was actually quite pretty, in her own way. She carried herself so well, and her one remaining eye glowed of striking wonder, even if it was tainted with veiny streaks of bloodshot red.

A horn sounded in the distance.

Niko became startled for a second before she remembered it was only the signal that her team had completed their quota for the day. Soft cheers erupted from the other workers on her row, as two older ladies with gleaming smiles walked by and patted her on the back. Little gestures like these reminded her how people in the fields were so much happier and friendlier than the Rift laborers were! She thought she might've spoken to more people today than during an entire week in the Rifts.

Yes, she definitely made the correct decision to switch to the fields, one hundred percent.

Happy to be done with the work day, Niko and Anda gathered their belongings and headed toward the rail station that flanked the fields. She half-hoped Kira-Tharn would be on the train that would stop for them, eager to introduce her new friend, but alas, she was not. It was likely that the Rift workers would still be drudging in those tunnels for another hour or so. Poor Kira-Tharn.

Oh well, her loss, Niko thought. She *did* try her best to get that woman to switch...

Niko simply stared out the window, admiring the terrain in the distance. Flat plains of ash were bounded by mountain ridges that dominated the horizon, with soaring volcanoes visible in some of the low-lying valleys. Though it was bleakness incarnate, something about this place was still so impressive. So *alien.*

"You seem happier now," Anda remarked, observing Niko rather perceptively.

Niko turned her attention back to her companion, raising one eyebrow in a questioning glance.

"You don't miss the Rifts much, I take it?" Anda clarified.

Niko widened her eyes and shook her head. "*Nooo.* Very glad to be done with that blazes-accursed hell-work."

Anda nodded. "I once worked there. Only for a few days, though."

"Oh?"

Anda turned her chin upward and stared out into the distance. "When I first came here, I had nothing, knew nobody. It was the only work I found."

She didn't say anything more, but Niko realized that the girl must have suffered whatever injuries she did after that. There would be *no* way she could've worked in the Rifts with only one eye. It was dangerous enough with two...

"The Rifts suck," Niko stated blankly.

Anda cocked her head to the side questioningly. Niko realized that she'd been using Arhandan slang.

"Oh sorry. A phrase from my hometown. It means they're horrible."

Anda nodded. "Ah. Horrible, indeed."

"Well, you sound smarter than me," Niko said with a smirk. "It took me way too long to figure out that breaking my body in the Rifts wasn't worth it."

"It wasn't my choice." Anda trailed off, suddenly looking glum.

"Oh, really?"

Anda didn't respond; she only stared out at the skyline of Alashadar as it materialized in the distance, which Niko took as a cue to change the subject.

"So," Niko asked, "where'd you learn to haggle so well?"

Anda pulled her eye back to Niko. "I learned how to deal with people growing up. I'm from one of the Meridian systems, so we never had Terion or money or anything, but dealing in responsibilities is the same principle. You offer your services in return for goods."

"Yeah, I guess that makes sense," Niko replied. "I was also raised in Meridian ways. I never made it past school, though."

"School?" Anda asked. "How old are you?"

"I just turned twenty-one the other day," Niko responded proudly. She was half-expecting a 'Happy Birthday', but she knew better. None of these people celebrated their traditions. "You?"

"Also twenty-one, though I will have ellipsed Sol One twenty-two times next month," Anda returned with a smile.

Niko didn't ask, but if Anda claimed to be working here for years, then that meant she had to have been so young when she started.

How awful.

"I always hear the An-Mara say Sol One when they talk about years," Niko stated. "I'm afraid I never learned what that meant."

"Sol One? Never? You never read the Legends? Nothing about Earth?"

None of it rang a bell.

"No. I was... kept in the dark for most of my upbringing." Niko didn't know how to address her involuntary ignorance without giving away too much about where she hailed from.

"Where *are* you from?" Anda burst out with the question that Niko had been bracing for ever since she befriended the girl.

"A *lonnnggg* way away."

That was all Niko replied with, and Anda seemed to accept it with a shrug.

"Must be," she laughed. "Well, Sol One is the star that Earth orbited a long time ago. According to the Legends, of course."

That didn't make things any clearer for Niko, but she nodded as if she understood perfectly. She learned it was best to just go with whatever weird cosmic nonsense people told her.

Interested as she was to learn more, she felt a little apprehensive about the conversation continuing to hover so close to her origins, so she decided to change the subject to something else entirely.

"Oh yeah, random thought!..." she started. "My friends and I are going to the race tomorrow night, and it would be super fun if you came along! I'm sure they'd love to meet you."

Anda seemed to hesitate, clearly taken aback by the impromptu invitation. Niko thought it would be fun for the girl, though. Besides, she was thrilled that she finally had a friend her own age and was eager to show her off to everyone else.

"Amon is welcome to come, too!" she added, hoping to sweeten the pot.

Anda hemmed and hawed, but still didn't commit.

"I'll make you a deal," Niko proposed, suddenly thinking creatively. "If I can barter one of those stools for less than fifteen hundred Terion, then you have to come with us."

Anda narrowed her eye at Niko, and after several seconds of what looked like intense internal deliberation, she nodded. "Okay, deal."

"Perfect!"

Niko's face lit up with excitement, but as the train pulled into Machine Row Station, she gulped. She had to actually follow through on her end. Would she be able to actually score the thing for fifteen hundred Terion?

CHAPTER SEVEN

7

The Invitation

THERE was something about this Niko girl. She seemed… *genuine*. A kindred spirit trapped in a hellish working cycle. The fact that she never once asked about the scars was so refreshing, unlike every single other person that lumbered by. She never even looked at them! She was one of the only people Anda had ever met that treated her like just a normal person.

Which she was…

Still, she hoped she made the right decision by allowing Niko to make that deal with her. Anda wasn't keen on flaunting herself around in public, but surely no harm could come from going to *one* race. Besides, she wasn't quite sure if the girl could even follow through and secure a stool for fifteen hundred Terion.

Sure, Anda herself could probably get one for under a thousand, but Niko was quite terrible at negotiating, from what she remembered the other day.

Poor girl, she laughed to herself.

As it was, Niko stood before the vendor now, silent and unmoving, the stool she wanted on clear display. Why *was* she simply standing there saying nothing? Could she not even work up the nerve to strike up the bargaining process? The girl was confident enough when it came to conversing with Anda, but when it came to bartering, she appeared to lose all sense of self-worth. Anda's instincts wanted so badly to take over and get the damn thing herself so they could be on their way, but she knew that Niko needed the practice.

Maybe she could give her a small assist at least...

She nudged Niko's elbow with her own and cleared her throat.

Niko started at the gesture, her eyes shooting wide as she glanced apologetically at Anda.

Good. At least that seemed to spur her into action.

"Umm, excuse me," Niko announced, much too softly to get the attention of the stool merchant, who didn't even turn around.

Niko looked to her with pleading eyes, but Anda only shrugged, returning a look that urged her to try again. Her new friend was undoubtedly desperate for help, but Anda restrained herself from taking over.

She will *learn this on her own.*

Niko rolled her eyes, but turned back to the vendor, who was still facing away, busy tidying her stall.

"How much for the stool?" Niko asked, this time actually getting the trader's attention.

Much better! thought Anda.

"That one?" the lady asked, pointing toward her wares as she peered appraisingly at Niko.

Niko nodded.

"Two thousand."

"Mmm, how about fifteen hundred?" Niko bargained.

Okay. Good start...

The merchant shook her head. "Eighteen hundred, minimum offer."

Niko looked to be on the verge of conceding defeat.

Don't you dare do it. That was the message Anda conveyed in the stare she directed toward Niko. She couldn't give up now! She barely even started...

Niko looked like she would be ill, but to her credit, she turned back to the vendor.

"Fourteen hundred."

Wait, what?

Why in the worlds was Niko going lower?

The merchant paused, taken aback the same as Anda was.

"Seventeen."

"Twelve."

Woah, thought Anda.

She was utterly dumbfounded. What an interesting psychology to employ!... And it seemed to be working!

The vendor examined Niko thoughtfully for a few moments, then nodded her head. "Twelve hundred."

Niko nodded back, looking as confident as ever, though Anda figured the poor wretch was probably a nervous wreck on the inside. The two completed their Terion transfer, then Niko walked away holding her prize, a plain harvesting stool, for twelve hundred Terion. Niko beamed, and Anda had to admit that she was quite proud of her new friend.

"Well done!" Anda showered her with praise. "That was an interesting tactic you used. How'd you know it would work?"

Niko's eyes widened as she shook her head. "I didn't! I actually messed up. And I realized I did as soon as I went lower with my bargain. But at that point, I just had to keep going along with it."

"Well, you were confident," Anda declared. "I think that's the lesson to be had there. Whatever confidence you felt during that bargain, use that for the next time."

"Was I really? I didn't even think about that, but maybe it was because I got mad," Niko confessed, laughing. "I didn't like the way she ignored me at first, then how she looked at me all dismissive."

"I suppose that's the secret then? Tell me what makes you mad, and I will be sure to push you next time you barter." The two young women giggled, Niko holding her new stool like a trophy as they walked through the marketplace.

When they passed underneath a neon banner advertising for the Trackripping Syndicate, however, Anda couldn't help but feel a small amount of apprehension about now having to commit to the outing tomorrow. Trackripping itself was entertaining enough, but being jostled around in a huge crowd of less than friendly superfans...

Not her idea of fun.

Even now, in the markets, she felt very exposed. People would often draw attention to her face, which she absolutely *hated*. Even if they weren't malicious about it, it certainly was still annoying.

She continued down the street with her companion, and cringed when she heard shouts emanating from one of the dingy fight clubs they passed, the thumping beat of the '*music*' in there making her all the more nervous.

The public in Alashadar was volatile, and any differences seemed settled by violence. That's just how it was out here, and Anda preferred to steer clear. The less she immersed herself in it, the better her chances of never again finding herself in a situation she couldn't control.

Niko seemed excited about the race, though, and Anda didn't have it in her heart to sway Niko from that enthusiasm. She was more than aware of an eternal sadness overlaid onto Niko's youthful energy, though it might not have been one that was visible when they first met. She saw it now, though; it was so obviously present in the corner of the girl's brown eyes. She had clearly been through a lot. Perhaps even more than Anda herself had been through, though she dared not ask Niko about her past. Not when Niko hadn't pried into her own...

"Who do you think is gonna win tomorrow?!" Niko asked, her eyes drawn to the glowing Trackripping ads that lined the towers that flanked them on this busy section of Machine Row.

Anda shrugged. "I don't know." It was the truth. She had no clue; she didn't follow Trackripping at all.

"Oh. I would assume Delmatic, but I also heard an interesting bit about Jon Wilhe."

Anda thought she had heard of Delmatic before, but she definitely had never heard of this Jon Wilhe.

"I don't really follow any of it very much," she replied frankly.

"Really?" Niko sounded surprised. "I guess I only follow it because there's nothing else to do in this cesspool."

"Hah!" Anda chortled. "I suppose that's true."

As much as the Trackripping brain rot was fun, Anda would much prefer to spend her free time reading and learning. This place wasn't known for its academic prowess, but a few years ago she had stumbled upon a treasure trove of old works in a repository tucked away off the main Avenue in NewCen. Mainly stuff from the Legends, but also some historical accounts from both An-Mara and Meridian sources, as well as some more technical literature in the realm of the sciences and engineering. Any of it would do nicely.

"Oh!" Niko squealed, grabbing Anda by the elbow and leading her toward a bright blue kiosk. "This is what I was looking for!"

Anda let herself be led by the arm as the two girls ended up in a long line in front of twin windows at the kiosk. She scrunched her nose at the odor of the people in line — a pungent fragrance, even filthier than the typical grimy background stench of the city. The class of character in this line was... *shady*, to say the least. Shady or desperate. Or both. Anda knew what this was...

A betting station.

"Please don't tell me you're thinki..." she started.

"I most definitely am," Niko cut her off, eyes gleaming with trouble. "Trust me, I have a good feeling about this."

Well, I don't... Anda wanted to say the words out loud, but she didn't even have to — Niko seemed to know exactly what she was thinking.

"I promise!" she begged. "I can't explain it. I just... I'm really feeling this today."

"How much?" Anda asked, holding Niko's gaze sternly. She really didn't approve of her friend being so frivolous with her obvious lack of Terion credit.

"Mmmm..." Niko hesitated. "I don't have much. I'm thinking twenty thousand."

A trivial amount by Anda's standards, but based on how little Niko seemed to have, it was not inconsequential.

"You sure?"

Niko nodded, lowering her voice to make sure the other gamblers in line couldn't hear. "I just have a really good feeling about this Jon Wilhe guy. I can't explain it."

So she already said.

Anda did *not* think this was a good idea. Not at all. Risking Terion was the wrong habit for *anyone* to pick up. All the multitudes of desperate folk that ended up indentured to crime lords in this city surely used the same argument Niko was using now...

"You do know that the EC's rig the system, don't you?"

"What are EC's?" Niko asked.

Oh, by the Mara... This girl was so fresh.

"The Entertainment Corporations."

"Oh. Well yeah, but this is different."

"If you do this long enough, you always end up on the bottom. They make *certain* of it."

"This is a race, though," Niko protested. "They have no sway over the outcome of the races. All the companies are competing against each other for bets."

Anda shrugged, sighing. It sounded like there wasn't much she could say to convince Niko to change her mind right now.

"Fine. But promise me that this won't become a regular thing."

"I promise!"

Niko had better hold to that...

Anda nodded at her, and only a few minutes later, they reached the front of the line, where Niko stepped up to the clerk. The pink and blue Gluoron logo ran across the top of the kiosk, along with a grid of screens in the background, all showing numbers, numbers, and more numbers. If Anda cared even the smallest amount, she would have bothered trying to decipher their meaning. But she didn't care. She refused to care. She would never engage in such reckless practices with her finances.

"How much?" the clerk asked.

"Umm, twenty thousand," Niko responded, placing her Terion badge next to the reader after the man lightly pushed it toward her.

"Okay, and your breakdowns?"

"Ummm..." Niko hesitated. "I don't know. How does it work?"

Good, Anda thought. At least she was new to this, which meant it wasn't a habit for her. Yet.

The man seemed annoyed beyond all belief. "Choose your Rippers, then choose which percentages you want to designate to each of them for certain finishing brackets."

Niko simply stared at him, then looked to Anda for help. Anda stepped back with her hands spread out to the sides. She wasn't about to be complicit in something as foolhardy as this.

"For example, you could say fifty percent to Delmatic for a win," the clerk said exasperatedly, "and fifty percent to Wenno Daks for a top three finish. Any breakdown is fine. And you can assign to the following brackets: winner, top two, top three, top six, top ten, or top twelve."

Anda got it; Niko should also. Just from talking with her, the girl seemed smart. Although her participation in such activity as gambling here in Alashadar did not reflect that intelligence...

"I'll do all one hundred percent on a Jon Wilhe top two finish."

The clerk glanced up through bifocals. He seemed surprised. "All one hundred percent?"

Anda became uneasy. If even this guy — who was so accustomed to wild gambling from habitual patrons — was taken aback, surely Niko's decision wasn't a sound one.

"Yes," Niko replied confidently.

Maybe teaching her to be confident in Terion dealings wasn't such a good idea after all... Anda thought wryly.

"Gutsy..." the clerk muttered. He shook his head, then typed Niko's requests into the console. "Okay, your receipt will be on your Terion statement."

The two girls stepped out of line, and Niko turned to Anda and shot her a sheepish grin. Anda only offered a tight-lipped grimace in return. She *really* did not approve of this.

At least the girl was smiling, though. A few days ago, Anda would have thought Niko to be a bona fide An-Mara, without so much a hint of amusement ever crossing her face. But the girl was not An-Mara, and Anda would've found it to be a bit cruel for her to adhere to that unhappy way of living. Anda held a great amount of respect for An-Mara culture, but the one thing she could never get over was how they prohibited themselves from social enjoyment.

Not even smiling, bah!

"Well, I guess I should probably get back home," Niko said. "Thank you for going with me. I know you don't approve of me gambling like this, but I promise I have a good feeling."

"It's fine," Anda lied. "As long as it's just a one-time thing."

"Yeah, yeah," Niko responded, avoiding her gaze. "Well, I'll see you tomorrow at the fields?"

Anda nodded.

"Cool. You're welcome to invite Amon too, if you want?"

Niko looked eagerly at Anda, as if she thought Amon was some close friend. Maybe he was, but Anda would prefer to go along without him. Niko didn't need to know their history.

"Okay, thanks. I'll pass the word along to him."

She wouldn't.

"Oh, and thank you for helping me get this stool," Niko added.

"Of course. You're a champion bargainer, now!"

Niko laughed, reached forward, and hugged Anda, who only stood with hands half-raised before Niko pulled away.

Well, that was a strange gesture... Anda thought. Where *could* this girl be from? Usually such displays of intimacy were reserved for much more familial situations. Her accent sounded Capital, but some of her phrases... and the social mannerisms...

Very strange.

No matter, at least the girl was happy.

"I'm looking forward to going to the race with you tomorrow," Niko beamed. "I'm feeling big winnings."

With that, Niko turned around and walked off.

Anda shook her head, half amused, but half concerned. Why would she have placed all of her twenty thousand Terion on a Ripper with such low odds of success? Did she know something nobody else knew? There was something about this girl... but she couldn't quite put her finger on it.

Anda, of course, had her own reasons for never, ever, *ever* engaging in the underworld of Alashadar, but she wasn't about to explain to Niko the full reason. She liked her, but they weren't nearly close enough for her to know any of that.

Niko finally made it home after way too long. Even Kira-Tharn was back, and had been for hours. Time seemed to fly by this evening, and Niko had no time but to go straight to Riiz's quarters for her lessons on machine tinkering. She was a little disappointed that most of it seemed like a math lesson instead — and math that she already had learned, for that matter. Riiz insisted that it was all important material, so she accepted his refresher course with good graces, reluctant as she was. He promised the next lesson would be more about the languages they use.

Now that she was home, though, she finally got a chance to rest. Her legs were screaming from her second straight day squatting and ripping those blazes blacksquashes off the vine for seven hours straight, and the smell that wafted from her was a reminder that she was *multiple days* overdue for a shower.

Niko looked across the room to Kira-Tharn, who was in a huff right now. What was going on? Was she fighting with Maro again?

At least Maro wasn't still here when Niko had arrived home just now... Niko's face went red at the prospect, but she supposed that Kira-Tharn deserved some happiness in her life. That woman worked so hard every single day, not to mention all she had done for Niko over the years. Niko knew better than to offer her a smile, but she nodded respectfully as she waked past to dump her new stool off in her room.

"I would be one to venture an assumption that you would have already been home," Kira-Tharn remarked.

"I went into town after work," Niko replied. "Then I had to go to tinkering lessons from Riiz, remember?"

Kira-Tharn nodded, then turned her nose toward Niko and sniffed.

"It would seem that you require a thorough washing, Niko Ryen," she smugly proclaimed.

"Thank you." Niko rolled her eyes. "*Thank you* for that commentary."

Niko shook her head embarrassedly, then marched down the hall to freshen up. Kira-Tharn wasn't wrong.

A few minutes later, Niko emerged into the living room feeling much, much better. She really had been needing that. The water was uncharacteristically warm, so she stayed in longer than she should have, Kira-Tharn's disapproving glare be damned.

"I do not believe a bathing of that duration is an intelligent use of Terion," Kira-Tharn began to lecture.

"I know, I know… But I was freezing, and I haven't taken one in days."

"That much was obvious when you entered the room."

Niko fought the urge to grin. The An-Mara couldn't laugh or smile, but Niko had come to learn that they most certainly had humor.

"It was only one shower. And besides, I have the Terion to spend."

Well, she *would* have the Terion to spend, after tomorrow.

Kira-Tharn seemed to sense the caveat, and narrowed her eyes at Niko, shifting in her seat to face her completely.

"I have completed revolutions around Sol One twenty-nine times, Niko Ryen," Kira-Tharn began. "I know when…"

"One of my friends from the fields used the same terminology," Niko interrupted, ignoring Kira-Tharn's point. "Sol One."

Niko didn't even think about it earlier, but she wondered if Anda was part An-Mara or something? It was strange she used that same An-Mara term: Sol One.

"It is a way to refer to what is also called one year," Kira-Tharn clarified, taking Niko's bait at changing the subject.

"Yes, yes, I know that much," Niko said. "My friend from the fields used the same phrase, but she's not even An-Mara. When I asked her about it, she said something about the Legends, and then something about some place I forgot the name of."

Kira-Tharn narrowed her eyes in thought. "Is it the place called Earth you speak of?"

"That's the name! What is that place?"

"In the Legends, the world called Earth is the birthplace of civilization," Kira-Tharn said. "The homeworld of the Nel-Mara, long gone many ages ago."

"Oh. Cool." Niko hoped Kira-Tharn wouldn't snap at her for the response being too casual, too disrespectful to the Legends, but she didn't know what else to say.

"I suppose you have never learned of the Legends, have you?"

"Not much," Niko replied honestly, shaking her head. "Only a little bit on the voyage over."

"I would not know where to begin for you, Niko Ryen, but there are many, many accounts that detail the history of the Nel-Mara."

Listening to 'many, many accounts' sounded rather tiresome right now, although she was curious to learn more about these Nel-Mara she'd heard so many whispers about over the years.

"What happened to them?"

"They disappeared," Kira-Tharn replied. "Many years ago. Over sixty millennia ago, to be more precise."

"How'd they disappear?"

"That is a very long tale for another time."

"Oh. Well, what did they look like, then?"

Kira-Tharn shook her head. "There are many conflicting and differing accounts, although it is known that far in their distant past, they resembled us. The Legends tell that our current form was engineered by the Nel-Mara to mirror their own biological ancestry at the Dawn of Civilization."

That would explain why all these different civilizations — An-Mara, Meridians, Arhandans, even An-Terino natives — were all of the same appearance.

"Were there any other intelligent species?" Niko asked. "*Aliens?*"

Kira-Tharn shrugged. "The Legends say that there were no others. Not anywhere in our galaxy, nor in the others nearby. The Legends even has a term for that phenomenon: the Paradox. During the course of billions of revolutions around Sol One, it was only ever the Nel-Mara. Or humans. Same thing, I would venture to assume."

That seemed highly unlikely to Niko. The galaxies each had hundreds of billions to trillions of star systems. There was no way that only *one* intelligent civilization sprang forth from such overwhelming possibilities, especially if their galaxy cluster was pushing twenty billion years...

"Who was this new friend you were speaking of such matters with?" Kira-Tharn asked.

"Oh, we weren't really speaking of that," Niko said. "I only asked what Sol One meant. But her name is Anda. I think you'd really like her!"

"You would do well to be cautious of how attached you become to strangers," Kira-Tharn warned, judging Niko from behind raised eyebrows.

"Anda is perfectly fine," Niko sighed. "Seriously, you should meet her."

Kira-Tharn muttered something under her breath that Niko couldn't quite hear. Probably one of those An-Mara curses she sometimes caught her spitting when she thought she was out of range of all listening ears. Niko decided just to let it go.

"And I know you'll say no, but I'm going to the race tomorrow night with Ravenna, Cryo, and Kyler. You're welcome to come along..."

"You are correct, Niko Ryen," Kira-Tharn said. "I will most unquestionably say no."

With that, Kira-Tharn walked past Niko without saying anything more, then disappeared into her room. Such a typical An-Mara goodnight. Niko shook her head and smiled.

Smiled.

It felt weird. Almost *new*. Before recently, how long had it been since she actually smiled? It had to be the Rifts that ripped away all human happiness and buried it deep. Though, Niko supposed it was long before she slaved away in those blazes-accursed canyons that she lost the joy in life. Still, she was so glad to be done with that nonsense. The fields were so much better than the Rifts, even if her legs were unreasonably sore.

She waddled down the short hallway to her own room, then shut the door. Tomorrow was going to be an exciting day, so catching up on much needed rest would do wonders for her. In the morning, she would wake up rested, go to work, then make the trek to NewCen for the big event.

———————

The next day in the fields was just like any other, as Anda mindlessly snaked her way up and down the rows, harvesting blacksquash after blacksquash with automated ease. She looked over at Niko, who looked much more comfortable today, proudly perched atop her stool to pluck the produce from the vine. The girl *had* to be sore, though. Anda remembered her own first week on the job, how her quadriceps burned like fire, even when she was resting. It was only thanks to good nights' sleep that she was able to come back the next week. And the next. And the next. And now, years later, she had this down to a subconscious art form where she hardly felt any exhaustion at all. At least not excessive levels of it.

Today, unfortunately, she *was* tired. She tossed and turned all through the night, and was embarrassed to admit that it was mainly because she was nervous about the outing this evening. Her days of attending social events were long gone…

And just how many friends did Niko expect her to meet? She absolutely detested every little thing about these Trackripping environments.

Anda sighed. She had made a deal with Niko, so she had no choice in the matter. She would go, and would do so without showing any semblance of disinclination. She had been raised to be tough, and she wasn't about to let one night of poor sleep trickle through to the surface. Not a chance.

"You look happy today," she said to Niko, who smiled at her enthusiastically.

"I'm excited for tonight. We're gonna have so much fun."

Anda huffed to herself. She highly doubted that *she* would be having any fun, but allowed herself to return the smile, nonetheless.

"Is Amon coming with us today?" Niko asked.

"No."

That's all Anda replied with, and Niko seemed to accept it.

"Oh, that's okay. Maybe next time!"

"Next time."

Niko looked at her sidelong, but didn't say anything further. Maybe she suspected some peculiarity to her relationship with Amon, but if that was the case, the girl possessed enough decency to not press.

Thank the Mara for people like her...

"Last row," Niko breathed. "This stool makes *all* the difference."

"I told you!" Anda was grateful for the change in subject. She didn't want the conversation to dwell on Amon one second longer.

"I thought I was going to be in the Rifts forever, but I really think I could do this long-term instead," Niko remarked, moving into position to complete her last few blacksquashes.

Anda stopped working and looked at Niko. Did the girl have such a low opinion of herself that she would be content to do *this* for the rest of her life? Niko had exhibited an increasingly peppy demeanor the last few days, but there it was again — that darkness that couldn't be completely hidden.

"Don't sell your life away too soon," Anda cautioned, shaking her head.

"I won't! It's just until I stock up on some Terion. I don't mean to stay here forever. We have a plan to..."

Anda perked up, but Niko cut herself off.

What was the girl about to say?

"Nevermind," she said quickly, appearing flustered, if Anda didn't know better. "Race you to the finish?"

"Very well," Anda replied, not letting on that she was highly intrigued about what Niko was about to reveal.

Was she really trying to get off planet? Is that what she was about to say? Anda had absolutely no clue why Niko was even living with the An-Mara at all, but it would certainly make things difficult for the girl to leave this place. Even if the rumors about the An-Mara using the Engines to destroy that one world were untrue, public opinion had shifted so hard against them that they were driven into such levels of poverty that practically no An-Mara would be able to secure transport off-world. Especially with the increasing Meridian encroachment onto this planet...

And besides, where would Niko even be trying to go? Obviously there was nothing else in the Bucon system, so she was either going to Aktun, the Ossion system, or the Capital system.

Given the girl lived with the An-Mara, most people would assume Aktun. But Anda was well enough aware that the An-Mara seeking refuge on An-Terino were *not* the kind that often made their way back to Aktun.

That left the Ossion or Capital systems, but based on what she had been hearing about how the An-Mara were being treated in the Capital system these days, it stood to reason she would most likely be bound for the Ossion system. She supposed Niko *could* be seeking passage to the Lamperian colonies, but those were much further away, and it didn't make sense that she would have been diverted this far off course if that was her final destination.

These suppositions were whisked away as the final horn sounded, signaling the end of the harvest day.

"Fourteen!" Niko announced. "How many did you get?"

"Twenty-three."

"What?! How?"

"I've been doing this for years. You've only been doing this for a few days."

"True, but still… Twenty-three, that's crazy…" Niko sounded rather disappointed.

So competitive!

Anda admired her for it. She herself was quite competitive, which maybe was one of the reasons they were getting along so well. Becoming friends, even? Anda was a little wary to develop actual friendships on this accursed Hole of a rock, what with her situation here and all… But she supposed it was a friendship of sorts.

"You'll get faster each day!" she encouraged. "Yesterday, you probably only harvested a third as many."

Niko laughed. Anda had heard her laugh before, but she noticed with each passing day, it was growing more relaxed, more liberated. It was also quite contagious; wherever Niko was from, it must be a world with such carefree youth.

"I think you're right," she admitted. "I was so bad yesterday, wasn't I?"

Niko flashed a smile that made Anda jealous. Of course, her own smile would never be what it used to be. A part of her wished she still had her old face, but she knew there was no turning back time, so it did her no good to wish for the old days. A waste of hope.

"You were… not great," Anda replied candidly.

Both women laughed as they picked up their stools and trudged over to the rail station.

"Well, I'm gonna make a vow that I will be as good as you within the month," Niko proclaimed, stubborn but playful.

"I will hold you to that."

Niko held her arm out, gripping Anda's forearm just like any Capital Meridian would when making a deal. Where *was* this girl from?!

"Do you know what time it is?" Niko asked abruptly, as they stepped onto the sleek train that would ferry them back into the city.

"17:40."

"Ugh, late finish today."

"Yes," Anda agreed. "We did our part, though."

Niko smiled at her. "Yeah we did."

"You'll get a pay raise next week if you keep it up."

It wasn't a lie. Ever since ROTO had purchased these fields, they were very quick to reward high performance with pay bonuses. Which was great... except that she hoped the ROTO people in the office wouldn't notice Niko *too* much. Heavens knew the girl could do without *that* attention to worry about.

"You think so?" Niko asked eagerly.

"Maybe." Anda shrugged.

"That would be awesome. I could use the Terion."

"Especially if you gamble it all away tonight." Anda smiled, meaning it as a joke, but Niko only stared nervously out the window.

"I hope not," she replied, turning back toward Anda. "I think we might need to head straight to the race tonight. I didn't expect that we'd get out so late. You okay with that?"

Anda was hoping she'd have time to freshen up before going to the Mara-forsaken Trackrippping race, but Niko was right.

"Hmm, yeah, it is late."

"My friends' place isn't too far from the rail station. We can drop our stools off there?"

Anda really didn't want to go to some unfamiliar residence in Machine Row, but she *definitely* didn't want to lug this stool around NewCen all night, either. No, thank you.

"Okay, sure."

"Cool. You'll like my friends. I know you will." Niko grinned back at her as the train accelerated off on its journey back to Alashadar.

It was a fairly short trip to the Machine Row rail hub, especially since Niko did a lot of talking about her friends. The girl was becoming more and more talkative by the day, which Anda was appreciative of. Niko was pleasant company, and it made the days go by *much* quicker.

After they exited the train, Anda reluctantly allowed Niko to lead her into the darkened streets, rather than boarding the adjacent rail that would take them to NewCen. She almost hesitated before continuing; it was not a path that she would have tread on her own. At least it wasn't Oldcity...

She suppressed a shudder and shoved those thoughts out of her mind.

"How far is their place?" she asked.

"Oh, not far," Niko assured her. "Down this way a couple k's, and then off the main path a few blocks."

Anda nodded, maintaining the confidence in her steps, not allowing Niko — or any of the passersby on the streets — to sense her apprehension. At least there was someone with her today, even if they were both slightly built women. As long as they appeared poised, no one would bother them.

Right?

It was marginally reassuring to assume that Niko was as uncomfortable as she was, because as soon as they departed the main thoroughfare, she picked up her pace. Anda made no complaints to follow suit as the streetlamps dimmed, but suddenly, Anda noticed her companion's demeanor perk up.

"Niko!"

Anda looked across the street and a handsome young man waved to Niko. Something about him seemed familiar, like she had seen him before in the city. Or somewhere.

"You didn't tell me your friends were so good looking," she joked to Niko, nudging her elbow.

Niko clicked her tongue. "Anda!..."

She laughed as Niko playfully tugged her by the arm across the street toward a residence, but stopped dead in her tracks, pulling her arm free, as another man stepped out from the doorway.

No.

Anda's face went ghostly pale, and she struggled to take a breath, as if the oxygen was sucked clean out of the air. She was frozen, the atmosphere around her nothing more than the vacuum of space.

She couldn't breathe. Couldn't speak. Couldn't move.

But she needed to act. Now.

"I... I'm sorry!" she managed to gasp, the words escaping in barely more than a whisper. "I have to go."

Before Niko could say one word — and before the man even saw her, thank the Mara — Anda dove around the nearest corner, then sprinted off down the street. The Mara be damned if any randoms paid attention to her odd spectacle — that was the least of her worries.

She muttered every curse she knew to herself as she hurried back into the light, refusing to look back to see if anyone followed. She hated herself for breaking her promise to Niko, but she couldn't be here. Not around *him*. Not right now.

She just hoped Niko wouldn't hate her also.

———————

CHAPTER EIGHT

8

NewCen Circuit

WALLS of black carbon windows stretched high into the sky, reflecting the lavish fluorescence of NewCen as far as the eye could see. Electric shades of pink, yellow, blue, and every color in between danced to life in the foreground, while the background was set with the familiar dark fade of Twilight, of course. The massive towers of downtown Alashadar were bisected by the Avenue, a thoroughfare of parallel railways and footpaths that streaked through the city in one direction, stacked atop each other on multiple levels. Most structures were gaudy, cube-like monstrosities, but some were topped with domes or spheres. And of course, there was the Skytower Palace, its impossibly thin tripod topped with an elegant, rotating disc. Far below, where Niko stood, the din of too many sources of music clashed loudly with the commotion from the sidewalks. Plazas at ground level teemed with shoulder-to-shoulder crowds, while wealthier revelers lounged profligately on elevated balconies. Massive monitors that hung from the buildings would normally display advertisements or entertainment shows, but today, all were fixated upon one spectacle, and one spectacle alone.

Trackripping.

NewCen Circuit, to be precise.

106

Most people scrambled to secure a place where they could see the finish line, but Niko always preferred to watch from the screens. She and her friends had originally wanted to see more of the track, but they had to settle on a spot near the corner of the Marindise, where only one turn was visible as it swept around the building's heights. However, three and a half massive displays were easily visible from where they stood, and they'd be able to track the entire race from this vantage.

The crowd around them was overbearingly obnoxious. Multitudes of scantily clad men and women alike clung to each other's arms, all of whom stared down their noses at Niko and her friends, their ridiculous hairstyles and sol-shades the epitome of extravagance. The elitism in this part of Alashadar was utterly ludicrous...

Whatever, Niko thought annoyedly.

Many of them were under the influence of something, anyway. Whether it be Cinto or alcohol, she had no clue, nor did she care. She simply ignored the chums and kept her eyes glued to the screens, where the Rippers were getting ready to start their race.

Twenty-four of the most famous stars on An-Terino sat in their karts, which were absurdly low to the ground, the wheels sitting just as high as the racers themselves. Most of the Rippers were obscenely egotistical; they each had pre-race rituals designed to either intimidate their opponents or to garner fan attention. Or both.

Delmatic, the track favorite, didn't even have his helmet on yet, and they were about ready to start the thing! He stood atop his kart, waving to the crowd, flashing his billion-Terion smile. His sleeveless shirt intentionally displayed bulging, muscled arms — probably flexed for extra effect — and his mullet of a haircut swayed in the light breeze. Arrogant ass.

Niko felt a small amount of annoyance, but her eyes were particularly drawn to the kart decorated in orange, where a relatively modest rider sat at the ready, both hands on the wheel. She had just dropped twenty thousand Terion on Jon Wilhe; she could only hope the intel she'd heard from that Shatter guard a few days ago had any merit...

The man seemed focused, though. A good sign.

Suddenly, the unbearably catchy chime of the Trackripping Syndicate reverberated over enhancers that littered the entirety of NewCen, accompanied by the booming of a very recognizable woman's voice. One could probably hear the racket from all the way out in the Rifts...

"WELLLCOOOOMMME TO TRAAACKRIPPINNGGGG! Tivane Fry here, along with the lovely Steven 'Turnslinger' Osinroler. The Trackripping Syndicate is proud to bring you NEWCENNNNNN CIRCUUUUIIIIIIIIIITT!!"

Deafening cheers erupted throughout the city as the giant screens all panned to the pair hosting the broadcast.

"Now Turnslinger, this is shaping up to be a season for the ages. Delmatic is proving why he's one of the all-time greats, but there are also a number of promising challengers."

"You're absolutely right, Tivane. I've been especially impressed by Wenno Daks. The way he's been steadily improving his finishes bodes well for his Tour standings."

"Yeah. I think we were all impressed by his near upset of Delmatic two weeks ago at The Belly, and I, for one, am looking forward to see what he can do today."

"Yep. I was floored myself. But I was also extremely impressed with Astine Rivers. Not many people focused on her race, since the duel between Delmatic and Daks was so intense, but her form looked amazing. A fifth-place finish was exactly what she needed to remain in the top six. She's only one of four women on the Tour this year, and I know she takes great pride in her success."

"I just love Astine. She's an amazing Ripper and such a great ambassador for the sport. Now Turnslinger, before we start, I'm sure all our viewers are curious... who did *you* put your Terion down on today?"

"Great question, Tivane! Today, I was feeling a little edgy. I put twenty percent on Delmatic for a win, of course, but I also put fifty percent on Daks for a top-three finish, as well as thirty on Morland Relm for a top-three finish. I've got a feeling that all of them can do some real damage today. How about you?"

"Personally, I put all one-hundred percent on a Delmatic win. Safe Terion is the best Terion." Tivane and the 'Turnslinger' both laughed in the fakest melody Niko had ever heard. She instinctively rolled her eyes.

"Yeah, Tivane. You can't go wrong with Delmatic. He's just flawless. The way he takes the turns is unbelievable. And the layout of NewCen Circuit only feeds into his strengths."

"Absolutely, Turnslinger. And for any viewers that may be

new, this is Trackripping, and we are at NewCen Circuit today! This is one of the newer tracks hosted by the Syndicate, and it boasts a ten-kilometer loop that winds its way in and out of our major sponsors: Alashadar Unlimited, Twilight Elegance, BlueWorld, ROTO, Gluoron Entertainment, the Marindise, Skytower Palace, and of course, Terion."

Niko watched the screens as a drone flyer sped along the course's layout, which was her favorite part of the entire Trackripping broadcasts, aside from the actual races themselves. The NewCen track was beautiful, she had to admit. The colors were striking, and something about the way it wrapped its way in and around the glorious towers of downtown Alashadar was breathtaking.

"Okay, I'm told it looks like we are ready to start in thirty seconds!"

"Yes, Tivane. This is where the Rippers really start to feel the nerves. Once you get going, it's smooth sailing. But this right here is the most nerve-wracking part of the whole race. Just look at their focus. Incredible!"

"You would know best! For viewers out there that don't know, Steven 'Turnslinger' Osinroler here is a two-time Tour champion, and we are honored to have him on our team for this season."

"The honor is mine, Tivane. Now here we go!"

The broadcast quieted, transitioning to the rhythmic countdown flashing on the screen, echoed by the countless denizens in the streets.

SIX!
FIVE!
FOUR!
THREE!
TWO!
ONE!

Goosebumps prickled Niko's skin as a blaring horn rang out across the streets of NewCen, nearly drowning out the thunderous roar of millions of fans, heralding the start of the race.

The gates opened and the karts accelerated out with such fury that Niko's breath caught. She'd seen several races before, but the power of these karts never failed to impress her. The forces these Rippers could endure... it was awe-inspiring. She imagined it felt much like that one time when she blasted off from Arhanda long ago.

She immediately buried that errant memory and focused on the race. Nobody would be traversing the turn around the Marindise for a minute or two, so she glued her eyes to the screen, as did everyone else around her. The crowd was raucously loud, each fan shouting at the Rippers they'd placed bets on like they were their coaches, as if they could actually hear them...

The sport looked insanely fun, if Niko had to be honest. At first glance, the tiny karts that the Rippers rode in looked like the playthings of children, but the velocity at which they hit the turns was heart-stopping. She'd tried her hand at virtual Trackripping before, but that certainly wouldn't be nearly as fun as the actual thing, sitting in those karts, low to the ground, racing around corners at breakneck speeds.

The competitors were all clumped together now since the race just started, but the pack would eventually thin out over the course of the six laps, at which point their speed would pick up even more.

She stood on her tiptoes and watched on the screen as the famous green and black colors of Delmatic led the pack around the first few turns. She didn't really care who won, so long as Jon Wilhe placed top two.

Watching her man in orange trail near the back, though, she wondered if she perhaps made a mistake. Maybe she should've bet on him for top ten? She had put down twenty thousand Terion, after all. A laughably small amount compared to what most people wagered, but for her, it was a lot. She really shouldn't be spending *any* Terion at all...

But, if by some miracle he was able to place top two, the returns on that finish were announced as 440:1. She would be getting 8,800,000 Terion if he was able to pull it off! Normally, she wouldn't have made such a reckless move, but for some strange reason, she felt subliminal confidence in her decision, almost like a gut instinct.

"And it looks like Delmatic is out to a comfortable start, Turnslinger. No surprises there."

"Indeed, Tivane. This is how he likes to do things. Get out early, then hold that lead the entire way. He's very good at hitting the turns at the perfect moment to keep any challengers behind him."

"Well, it seems like he is doing just that. But it looks like our other top competitors are right there along with him!"

"Yes, it's going to be a very exciting race! The thing with this track is that there are *a lot* of turns. So many chances for Rippers to make up lost time on this course. All it takes is one mistake and bam! — you're at the back."

"Well, Turnslinger, we'll have to see how this one plays out. Looks like the pack is heading into the first long straightaway as they pass from the Alashadar Unlimited mall toward Twilight Elegance."

"Yeah this is where position is everything. You really want to get to the inside for that right turn coming out of the straightaway. See, notice how Delmatic and Astine Rivers were able to hit that turn perfectly, and now they've solidified a one-two position."

Niko watched as all the karts zoomed out of that straightaway and into the turn at a speed that made her uncomfortable even watching. As if her unease was a portent, she watched in slow motion as two Rippers right next to Jon Wilhe competed in a wild dash for the inside spot at the same time.

Wilhe slowed down, but Niko couldn't tell if he avoided the collision or not. The crowd around her let out a collective groan as multiple karts spun and tumbled across the track, shards and splinters of the wreckage tumbling along with them.

"Oooh! Looks like we have a crash already! Can you tell who that is, Turnslinger?"

"Difficult to tell from this angle. I saw an orange kart in there somewhere. Who is orange?"

"I believe orange is Jon Wilhe."

"Yeah you're right, Tivane. Orange is Jon Wilhe. Tough break to all the Jon Wilhe fans out there. Not a track favorite by any means, but he was doing so well this Tour in his own right. A promising up-and-comer for certain."

No.

It couldn't be Jon Wilhe.

Niko's jaw tensed as she subconsciously bit her lower lip hard, craning her neck to get a better look at the screens.

"Oh wait!... I see Wilhe right there on the turn. Looks like a false alarm."

Niko let out a sigh of relief. Sure enough, she caught a glimpse of an orange kart speeding away from the wreckage. Although any crash was terrible, she was selfishly glad that Jon Wilhe was still in the race.

"Yeah you're right, Turnslinger. I'm getting reports that it wasn't Jon Wilhe, but in fact Dingo Walalam and Max Elsireon who have collided."

"Yes, I see it now. It was definitely those two karts. Ooof, that looked like a terrible crash. I do hope they're okay. Do we have any reports, Tivane?"

"Emergency personnel are on the scene as we speak. We should get reports momentarily."

"This is a really early crash, but not unheard of on this track. Those tight turns that come just after those high-speed straightaways are particularly hazardous. Rippers need to really be paying attention in those moments. If you don't switch your wing pressure in time, you lose all traction."

Niko jumped when a voice shouted in her ear.

"Not our Ripper, right?!"

Ugh! The blazes!

Kyler.

He didn't need to shout so loud! He could've tapped her on the shoulder or something...

Niko shook her head in reply. She'd been so focused on the race that she almost forgot she was here with her friends. Coming here with them had been the plan all along, of course, but after Anda left unexpectedly, Niko closed in on herself and became a little antisocial, as she sometimes did.

She knew she shouldn't dwell, but there was something so odd about how Anda bailed. The way she looked directly at Ce-Ellum with a look of such deep panic gave Niko bad, bad feelings. She'd already been thinking how it made sense that he might be some high level Alashadar gangster, but now this... It was just one more piece of the puzzle that was starting to stack up against the man in her mind.

It was a random thought, and she hoped it was only unfounded paranoia, but she got the awful feeling that Ce-Ellum may have had something to do with Anda's disfigurement. There was nothing spoken or obvious, it was just an intuition. Maybe she was only spiraling and imagining things...

Probably.

Niko looked over at him now, his dark hair and solid complexion silhouetted against the neon blue and green logo of the Marindise. Just enough light reflected to illuminate his beady, black eyes, which were supremely focused on one of the screens. He stood nervously rigid with clenched hands, and if Niko wasn't mistaken, it was Jon Wilhe's kart he watched. Why so tense?

Her concern over Ce-Ellum's intentions faded as a massive wave of cheering erupted.

"Wow! What do you make of that move, Turnslinger?"

"Absolutely unbelievable, Tivane! What a move! The way she maneuvered just to the inside of Delmatic's wheel… Masterclass."

"Those two are really setting the tone on this first lap, but it looks like the rest of the pack won't let them get away just yet."

"Yeah, Tivane. The one thing about Rivers and Delmatic jostling at the front is that it will slow them down just enough to leave opportunity for the others to keep up."

"It sure does look like there is a considerable pack that is right on the heels of those two, doesn't it Turnslinger? Morland Relm and Wenno Daks, number two and number three on the Tour right now, are right there. And Marl Vikers, the Tour number four, isn't far behind!"

"It's anyone's race at this point, Tivane. But we have to remember that they're only on lap one out of six. There is so much time for anything to happen."

At that moment, Niko's attention was drawn to motion on the sweeping turn at the top of the Marindise. Like the buzzing of wasps, karts raced by as the turn ducked back into the building. Soon, all twenty-two of the remaining Rippers had passed, and Niko wouldn't be able to see them again until the next lap.

Seeing them with her own eyes was completely anticlimactic. Watching from the screens was a vastly superior spectating experience in every way. The only reason to go in person was to feel the rush of the atmosphere, which was exciting in its own right, being among the fans who screamed and cheered with all of their soul. Many levied nasty taunts against each other, and some more aggressive fans even resorted to fistfights, though Niko preferred to stay far away from any such scuffles. Security was tight within the confines of each entertainment venue, but out on the streets things often became lawless.

"Now, Tivane, let's see how this next turn after the straightaway unfolds."

"Yeah, Turnslinger, we had a terrible crash on the first one of these a few minutes ago between Dingo Walalam and Max Elsireon.

Everyone will be glad to know that we have received reports that both Rippers are unharmed from that crash. However, their karts have been damaged to the point where they are unable to continue tonight."

"Such a shame for both Rippers, Tivane. Both of them were vying for a top six spot before the Tour concludes in a few weeks, but this DNF surely puts them out of contention."

"Yes, it looks like it will, unfortunately. Both Walalam and Elsireon had fairly high returns for top six finishes tonight, and there are sure to be many upset bidders out there." Both Tivane and 'Turnslinger' chuckled.

Niko told herself that she was relieved to hear that neither of the two Rippers were hurt, but truthfully, she was only really glad that Jon Wilhe wasn't caught up in the crash. She had always prided herself on her empathy, but that sentiment had withered away into nothingness over the last few years. Maybe she needed to take a long, hard look at herself... What would her family have said about that?

She huffed to herself, then shoved any sense of nobility tucked away where it belonged, returning her attention to the screen where Wilhe's kart was visible doing battle with three others near the back of the pack. At least he was keeping up, but he really needed to make a move. Sure, there were over five laps remaining, but he wouldn't want to get too far behind. It would be impossible to make a move to the front once you ran out of time on the track. By lap four or five, he really would need to establish himself near the front if there was any chance of him getting into that top six, let alone top two.

You idiot, she scolded herself, suddenly acknowledging the serious doubts she harbored about a top two finish. She really should've just put all her Terion down on Delmatic for the win, even if the returns were minuscule. Or perhaps even Astine Rivers for a top two or three finish. That was probably her favorite Ripper, anyway. But even Astine's odds of a top two or three finish were a little lower. Most people had predicted Delmatic, Wenno Daks, Morland Relm, or Marl Vikers for those top spots.

As the race progressed, Niko beheld the screens religiously, the Ripper POV's addictingly thrilling to watch. She wished she could be right there with them, along for the ride in one of the karts, or even piloting one of her own. It looked so incredibly fun — probably even more fun than those railcoasters she'd once ridden at Alashadar

Unlimited. The speed that the Rippers hit the turns with was unreal. How did they not go flying off the sides?!

She watched as the karts raced around turn after turn, weaving in and out of the giant pleasure palaces that lined the streets of Alashadar. And each time the leader — who of course happened to be Delmatic — completed a lap, the telltale horn would sound, along with a rise in volume from the crowds. Finally, after several long, stressful minutes, she heard it.

The sharp, five-note chirp that signaled the final lap.

"And here we are!" Tivane Fry cried over the broadcast. "Delmatic leads the pack into the last lap, as expected. But hot on his wheels are five other Rippers!"

"We couldn't have scripted this race any better, Tivane."

"No, we could not have! Five of the top six on the Tour right now are locked into a battle for NewCen Circuit!"

"And then we also have Jon Wilhe cracking into this pack, as well. Kind of a Night's chance, really... But truthfully, he has been impressing the Daylight out of me."

"Absolutely, Turnslinger. He recently squeaked into the top twelve in the Tour standings, but if he can keep up with this group, he might earn enough points to break into the top ten."

"Yeah, Tivane, I agree one-hundred percent. It looks like he's locked into the fourth spot right now, but this lead pack is so tight that any one of them can take this race."

Niko dared to hope. Her fists had been clenched and her teeth gritted for at least ten minutes now, every ounce of her praying that her intuitions would prove savvy. She hadn't let herself dream ever since she'd lost her homeland several years ago — she hadn't even come close — but she still followed those... *instincts*... on occasion. Those ones that ran deeper than everyday intuition.

She watched ever so anxiously as the karts completed their last lap, screaming around each turn one last time, the iconic locales in the background blurred from the speed, as the broadcast followed the leaders.

The shouts became even louder, if that was possible, when the lead pack raced for the finish, no one kart pulling away or making any daring moves. Jon Wilhe needed to do something soon if he was to get top two...

Somebody was sure to make a move, but all six of the Rippers seemed to be playing it safe this entire lap. Biding their time. Waiting. Until...

The crowd roared, gasping as one when three of the karts that held everyone's attention collided. Niko froze as the events played out in slow motion.

The blue and yellow kart skidded sideways, making contact with the green and purple kart.

Both karts slid and bounced into the guardrail, spinning uncontrollably.

The pink and white kart shot the gap between the two unsuccessfully, but somehow managed to temper the inevitable crash between all three, who were now facing backwards.

The all-red kart slowed to avoid the tangle, but became trapped in the back.

The green and black kart, ahead of the mess, was home free. Delmatic. *Ugh.*

The orange kart accelerated to avoid the crash, and somehow squeaked through without getting caught up.

Only then did Niko breathe; Jon Wilhe had made it through. *Jon Wilhe made it through!*

"By the will of the Nel-Mara, Turnslinger! What in all of the worlds just happened?!"

"I have no clue, Tivane. It looked to me like Vikers may have clipped Daks on that turn. I'm stumped as to how nobody wiped out."

"All four Rippers caught in that near-disaster are now on their way again, but Delmatic and Jon Wilhe have pulled away significantly!"

"Yeah, Tivane, I don't see the other four catching up at this point. This looks like a two-man race to the finish."

"And what a finish it will be! Wilhe has now pulled even with Delmatic on this final straightaway!"

The roar of the crowd became earsplitting. Even the announcers were yelling unintelligibly through the broadcast as the two Rippers dueled for the win. Niko thought the giant screen display seemed to be shaking, rattling from the thunder of the crowds that packed NewCen to the brim. The buildings themselves may have even been quaking.

She couldn't believe it. Jon Wilhe was in the top two! All he needed to do was not crash...

But he didn't seem to share her wishes of playing it safe. Of course, he wanted to do whatever it took to win.

He pulled even with Delmatic, and Niko held her breath, as if any motion on her part would shake loose some butterfly effect to send her Ripper crashing and burning. His wheels made contact with Delmatic's as the finish line neared ever closer.

She would've closed her eyes, but she couldn't bring herself to look away. Too much rode on this.

Four hundred meters.

Three hundred.

Two hundred.

One hundred.

The booming sound of the final horn resounded across the streets of Alashadar as the wheels of Delmatic's green and black kart crossed the finish line, not one meter ahead of second-place Jon Wilhe.

CHAPTER NINE

9

An Idea

THE streets shook under the trample of the crowd, a living tide that surged back and forth with electric festivity. Banners spiraled into the air, and the sky lit up with a thousand fireworks of every color.

NewCen was in a frenzy, and rightly so. It was one of the closest races of the entire season so far, but Niko wasn't thinking about that. All she could think about was the enormous payout she was about to receive.

Her fingers curled into fists in her pockets to keep from trembling after watching that exhilarating finish, but now that it was over, she could finally breathe at least.

No reason to be surprised, though. She *knew* this would happen. Something deep inside — her instincts, she supposed — *knew* that this gamble was the right move to make tonight. Even still, shock whizzed through her.

She was getting paid.

And getting paid big. Not nearly enough to cover the costs of leaving this place, but a significant chunk, nonetheless. Much more than *any* of her friends had made thus far. The excitement of telling them couldn't wait, so she looked around for any of the Gluoron betting stations to cash out immediately.

Across every screen, Delmatic swept out of his kart in triumph and made a rude gesture at Jon Wilhe, as if his competitor hadn't just pushed him to the brink, before turning to the crowds in celebration.

What an ass, thought Niko. *If Riesen was alive, he would put that arrogant chum in his place...*

The stray thought struck Niko unexpectedly, exacting a smile from her. Riesen *would* be an amazing Trackripper; he was the best at everything he did.

The shouting grew louder around her as she slipped through the masses, where she spied a nearby Gluoron station off to the side. She knew she'd better collect her payout before the crowds became too thick.

Only then did she realize what the deafening commotion was about: Astine Rivers had finished in third place, ahead of Wenno Daks, Morland Relm, *and* Marl Vikers. A night of huge upsets. The top three were Delmatic, Jon Wilhe, and Astine Rivers, which the two announcers were repeatedly stressing was an incredibly low odds finish order. Some people would be getting extremely rich tonight, but most people were losing big...

And *that* had turned NewCen into a fledgling riot.

"It was rigged!"

"They rigged it!"

"Rigged!"

The shouting grew louder, transforming into a chant.

"RIGGED! RIGGED! RIGGED!"

Niko quickly finished her transaction, hands quivering from the nerves as eight million Terion was transferred to her account. Not the 8,800,000 she thought she was getting — the clerk explained that Gluoron's cut was eleven percent, as agreed upon when placing her bet — but she didn't have any time to complain. Besides, it was more Terion than she had ever dreamed of having in her account.

She scampered away, partially assisted with a violent shove to the side as a mob of angry spectators rushed the betting station. Niko was only able to stare, looking on in horror as the clerk she had just dealt with thirty seconds ago was pulled through the windows and beaten, right there in plain sight. Dozens of crazed fans kicked and stomped without any regard or reason.

"RIGGED! RIGGED! RIGGED!"

She'd heard stories of the lawlessness of Alashadar, but had

119

never seen it firsthand. If she was a braver person, she would've intervened. But there was no way she could. What could she do against dozens of angry men? She averted her eyes after seeing the poor man's arms forcibly twisted in an angle that no arm should ever bend, wishing she didn't have to hear the piercing screams that accompanied it. Were they going to kill the guy?!

Blazes, this was worse than she could've imagined!

In a past life, she might have cried at the savagery. But she had seen things — far worse things — and had become hardened to this type of occurrence, for better or worse. Either way, this was unbelievable. Why would these people do this?? Everything in the betting station was protected with Terion encryption... what did they expect to accomplish with this assault?

A young woman, alone, with a Terion badge in her hands however...

Suddenly, realizing just how much Terion had been transferred to her badge, she felt very exposed. If someone, anyone, witnessed her transaction a minute ago...

Her breath hitched, and the noise around her dulled as her pulse pounded in her ears. What should she do?? What *could* she do?

Think, Niko! Think!

Her mind raced and raced, until she decided to smoothly walk away to not incur any suspicions. Yes, that would be the best choice. But damn it all, she wanted out of here, and couldn't help herself when she turned to run back to her friends.

And then she tripped.

Or was she tripped on purpose?

It must've been the latter, because now there was someone behind her, clinging to her leg. And they wouldn't let go...

"It was her!" the man yelled, his tone vicious with desperation. "The clerk said it was *her* he gave the Terion to!"

To Niko's utter terror, more men heeded the call and stalked menacingly toward her. The man who held her leg effortlessly pulled her backward, and she screamed. She was embarrassed to do so, but she *actually* screamed.

Just then, however, another mob came from the opposite direction and slammed straight into the men attacking her. Fists, legs, anything and everything, were caught in a whirlwind that raged above her. She felt the man's grip slacken for a split second, and that was all she needed to kick free.

She felt and heard the sickening crunch of his finger— and his violent curses toward her — but she continued to kick and thrash as she frantically searched for any purchase to scoot herself backward.

An unstoppable wave of people surged overhead, all other sounds drowned out by their clamor. Niko's arms and legs were trampled, and the electric lights of NewCen became blotted out by the bodies around her as she attempted to wriggle her way out.

Suddenly, her ears rang and vision blurred as she lost all orientation of left and right, up and down.

What the blazes!? Did someone just kick her in the back of the head? Awareness faded for a moment, but she continued to pull herself out of the chaos toward freedom. Toward life.

But before she even scooted five meters, another hand reached out and grabbed her by the collar, hauling her across the ground with ungodly force. She screamed again, hoping her friends might hear, but...

"Niko! Blazes, it's me! I've got you!"

Niko whirled around to face Ravenna, who was shoving men and women to the side as she parted the roiling mass of people. The crowd thinned after a few seconds, most of those remaining stepping aside on their own free will, wise enough to avoid Ravenna's onslaught. Soon they were at the edge of the street, where she was glad to see her other friends rushing toward them.

"Blazes, girl! What were you *thinking*?!" Ravenna smacked her on the side of the head, causing her vision to dim once again.

If she didn't already have a concussion, Ravenna seemed dead set on giving her one. Niko had never seen her so angry in her entire life — which was saying a lot, considering she had witnessed the girl rage like a firestorm several times firsthand.

"I... I..."

"You could've gotten yourself *killed*! And *not* in a good way..."

Ravenna gestured to the crowd, who were now tossing one of the clerk's torn-off arms around as if it were a Field ball. It was a stomach-churning sight, but Niko didn't react in the way that she might once have. She only shuddered mildly, staring blankly toward the spectacle, glad that it wasn't her own arm being thrown around. Then her eyes met those of the man whose finger she just broke.

"We need to get out of here," Ce-Ellum astutely butted in, diffusing Ravenna's anger. "Follow me!"

Ravenna gave Niko one last glare that could've melted the hair off her head, but she turned and followed, as did Niko. She did not dare look back as they rushed off the scene, praying to every imaginary deity that they weren't being followed by any of those bloodthirsty rioters.

After a few breathless moments, they made it through the doors of the Marindise, whose environment was in stark contrast to that of the street just outside. The overwhelming, decadent atmosphere inside the entertainment venue, along with its charming background music, barely even registered to Niko. The only thing she could focus on was following her friends up a zig-zagging row of escalators, and finally, onto a train bound for Machine Row.

Niko settled onto a seat, closed her eyes softly, and squeezed her head with two hands. Blazes, her vision would *not* stop spinning.

After a minute, she finally opened her eyes wide enough, chagrined to see a massive riot amassed out the windows below. How did things turn to blazes so quickly? Even worse, she could make out dozens of armed figures encircling the furious mob. Lines of smoke were fired into the crowd, followed by the flashes on the muzzles of their weapons.

The blood curdled in Niko's veins.

"Don't worry," Ce-Ellum said, noticing the look of horror stamped all over her face. "Crowd-control projectiles only. Though, they'll probably wish they didn't attack EC property by the time the interrogators are done with them."

Of course he would know their interrogation methods, if he was in league with those thugs…

However, once she had a chance to catch her breath, Niko realized she was eternally grateful to Ce-Ellum for leading them away from that mess down there. Maybe she'd been too hard on him all this time. Maybe she should thank him.

She turned to do just that when a metallic, tapping noise sounded as he settled back into his seat. Her attention was drawn to the sound, down to his leg.

A prosthetic leg.

Of course he would have a prosthetic leg…

It was so stereotypical — he was a spitting image of what she knew the Oldcity gangsters looked like. How did her friends never connect all the dots? It was well known that the underlings of some of the crime bosses in Alashadar were required to give up half a limb of their choice if they failed their lords in any way. Most chose the weak leg. Such a savage, primitive rite, but that was just how things worked out here — as she was beginning to experience personally, if her run-in with the mob outside was any indication.

"Thank you," Niko offered with wide eyes, pretending to not notice his leg. "Thank you for getting us out of there."

"Of course." He pressed his lips tight and nodded in return. "So, how much did you make out with?"

"Oh, *please* tell me you didn't bet tonight, Niko…" Ravenna groaned.

"I… Well, I won, at least," she admitted quietly.

Ce-Ellum returned her gaze calmly with deliberate confidence, while Ravenna had her arms crossed and looked like she was about ready to throw Niko off the train. Cryo and Kyler just raised their eyebrows in surprise.

"How much?" Kyler asked.

"Eight million," she whispered.

"Holy bla…!" Kyler half-shouted, before quieting his voice, realizing they weren't the only people on board. "Holy blazes! Eight *million*?!"

"Shhhh!" Niko nodded, and her friends looked around at each other silently for a few seconds.

"It was a risk," Ravenna said, still glaring at Niko with the look of a predator.

"I just… I had a feeling," Niko shrugged, looking away.

She thought she could make out a small smile forming on Cryo's lips, but then caught a similar expression from Ce-Ellum, which unsettled her once again. If that chum tried to take her Terion somehow…

"Blazes, why didn't you tell us?!" Kyler exclaimed, still attempting to quiet his enthusiasm. "If we all placed that bet, we could be getting off this hellhole!"

Niko shrugged. "I wanted it to be a surprise if I won."

"Oh, it was a surprise, alright." Ravenna still looked furious.

"Did you bet on Wilhe?" Ce-Ellum asked.

Niko hesitated, but replied. "Yes…"

"So did I," he responded.

All heads turned toward him.

"But for future reference," he continued, "don't *ever* cash out immediately. Things can get ugly pretty fast out here."

Niko and her friends didn't talk much the rest of the trip, since a few nearby passengers looked a little *too* interested in their conversation. But now that they were back at her friends' place in Machine Row, the conversation was started anew.

It was more of the same: Ravenna scolding her for being so reckless, Cryo doing his best to hide his amusement and pride, Kyler talking about what they would do with *her* Terion, and Ce-Ellum… well, she couldn't get a read on what Ce-Ellum thought of the whole thing.

Would it be too far-fetched to imagine that he'd try to steal the Terion she just made? She really wished she didn't say anything at all about her winnings, if he was indeed involved in the Alashadar underworld. Even if he did help save their hides back there…

She wished Anda was with her now. She needed an ally against this ridiculousness, especially if Cryo wasn't going to speak up. She didn't know Anda super well yet, but her speech was so smooth that she imagined the girl could diffuse a bomb in a hurricane. Which was exactly what she needed now.

"I'm just getting the feeling that *none* of you realize how dangerous that was," Ravenna accused.

"That's what we have you for!" Kyler quipped, a smile mischievously spreading across his face. "I saw how you pulled Niko out of there like it was nothing."

Ravenna now turned on him. "And what would you have done if I wasn't there? If I hadn't heard her?"

The group had no response to that. Not even Niko had a response to that. What *would* have happened if Ravenna hadn't heard her? Would they have ripped her arms off and left her to die like the clerk?

Niko was surprised when Cryo finally spoke up. He hadn't really said much this whole time, but his gaze became deeply thoughtful, as if she could see all the wheels turning at once.

"Niko, before we left Arhanda, how much did Ajane teach you?"

The question caught her off guard, so she hesitated.

"What do you mean? Like self-defense?"

He shook his head. "I mean with your instincts. Your psychic intellect."

Oh. That.

She had done her absolute best to ignore all of that ever since they'd lost Ajane. Ever since they'd abandoned their home. She hadn't even once tried to reach out to *anybody* in a dream. Not her family, who was probably dead; not Daren, who was on another world, hopefully alive; and not even Jack, who she knew was out there somewhere on this planet — alive, for all she knew. But she supposed her instincts still did her favors when she wasn't paying attention.

She was about to explain to Cryo what exactly Ajane trained her on, but then she saw Ce-Ellum staring at her intently from the shadows and lost her nerve.

She only shrugged. "I don't know."

Cryo seemed to look right through her, reading her with knowing contemplation.

Niko hated that all the attention was on her, so she tried to deflect it elsewhere. "How much did you put on Jon Wilhe?" she asked Ce-Ellum.

He shifted from his perch against the wall and came to stand over the table they all sat at. "Two million Terion. One-hundred percent on Wilhe top six."

Niko could almost hear the jaws dropping. Two million?!

"Blazes!" Kyler blurted out. "I didn't know you were rich!"

"Hah!" Ce-Ellum snorted. "I would hardly call that rich."

"Richer than us..." Kyler responded. "Well, other than Niko, now."

"What were the returns on that?" Cryo asked.

"4:1"

"Damn! So you get eight million, also?!" Kyler exclaimed.

"Yes."

Ce-Ellum seemed so calm about it, like gambling and winnings of this scale were business as usual. Maybe instead of waiting to let him steal their Terion, they should strike first and steal his...

"Okay," Kyler started, "I have to ask... Why are we beating our heads against a wall and wasting time creating some super machine when we can just have Niko and Ce-Ellum bet on Trackripping to get us out of here?"

The silence in the room seemed to say it all. Kyler actually was speaking reason, and his proposal was far less daunting than her unspoken plan to steal Terion from a criminal kingpin.

"Gambling is just as it sounds," Ravenna said. "Eventually you lose."

"Maybe in the big EC venues, yes," Kyler responded. "But Trackripping is a sport. It's different."

"Yes and no," Ce-Ellum intervened. "It can be rigged. I've... I've seen it happen many times before. Ven is right. The system is designed to make the EC's win in the long run. If we start playing against them long-term, they eventually win. And we eventually lose."

"Well, why did you bet on Jon Wilhe tonight, then?" Kyler asked.

Ce-Ellum tilted his head to the side. "I always like to support him."

"Wait, do you *know* Jon Wilhe?" Niko blurted out.

Her heart skipped a beat as she put it together — one of Jon Wilhe's sponsors was Vulture, a front for one of the most notorious gangs on Alashadar. She didn't dare say anything else in front of Ce-Ellum, but she would most *definitely* be bringing this to the attention of her friends later. They should *not* be associating with this guy.

Ce-Ellum slowly nodded, all eyes upon him. "I do."

"What the blazes?!" Kyler shouted. "Actually?!"

"Yes."

"Woah!" Kyler looked absolutely flabbergasted. "Well, since we have an *in*, we should be using that. You could ask him about his chances before each race, and if he gives you an honest answer, we can all place our bets accordingly. Even if we win only a little bit each time, added together we can get enough Terion pretty quickly to leave this place."

"That's dangerous territory, right there," Ce-Ellum cautioned. "If the EC's sniff out any foul betting, their justice is swift and brutal."

"So each of us uses a different EC each time," Kyler went on. "And we each rotate. Unless Terion collects data centrally, I think we can..."

"They do," Ce-Ellum interrupted. "Which is why we need to

continue with our work on the Infinity Machine."

Kyler sighed. "I guess you're right. But it can't hurt to place small bets. I can't imagine anything under a million Terion would be flagged by their system."

"Probably not," Ce-Ellum admitted.

"So let's do that for the next race," Kyler declared. "Would you be able to talk to Jon Wilhe and see what his chances are?"

"I can try," Ce-Ellum said. "But using Niko's... *psychic intellect*... might be more beneficial."

The slight smirk that tugged at the corners of his mouth made Niko feel squeamish to the maximum. Why did Cryo have to talk about that in front of this stranger? This *gangster*...

"I don't like it," Ravenna said abruptly.

"You have to admit that it's a good way to get our Terion faster," Kyler pushed. "Even if it's just a little bit each race. I don't know about you guys, but I'm sick of this place. The Capital system sounds *way* nicer."

Ravenna sucked air through her teeth and shook her head, but didn't protest any further.

"Like I said," Ce-Ellum stated, "we need to still be working on the Infinity Machine. It's even more important now if we're going to be methodically sticking our noses into Trackripping betting."

"Yeah, yeah," Kyler grumbled. "I'll work on something that can help mask our betting patterns. I'm all in for this."

In typical fashion, Ravenna snapped to her feet, kicked her chair in, and stormed down the hall without saying any farewells. Niko wondered how she and Kira-Tharn never became great friends. Sometimes, they were the exact same person.

"Just admit it. Aren't you guys so glad to have me around?" Kyler beamed, taunting Niko with a flashy grin. "A man full of brilliant ideas."

Ugh! That cocky, blazes-accursed asshat!

Niko was about ready to punch him in the face. Although, she did have to admit that it was a pretty good plan — better than her foolish notion to steal from Ce-Ellum, that was certain — which made her all the more frustrated.

10

On the Job

THE heat was brutal today, though not unexpected. The last three days were Venting days, where the atmosphere would be adjusted by the Engines — well, not *Engines* plural, but the one functional *Engine* on this whole planet. These adjustments weren't needed often, but they were becoming more and more frequent. Apparently, the atmosphere was turning more dynamic with the increasing number of Rifts being excavated.

As annoying and uncomfortable as the heat was, however, Niko supposed that it beat the alternative, which was planetary devastation. Because of An-Terino's proximity to Bucon, the cosmic rays were much more destructive to the atmosphere, the top layers easily stripped, and the surface exposed to ionizing radiation.

To protect against this, not only would the Engine vent more greenhouse compounds into the atmosphere, but it maintained the planet's magnetic field, which was crucial in defending the surface from the high flux of Bucon. Without the Venting, the whole planet would snowball into unlivable conditions: there'd be too much harmful incoming shortwave radiation, while simultaneously losing too much outbound longwave radiation in the energy balance. The Daylight zone would become even more scorchingly hot than it already was, and the Night surface would become completely frozen. The thin band of Twilight in between would then become a zone where a hurricane of alternating tendrils of searing hot and freezing cold would rage endlessly — if any atmosphere even remained at all.

At least the planet was rife with vulcanism, Niko supposed, because one lone Engine wouldn't be enough to keep the planet habitable. Even though stars like Bucon were the most common type in the galaxy, Niko was beginning to learn why life never popped up naturally in these systems. If people thought this place was bad now, they had no idea of the hellscape it could potentially become without human influence.

Whichever Nel-Mara initially decided An-Terino was a good place to build a society must've been some sort of sadist. Maybe it's why they abandoned further construction of the Engines and left the terraforming incomplete. But then there were the Meridians who, years ago, came back to finish the job...

Arrogant idiots, the lot of them. It was such a terrible, wasteful idea, even though they only decided to do so assuming that Bucon was old enough to have aged past its most volatile phase of youth. This place was unsustainable, to say the least. Niko just hoped she would be out of here before it was too late.

She had learned much in her studies of planetary science over the last several years, and then had also been learning of the history of the galaxy from Anda, Kira-Tharn, and Riiz. A new curiosity of hers was why no other intelligent civilizations besides that of the Nel-Mara had emerged. What did Kira-Tharn call it? The Paradox?

It was so strange, even with the knowledge that these planetary systems like Bucon's were so inhospitable, that they should be the only intelligent life forms. Even here, in a completely alien world, society was so similar to her own that she was raised in. All humans, all speaking the same language, and all aware of the same histories.

One day long ago, she might've been skeptical of the reason why — that all of the different civilizations around were only present because the Nel-Mara had terraformed and seeded these worlds with humans, even interjecting cultures and languages from their own epoch called the 'Dawn of Civilization' — but after all she'd experienced in the last few years, none of it was too much of a shock.

Niko's attention was brought back to the present, her muscles protesting as she leaned forward to snap another blacksquash off the vine. The heat made everything *so* much more difficult today, but the most annoying part was the winds, which were sure to linger for several days after the Ventings.

During these events, the high pressure zone from the middle of the Daylight fanned the hot air outwards stronger than normal, sweeping past the population center in the Twilight and into the Night. Because of this, harvesting the blacksquashes became a struggle, the blasts of hot air continuously threatening to pitch their bins of produce into the air. Even Anda's haul looked far smaller than usual.

She couldn't believe that ROTO expected them to meet the same daily quota as on a normal, non-Venting day. She'd already worked an hour past the normal quitting time, and they still had another row to complete! This *almost* had Niko wishing that she still worked in the Rifts.

Almost.

One reminiscence about the conditions in the Rifts after a Venting day was all she needed to feel grateful to be working in the fields instead. Seventeen workers had died during that last Venting day shift in the Rifts!

"Almost done," she muttered.

She hadn't conversed much with Anda today since the work was so taxing, but she wanted to catch up with her friend. The last few days offered no chance to see her, of course, since they didn't work during the Venting. What Niko really wanted to ask was what happened the other night when she disappeared before the Trackripping race.

"Almost," Anda panted, visibly struggling today. Niko perhaps had collected even more blacksquashes than she did, which would be a first.

"You okay?" Niko asked with earnest concern.

"I am," Anda replied, her face returning to unreadable calm, as if it were a simple choice for her.

Niko stopped plucking squashes and paused to look at her friend, her eyebrows scrunched in doubt.

"Oh, hush." Anda returned the glance. "I'm fine."

"Okayyy, if you say so…"

"I have much on my mind."

"Is that why you left the other night?" Niko didn't want to

impose on her new friend's business, but the words were out before she really thought about it.

Anda paused, taking a deep breath, probably weighing her response.

"I'm sorry for that," was all she said.

"It's okay," Niko replied.

She wouldn't push the issue any further. If Anda didn't want to disclose what had spooked her so badly, she didn't have to. Even though she did suspect that it had something to do with Ce-Ellum...

Still, Niko wouldn't be *that* type of friend that pried things out of people. Not like Kate.

Niko winced at the thought. The smallest memory of her long deceased sister, even a less than flattering one, threatened to uncork the flood of sorrow that lay bounded by the wall that had done so well to hold back her emotions over the last few years.

"I wasn't feeling great, so I had to leave," Anda clarified without making eye contact, her attention instead focused on the harvest.

Niko got the feeling that wasn't the entire truth, but she would just leave it be. Neither of the two said anything else for the duration of their shift.

Anda was so incredibly exhausted today. After leaving Niko the other night — which she felt awful for — she didn't manage to sleep at all. Not one minute. Even the following few days, which were days off from work due to the Venting, she only managed short naps. Her mind was instead preoccupied by that guy that masqueraded as one of Niko's friends.

She seriously debated telling Niko what she knew of the man, and she could feel Niko's unspoken desire to know what happened the other night, but that would entail going down a road that she wasn't ready to discuss just yet. The scars ran deep there, and she ultimately decided that she didn't know enough about Niko to open up to that extent.

Maybe someday.

She also felt regret for being socially awkward today, barely uttering but a few words to Niko all day. Sure, the heat was making things unpleasant, but most of her introversion came from being lost in her own thoughts.

She was startled — something that rarely happened to her — when the final horn sounded as they finished harvesting the last row.

The two older ladies next to them, Marial and Nuna, congratulated her and Niko, and she returned the favor with her best smile, choosing to dispel all that weighed upon her mind.

"A tough day," Marial said to them. "You ladies are wondrous."

"You, as well," Anda offered back, grasping her hands in the traditional Ossion manner, crisscrossing one over the other. Both of these ladies clearly hailed from that system, their accents and customs mirroring everything Anda knew of that place, as well as their telltale red hair and freckles.

"And you, young lady, we have not learned of your name," Nuna said, grasping hands with Niko.

"Oh, sorry. I'm Niko."

"What a lovely name," Nuna purred. "And where do you hail from, Niko?"

Her friend paused ever-so-slightly at the request. It probably wasn't noticeable to Marial and Nuna, but Anda had spent enough time with her the last few days to know Niko was made uncomfortable by the question.

"Umm, I lived with the Meridians, then with the An-Mara."

Not exactly an answer. Strange. The girl was hiding something. *Her prerogative*, Anda supposed.

"Well, we are blessed to have you among us here," Nuna said to her.

"I'm glad to be here also," Niko replied politely.

Anda nearly snorted. She knew *that* was a lie. Nobody was glad to be here.

"Until tomorrow," Marial and Nuna both echoed, bowing in their Ossion farewells.

"Until tomorrow." Niko and Anda returned the gestures.

"I love those ladies," Niko commented as they walked off the fields. "They're so sweet."

"Yes, they are."

"Where do you think they're from?" Niko asked. "I should've

asked them, since they asked me."

"They are from the Ossion system," Anda replied. "So either Ossion or Proteia."

Anda studied Niko from the corner of her eye. Surely she would know of the Ossion system? After all, that was her best guess at where Niko's ultimate destination lay.

"I'm not familiar with that system," Niko admitted. "Where is it?"

Very strange.

Anda looked skyward and pointed at the bright star at the center of the Ossion system, which just so happened to be visible today. Everyone just called the star Ossion, even though that was technically only the name of the most settled planet there. How did Niko *not* know about that system? This poor girl must have led a very sheltered life, indeed.

It looked like Niko was about ready to say something else, but Amon appeared out of nowhere.

"They need you in the Cinto fields tonight," he announced to Anda, unbothered by Niko's presence. "Shatter is unloading a huge shipment we need treated. And there are going to be many more in the coming weeks."

Niko's eyes widened, darting back and forth between Amon and herself. Anda sighed. Not only was she exhausted, but now she felt compelled to explain why she was needed in the Cinto fields.

"Right now?" Anda asked.

Amon nodded. "At 19:00."

Anda sighed again, nodding. Amon offered her a sympathetic half-smile, but turned around and headed back to wherever he came from. The office, probably.

"Anda?" Niko asked concernedly.

Here we go...

"Everything okay?"

"Yes," Anda replied. "It's... it's complicated."

"That's okay," Niko said. "You don't owe me an explanation."

Ugh, the blasted girl is too nice! Anda thought. She felt obligated to explain everything to her on those grounds alone. *I guess I am going down that road...*

"It's fine," she said. "I... I owe a debt to ROTO. It's a complicated arrangement — a time debt rather than a monetary debt. I get paid well, but I'm stuck here until my time is paid off."

Niko stared at her with scrunched brows. "I don't get it. How'd you get stuck with that?"

"They intervened... well, *Amon* intervened... and got me out of a tough situation. Saved my life, really. He was indentured to ROTO, though, because of a gambling debt he owed them. So when he brought me in, they agreed to save me on the grounds that I give them a certain amount of service."

"So now *you're* indentured to them? They couldn't just save you out of goodwill?!" Niko looked at Anda with utmost genuine concern.

Anda grunted a scornful laugh. "Nothing is done on this planet out of goodwill. Have you not learned that by now?"

Niko just shook her head and looked at Anda with pity.

"Oh, *please* don't give me that." If there was one thing Anda hated more than anything, it was being treated with pity. Niko never did that before, and it was the one thing she most appreciated about her. "I'm fine. It's not a horrible arrangement. I'm alive because of it, and besides, I get handsome paydays."

"But aren't the Cinto fields... *toxic*?" Niko asked.

"We do wear proper gear, you know..." Anda responded, sighing. "I didn't want to tell you about it before, because I didn't want you to react the way you are now."

"I'm sorry!" Niko squeaked. "But I consider you my friend, and if you're in any danger, or if you're blazes *indentured*, then that bothers me."

"I promise I'm fine," Anda assured her. "But what about you? You always say 'blazes this' and 'blazes that'. Your phrases and world views are so unlike those of any people I've come across."

"I..." Niko hesitated, taking a deep breath before continuing. "I'm from a world called Arhanda. It was the one the An-Mara destroyed a few years ago."

Anda maintained a peaceful visage, but she shuddered inside. No wonder she could sense the darkness inside this girl. Losing a home permanently would hollow out anyone. She had heard of that world before, and the rumors that its people were manipulated by Shatter. This girl must carry some profound scars...

"But please don't tell anyone about this, ever," Niko pleaded. "I was sworn to silence about it. A few of us came here about a year ago. We've been trying to get off planet, but we don't have the Terion."

"Of course I won't tell anyone," Anda promised her. "And I'm sorry about your home."

Niko nodded. "Thank you. It's... I've come to terms with it, I guess."

She reached out and touched Anda's arm. This physical intimacy must be one of the customs of her people. Strange, but not unwelcome.

"I was forced to leave my home, as well," Anda said sympathetically. "It's not remotely the same, because mine still exists, but I know how difficult it is to leave under difficult circumstances."

"Yeah." Niko looked up at Anda tenderly. "But if neither of us left, we would've never met. And for that, I'm glad we did."

"Me too." Odd as it was, Anda was telling the truth. She *was* glad for the opportunity to know Niko.

Niko reached forward to embrace her in a hug, which Anda lightly returned.

"I guess you need to get going now?" Niko asked.

"Yes, unfortunately."

"If there's anything I can do to help, please let me know."

"I'll be fine," Anda laughed. This girl sure liked to fuss over her well-being, and they'd only been friends for a week.

"Okayyy. I'll see you tomorrow?"

"Yes, I'll be here."

Niko reached in for one more hug before turning away, but before she had taken ten steps, Niko called back to her.

"Oh, Anda?"

"Yes?"

"I did have a question. I don't mean to pry further, but it's about that guy you saw at my friends' place. Ce-Ellum. It looked like you knew him, and not in a good way. I... I need to know if he's someone my friends need to stay away from."

Anda paused. So Niko did notice the other night. She needed to phrase her words carefully.

"I know who he is."

"I just have a strange worry that he's involved in the Alashadar underworld," Niko continued, "and that he'll betray my friends."

"He does work in the underworld," Anda confessed after a few seconds. "But I don't think he's the type to go around people's backs."

"I just get really bad vibes from him," Niko said. "I can't explain it."

Anda shrugged. "What do your friends think?"

"They said what you said, basically. That I should trust him."

"I'm not saying you should trust him — or anyone — implicitly. Keep an eye on him if you need to." Anda paused, seeing the apprehension written all over Niko's face. "If it makes you feel better, I only avoided him the other night because I didn't want to get caught up in his business, is all. I'm already entangled in the underworld enough."

It was the truth. She absolutely did *not* want to get caught up in that man's business…

There was some more that she hadn't mentioned, of course, but she already told Niko far too much tonight. She wasn't about to delve into her entire history and spill everything. Besides, she needed to hurry over to the Cinto fields…

… And that brought worries afresh — whatever Shatter had planned wasn't good. Increased Cinto shipments could mean a number of things, but Anda hoped that it wasn't what she thought.

"I'm afraid I must leave now, though, Niko. I can't be late."

"Okay. Good luck. And I'm sorry for prying into your business so hard." Niko shot her a grin that appeared mixed with a grimace.

Anda smiled back. "I'll see you tomorrow. Thank you… for talking to me tonight."

CHAPTER ELEVEN

11

The Cinto Scheme

"SORRY."

Niko's mind was more than preoccupied. She couldn't believe what she'd heard from Amon.

Shatter.

Involved with Cinto.

And not only involved — they were *deliberately* increasing its presence on An-Terino. But why?

It was probably information she should tell her friends, since they'd been very interested in Shatter's business the other night. Best to keep them all in the loop.

"It is of no consequence, Niko Ryen," Riiz replied. "We will continue tomorrow."

"Thank you," she winced. "I'll see you tomorrow."

She should've been more focused on her tinkering lesson with Riiz tonight, but after all the bombshells from her conversation with Anda, focusing was nearly impossible. Even Riiz noticed that her mind was elsewhere and ended the lesson early.

Niko wanted to learn more. She really did. But realistically, she knew that she wasn't in a state to retain all this new jargon effectively, so she accepted his judgment to continue the lessons another day.

The one good thing was that he introduced Niko to the communication program they used, so now she had a way to connect securely with her friends. She didn't completely trust it, but Riiz seemed to, so she'd take his word for it. Maybe testing the thing out would give her an opportunity to tell her friends about what Shatter was planning with the Cinto. Maybe they could shed some more light on that.

She said her farewells and walked across the open square to her own quarters, where she barged in to find Kira-Tharn sprawled out on the floor. It looked like the woman was performing some stretching routine, and an odd one at that. She looked absolutely ridiculous, her legs splayed into some contortion that looked downright painful.

"You okay?"

"I am perfectly fine, Niko Ryen."

"Doesn't look that way…"

"I am providing my muscles with the necessary care for optimal recovery."

Of course she was.

"You should seriously think about switching to the fields," Niko suggested once more. "It's hard on the legs at first, but overall it's way easier than the Rifts."

"I am content with my placement, thank you very much."

Niko raised an eyebrow at her in skepticism, drawing a disapproving frown in return.

"I have told you before, Niko Ryen. The Rifts provide much more Terion credit than do the fields. *One of us* must provide ample credit to pay for living costs."

"The starting pay, yes. But you can get promoted in the fields much easier than in the Rifts. No way that clown Armond-Dei ever promotes you."

Kira-Tharn continued to glower at Niko, but did not respond. She must've known it was true.

"Anyway, here… I have something to show you," Niko said. "But you have to promise not to be upset with me."

"What did you do this time?" Kira-Tharn immediately sat up, narrowing her brows at Niko judgmentally.

'What did you do this time?' Ugh!! Niko nearly made a face. Why did no one trust her to just live her life her own way?

"Nothing bad," Niko promised. "I just got some Terion from the race the other night."

Kira-Tharn glared daggers at Niko in return. "You gambled."

"Yes, but…"

"I warned you of that activity many months ago, Niko Ryen."

"I know, but I…"

"It is not a practice that is sustainable," Kira-Tharn continued. "Nor is it proper. If you wish to abide by the Time, that is something you cannot engage in."

"I don't *wish to abide* by every word of the Time!" Niko burst out. At this point, she was so sick of tiptoeing around Kira-Tharn's touchy attitude when it came to the damn Time. "Of course I love being with the An-Mara here, but I *do* want to live my life every now and then. I just… I feel so trapped."

"If you become addicted to gambling, *then* you will know the meaning of feeling trapped."

"I am not addicted!" Niko protested. "This was the first time I ever did it!"

"The sensation of winning will incur the desire for more."

"No! I…" Niko stopped. She was going to tell Kira-Tharn that she would never gamble again, but she remembered that betting on these races was now part of the plan that Kyler had introduced. "I just… I promise it won't be an issue."

"See that it does not become one, Niko Ryen."

"It won't."

Kira-Tharn finally broke the unblinking stare she'd been leveling at Niko, turning her dark eyes toward the ceiling as she lay back down, returning to her peculiar stretches. Niko took this to mean that the conversation was over, so she trudged down the hallway to her room and threw herself on the bed, yelling into the blankets.

Why must her friends be so dismissive?! Couldn't *one* person actually have the decency to *thank* her for winning eight million Terion for them, rather than lecturing her like she was some child?

Of her friends, only Cryo and Kyler hadn't looked askance at her, and it was Kyler, of all people, who seemed the most impressed. Which reminded her — she needed to let them know about the new information regarding Shatter.

Still facedown on her bed, she reached across to her pack and pulled out the console that Riiz had loaned her for tinkering lessons, loading up the communications program like he'd shown her earlier. The thing looked ancient, the screen's pattern only made from rudimentary pixels, though she understood a fancy console screen wasn't required to learn the tinkering languages that her friends used. Her eyes were drawn to the corner of the display, where a countdown ticked on.

Twenty-three.

Twenty-two.

Twenty-one.

Twenty...

Nothing urgent there, Riiz had told her. The countdown recycled every sixty seconds, upon which a new encryption key would be randomly generated. These encryption keys were shared, but only among users of the program, and they were designed to keep their transmissions secure. Nobody from Terion, Shatter, or anyone else would be intercepting them. That's what Riiz said, at least.

At the bottom of the screen was an open bar-like space where she could type — yes, *type* — symbols in to create a message. She had seen machine tinkerers pressing buttons to type messages before, but she herself never had to do that; she'd been so dependent on the damn Uts to send messages with her thoughts. Typing seemed so old-fashioned.

What should she input though? She didn't completely trust that it was one hundred percent secure, so maybe something generic to start.

This is Niko. Can anyone see this?

She then hit the enter key as Riiz had shown her, and waited. And waited.

And waited.

She was about ready to close the thing and head to sleep when a line of text appeared underneath her message.

niko!? this is kyler

Usually, she wouldn't be all that excited to hear from Kyler, but communicating on this machine her friends built gave her a strange rush.

Riiz taught me how to use this. He said it's secure. Is it?

This time, she waited barely two seconds before she received his reply.

yes

In matters of machine tinkering, she would trust what Kyler had to say. If this was actually Kyler...

Okay, good, she replied.

what u need? Kyler asked.

Are you sure no one can be reading in on this? She just wanted to be certain.

...

Okay, point taken. At least the rudeness of a '...' gave her more confidence that this was indeed Kyler, and since he was already easily annoyed by Niko's lack of machine literacy, she didn't want to irritate him further. Best to get to the point.

Well, I heard some stuff about Shatter today that I thought you guys might want to know about.

like what

Niko paused for a moment, giving herself a chance to compose her thoughts and send them out in a coherent, yet concise, manner.

Apparently they're shipping a bunch of materials to the ROTO fields. Materials that are going to be treated for Cinto production.

There was a short pause before Kyler replied.

what u mean by a bunch? he asked.

I just heard a huge shipment was inbound tonight, and that a bunch more were expected in the coming weeks.

how do u know this?

Hmm, how could she phrase this without throwing Anda under an Alashadar train?

I heard it straight from a man at the fields. He was requesting someone's presence for the treatment of these materials, whatever that meant. He said the shipment was from Shatter and that they were expecting a lot more in the coming weeks. That's all I heard.

A couple minutes went by without a response. Niko considered he might've been done with her, and was just about to tuck the device away when another line of text appeared.

niko, this is cryo. who did you hear this from?

Okay, much better to be dealing with Cryo than Kyler. Still, she didn't want to clue any of them in to Anda's involvement.

I overheard a man at the fields I work at asking another worker to meet in the Cinto fields. He said that there was a huge shipment from Shatter and that there would be more in the coming weeks. That's everything I heard them say about it.

ok interesting. thanks.

What do you think this means? she asked.

She was worried he wouldn't respond quickly, but to her surprise, she only had to wait a few seconds before he explained it all in detail.

we suspected shatter was working alongside terion to flood this place with cinto to keep the population happy and dumb. not only cinto, but trackripping, droneripping, pit fighting, concerts... all sorts of entertainment to keep everyone oblivious to increased surveillance and control. they're using that riot from the other day as an extra excuse to ramp up security in newcen and machine row.

Well. Niko supposed that made sense. She'd seen a ridiculous amount of news related to that riot, and while she agreed that it was bad, she wasn't sure that it justified a massive crackdown on freedoms.

this is one of the things that'll make it way harder for us to hack into terion, he continued. *but at the same time, it's giving us a window. when they take parts of their system down for expansion, sometimes there are little holes we can exploit.*

Was this what they were excited about the other day when she was first telling them about her experiences in the Shatter yard?

Is there a connection between this and Minedyne? And the Meridians? she asked.

yeah. turns out minedyne IS shatter. or a part of it at least. and the fake meridians that we knew of on arhanda are a part of shatter also. i think callum and jack would have more info for us. i'll reach out.

Niko's jaw flopped open while reading this last message over and over and over. Minedyne *was* Shatter? And the Meridians in charge of Arhanda were also Shatter?? Cryo's message laid it all out so nonchalantly, but this was anything but everyday information.

you coming over for the race in three days? he asked, after Niko didn't respond for a few minutes.

Yeah, of course.

ok awesome. i'll get in touch with callum and jack and we'll keep you updated on this whole thing. if you hear anything more about the cinto at your fields, let us know.

I will. See you in a few days.

cya

After that, there were no more exchanges for the rest of the night, but Niko continued to stare at the screen regardless, reading and rereading the entire conversation.

———————

The next day at the fields, Niko still had Shatter, Minedyne, Cinto, Meridians, and everything else all swirling around in her brain. She debated telling Anda what her friends had been discussing, but thought it best to keep it under wraps for the time being. Even if she and Anda *had* opened up to each other yesterday, her friends still depended on her discretion. After all, they were still planning to infiltrate the security system of the closest thing this planet had to an authoritative body. Dangerous stuff.

"How're you feeling today?" she asked Anda, simultaneously plopping another blacksquash into the bin.

"Tired."

"How late did they make you stay?"

"Late," Anda replied. "Or... early, rather."

Both women laughed, but Niko imagined neither of them thought it was actually funny. This blazes corporation had the gall to indenture this poor girl just because she couldn't pay them back? And for something she had no control over?... Anda was right, there was no such thing as goodwill on this world.

"How many hours did you get until you had to be back here?" Niko asked, narrowing her eyes at Anda.

Anda looked up at her, but all she replied with was, "I'm fine," before she continued to work along the row of vines, rattling off blacksquashes at an accelerated rate, even by her own standards.

The woman was on a mission. Niko was beginning to wonder if she came straight here after doing whatever work she had to do in the Cinto fields, and was just on a hot streak out of pure spite.

"You should take it easy. I can pick up your slack," Niko offered concernedly. She remembered Anda hated pity, but she wasn't going to let her friend work herself into complete exhaustion.

Anda shook her head, not bothering to stop. "I promise. I'm fine."

Niko stopped to look at her friend — who appeared fine physically — but Niko knew if she were in Anda's position, she

143

would be frustrated beyond all belief. "Okay."

The two worked for several more minutes in silence before Niko spoke up again.

"Did you wanna go to the race with me in two days?" she asked.

"I can't," Anda replied, shooting Niko an apologetic frown. "I'm sorry. They need me at the Cinto fields again that night, and they made it seem like it was more important than normal that I be there for that one."

"Oh, okay."

"I'm sorry, I'm letting you down with these races," Anda laughed. "I'm not trying to ditch you, I swear. I may not follow Trackripping, but they are still fun to watch."

"No, it's fine, I promise!"

"I will go with you to the next one after that. Even if I have to find an excuse to skip my shift."

"Are you allowed to do that?" Niko asked carefully. "Like with your... you know... your indentured servitude."

Anda shrugged. "It's not as bad as it sounds. I can miss every now and then if I'm 'not feeling well'."

"I don't want to put you in a predicament," Niko said. "It's totally fine if you don't go! I have all my other friends that I go with anyway."

"Just flaunting around our social life now, aren't we?"

Anda's mangled mouth looked like it was sporting a smirk, and Niko burst out laughing.

"Oh trust me, compared to the friends I grew up with, I am *far* from social."

"Me too," Anda admitted with a chuckle.

"But seriously," Niko said, "I'm not upset you can't go to the race. Besides, you'll be making some big time Terion out here instead."

Anda snorted in response.

"How much do you make anyway?" Niko asked curiously. "If you don't mind me asking."

Anda stopped working and looked up at Niko, holding her gaze. "It doesn't matter. It's not worth it. Don't you get any ideas."

"Oh, no, no. I wouldn't." Niko spread her arms in innocence. She certainly had no desire of selling herself into indentured servitude. No amount of Terion would be worth that.

"The extra Terion isn't even that good," Anda said. "Every time

I work the Cinto, it's basically only a charity bonus for my... expertise."

"I saw your haul from the markets last week, though. You must have a decent amount?"

"Ehh. A decent amount," Anda shrugged. "On that topic, though, you never told me how much *you* won the other day?"

"Eight million." Niko uttered the number as meekly as possible in the hopes that Anda wouldn't lambast her for gambling in the first place.

"Wow. That's more than you've ever had, I take it?"

Niko nodded, relieved the scolding never came. How refreshing it was to have a friend that didn't light into her at every opportunity...

"I'm happy for you!" Anda smiled at her. "You should keep that credit safe, though. My advice is to get out while you're ahead. No more betting."

"I..." Niko started. How was she going to explain this to Anda. "I would, but one of my friends has a plan to place... *informed*... bets. We have someone who knows one of the Rippers, and he thinks he can find out reasonable likelihoods of finishes."

"I'm not one to tell you how to conduct your business, but be careful with that world. They play by different rules." Anda paused for a second, looking at Niko thoughtfully with her light blue eye. "I told you of Amon's gambling debt... Well, before he incurred that debt, he wasn't some crazed, irrational gambler, but rather the opposite. He used statistics and maths to his advantage, calculating the odds in his favor. But when ROTO caught on to what he was doing, they planned a trap and swindled him, and he lost everything.

"I'm not saying you shouldn't try to win. Just... be careful is all. Listen to your instincts. Be aware of your surroundings. And make sure you always have support from your friends around you."

"I know, I know," Niko sighed. "Some of my friends are worried about it, too, but I really think the Trackripping betting is different than those games inside the big EC venues."

"Yes, and no," Anda said. "It is still run by all the EC's and ultimately designed to make them money."

"Yeah," Niko acknowledged. "My friends have said as much, also. But they were the ones who wanted to go ahead with this plan, and they have my back."

She didn't tell Anda about Kira-Tharn or Ravenna, who were

fervently against the idea.

"Good," Anda said.

Niko imagined Anda didn't really approve, but at least she wasn't talking down to her — if anything, she was being perfectly understanding about it. All the same, Niko wanted to talk about something else.

"So why is Shatter flooding the world with Cinto production all of a sudden?" she asked.

It came out before she thought about it. She already decided to *not* talk about what her friends suspected with Shatter's Cinto scheme, but her big mouth had other ideas, apparently.

"What do you know...?" Anda asked guardedly.

"Oh, nothing. Nevermind."

Anda tilted her head sideways at Niko. She probably knew she was full of nonsense.

"I just... my friends and I were talking."

Oh please shut up, Niko. Just stop talking.

"About the Cinto production? You didn't tell them of what was happening here did you?"

"I... I did," Niko admitted. "But I swear I didn't mention your name! They've just been investigating Shatter on their own and it was something I was only asking them about."

"Why have they been investigating Shatter?"

It was already too late. Niko had already blabbed too much; there was no going back now.

"Oh, it's nothing serious," Niko said. "They've seen stuff from a company that controlled our old planet — Minedyne — and they've connected it to Shatter."

Anda peered thoughtfully at Niko, but didn't respond.

"They're importing stuff that has both logos on it, as well as the Meridian Crescent," Niko continued. "I've seen that with my own eyes. And now they think that Terion is in on it too, and that they're flooding the world with Cinto and entertainment to trick the citizens into ignoring increased control by Terion and Shatter."

Anda continued to stay silent.

"I don't know," Niko said sheepishly. "That's just what we were talking about. I'm not really sure about any of it, to be honest."

Niko bowed her head, wishing she never said anything at all. She shouldn't have tried to change the subject; she should've just let Anda continue to tell her how dangerous gambling was.

"They have good instincts," Anda finally said, quietly.

"Wait, so it's true?" Niko perked back up.

"More or less. But distracting the population is a process that will take many years."

"Oh, I was hoping my friends were just being paranoid," Niko said. "But I guess I mostly believed them. Either way, I hope we'll all be gone before long."

"Me too," Anda agreed.

This was the first Niko heard the girl say that she hoped she wouldn't remain on An-Terino forever.

"Yeah? You want to get off-planet also?"

"Of course," Anda said matter-of-factly. "Who doesn't?"

Niko laughed. That was very true, she supposed. "Do you have a plan for it?"

"No plans," Anda confessed. "Just dreams."

"I guess you gotta start somewhere, right?"

Anda only nodded, still intently focused on ripping blacksquashes off the vine. Niko smiled to herself, imagining that maybe someday when she left this dump, Anda would be able to come with her.

So the women worked industriously in the fields, harvesting their quota in record time, despite the lingering heat from the Venting. And when it was time to go home for the evening, they put on a good face, both of them fantasizing of better days ahead where they wouldn't be shackled to this lifestyle.

———————————

12

Return From the Salvage Yards

"LOOK out!" Ce-Ellum hollered.

Niko stood frozen in panic. What was *he* doing here?! She hoped that guy would *never* learn where she lived. She should've heeded his warning call though, because just then, a small flat kart zipped around the corner, nearly taking her out before she could react.

She let out an involuntary screech, one that she might later be embarrassed about.

"What the blazes?!" she spat.

The kart skidded to a halt and out popped Cryo.

"Niko!" he exclaimed. "I'm sorry!"

"It's okay," she hoarsely replied, staring dumbfoundedly at the scene before her.

Cryo. In a Trackripping kart. What the blazes, indeed.

What was going on? Where would he have even gotten one of those things from?

"You wanna try this thing out?" he offered, walking her way with a helmet in his hands.

She *had* always wanted to try it, obviously. But not here. Not in a busy neighborhood. And not around all these An-Mara, who largely despised Trackripping. If not despised, they strongly disapproved, to say the least.

"Maybe later," she squeaked. "What're you guys doing here?"

"Riiz invited us over for dinner," he answered, turning to give the helmet back to Ce-Ellum, who now approached both of them.

"What'd you think?" Ce-Ellum asked.

"Was amazing," Cryo said. "Thanks for letting me ride over."

"Of course," Ce-Ellum replied. "I figured you'd appreciate the updates I gave it."

So it was *his* kart then.

"Yeah the straightaways were so much faster with them," Cryo acknowledged. "And the turns didn't suffer, either. Good stuff."

"I'll see if Vulture can let us onto one of the tracks," Ce-Ellum offered. "Once we replace the main-body fasteners with the lighter alloys we picked up, I think you'll notice even more of a difference from the last time."

Wait, had Cryo raced before? It sure seemed like it, the way they were talking like he was intimately familiar with it all... It honestly wouldn't have surprised her; Cryo was a man of many talents.

She didn't like how they were talking about doing business with Vulture, though. If she was getting reprimanded for gambling, then why wasn't Ravenna all over *them* about their association with one of the most notorious gangs in Alashadar?

A bit of a double-standard, no? she thought in irritation.

"You sure you didn't want to try, Niko?" Ce-Ellum asked her.

"I'm okay for right now," she told him. "But thank you."

Ce-Ellum shrugged. "Suit yourself."

"You guys should be careful around here, though," she said to both of them. "The An-Mara aren't fans. And besides, people are walking around the corners all the time. You don't want to hit anyone."

Blazes, she sounded so bossy. And to Cryo of all people! But they really should be more careful...

"Yeah, you're probably right," Cryo admitted with a wince.

"Did you guys drive that thing over from Machine Row?" Niko asked.

"I did," Cryo said. "The rest of them rode the train. They had to hit up the Salvage Yards before heading over tonight."

"I didn't even realize there was enough flat terrain between here and there," she said.

"I had to veer out of the city for that section right before the An-Mara quarter. Otherwise the streets connect."

"Oh, maybe I'll try it out over there sometime," Niko said. It *would* be fun, after all. "What'd you guys need to get at the Salvage Yards?"

"We got some materials we're gonna use for this kart, and then just some parts for the machine we're working on."

"The Infinity Machine?"

"Yeah. You know about that?"

"Mhmm. You guys mentioned it the other night. And Riiz told me a little bit about it also."

"Right. Well, we're having trouble keeping the states of the particles stable for long enough to run calculations, so we're trying another approach. Instead of cooling the thing to low temperatures the way we were doing, we realized we could utilize lasers a lot more."

Niko had no idea how keeping particles stable had *anything* to do with running calculations. She would just have to trust him on this one. And how would they find materials for *lasers* in the Salvage Yards?

"Riiz told me *of* the Infinity Machine, not how it worked," she laughed.

"I guess you'll need to see it for yourself. It's hard to explain. I'll show you next time you're over at our place."

Niko nodded. "Okay, for sure."

If Cryo said it was hard to understand, then she knew it surely would be a *mystery* to her. She wasn't sure she wanted to commit to learning its workings if that was the case. Maybe if she got a decent night's sleep for once...

She thought she'd be feeling more rested after switching out of the Rifts, but Riiz's tinkering lessons were dragging out her fatigue. The physical toll was lighter, sure, but it was the mental exhaustion that was affecting her.

"Did you wanna eat with us?" Cryo asked.

"Mmm, I told Kira-Tharn I'd make a dinner up tonight. Since tomorrow is the race and I'll be gone then."

"I just spoke with the one called Kira-Tharn," Riiz announced, Niko whirling around to face him. Blazes, he came out of nowhere. How long had he been out here? "She asserted that you will both be joining us for dinner, but do feel the option to make your own choice, Niko Ryen. I do understand that the one called Kira-Tharn can be... controlling... when it comes to your decisions."

Ugh, Kira-Tharn! The blazes woman... Niko couldn't very well decline, now that she'd been invited personally.

"Sure, I'll go to dinner. Thanks."

"Don't steal all of our enthusiasm," Ce-Ellum chided her.

She directed a less-than-pleasant glare in his direction, though she did her best to soften it upon reminding herself that this was an Alashadar gangster she was giving attitude towards.

"Sorry, I'm just tired is all."

"Not to worry, I was only jesting," he said with a grin.

She attempted her best to return the smile. Hopefully it didn't look as hollow as it felt...

"And I do apologize, Niko Ryen, but we will not be able to hold our tinkering lessons today because of the dinner," Riiz spoke up. "Perhaps tomorrow we can double our lesson?"

"That's fine with me," Niko replied. "I'm beat for today, anyway. I might head inside to wash up. I'll see y'all in a few minutes."

She knew she was behaving like Kira-Tharn or Ravenna with her abrupt exit, but she really didn't have the energy for pleasantries. She hauled herself into her quarters, where Kira-Tharn was just on her way out the door to meet her friends across the lot.

"You will join us for dinner tonight at the quarters of the one called Riiz Alke-Tani," Kira-Tharn commanded. "Do try to hurry, Niko Ryen."

"You could've given me more warning," Niko huffed. "But don't worry, I'll be over there. Just give me a few minutes."

She stalked down the hall without granting Kira-Tharn the satisfaction of saying anything else, then took a little longer in washing up than she otherwise would have before heading back out to Riiz's quarters to join her friends.

She had no idea Riiz was such a good cook. They had a great meal by An-Terino standards: blacksquash soup with sides of spread-biscuits and dressing.

And all spiced with Cinto.

The herb was becoming more common among all dishes, just as her friends were worried about. Of course, she would never consume enough to *ever* become impaired by its influence. That did not sound appealing whatsoever. No, thank you.

Besides the good food, there was no fighting, no excessive business chat, and no scolding of Niko for her Trackripping gambling. Up until this point, the only talk of business was when they discussed a little bit of what they got from the Salvage Yards. Other than that, it was all leisure conversation. Trackripping, Droneripping, things like that.

Riiz and Kira-Tharn even got to talking about their homeworld, and Niko was enthralled. She wished she could see Aktun in person. The Palace Main Square they spoke of seemed nothing short of amazing: architecture more grand than Alashadar, Sol City, and everything she'd ever seen combined, so they claimed. They also spoke of the academies they attended, adventures they had, and their life experiences growing up in An-Mara society.

Niko found it particularly interesting to hear that as advanced as she knew the An-Mara to be, they admitted that their civilization was far technologically inferior to the Meridians. The real Meridians, that was. From her experiences on Arhanda, the An-Mara were the dominant force, but both Riiz and Kira-Tharn made it clear that the Meridians on Arhanda were but a shadow of what the actual Meridian civilization was. They also made a point to mention that the real Meridians were far more pompous, as well.

Hearing these tales of Aktun made Niko wonder how Daren was faring, if he was still alive. She supposed he would be, but a lot could happen in five years. However, nobody else brought Daren up in the conversation, so she left it alone.

"Soooo, what time are we meeting up for the race tomorrow night?" Kyler asked. "Like 19:00?"

"The Rifts are a little further than the other races, so we'll probably leave from our place at 18:30," Cryo said. "That work for everybody?"

Nods, shrugs, and grunts of approval circled the room.

"Oh that's right, I haven't seen this new track yet," Kyler said. "What's it called again?"

"Excavation Run," Cryo reminded him.

"It's the new track they purchased from Terrovian Aquatics," Ce-Ellum elaborated. "It quite literally runs through an excavated Rift system, right next to the aqueduct, through tunnels and around old mining equipment that was left there. This is the first year they'll race it on the Tour."

"So about that," Niko interjected, "do we know who we should be betting on?"

"Good point," Kyler agreed. "We haven't really talked about that. Ce?"

"I'm sorry," Ce-Ellum apologized. "I didn't get a chance to talk to Wilhe. We should probably play it safe and just go with Delmatic. Maybe extra safe and say one hundred percent on Delmatic top three."

"I agree," Ravenna said. "Play it super safe. I think we're pretty crunched for time, though. I don't think we'll even be able to make it to any of the EC stations before the betting closes."

"Hmmm, that's true," said Kyler. "Niko, do you have any time to go to the stations?"

"I could," she said. "You want me to take your badges and put down anything?"

"Oooh, that's an idea!" Kyler squealed. "I was thinking just for you, but yeah, take ours. Do you have time to go tonight? I'll need my badge back by tomorrow morning."

"Yeah, I guess so."

"Okay, we can get some decent Terion if Niko puts all our bets in," he announced to everyone. "Hand 'em over."

Slowly, everyone who wanted to participate handed their badges to Kyler, who handed them to Niko in turn. Even Ravenna handed hers over, albeit reluctantly. Of course, Kira-Tharn and Riiz kept theirs, gambling being against the Time and all. Ce-Ellum kept his, as well, claiming he needed his badge tonight. It was fair, Niko thought, even if he was lying. If their positions were swapped, there would be no way in the blazes she would give her Terion badge to a stranger. Especially not him.

In fact, Ce-Ellum claimed that he was late for some urgent business in the city, so he offered everyone his farewells and told his friends he'd meet them later.

The abruptness of his departure only served to deepen Niko's distrust of the man. The guy was hiding something. Why in the

153

blazes did no one else see it?!

She half-sighed after he left, then turned back to everyone else. "I'll bring them back by your place tonight. You guys will be there, right?"

"Yeah, we're going back right after we clean up here," Kyler said. "Thanks, Niko."

Wow.

Kyler. Being polite? This was new.

"You should have someone go with you, though," Ravenna advised. "I don't like you going into town by yourself."

True. She didn't like it herself.

"Kira-Tharn? Can you go with her?" Ravenna asked.

"I do apologize." Kira-Tharn shook her head and frowned. "I already have a prior engagement with the one called Maro Del-Fiiz tonight. But I do concur — the one called Niko Ryen must have an accompaniment if she is to traverse into the city."

"If no one else can provide that accompaniment, I will," Riiz offered.

"But we need you on the system tonight," Kyler said.

"Kyler's right, we need you to pl…" Ravenna started to explain why they needed Riiz, but was cut off by a sharp knock at the entrance.

"Oh! Looks like they're finally here," Kyler shouted, as Riiz got up to open the door. "It's about damn time."

Finally here? Were they expecting someone else tonight? The room was already packed to the brim with all her friends. Who else would they even be expecting?

Niko's questions were answered as Riiz opened the door wide, her heart dropping to the floor as she stared at the two figures who stood outside.

———————

13

Visitors

"LOOK who the forest cat dragged in!" Kyler yelled, kicking his chair out and springing across the floor to greet the visitors. "Took you guys long enough."

In Meridian fashion, he gripped forearms with each of them, then Cryo did the same, followed by Ravenna. Niko would've gone up with the rest of her friends to rush the newcomers, except she could only stare, incapacitated while her heart burned a hole through her chest. She had yearned for this moment for so long, but now she had no idea what to even say.

"Hey, Niko," Jack said, sweeping across the room to greet her. He stopped just short as she made no move to get up.

"Hey," she responded plainly, her face showing no emotion.

Blazes. She was *sooo* happy to see him, but she was also angry at the same time. *He* hadn't made a single move to contact her this entire time!

Just let it go, Niko, she told herself. *Be happy to see him.*

She was happy, after all. Really happy! She hadn't felt a fluttery feeling like this in a *long* time. But by the Mara, she refused to be some pathetic, drooling mess over this guy — this guy who'd left her hanging for months and months! Years, if she had to be honest, considering he'd never made any move to progress past anything besides mere friendship.

The others in the room must have sensed the tension, because the lively reunion from seconds ago had gone as silent as space. Finally, after too many awkward seconds, Callum broke the lull.

"It's good to see you, Niko," he said, his gravelly voice contrasting with the warm tone.

"You, as well," she said with a wide grin, finally standing up and embracing him with forearms, then doing the same to Jack, who took the formal greeting with a wince.

What, did he think he was getting a hug? ...

"Sorry we missed the dinner," Callum said. "We got caught up in the Row on the way over here. They're really increasing patrols and security. Heaps of checkpoints over by the Terion facilities."

"Yeah," Kyler said. "It's annoying as blazes. And don't worry about it, you didn't miss much. We were just arguing over who has to babysit Niko while she goes into town."

Babysit!? That little... She was *not* some helpless damsel who needed *babysitting*.

"Jack, I know you just got here, but would you be able to go with her?" Ravenna asked, inviting him along without any consultation from Niko. "We don't like her going into town alone these days."

"I do not ne..."

"Yeah, of course," Jack quickly assented, cutting Niko's protests short. "Like right now?"

"Mmhm. She has all our Terion badges and needs to get them back to us tonight."

"I'm right here, you know?" Niko said angrily. "I'm perfectly capable of speaking for myself."

"Debatable," Kyler muttered.

Niko flashed him a red-hot stare, but chose not to say anything inflammatory. The whole evening had gone by without devolving into a single argument; she wouldn't be the one to start now.

"You *have* appeared to be struggling to form words," Kira-Tharn called her out, supporting Kyler's claims. "The one called Ravenna Night only spoke up to expedite your departure to the city."

Niko could've throttled Kira-Tharn right then and there. And Kyler. And Ravenna. How was this long-awaited reunion with Jack and Callum turning into one of the more embarrassing moments in recent memory?

"I..." she started. "Fine. Come on, Jack. Let's make this quick." Niko stood up and stormed over to the door.

Kyler let out a long whistle, and she could've sworn she heard snickering from behind her back, but she refused to acknowledge it by turning around. This whole sequence brought her back to feelings of when she was a teenager — where everyone around her would treat her like nothing more than a child. They might as well have gone back to calling her 'kid'...

She walked briskly across the open square between all the dilapidated residences, forcing Jack to skip a few steps to fall in line with her. Niko was all too content to complete the journey to the city in silence, but as soon as they rounded the corner, Jack spoke up.

"I'm sorry," he said.

"For what?"

"For everything. For not seeing you in months."

Niko shrugged. "I know you had a job to do. And I know you were supposed to be undercover and keeping things secret. It's okay. You don't owe me an explanation."

"I do owe you that much," he said, appearing genuinely remorseful. "You're my friend."

Friend!? Was that all he saw her as? Niko could've exploded, but before she reacted in a way she would regret, something about his face soothed her temper. His green eyes looked... sadder. Older.

Of all the blazes, she could've melted. She still might. How could she be so cold and restrained right now? She should be ecstatic for the opportunity to reconnect with him, regardless of whatever frustrations she felt.

"You *don't* owe me," she said, lightening her tone. "I promise it's okay. How've you been, though?"

"Busy. We've been back and forth all over the city for months, and then just yesterday we got back from a week out in the Daylight."

Niko grimaced for him. "Ooof, a week in the Daylight? That's rough. What for?"

"There's a new Shatter complex that opened way out there. A solar harvesting installation, rightly called the Frying Pan."

"It's about time they started making some more harvesting facilities. Just this morning, the power went off again. It's been doing that more and more every week."

"Oh, that's lame. Sorry to hear that," he said. "But I don't think they're rerouting any to the city. This power plant is only for the refineries they're building out there. Kind of like how the one in Machine Row next to Terion is only for Terion."

"Figures," Niko grumbled. "What are the refineries even for? Last week, I overheard Shatter talking about Minedyne imports. Stuff from Arhanda. Lanthanides, I've heard them called?"

"Mmhm," Jack mumbled. "That's exactly what's being refined. This planet doesn't have much in the way of important resources for the expansion they're planning, but it does have an endless supply of easily harvestable sol-light available, which can power the refineries indefinitely. And not only is it cheap to build those harvesting facilities — but the labor is also cheap out here."

"That makes sense. So you guys went out to this complex, and then what?" she asked.

"Took stock, crunched numbers, found out what's coming from where. All that good stuff," he replied.

"And where is it all coming from?"

"Like you overheard, some of it's coming from Arhanda. But the thing my dad's worried about is the shipments coming directly from the Capital system. Batteries, mainly. And lots of them. He thinks the Meridians might be trying to take over this place."

Niko let out a sharp laugh. "Is that necessarily a bad thing? I mean, this place can't get much worse, can it?"

Jack peered at her, *really* peered at her, raking over her dirty and unkempt appearance. If she showed even a fraction of the exhaustion she felt, it wouldn't be hard for him to tell how worn she was.

"What happened to you, Niko?" he asked.

"Pfft, thanks," she said wryly. "You sure know how to flatter a girl."

"That's not what I meant! You look great, as usual," he backtracked, causing her heart to leap with the compliment. "But you look so... *tired*. Where've you been working all this time?"

"The Rifts, mostly." She didn't add that little detail about working ten hours a day, seven days a week, because she didn't want to deal with him being fussy right now, as sweet as it might've been.

"Phwooosh!" he exclaimed. "The Rifts?! I'm so sorry..."

"It wasn't that bad," she lied.

"The Rifts sure *sound* bad, from everything I know of them," he said dubiously. "Are you okay?"

"Yes, yes, I'm fine. And I quit anyway. I'm working in the fields now."

He looked sideways at her as they rounded the corner of a street, the clotheslines forming a sort of tunnel, the ropes haphazardly strung from one stack of residences to another. "That's not much better, you know... Why don't you find an inside job or something easier?"

She stared at him. He knew her better than that...

"Do I look like an inside person to you?" she snapped.

"You're right, you're right!" he yielded. "But the Rifts? And the fields? There's gotta be a better way..."

"And what is this better way you speak of? Going undercover and disappearing for months at a time?"

It was a cheap shot, one she instantly felt bad about, but the point she was trying to make was a legitimate one. What else was she expected to do? She didn't possess any skills that would net her a better job. The fields or Rifts were about as good as she could hope for.

"It's not my choice, you know," he said defensively. "We talked about this when we came here, that my dad and I would need to work into Shatter..."

"I know, I'm sorry," she admitted. "That wasn't fair for me to say. We're all just doing what we can to survive."

"Survive, and eventually get out of here," he murmured.

He was right. He *was* doing his part to hopefully get them all out of here. It's not like he enjoyed being separated from her and the rest of her friends for all these months. At least she hoped that was the case...

Niko stared grimly ahead as they walked toward the rail station, its red tinted roof peeking out from the silhouette of blocky buildings in the distance. Neither of them said anything more until they got there, at which point Niko pulled Jack onto a train bound for NewCen. Normally, she would've taken one to Machine Row, where the closest betting stations would be, but she instead opted to take the longer ride to NewCen, if only to avoid all those supposed security checkpoints. It had nothing to do with squeezing out a few more minutes to catch up with Jack.

Nothing to do with that... she lied to herself.

"Where are we going, anyway?" he asked, chuckling lightly.

"No one told me anything before they shoved us out the door."

"I'm placing some bets on the race tomorrow."

He looked at her skeptically, grinning as if she were kidding him.

"I'm actually so serious."

"Not joking?"

"Crescent to heart," she promised, holding the Meridian C to her chest.

"Woah, since when did you become a gambler?! That's rad as blazes!"

"I'm glad you think so. Everyone else has seen fit to yell at me about it," she said, rolling her eyes. "Except for Cryo, Riiz, and blazes Kyler."

"I actually don't think it's a bad idea, at all," he said. "But there are smart ways to bet. You just gotta go easy with it. Can't win big too many times in a row."

"Yeah, well I won big last time," she said casually.

Jack raised an eyebrow at her. "Oh yeah?"

"Eight million."

"What?!" It sounded like he nearly choked on something. "You're not kidding?"

Niko shook her head.

"Phwooosh…" he exhaled.

"Yeah."

"We only need thirty million to get all of us out of here. A couple more wins like that and we could be off!"

Niko knew all too well. She'd been tracking that thirty million number ever since they landed here over a year ago.

"I'm gonna pass on any bets tonight, though. I haven't followed Trackripping at all this season," he remarked. "I've been gone for way too much of it."

"Where else have you been?" she asked, lowering her voice. "What else have you guys been investigating?"

"Well, we're still trying to find that one guy. Kezane."

"Oh yeah, Riiz always mentions him. I feel like the dude is a ghost. You sure he's even here?"

Jack nodded. "Oh, he's here all right. Alashadar is a huge place, but An-Terino is way huger. He could be anywhere."

He paused, and Niko knew there was a 'but' coming.

"*But…* my dad and I think we've narrowed a possible

workshop down."

"Oh, right. Riiz said something about that also. He said you guys found traces of him living in Oldcity? And now he's somewhere out in the Night?"

"Yep, so you heard."

Niko nodded. "But how in the blazes would you even find him if he's out in the Night wilds? How could anyone even live out there?"

"I don't know," Jack replied honestly. "But I do know that there're some settlements out there. Don't ask me how or why anyone in their right mind would *choose* to live there…"

"So you guys plan to go out there and search for him?" Niko asked.

"I don't know." Jack furrowed his brows and looked down. "My dad has a contact who's been to one of the settlements. He's waiting to hear back, but that's where we go next. If the contact ever gets back to us."

Niko sat silently for a moment as the train slowed down, nearing its destination. She had just gotten Jack back; he better not be off and racing into the Night searching for that blazes Kezane guy. Riding out into a land covered by pitch darkness and beyond freezing temperatures seemed like an extremely dangerous fool's errand if she'd ever heard of one.

"Why do you guys even want to find this guy so bad?" she asked. "I mean, I've heard Riiz's excuse enough times. But is it really about this whole Machine business."

Jack shrugged. "It's not just the An-Mara that talk about Kezane. My dad seems pretty intent on finding him also. And he's only ever once talked about that Machine… but when he did, he seemed really spooked. Like really, *really* spooked. I've never seen him scared of anything in his life, so I trust that it's real from that alone."

If it was as bad as Riiz described…

A shudder shot down her spine.

An artificial intelligence so menacing that it could overrun entire civilizations and snuff them out entirely in a matter of hours. How would such a thing even be possible? Wouldn't there be *someone* out there that could stop this thing? Someone other than a lone person? The Meridian blazes Empire, perhaps?

"And how is this Kezane guy supposed to help even the

slightest amount? If it's so invincible as everyone describes…"

"That I don't know," he admitted. "I'm with you there. Like I don't totally see what my dad's obsessions are with this guy. And I don't know what he intends to do once we find him. *If* we find him."

The train came to a complete stop, and Niko and Jack filed off into the bustling station, changing the subject since they were now surrounded by the massive crowds of downtown NewCen. Niko strode to the nearest betting station — an orange ROTO kiosk right outside the exit to the rail depot — with Jack in tow, then stood in line. To her dismay, she realized she hadn't put any thought into who she was actually betting on, spending all her preparation time talking with Jack instead.

Should she do what her friends suggested? One hundred percent on Delmatic top three? The returns would be so low there… They would barely get anything at all! It practically wouldn't have even been worth the trip out.

Jon Wilhe on the other hand…

The returns for a Jon Wilhe win were still very lucrative. 12:1.

She didn't entertain that idea too much, though; it would be far too risky, and her friends would wring her neck if she even considered putting their Terion down on something so sketchy.

A top two finish, however, would be 3:1. Nothing compared to what she won the other day, but still significant. If she pooled all her friends' Terion together, that would increase their coffers by nearly thirty million and they could get off this place once and for all. Very tempting…

However, she heard a voice in the back of her head urging caution. Maybe a top three Jon Wilhe finish? That sounded reasonable. He was no Delmatic, but he *was* becoming a clear secondary favorite. And based off hearing the talk of people in line, this particular track was very favorable for Jon Wilhe.

She looked for the returns on a top three finish. 4:3.

Not great, but not insignificant, either. That would net them about five more million, and every little bit helped.

Hmmm. So many choices…

Play it safe. That's what her friends had requested.

She was now next in line, though, and the person in front of her was almost finished. She needed to decide quick.

"Terion?" the clerk asked, once the patron in front of her stepped away.

"Umm, eight million," she replied. So much for playing it safe. Oh well, she'd make up for it with a relatively safe choice on outcomes.

"Breakdowns?"

"Mmmm, one hundred percent on Jon Wilhe top three."

"Smart choice."

She smiled back at the clerk. "Thanks."

"Thank you. Next!"

Niko then stepped out of line with Jack, who stared at her with wide eyes.

"You put down all *eight million* of your Terion?!"

"You don't approve?"

"I..." he exhaled through puffed cheeks. "That's just a lot. What if he doesn't place top three?"

Jack did have a point. Niko hadn't even considered that possibility. And worse, she didn't even listen to her instincts tonight. Last time, she'd had a distinct gut feeling, one she didn't have right now.

Blazes, she scolded herself. *Was this a bad idea?*

Jon Wilhe already helped her once; he'd come through again. He would. He had to. A top three finish from Jon Wilhe was actually highly favorable, according to all the experts. He nearly beat Delmatic last week! Placing top three tomorrow would be easy.

No, she shouldn't be worried. It was too late for second guesses, anyway.

"I'm pretty sure he's got this." She said it as much for herself as for Jack.

"If you say so."

She knew Jack was too nice to question her choices, but she could feel the skepticism oozing from him like sweat in the Daylight.

"Yeah. He's got this. Come on, let's go to Gluoron next."

She grabbed his arm and walked over to the blue kiosk across the plaza from the ROTO betting station, doing her best to ignore the butterflies in her stomach as she did. Whether it was from holding Jack's arm or from throwing that much Terion on the line, Niko did not know. Maybe it was both.

So they walked and talked, only taking breaks for Niko to place her other bets. For better or worse, she bet all of her friends' Terion on a Jon Wilhe top three finish, doubling down on her convictions that he would score those results for her. And after finishing

Ravenna's badge last at the Twilight Elegance station, they slowly walked back to the rail station.

"You're probably not hungry, are you?" Jack asked, one eyebrow raised keenly.

"I'm pretty sated," Niko replied. "But how about you? We can stop for food if you're hungry."

"It's okay," he said, the faintest tinge of disappointment hidden in his voice. "I can wait until we get back. Everyone was expecting us back, anyway, right?"

She'd started this outing still frustrated with Jack, but now she was beginning to feel more freedom than she'd felt in ages. Besides, she was still upset with her friends; she'd take as long as she wanted in the city tonight. They could all go to blazes.

"No, no," she pushed. "Let's get something. I can do dessert, if nothing else. I still have a little bit of Terion left, and then tomorrow I'll have a mountain of it!"

"You sure?"

"Yes! What're you hungry for?"

"Ummm, I can do anything."

"For the love of the Mara, Jack Sehs, please choose something."

"Okay, okay," he relented. "You sound like a damn An-Mara though, all pushy, and calling me by first and last name."

She snorted. "Actually, *the one called* Kira-Tharn would let me have it for using the word 'Mara' as an interjection. As she has many times…"

Jack laughed at that, beaming back at her.

Blazes, his smile was beautiful…

She didn't realize how badly she missed it. His smile, his laugh, his very presence. It all brought her back to those long years aboard the ship bound for An-Terino, where on so many days she had nothing to do besides keep company with Jack. Those were some of the worst days of her life, yet they were also some of her most iconic. Spending time with him was something that had become part of her, and those pieces of her had been ripped away this past year with him missing.

"Choose somewhere, though. I'll pay," she offered.

"Well, if you're paying, I'm choosing something cheap," he threatened.

"Jack." The simple saying of his name had him yielding,

although maybe it was more the no-nonsense expression she gave him. Maybe she was turning into an An-Mara, after all.

"Okay, okay... Ummm, how about poultry. That sound okay to you?"

"Poultry it is!" she proclaimed. "I know a place in Alashadar Unlimited if you're up for going that far into town?"

"I'm in!"

"Excellent. It's really good."

She'd be able to afford it, but poultry *was* getting more expensive. The farms that raised the birds were facing an ever-increasing demand from Shatter, driving up the prices for everyone else. That was one of the other bad side effects from the growing Shatter presence here. Among other things...

She wasn't about to tell Jack about the prices, though. Even though both of them were as good as forced to go on this little outing by their friends, it had been rather enjoyable so far, and she wasn't going to ruin the night on account of a couple Terion. After tomorrow, she would be swimming in it, anyway!

She linked her arm through his and yanked him away down the Avenue, strolling past all the big EC's, their dazzling radiance lighting the way. On their way to Avion Flavor, the poultry restaurant, Niko became distracted by a number of attractions, pulling Jack along with her. Live bands, impromptu street acts, and amateur magicians were out in force, probably lured by the bolstered crowds here for the pre-race Trackripping hype, plus the rush hour of last minute bets.

They threaded their way through the bustle, but once inside Alashadar Unlimited, Niko couldn't help but detour from shopfront to shopfront, browsing through the many high-society boutiques that lined the perimeter of the halls, even though she had no intention of spending any Terion. Even with big winnings, it was still prudent to save up for their exodus to the Capital system. Merely looking through everything was the fun part, anyway.

She did, however, *have* to drag him on her favorite railcoaster in the city, of course. He'd never been on one before, and a thousand Terion for the both of them was well worth the price to see his face, doused with nervousness and exhilaration. The ride took passengers to the highest levels of the mall before plunging them down an impossibly steep drop that had to be at least two hundred meters high, then whipped them around turns that caused her vision to dim.

It was *so* fun, a moment of pure bliss in this existence that had otherwise become so dull and pitiful over the months. The best moment of the whole ride was at the very end, when she looked over at Jack to see the most relaxed, content smile plastered across his pretty face.

"Phwooosh," he panted. "That was... *intense*."

Niko flashed a glowing smile back at him. "I knew you'd like it! Especially since you threatened to ride out one of the Fleetnesses out of your pod that one time..."

Niko rolled her eyes as they both laughed at that recollection.

"I wasn't *actually* going to do that," he said, spreading his hands wide. "I just wondered what it would feel like."

"It would probably feel like that helix at the end of the ride right there. Except instead of lasting ten seconds, it would last a week!"

After steadying their wobbly legs, the two continued through the mall to the upper levels until they came upon a wide doorway framed by exotic trees, fluorescent blue light illuminating the edges. The Avion Flavor logo was visible through the trees, and Niko and Jack walked in.

Niko had been here before, but she forgot how the opulence of this place made her feel unwelcome. Even the music had a sort of upper-class polish, the instruments being some Niko wasn't sure she'd ever heard before. The stares of the patrons around them oozed with elitism, but Jack didn't seem to notice. As always, he simply grinned back at everyone around him, going about his business like he belonged there.

The pair had to wait a few minutes, but were eventually seated at a table underneath a waterfall, the imported ferns making it feel as if they'd been dropped straight into the jungles of Equatorial Territory back on Arhanda. To complete the rainforest ambiance, colorful birds chirped overhead, their brilliant plumage lit by the flickering lantern that sat on the carved wooden table between them.

They placed their orders, received their food shortly after, and ate their fill, to which Niko gorged herself on a full meal, even after the one Riiz had made for them not three hours prior. She should've felt bad, but she refused to judge herself for it. The poultry was *so* good. Something that flavorful was probably loaded up on a *lot* of Cinto, but she didn't care. Not right now. She hadn't eaten that well in months.

After they were finished with their meal, and now that she was well and truly sated, Niko figured they should probably head home. She and Jack continued their conversation from the restaurant, which was mostly Niko talking about her time in the Rifts, and now in the fields. She told him of everything she could remember — everything from Kira-Tharn and her new fling with Maro Del-Fiiz, to her own tinkering lessons she'd begun with Riiz, to her new friendship with Anda.

She talked about herself for so long, that once they were on their way back down the Avenue, she was all too happy to let Jack do more of the talking, especially when he told Niko of some of his adventures.

Yes, adventures, she thought bitterly. While she had to be stuck excavating Rifts and plucking blacksquashes all day long, he was out on bold quests and grand excursions across the planet.

But she was enthralled by his accounts, like the one where he and Callum had to infiltrate one of the Shatter offices, then escape before they were caught or identified. The way Jack told the tale, it had culminated in a thrilling, high-stakes chase all the way down the streets of Oldcity. Luckily they'd managed to slip into a dance club and masquerade as partiers. She would've paid good Terion to see Callum pretending to dance in a club...

And then there was the other, grimmer story where Shatter sent them as part of a recovery team into a mine where the workers had accidentally dug into a dike near an active volcano a hundred kilometers north of the city. A billion Terion worth of equipment was left abandoned, and their team was sent to recover it, along with any survivors — which there weren't any, unfortunately. Sending more people into a situation like that seemed really dumb to Niko, but Jack just shrugged and told her Shatter only cared about their missions and resources, not about their teams. Luckily, there hadn't been any more volcanic activity while Jack and Callum were there.

Niko listened intently as Jack rattled off one recollection after another, so engrossed that she barely remembered stopping at Machine Row to hand the Terion badges back to Cryo, Ravenna, and Kyler. After promising to meet them at 18:30 to head to the race tomorrow, she and Jack continued on to the An-Mara quarter. He and Callum would be staying with Riiz, so she was happy to squeeze out an extra few minutes talking.

The time passed too quickly, though, and she was disappointed when they rounded the final corner to her residence block. She wished this night could have gone on and on and on, but she had to admit that she was extremely tired, not to mention her head was swimming with dizziness, probably from the damn Cinto they'd added to the poultry. Tomorrow was going to be a big day, with the race immediately following a long shift in the fields, so she would do well to get some sleep.

"Thanks for tonight," Jack said, standing in front of Niko, now back in front of her quarters.

"You too. I missed you."

Should she hug him now? Should she *kiss* him now?

No, that had to be the Cinto talking…

She waited for him to make the move, part of her daring to hope for something special, but to her frustration, they only stood awkwardly in front of each other for a few seconds. Finally, she raised her hand up and waved goodbye before walking back to her own quarters. She would've cursed her own gawkiness, but she didn't even have the energy to do that. Besides, she was still feeling quite good. What a night that turned out to be…

It wasn't a *date*, she reckoned. Especially because Jack never made a move back there. And because he called her a *friend* earlier.

Idiot.

She wouldn't consider anything a date with Jack until he stepped up and professed his feelings. But still, she hadn't had that good a time in many years. Maybe ever.

When she finally lumbered into her own quarters, she ignored the questioning look from Kira-Tharn and went straight to her own room, collapsing onto her bed. She was still smiling when she fell asleep with all her clothes on.

CHAPTER FOURTEEN

14

Excavation Run

NIKO hadn't been back to the Rifts since she quit over a week ago, and although it was only a few days, it felt like much longer. Maybe it was her brain's subconscious desire to never come back here.

The oppressive heat this far into the Daylight melted her into a puddle, the sweat clinging unbearably to the abundance of protective layers that all spectators wore for their own safety. It was a place she would've been all too happy to never return to, were it not for the race that was about to start.

Her work shift today hadn't been terribly overbearing, but it was a work shift nonetheless, and that compounded with her exhaustion from the late excursion last night had her wishing the race would just start already.

The one good thing about the dreadful conditions here was that there were far fewer in-person spectators than there were at the NewCen Circuit last week. Niko and her friends were even able to find a comfortable place in the stadium in full view of the finish line straightaway.

She peered down the line, where the track was blurred with thick haze. Probably a mix of the smoke that drifted down from the power plants in Machine Row and the thick layer of dust that hadn't quite settled after being agitated by the Venting. It was an ugly day, even by An-Terino standards.

Suddenly, a familiar voice boomed over the sound enhancers, their quality much lower than the first-rate acoustics in NewCen.

"WELLLLCOOOOOOOME TO TRAAAACKRIPPINGGG! I'm your host, Tivane Fry, and I'm here once again with the lovely, exquisite, magnificent, superb, *unparalleled* Steven 'Turnslinger' Osinroler! Today, the Trackripping Syndicate is proud to present EXCAVAATIONNNNN RUNNNNNNNNN!!"

The crowd may have been smaller than in NewCen, but no one in the stadium would know the difference, the way it trembled mightily with roaring applause, drowning out the rumble of the kart engines as they began to start up.

"Well, thank you for that glorious intro, Tivane. You're looking quite excellent tonight, yourself."

Both hosts laughed that same fake, made-for-presentation laugh that Niko had heard all too often. She put up with it, though, for the sake of enjoying the spectacle.

"My appreciation, Turnslinger. My appreciation. Now for those who may be new here, we are the Trackripping Syndicate, and this is the newest track in our fleet, Excavation Run. It is exactly as it sounds, a course that winds its way through the excavated tunnels of an old Rift system, purchased from Terrovian Aquatics for the modest sum of ten billion Terion. Rippers must brave the searing hot temperatures of Daylight, avoid the leftover mining equipment, and race around twenty-nine blind corners on each of the six four-kilometer laps."

"Yes, Tivane, this is one of the shorter tracks on the Tour, but it's a technical nightmare for all of the Rippers. They're really going to be tried and tested tonight."

"Absolutely, Turnslinger. It's a track like no other, especially considering the Rippers have to endure the elements of Daylight. Just sitting here in our booth has me sweating more than a blacksquash worker."

Rude, Niko thought, suddenly becoming embarrassed of her trade. Hopefully no one in the crowd could tell that's where she worked.

"That's one of the big challenges here, Tivane. The Rippers need to maintain utmost focus on these races, but it gets significantly more challenging in this heat, especially when they traverse the long roundabout on the far end of the course. There will be about twenty seconds where they are completely exposed to Bucon before ducking back into the aqueduct system."

"All the sudden, the booth doesn't sound so bad, Turnslinger! But where are those drinks we ordered?!" Tivane and Turnslinger burst out in that laughter that annoyed Niko oh-so-much. "Now, for those who may not know, Steven 'Turnslinger' Osinroler is a two-time Tour champion, so his insight is unrivaled, except by Delmatic himself, perhaps."

"Thank you, Tivane, you flatter me! But I agree, I would most definitely trust what Delmatic has to say more than me," he laughed. "Although, maybe not on fashion... What in the worlds is he wearing?!"

"I do not know, Turnslinger. I do not know. It looks like some sort of fluffy headband, but with a streamer that flows all the way down to the floor. If I were him, I would be worried it would get caught in my wheels!"

"Yeah, Tivane. I, for one, wouldn't be caught dead in the Night wearing something so outlandish. He's always pushing boundaries, Delmatic is, but I suppose that's the mindset that makes him so good."

"Aye, Turnslinger. It can be argued that we do owe him some leniency regarding his wardrobe choices, so long as he continues to dominate the sport."

"I suppose you are right about that, Tivane. No arguments here."

"Now Turnslinger, you've never had to race this track during your time on the Tour, but which of our esteemed Rippers would you say this track favors?"

"Great question, Tivane. This is an extremely technical race, so of course I'd have to go with Delmatic, who's undoubtedly the best technical Ripper to ever live. I think the only track on the Tour he might face stiff competition on, other than last week's burner, is the one coming up next month, the Century. That one is far less technical, and more about fortitude and daring. Whoever has the most guts will take that one."

"I agree, Turnslinger. Delmatic is going to be too good tonight. He excels on these races with the tight turns. If he gets to the lead early, I don't see anyone getting around him."

"That's his strategy. And it's served him well thus far. If

anyone else wants a chance, they're going to have to take the lead almost immediately."

"Now, we can't forget about last week's runner-up, Jon Wilhe."

"Definitely, Tivane. You absolutely cannot count him out. He has been surging in recent weeks, even before last week's near-win. He's also one of the Rippers that thrives on turns, so I think he has a real shot at winning tonight, or at the very least, top two or three."

Good, Niko thought. It sounded like her bets were well placed.

"Any other Rippers to watch for tonight?"

"Well, anyone on the Tour has a chance to win on any given night, but some of my other favorites will come as no surprise. I like Wenno Daks, Morland Relm, and Marl Vikers, as well."

"Those are all amazing Rippers, Turnslinger. And fans haven't been letting us forget Astine Rivers, either. She's one of my personal favorites."

"Yes, of course, Tivane! How could I forget her? She had a third place finish last week, and has moved up to fifth position overall on the Tour. She is well-poised to take the fourth spot if she can place ahead of Marl Vikers tonight."

Niko had been so engrossed in the broadcast that she jumped at the sharp nudge to her ribs.

"Jon Wilhe. Top three. Right?" Ravenna shouted in her ear to be heard above the din. She looked exceptionally tense right now.

Forget losing the Terion; Niko would be way more worried about a wrathful Ravenna than any amount of lost Terion if she somehow failed the bet.

Niko nodded. "It sounds like he's a pretty safe choice on this track."

Ravenna widened her eyes and pressed her lips tight, as if to say, '*He better be*'.

"Okay, Tivane, it looks like the racers are all ready," Turnslinger announced, quieting the crowd. "Oh wait, no. Sorry about that. Short delay… Delmatic is holding everyone up with his hair accessory. He's back on top of his kart wrapping it around his head."

"He is too funny," Tivane chuckled. "Always creating some sort of distraction to mess with the other racers' mindsets at the starting line."

"Not a bad tactic," Turnslinger mused. "Okay, there we go! Now we are ready."

"Yep, there it is, Turnslinger. The thirty second countdown."

"Like we always say, this is where the Rippers really feel the nerves. You have to dig into your inner focus and summon all the concentration you can. These first seconds out of the gate are sometimes the most important ones."

"Especially on a track like this."

"Correct. This opening dash is going to be so critical. Keep an eye on the green and black kart in the center of your screens. Everyone will be gunning for him."

SIX!

FIVE!

FOUR!

THREE!

TWO!

ONE!

The horn that signaled the start of a Trackripping race echoed through the dust.

"And they're off!"

Niko followed the advice of the Syndicate broadcasters and watched Delmatic's green and black kart shoot out like a bullet. Except this time, there was a faster bullet. The orange kart she knew as none other than Jon Wilhe's held a half-kart advantage over Delmatic's, and vanished around the turn in first position.

"Wow!" Tivane exclaimed. "Will you look at that?! Just like we talked about! All the Rippers seemed focused on that start, Turnslinger, and it looks like that is Jon Wilhe in the lead! His second place finish last week really did him massive favors as far as starting position went. As you all know, the higher a Ripper places in the previous week, the closer to the front they start for that next race."

Niko held her breath as she turned her attention to the big screen overhanging the opposite side of the track. Her visor was grimy, but she knew better than to remove it for cleaning. She had done that last week and her lungs paid the price. She'd just have to deal with it and watch the race unfold through cloudy vision.

"Wow indeed, Tivane! Like we were talking about in the pre-race show, Jon Wilhe performed some straightaway adjustments to his kart's engineering, and it seems those have paid off. He is going to have an *enormous* advantage from this position in the lead, especially because of his technical prowess on the turns."

"I admit I was skeptical when he was talking about it before the race. We talked about the possibility of his performance being sacrificed for that extra speed."

"Yes. At first glance, the only straight parts of the track are the finish line straightaway and then that long, smooth roundabout at the far end. So it seemed like a waste to sacrifice turn speed for straightaway speed, but I actually think it was a brilliant adjustment to make. Look, nobody can get around him on these turns now! Not with the track being so narrow."

"You're right, Turnslinger. They're not even going that fast. Quite slow, really. But if no one can get around him, it won't matter."

"Yep. And then the only chance they have to pass is on the straightaways, and that's where his kart's top speed has the huge advantage, anyway."

"Delmatic might be in real trouble here, Turnslinger. What's your expert analysis?"

"Well, Tivane, it's still very early in the race, and Wilhe has a lot of concentration to execute, but I agree. Delmatic is going to have a tough time. And not only a tough time with Wilhe, but with everyone else now stuck in a giant traffic spike, he'll have to fend every other Ripper off on the straightaways. This just might be the most ingenious strategy Wilhe could have pulled off. If Delmatic takes top two tonight, he will have as good as wrapped up the Tour championship. But now with Wilhe's strategy, Delmatic might be in jeopardy for the first time in... well, a *long* time."

Niko's eyes were fixed to the screen, focused on the Rippers as they raced around corner after corner. The remnants of old mining equipment stuck out of the red-orange haze like ugly obstacles, ones that Jon Wilhe expertly used to his advantage to keep every other Ripper on his tail, no matter how fast or slow he was going.

Should she have *instead* bet on him for the outright win? She desperately wished she could've changed her bet to be top two, at the very least. They would be leaving this place if she had! Ugh!

"Kyler!" she hissed. "There's no way to change bets is there?"

He shook his head, eyes squinted and lips pursed through his mask.

"Blazes! I should've bet top two!"

"Top one even!" he replied.

"Hush, the race has only started!" Ravenna shouted to both of them. "I'm not so sure you made the right choice with top three!"

"Yeah, but the announcers were even saying whoever can get to the front early has a *huge* advantage. And with the adjustments made to his kart, they think he's a certain victor."

"We'll see..." she repeated her doubt.

Niko turned her attention back to the screen, where the mob of Rippers emerged from one of the narrow Rift tunnels into the long roundabout that took them out into the open.

"Here is the critical moment in the lap!" Turnslinger announced. "If Delmatic can sneak around Wilhe, I don't think anyone can touch him."

"Yes, Delmatic fans will rightfully be on the edges of their seats on this section. Let's hear some noise for these Rippers!"

In response, a deafening roar began to crescendo, engulfing the stands around Niko.

"Oh wow! I don't believe it!" Turnslinger shouted. "Not only can Delmatic not pass him, but Wilhe is *extending* his lead! Those straightaway adjustments are truly brilliant! I don't know what they are off the top of my head, but I do know they were approved by the Trackripping Syndicate. Can we pull up those stats, Tivane?"

"Absolutely. Let's see... Ohhhh wow. It's a Vulture impulse drive, powered by a solar harvester outfitted to the left side of his kart. What do you make of that?!"

"Ingenious, Tivane. Completely ingenious. For those of our fans unfamiliar with an impulse drive, it's a system that creates an explosion of sorts behind the kart. That explosion delivers a large force over a short period of time that will accelerate the Ripper to great speeds. All karts have them, but this one looks noticeably more powerful, and enough energy is harvested to power it with that solar outfit. Brilliant. Just brilliant."

Niko looked sideways as Ce-Ellum slapped Cryo on his back, the two sharing a genuinely proud smile.

"I knew it would work," she heard Cryo say.

"You called it," Ce-Ellum beamed at him.

Did *they* have something to do with this?! She recalled their conversation about the adjustments they made to the karts, then also remembered how Ce-Ellum knew Jon Wilhe. She was about to ask Cryo, when...

"WOAH!" Tivane thundered. "That might have been a little too much speed! He's lucky he didn't burn right there!"

Niko's heart stopped for a moment as she watched Jon Wilhe slam into the side barrier, bouncing off with some speed-wobble. Luckily, he maintained his bearing and continued on. She blew out all her air at once, only after he was in complete control again.

"Very close call, Tivane. He'll need to manage that speed coming into the turns a lot better. He's got a great advantage here, and now his own worst enemy is himself!"

Cryo and Ce-Ellum chuckled to each other, while Ravenna and Kyler looked as if they'd seen a Nel-Mara. Niko figured she looked like the latter, also. She gripped the rail in front of her, knuckles white as Jon Wilhe's orange kart navigated the labyrinth of tunnels and aqueduct corridors, luckily without anymore errors. After another minute, she heard the distant buzzing of a kart just before she saw an orange blur come screaming around the corner.

A sharp boom echoed through the narrow Rift as he hit the straightaway. That had to be the impulse drive.

"And that is one lap down!" Tivane yelled. "Unbelievable. Jon Wilhe is holding a ten second advantage over second place Delmatic. And with this impulse drive, I only see it increasing!"

"I think this one's a done affair," Turnslinger concluded. "This was something nobody was expecting! We all knew Jon Wilhe *could* win... But in such dominating fashion? This is unreal. Wilhe's engineering team must be beside themselves. Just unbelievable."

Niko watched as the rest of the field scrambled through the finish, Delmatic barely holding off every other Ripper in the tour. She smiled to herself as she imagined that arrogant chum stewing in his misery. *Serves him right.*

She crept up beside Cryo, yelling into his ear to be heard above all the shouting. "Was this impulse drive the thing you were talking about yesterday? Was this *you guys*?!"

He grinned back at her, holding his forefinger over his lips and nodding.

"Wh... How?"

"Later," he replied. "After."

Blazes, she needed to know now! She was going to demand answers, but she had plenty excitement to keep her occupied at the moment.

If her friends could help Jon Wilhe to a win here, they could do it at the next race. Then she'd bet everything on a win for him, and they'd be off this damn planet once and for all!

An uncontrollable, dumb smile was stamped onto her face as Wilhe completed lap after lap, extending his lead further and further with each one. The heavy layers of protective clothing was intolerably uncomfortable, but somehow that didn't even matter. Not even the sweat that drenched every centimeter of her body could dampen her giddy spirits. They were going to get off this Hole of a hell-dump soon! Only a few more weeks...

Even Ravenna's perpetual glower seemed lightened after the five beeps sounded to signal the final lap. Jon Wilhe now held a *forty-two* second advantage over the second place Ripper, who was now Astine Rivers. She had overtaken Delmatic on the last straightaway, to Niko's eternal amusement. Even the announcers had stopped focusing on Wilhe because his victory was already sealed.

"Would you look at that!? Rivers has now passed into the lead! Well, not *lead*... but you know what I mean."

Turnslinger laughed. "Yes, it's easy to forget that Wilhe is even in the same race. But that was an incredible move by Rivers, Tivane. She had been waiting for that smallest mistake from Delmatic, and then capitalized on it. Let's take a look at that replay."

The screen panned away from Jon Wilhe, and to the pink and white of Astine Rivers as she cut inside of Delmatic. Niko was ultimately pleased to watch him being passed by Astine in slow motion. He'd always been such a chauvinistic animal, Delmatic had been, and would surely be fuming after being passed by a woman.

"You can see it right there, he tried to glance at the screen to check where Wilhe was, and then bam! Rivers cuts right to his inside. What a move! Delmatic really only has himself to blame."

"Yes, Turnslinger! I'm sure Delmatic fans feel like they're on Daylight cinders right now. A very disappointing day for him, indeed. He was more than clear about his goal of becoming the first ever Ripper to win a first place victory on every single track in the Tour, but it's looking like that won't be happening this season."

"Yep. It will take nothing short of a miracle to beat Jon Wilhe at this point. It's even an uphill fight for Delmatic to take *second*! The betting stations are going to be a mess."

"Oh, I don't doubt it! The good news is, Terion and Shatter have teamed up to enhance security at all the EC stations tonight. After the riots last week, they aren't taking any chances."

"Yeah, Tivane. I know a lot of folks are upset with the

crackdowns, but everyone should truthfully be grateful for it, especially during an event like tonight."

"Yes, I know I am! We at the Trackripping Syndicate are really supportive of all that Terion and Shatter are doing together these days. You all saw the collective pre-race message from our Rippers supporting them. If our Rippers are fans, then everyone most certainly should be. In fact, let's hear a huge ovation of support for our friends at Terion and Shatter!"

Niko was most definitely *not* a fan, and she was disappointed to hear the earsplitting whooping in favor of them. She was so annoyed at the mindlessness of all these people.

Drones, the lot of them. Could they not muster any small amount of thought for themselves? Terion and Shatter were actively shutting down freedoms, and the people overwhelmingly cheer for them? She supposed it was a smart move — getting all the Rippers and celebrities to endorse them. It all felt eerily similar to the Meridians and their propaganda campaign back on Arhanda.

Whatever. It's not like she really cared. As long as she was getting out of here soon...

"It is wonderful to hear such deserved respect," Tivane hummed. "You are all great and wonderful citizens of An-Terino! Now back to our race... Wilhe is just now rounding the long corner into the open Daylight, and all the rest of the Rippers are in single file, zipping through the Rift caverns."

"Yes, Tivane. Wilhe has now extended his lead by *fifty* seconds! It's the last lap; he could practically get out and push his kart and still win."

The two broadcasters burst out in laughter, as if they would love to see Wilhe do just that.

"But the race for second is hotly contested," he continued. "Delmatic is nipping at Rivers' wheels, but Vikers and Relm are right behind him. Daks, surprisingly, is in eleventh position."

"Yeah, Turnslinger, I like Wenno Daks, but I see him dropping considerable points here. Not what you want heading into the Oldcity Blitz, the Tour's penultimate race. After that, all that's left is the Century, coming up next month, like you said."

"Very unfortunate for him indeed, Tivane. We'll have to see how things shake out after the final results from tonight, but I think Wilhe might shoot up to top six, and Daks might just drop."

"If the places stand as they are, nobody would have believed these results an hour ago."

"It is wild, Tivane. Now we have to remember, there are still a few places where Rippers can make their moves. The pack will come up on the roundabout in a few seconds here, so we'll have to watch closely."

Even Niko herself had stopped watching Jon Wilhe. She had instead turned all her focus to rooting for Astine Rivers to beat that blazes chum Delmatic. What a night this was turning out to be!

Two nights in a row, she reminded herself, remembering her outing with Jack yesterday evening. She was sad he wasn't here with her tonight, but she'd see him again soon enough.

"OOOOH! OUCH! And just like that, Turnslinger, anything can happen!"

Niko watched as one of the karts in the middle of the pack, a green and pink striped kart slammed into a yellow kart, sending both of them tumbling into others. The dust hadn't even settled, but it looked to be four karts that lay in wreckage underneath the sol-light of Bucon.

"That's a bad place to wipe out, Tivane. You do *not* want to crash in the Daylight. Emergency crews are on their way, but they are fully exposed to Bucon until they are recovered."

"Yes, we will keep all patrons updated on the situation, but it looks like Wenno Daks was very fortunate to avoid that collision by mere centimeters. And now Rivers, Delmatic, Relm, and Vikers look like they are clearly ahead of the rest of the pack, where everyone else has been slowed down by the crash."

"Those four front-Rippers struck luck indeed! And I think most people missed it, fair enough, but Relm was able to take over the fourth position from Vikers. Great move, too! Delmatic wasn't quite able to steal that spot from Rivers, but he'll have one more chance at the finish line. That is, as long as she keeps him behind her in the aqueduct tunnels."

"I did see that move! Very skillful. This last half of the lap will be very interesting now that the field has opened up," Tivane said. "Now, I have terrible news for fans of Dingo Walalam and Max Elsireon, but it's looking like those two were involved in the crash. *Again!*"

"Wow. Just, wow. Those two can't catch a break. They had such high hopes for the Tour this year, but with crashes in back-to-back weeks, there is no chance that either of them can secure a top twelve finish this year. What a shame."

"Shame indeed, Turnslinger. Now, I'm receiving reports that all four Rippers are alive and conscious, and they will be rushed to the medical center as soon as possible. Our thoughts go out to them and their fans."

"Absolutely, Tivane. I always take a moment to think of w…"

Turnslinger was cut short as an earsplitting pop cracked like a whip through the air. It wasn't on the broadcast, but rather inside the arena.

"OHHHHH NOOOOOO…" Tivane shouted. "NOOOOOO! What happened?!"

"I… I… don't know, Tivane. I can't believe it…"

Niko was confused at first, but her eyes scanned down the line to a dusty cloud that appeared to be skidding forward.

A cloud that rained debris, pieces of wreckage pinwheeling from a kart that was tumbling head over wheels.

An orange kart.

The silence of settling dust was the only thing that ensued for a few short seconds, then all pandemonium broke loose. The piercing shouts of everyone around her made it impossible to hear anything intelligible as the crowd tugged her back and forth. Niko was but a weed in a windy field, forced to sway in whichever direction the masses dictated.

She rose onto her tiptoes, desperate to get a look at what the commotion was about. She cursed her own height as much taller fans now surrounded her on every side, the crush of bodies shoving her this way and that. The announcers' broadcast had even paused. How was she to know what happened?

Whatever it was, it couldn't be good. The last thing she remembered seeing was pieces of an orange Trackripping kart doing cartwheels down the straightaway, only meters from the finish line. The murmurs around her eventually became clearer and clearer, and the words were nothing she'd want to hear in her worst nightmares.

"Jon Wilhe!"

"It was Jon Wilhe!"

"Jon Wilhe's crashed!"

No.

She craned her neck, hoping to see for herself.

There's gotta be a mistake. Maybe it was after he crossed the finish line? Maybe it wasn't a crash at all?

Panicked thoughts poured from her consciousness. She had to have heard wrong. She had to have *seen* wrong.

In the distance ahead, she peeked enough of a glimpse to spy Ce-Ellum pushing his way through the crowd. How did he get over there so fast? Fans parted for him, infuriating as it was to watch, and he momentarily disappeared from view.

"What happened?!" she shouted to Cryo, tugging on his shirt.

Wide-eyed, he made firm, direct eye contact, then subtly shook his head. "It's not your fault," he mouthed to her.

"What happened?!" she screamed louder this time.

"*You* lost us all our Terion is what happened!" She heard the accusation from behind her.

Ravenna.

And looking more dangerous than Niko had ever seen her.

Niko's vision suddenly turned starry, her ears ringing with a high-pitched hum. What the blazes?!

"Ven!" Cryo yelled. "No! It is *not* her fault!"

"She took *our* badges and bet *our* Terion!"

Blazes, did Ravenna just *hit* her?! Her jaw stung as she reached to rub it, even through the mask on her head. The woman was lightning quick; she didn't even sense it coming. Niko hadn't cried in years, and wasn't about to start now, but she suddenly felt so... hurt. So insignificant and worthless.

"If you're looking to blame someone, blame me," Cryo challenged. "It's all of our faults. *We* came up with this plan. *We* could've shut it down."

Ravenna now directed her ire toward Cryo, her fierce, violet eyes glowing through her visor without blinking, but she didn't say anything. Oh, she was *pissed*.

And Niko didn't blame her. Cryo, the noble chum, always tried to take accountability for everything, but she wasn't going to let him on this. This was *her* fault. And her fault alone. *She* was the one who first gambled. *She* was the one who spent their Terion. *She* was the one who chose Jon Wilhe instead of Delmatic.

Blazes, what had she done?

Unblinking, she stared emotionless into the distance, while the screeching voice of Tivane droned on in the background.

"Did you see that Turnslinger?!"

"I certainly did! She skillfully avoided the debris, but that evasive maneuver just cost her the victory! What an unfortunate turn of events!"

"Well, an unfortunate turn of events for everyone besides Delmatic," Tivane corrected. "And against all odds, he remains our champion once again!"

Cheers erupted, but Niko could care less. Ignoring even the stinging on the side of her face, her eyes became fixed upon a grisly sight in front of her.

On the sandy track below, being dragged to the side by Ce-Ellum — *Ce-Ellum*, of all people! — was the limp body of a Trackripper.

Jon Wilhe, certainly.

How Ce-Ellum got down to the track was beside Niko's concern. The more peculiar issue was the look on the man's face. He ordinarily looked so haughty and composed, but grief now flashed through his dark eyes.

One look at him, and Niko knew it was genuine pain. Gangster though he might be, he was still human, and surely felt human feelings. Jon Wilhe was his *friend*, and he was hurt. Badly. Ce-Ellum yelled something to those around him, but Niko couldn't make it out.

Cryo rushed forward, leaping over the barrier to join him, dropping nimbly at least four meters to the ground below. The two worked in tandem to lift Jon Wilhe over to a set of doors on the side of the track, supporting his head as they did. A crew of emergency workers rushed out and took over, hefting him onto a gurney and wheeling him out of sight.

Niko was left on her own to panic for several minutes, not brave enough to face Ravenna or Kyler. When Cryo and Ce-Ellum finally joined the group again, she was horrified to see both of them covered in blood.

So much blood.

Blazes! Would Jon Wilhe even survive? If Cryo only held the man for less than thirty seconds and was covered in that much blood...

"I can't believe that, Turnslinger! Look at the replay! It looks like fragments of a rock blew out one of his wheels, then he hit the larger piece of it, and that was enough to flip the kart off its right-side-up." Tivane continued her broadcast, enthusiastic as ever.

"My question is, where did that rock come from?" Turnslinger posed. "It looked to me like it was *thrown*."

"It very well may have been, but the rules are clear. Outside influencers may be detained by the Syndicate — and will most surely face swift and firm justice — but race results may not be overturned, no matter what."

"Such a shame for Wilhe. He deserved that race through and through. And I'm not sure I approve of Delmatic's gestures right now."

Sure enough, Delmatic was standing over the wreckage of Jon Wilhe's kart, making obscene gestures that made Niko's blood boil. She was already seething about what was *stolen* from her, but now she had to watch Delmatic gloating over...

Wait... Was that chum *urinating* on Jon Wilhe's kart?!

Niko squeezed her eyes closed and clenched her fists, her vision turning red as she shook with anger. What an abominable human being. A truly despicable monster. *He* probably had something to do with the rock that was thrown.

"Very tasteless," Tivane admitted, "if Jon Wilhe is indeed deceased."

"I don't see how he could've survived. The way his kart just *disintegrated*... And the state of his body when those fans pulled him off the track..."

"This is a very grim moment for Trackripping. But at the end of the day, Delmatic *is* the champion."

"Very true, Tivane. Champions just somehow find ways to win. Though I think Delmatic should be a little more humble after it was only pure luck that secured him the victory today. He could have very well taken third place, and I think a little humility would go a long way for him right now."

"Agreed. And amidst all the finish line drama, many fans may have missed an incredible finish from the top four. Rivers was forced to swerve to avoid colliding with Wilhe's kart, and Delmatic used that distraction to pass her right at the very end to secure the victory. Relm barely held off Vikers, but both of them passed Rivers in a photo finish. All three karts were separated by less than two meters!"

"It was an unbelievable finish, Turnslinger! And just now we are seeing more photo finishes! Looks like Wenno Daks just held off four Rippers by about two meters, as well!"

Niko couldn't fathom how the announcers were so quick to move past Jon Wilhe's crash. They were announcing the damn race as if they didn't just watch that brutal, brutal crash. Or the fact that it was sabotage.

Sabotage.

Surely that would account for *something* when it came to her bets? There was no way she could lose that Terion from an illegal move like that. Right?

"Now, Turnslinger, I'm getting reports now that Jon Wilhe has indeed died. I say again, I am very sorry to announce the tragic news that Jon Wilhe is deceased. Our thoughts go out to him and all his fans."

Dead. He was dead.

"What a tragic day, Tivane. That may have been the most impressive performance I have ever seen. For him to not only miss out on the win, but to lose his life like that... Just heartbreaking."

"No doubt his performance will go down in Trackripping history, Turnslinger. That was one for the ages."

Niko turned to frantically ask her friends if there was any way to recover her bets because of the sabotage, when she noticed Ce-Ellum looking down, quite distraught. His face was largely stoic, but she knew that look anywhere. She'd worn it well herself in the days after her flight from Arhanda.

Though Niko was far from ready to trust the guy, she pitied him. No one deserved to lose a friend. The Mara knew she'd felt grief like that before, and it wasn't a good feeling.

She tapped Cryo on the shoulder and asked as quietly as she could, "Is there a way the sabotage makes it so the bets don't count?"

He exhaled deeply through his mask and shook his head. "All places are final, no matter what happens."

"But..." she started, "that's... that's so unfair!"

"It is," he replied calmly.

"We *told* you to be careful," Ravenna hissed. "But you didn't listen. You *never* listen!"

Niko opened her mouth to protest, but Ravenna whirled around and stalked off. There was nothing Niko could say or do to make it better right now. It was all bad. And it was all her fault.

Kyler looked at her with an unreadable expression, then turned and walked away from her, as well, leaving to follow Ravenna. Blazes, it would've been better if he made some snide comment like he always did.

She hated herself wholly and completely. How long would it take them to get off this Mara-forsaken hellhole of a planet now? Months? Years? She didn't even know. She didn't *want* to know. It didn't matter at this point.

She should've been more concerned about Jon Wilhe as a person — it looked like Ce-blazes-Ellum even showed more humanity than her — but all Niko could really care about was her dashed hopes of getting off the planet.

Blazes, since when did she lose her sense of empathy??

She hated herself even more when Cryo came and put a soothing hand on her shoulder.

"Don't worry about them," he said. "They'll come around. It's not your fault."

But it was her fault. Oh, but it was.

CHAPTER FIFTEEN
15
Making Amends

"**THEY'LL** come around," Anda said, echoing Cryo's words from the night before.

Ugh! Why did she have to be so infuriatingly understanding about everything?

Part of Niko almost wished she reacted how Ravenna, Kyler, and Kira-Tharn had, shredding her for her poor choices. It's what she deserved, after all.

"I'm not so sure," Niko replied. "You should've seen their faces. It was beyond disappointment. I think they *hate* me."

Anda let out a huff. "With everything you've been though together, I doubt they *hate* you."

Niko bowed her head, the air deflating from her lungs as she stooped down to twist another blacksquash off the vine.

"It was like ten million Terion. Now we have next to nothing."

"You'll earn it back," Anda encouraged, waiting for Niko to look up before continuing. "But the proper way, not by gambling."

"*Proper!?*" Niko bit out. "There's nothing *proper* about any of this. They *cheated*, Anda. They threw a rock in front of him! And he *died* because of it."

Anda's stoic face gave away no hints of a reaction; she only continued to work in that automated fashion reminiscent of those produce-harvesting machines back on Arhanda.

Niko sighed. "You should've seen the way that chum Delmatic gloated over his win. It was disgusting. He *peed* on Jon Wilhe's kart, after he crashed and died. How can people get away with that?"

Anda snorted. "People get away with *far* worse than that here."

"I just... I don't know... What am I to do?"

"Keep working for now. And continue learning machine tinkering. You can get a much better-paying job with that skill."

"I know. I'm trying. It's just a lot."

"I can help you, if you need to learn more."

Niko paused. "You know of machine tinkering?"

"A bit," Anda shrugged, still focused on her harvesting work.

This girl was such a puzzle. It didn't exactly surprise Niko that she knew of machine tinkering, though; she seemed exceptionally intelligent.

"Why don't you get a better job, then?" Niko asked.

"I don't have a choice. Indentured... remember?"

Ah, that's right.

"Besides, I get paid well enough for my *other* work. And I'd much rather be outside."

Niko became lost in thought for a few seconds and stopped pulling blacksquashes, prompting Anda to look up. She suddenly had an idea — an idea to potentially make back all of her lost Terion.

"Can I..." she started. "Do you think they'd let me work in the Cinto fields with you?"

Anda completely stopped her own harvesting and met Niko's eyes. "Do *not* entertain that idea, Niko," she said sternly. "Not for one second."

Blazes, the woman sounded like Kira-Tharn. Even more intimidating, actually. Her one eye did not blink — did not even twitch — as she stared Niko down.

Point taken.

"If you think your situation is bad now, you have no idea," Anda continued. "Desperation is death here. Look at this."

She held Niko's gaze as her two hands waved across her face, as if unveiling her scars for the first time. Niko only stared meekly back. Blazes, she felt foolish for dwelling on her own woes.

"Do you want to know how I got these?"

"Anda, I..." Niko started, shaking her head. "I didn't mean to...

187

I'm sorry."

"You don't have anything to be sorry for, other than feeling sorry for yourself. I'm only offering so it may help you from going and doing something reckless."

Niko turned her head down in shame and accepted.

"It was shortly after I came here," Anda began. "I told you of how I worked in the Rifts... Well, my foreman... he withheld my first Terion payday. When I confronted him, I was rather aggressive about it. Foolishly, I thought it was because of my confidence that he gave me what was owed. Little did I realize there was a more sinister plan.

"He then told me there was an opportunity to make even more Terion, and to meet him at this address in Oldcity. Ignorant as I was, I did so. When I entered, I realized I was in a den of thugs in the heart of the underworld. They expected me to work for them — tasks they wouldn't explain — and made it clear I was in no position to refuse, and that payment was optional, according to them.

"Invincible as I thought I was, I turned to leave, and when one of them barred my way, I punched the man in his throat — *hopefully* crushing his trachea. But then three, four, five — I don't know how many more — they all grabbed me at once. I fought back with every shred of being in my soul, but they beat me and beat me and beat me. At that point, I thought I was going to die. It was a weird sense of peace — mentally surrendering like that — if not for the pain. And the pain... well, it was bad..."

Niko nearly vomited as Anda described in detail the level of torture she endured. How could someone even live through that?

"The last thing I remember before waking up on a table in the ROTO offices was the smell of burning," Anda continued. "My flesh. My hair. Me.

"According to Amon, he was walking by on the streets when he saw my body, burned and naked, dumped on a heap of trash. Whoever did it certainly thought I was dead, or well on my way to death. Amon grabbed me, covered me with a sheet of fabric from that same trash pile, and hauled me all the way to ROTO, and that's when they saved my life. But because he owed them, so now I owe them also."

Niko was speechless. What could she possibly say? She might have tried to tell Anda she was sorry that happened to her, that nobody should ever have to endure that in a million years, but that wouldn't come close to cutting it. Blazes, her own misfortunes were *nothing* compared to Anda's...

"Did you ever find out who it was? Did they ever get caught??"

"Of course not. My memories of the event are foggy at best. Besides, this is Alashadar... Like they say when you first get here, 'welcome to the bleakness'. There are fifty million people in this city and no central authorities. There is no law. There is no justice. Which is why *you* need to keep a rational mind. Even on my deathbed, I would choose never to sell myself to ROTO like happened. I went from being one type of victim to another, now little more than a slave. The lesson is... do not involve yourself in the underworld here. Even for something as tame as Cinto farming."

"I... I..." Niko stammered. To her embarrassment, she struggled to form the sentences she wanted. "But I need the Terion. *Because* I need to get out of here."

"Find another way."

"There is no other way!" Niko protested. "I *need* to make it up to my friends by getting their Terion back."

"Any other way is better." Anda held firm. "Become a damn Trackripper, for all I care. Just *do not* sell yourself into the underworld. Because then there is no leaving this place. Ever."

Niko sighed. Maybe she should be a Trackripper. That was just about as fantastical as earning Terion legitimately through ripping out blazes blacksquashes for the rest of eternity.

"I..."

"Promise me you won't sell yourself into service," Anda pleaded. She stared intensely at Niko, her one eye glowing against the low sol-light from Bucon. Blazes, with that look — the one with the intensity of a thousand sols — there was no way Niko could refuse.

"Fine." Niko gritted her teeth through closed lips, then returned to harvesting the blacksquashes. It was going to be a long shift, especially if she would spend the entire time wondering how she'd ever pay her friends back.

After her workday was over — which *did* prove to be a long shift — she took the train with Anda and Amon back to the city center. It was an awkward, silent trip, and Amon surely wondered what the blazes was going on between them. It wasn't like there was any drama, though; it was just that neither of them cared to talk about anything. What more was there to say, after what Anda had told her?

Niko only muttered half-hearted farewells as she parted with the pair at the rail station, then drifted toward her friends' place in Machine Row with dragging steps. It was about the last place she wanted to go, but she owed them.

Maybe Anda and Cryo were right. Maybe they would come around...

Probably not. It was more likely that she'd be chewed out by Ravenna again. And Kyler. But he was an idiot and could go to blazes. *He* was the one who was all about betting the Terion in the first place. He even wanted to put all of it on a Jon Wilhe *win*. The gall he had to call her a '*blazes-accursed fool of a chum*'...

Thinking of her last conversation with them made her stomach lurch, and for a heartbeat, she considered turning right back around. But no. She steeled her nerve and continued on. She knew she owed them. She had to find some way to make amends.

As she stepped up to their door with butterflies churning, she clamped her jaw shut to keep her teeth from chattering. Finally, after unsuccessfully quieting her storm, she found enough courage to raise shaky hands to the door, and knocked.

Luckily, Cryo answered. He gave her a sympathetic smile, a pat on the shoulder, and invited her in, where to her chagrin, the others were lounged in the living room. Ce-Ellum looked at her with a deeply set grimness, but still offered a tight smile. Ravenna and Kyler, on the other hand, only scowled at her.

For blazes' sakes, even Ce-Ellum was more civil toward her than Ravenna and Kyler... Although, it wasn't Ce-Ellum's Terion she squandered. The others *did* have a right to be upset. But surely they understood how badly she'd been cheated out of that Terion...

"Come to beg?" Kyler sneered.

Niko ignored him as best she could. "I was doing some thinking, and..."

"That would be a first," he interrupted.

Niko looked to Cryo to save her through diplomacy, but he seemed to be ignoring Kyler as much as she wished she could've.

"I was doing some thinking," Niko continued, "and what if I became a Trackripper? And if not a Trackripper, what about a Droneripper?"

The living room was silent for a few seconds, before Kyler burst out into laughter.

"You?! A Trackripper?"

Kyler almost rolled out of his seat in his own smug enjoyment, snide as he was. Ce-Ellum smiled, but didn't join in the full-fledged mockery. Cryo seemed annoyed with Kyler, and Ravenna showed absolutely no reaction whatsoever.

"Or a Droneripper," she protested. "It might be a way to get some Terion faster than we have been."

"Faster than *you* have been," Ravenna corrected, speaking up.

"There is no way in the blazes that you would ever be able to be a Trackripper *or* a Droneripper," Kyler jeered.

"I'd be better than you!" she challenged.

"No, I very much doubt that."

How could Kyler have so much attitude? Niko was trying so hard to remain calm because she knew she *had* been in the wrong by betting all their Terion, even if she *did* get cheated out of it. But by the Mara, it was too difficult to hold back from defending herself...

"It was just a thought," she muttered quietly.

"A idiotic one." Kyler just would *not* shut up. Nothing new there.

"Actually," Ce-Ellum interjected from the shadows, "if you all were looking for quick Terion, Niko might not be able to take Jon Wilhe's place — but Cryo might."

Kyler stopped laughing, and even Ravenna sat up straight.

"Hear me out," he continued. "Vulture is going to press me to replace Jon Wilhe, but I've seen you Rip, Cryo, and I think you could actually do the last two races. Neither is so much technical, as they're mostly about pure speed. Which you know."

"You can't be serious," Ravenna said.

"I do not jest," he replied. "Cryo may not boast about his skills, but I assure you, he is quite capable."

Ravenna shot a questioning glance to Cryo, and the two shared that look that Niko always imagined to be silent conversation.

"I could do it," Cryo responded plainly. No emotion, no pride. Just quiet confidence.

"You're not joking?!" Kyler blurted out. "Here I thought Niko had the dumbest idea in the worlds — and maybe still might — but I wasn't expecting you to be able to actually perform on the Tour!"

"It's just two races. Two mostly non-technical races that Cryo has more than enough qualifications for," Ce-Ellum elucidated.

Niko was grateful that the attention had shifted from her, but she suddenly became very concerned for Cryo. If Jon Wilhe — a seasoned Trackripping veteran — was killed, how could Cryo expect to fare?

"You're sure you can be safe?" she asked.

"Niko, just a second ago, *you* were about ready to volunteer. Now you're doubting someone with actual Ripping experience?" Kyler asked.

He had a point.

"I'll be fine," Cryo promised her. He then turned to Ce-Ellum. "I'll do it. You can let 'em know."

"Perfect." Ce-Ellum straightened from his typical slouch against the wall, heading for the door. "I actually need to head into the office tonight, anyway. The whole place is a mess right now."

"I can imagine," Cryo murmured. "Tell everyone... we're sorry for their loss."

Ce-Ellum nodded, then disappeared into the Twilight outside.

The door had barely closed when Ravenna then turned her ire toward Cryo. "You should *not* be agreeing to this."

"I can do it," he defended. "I've seen the courses, and I've even been able to Rip on part of them before."

"You know I'm not worried about your capabilities," she argued. "It's the uncontrollables. It's the other Rippers. It's this damn underworld. None of it feels right, and you know it. And *you*, Niko, none of this would even be an issue if you would've just *listened*!"

"I'm sorry," Niko squeaked, as she instinctively cowered from Ravenna's direct verbal assault.

Ravenna took a deep breath, but didn't accost her further. A moment of quiet ensued, with Cryo sneaking eye contact with Niko, offering her a tight-lipped expression of commiseration. Both of them were currently on the receiving end of Ravenna's indignation, as justified as it might've been.

"You're right to not trust this underworld, Ravenna", Niko said, sucking up with a small amount of goodwill toward Ravenna. "I've heard some... *stories*... and I don't trust it at all. In fact, how well do any of you really know Ce-Ellum?"

"For the last time, he's fine," Kyler sighed dramatically. "You sure you're not just jealous he replaced you in our group?"

Well, that sure was a cheap shot...

"I'm serious. The guy is a stereotypical gangster, straight out of the Oldcity underworld. Have you guys even noticed his leg? And what about all of his contacts? Vulture? I mean, c'mon!"

"Niko, you're being really judgmental," Kyler accused. "Ce-Ellum is fine. He's our friend."

Blazes, Kyler, shut up! she wanted to say. Why did the guy *always* have to be so problematic?

"I just get a *feeling* around him," she objected. "I haven't talked about *that* in a long time, but I swear I get *it* around him. The guy is hiding something."

"Well, as far as we're concerned," Ravenna rebutted, "you've lost all credibility where your *feelings* are concerned."

"Yeah, your *feelings* are why we're broke," Kyler jumped in. "Maybe you should shut up and let the adults decide here."

"Kyler. Ven. It's *not* her fault."

Cryo intervened on her behalf, but it was too late. She was done taking this from her friends. She tried making amends. She tried being nice. She tried warning them about Ce-blazes-Ellum, for the love of the Mara. If they weren't going to respect her as a human being, she was done for tonight. She would talk to them again when they decided to pull their heads from their asses.

———

Niko left her so-called friends' place in Machine Row fuming in frustration. At first, it was all she could focus on, but as the walk dragged on, the anger cooled just enough to notice her surroundings, and with that clarity came a deep unease. After recalling Anda's horror story, every stranger became a potential threat, someone to avoid at all costs. She put her head down and hurried her steps, only letting herself breathe once she reached her own corner of town.

She burst into her quarters, and immediately wished she was elsewhere after catching Kira-Tharn's unblinking glare. What did the blazes-accursed woman want now? Probably to yell at her some more about the gambling debacle, just like everyone else…

Niko didn't even give herself a chance to find out. She stormed down the hall, threw her belongings on the bed, then left her quarters just as quickly. Even if she didn't have tinkering lessons with Riiz, she still would've left. Kira-Tharn had been so self-righteous about the lost Terion, preaching down her prominent nose as she lectured Niko about the Time yet again. Niko just could not deal right now.

She huffed across the lot to Riiz's quarters when she spotted Callum and Jack loading up some strange looking vehicle. The thing was bulky, with tank-like armor and massive wheels, as if it was built for an expedition on some asteroid. Where did they even get this thing? And where the blazes were they off to?

"Niko!" Jack called out.

"Hey."

"We were waiting for you!"

"I had work."

"I know! But Riiz was adamant that we wait for you. He wanted to tell you that he was leaving with us."

"Okay." Great, now Riiz was leaving. "Where're you going?"

"Into the Night. We heard from our contact."

Now? They were leaving now? The *one* thing that was making life bearable was that Jack had returned, and that he was being nice to her and giving her the attention she'd been craving. Now he was up and leaving??

Wonderful. Just wonderful.

"I know you have work, but…" he started. "Maybe you could come with us?"

She perked up a little at the invitation. Oh, how she wanted to. But she *did* have work.

"For how long?" she asked.

"I don't know," he replied. "Maybe a couple of days."

"I… I can't lose my job. I already lost everyone's Terion."

Jack shrugged. "Can't you always get hired in the fields?"

She didn't know if it worked like that. She supposed she was hired rather easily in the first place… but would it be different if she just no-showed for several days, then started back up again?

"I don't know. Are your dad and Riiz cool with it?"

He shrugged again. "I don't need their permission to invite you. I would love it if you came along."

The blazes man sure knew how to tug at her heartstrings. She really *did* want to go, if for no other reason than to escape the hell she'd created for herself here. The Night, as bad as it sounded, couldn't be as bad as her existence in this dump of a city.

"You know what — sure. I'll go."

Jack's face lit up. "I knew you'd say yes!"

Niko rolled her eyes. She wished he'd show the same enthusiasm when it came to admitting his feelings for her... Of course, she hadn't admitted hers either, but she wasn't going to until *he* did, yearnings be damned.

"I need to tell Kira-Tharn, and the rest of everyone..." Niko paused, scratching her head in contemplation. "Actually... to the blazes with them. They'll figure it out when I'm gone."

Maybe that way, they'd think twice before treating her like dirt next time.

Jack looked askance at her, narrowing his eyes. "You might want to say *something*. Although, I'm sure we can send a message to them."

"Niko! How are you holding up?" Callum called. He and Riiz walked out carrying a couple boxes of equipment.

"I'm okay," she lied.

"She's coming with us," Jack announced.

Callum raised his eyebrows in surprise, but then just said, "Welcome aboard. Did you need to bring anything?"

"Umm, how long are we gonna be gone?"

"Should be a few days. Two or three, I'm hoping. But you might want to plan on three or four, just in case."

Three or four? ... She really hoped ROTO would keep her on in the fields after no-showing for three or four days...

"Okay, let me just grab a few things. I'll be fast."

She scurried across the lot, marched back into her quarters, and gathered a few belongings, ignoring Kira-Tharn's inquisitive gaze as she stormed right back outside. After the scolding Niko took last night, she wasn't about to give that woman any friendly goodbyes.

"When are we leaving?" Niko asked. She wondered if she had time to let Anda know. That girl, at least, deserved enough respect to hear it from Niko.

"Now," Callum responded. "Got everything you need?"

Well, so much for letting Anda know. She'd just have to explain it all when she got back.

"I guess."

"Good. There should be plenty of room for you to sit in the back."

"Thanks."

She walked to the tail end of the articulated vehicle and climbed in, dumping her bag carelessly on the floor. It was roomier than she expected, but maybe that was because there wasn't much luggage from the others. Should she have grabbed more food?

Whatever. Not my problem. Though, it would become her problem if she ended up stranded in the Night with nothing to eat...

She pushed that foolish thought aside. There was no way Callum Sehs went anywhere unprepared.

An accordion-like passageway connected to the front of the vehicle, but she was content to enjoy the privacy back here, stewing in her own misery for a little bit. Although, it would be okay if Jack kept her company. That would be fine. Welcome, even.

To her annoyance, however, all three of her companions piled into the front of the vehicle. She supposed they did have business to attend to, as they immediately began discussing the logistics of the travel for the day. Niko listened in, but didn't eavesdrop too intently. Her mind was still swarming with thoughts from what Anda had told her. She'd probably fall asleep soon, anyway.

Her eyes were almost closed when the connecting door burst open and Jack stood there, smiling broadly.

"Alright, off to find Kezane!" he said excitedly. "All good?"

"All good."

Niko, tired as she was, managed to eke out a soft smile at his youthful enthusiasm as he disappeared to the front once more. And as they set off into the dead of Night, the rumble of the vehicle lulled her to sleep.

―――――――――

PART TWO

The Wilds of An-Terino

CHAPTER SIXTEEN

16

Into the Dead of Night

PITCH black darkness, as far as the eye could see. When she looked out the front window, at least. Behind, a faint hue of reddish purple still clung to the skyline, but that was now only the tiniest sliver pressed between the horizon and the Night sky above, dimmer even than the embers of a dying fire. A few stars were visible away from the city's light pollution, but only the brightest ones could be seen through the dusty haze of the atmosphere.

Niko's attention was drawn to one in particular — a yellowish-white sol that hung low to the ground — and it was strange to think that faraway dot had once illuminated her life every day for sixteen years. In the early days of her arrival to An-Terino, she had refused to even look in its direction, but she supposed she was past that stage of grief now. She didn't really feel *anything* anymore, looking at it tonight. It was just another star. Though, something about its color brushed her with an inexplicable satisfaction, a ghost of a memory she couldn't quite bring into focus.

"I'm about ready for a bio break," Jack announced out of nowhere.

Callum and Riiz were sleeping in the back, and Niko had meanwhile migrated to the front to keep Jack company while he took his turn at driving. She had since become his de facto navigator, much enjoying the opportunity to pore over maps of the terrain. Old-fashioned paper maps, just like her father used to show her when she was young.

She never realized the Rifts existed way out here. The excavated valleys they traversed almost seemed like giant roads at first, but the bumpiness of the ride told a different story. This place was wild. Which made it especially surprising to see what looked to be settlements marked on the map.

Settlements! Out here?!

What a strange world…

They'd been traveling for over twelve hours, and according to the map, they'd made about three hundred kilometers. Not the fastest land craft she'd ever traveled on, but it wasn't bad progress considering they were traversing unpaved terrain, cliffs and all.

"Yeah, me too," Niko agreed. "When does your dad take over?"

"Soon. I wouldn't complain if he did now. I'm getting a little sleepy."

"Sorry," Niko winced.

She didn't mean to ignore him; she was just so engrossed in the maps of An-Terino that she'd barely spoken to him at all.

"No, you were a lifesaver. I would've fallen asleep long ago if you weren't here."

Niko returned his smile, then pointed to a tall outcropping of rocks, slightly behind them to the right, its silhouette barely illuminated by the faint glow of the horizon.

"That work for your bio break?"

"Yeah, that'll do."

Jack turned the vehicle toward the mountain, which was farther away than looked at first glance. It wasn't exactly a mountain, though; instead it turned out to be a field of massive boulders piled atop one another, the aftermath of some ancient volcanic tantrum, like most of the landscape here. None of these remnants came as a surprise — on a world with tidal forces this strong, its interior was undoubtedly restless.

A grumble sounded from the rear compartment when Jack opened the connecting door. Niko nearly chuckled; that grumble would probably be the closest thing to a complaint from either Callum or Riiz.

"Bio break!" Jack announced.

Niko was about ready to go outside ahead of everyone else, when Callum shuffled to the front and yelled, "Wait! You need some layers first!"

Right. What was she thinking trying to stroll out into the Night with only a shirt and light pants on? *Idiot.*

"Way too cold out there. It's about 190 K."

190 K! Holy blazes.

Callum tossed her a thick jacket, as well as a blanket to be donned like a poncho. The thing was heavier than any layer of clothing she'd ever worn, but when she stepped outside, she was grateful for it. Even so, the air she inhaled burned. Not like the scorching hot Daylight air she accidentally gulped in the other week, but one with a chill so sharp it stung. When she blew her breath out, the droplets froze almost instantly, forming icicles in her nose.

Blazes!

She once thought the Green Coast winter was about as cold as it could get, but this… This was something else entirely.

Niko scrambled around a few large rocks, finished her business as quickly as possible, then practically sprinted back to the vehicle.

She could barely stand two minutes of this frigid inhospitality — how would it be possible for anyone to *live* out here?! Would they actually find any settlements? This Kezane guy must be a masochist to willingly set up camp out here…

"Everyone all good?" Callum asked, once back inside.

"Yep, yep," Jack replied.

Niko nodded breathlessly, her lungs still recovering from their battle with the knife-cold air. The rush of heat as she entered the vehicle was in staggering contrast to the 190 K outside.

"We're just going to drive straight through until we get to that first settlement," said Callum.

"How long will that take?" panted Niko.

"At this rate, only about six more hours."

Not as bad as she imagined.

"Once we get there, we meet our contact," he added. "Hopefully Kezane ends up being somewhere in this settlement, but I think we can expect them to be a little hush-hush with strangers. There's a reason these people have fled all the way out here."

"Do we even know what he looks like?" she asked.

"Yes, I do," Callum declared. "I've only ever seen him in person from a distance, but he was very famous back in the Empire.

I know what he looks like well enough."

She remembered the stories Riiz told her of Kezane Pfase, the once in a generation talent who was meant to be their salvation. He was a Valanse commander who had risen to the highest ranks of the Meridian Empire, but had also been a righteous defender of the people, unafraid to call out the hypocrisy of the Meridian elites. Before Riesen, it was Kezane who was considered to be that Child of the Nel-Mara.

Years ago, however, he was sent off by the Meridians to go investigate the Machine in the hopes to stymy its expansion. When he never returned, people obviously feared the worst and all sorts of rumors spread…

He and his entire crew were killed.

No… he survived but was taken prisoner.

Actually, he deserted the Empire and defected to the Machine.

Wait, no. He deserted the Empire and defected to the An-Mara.

The gossip was a mess, and it was impossible to know what really happened, but Riiz was convinced of that last scenario. Kezane never surfaced on Aktun, but a few years ago, there were reports of him on An-Terino. The An-Mara believed the Machine was a real threat, and if there was a chance at defeating it, Kezane would hold the answers. Or so they all said. This is what drew an influx of An-Mara here in recent years, and was the reason they searched for him now.

"Has your contact at this settlement seen him?" Niko was suddenly full of questions.

Callum shrugged. "I've never met the contact at this settlement. My contact in the city, however, *has* seen him — though not for a few weeks. He swears the people of this settlement have been working with Kezane, and if anyone knows of his whereabouts, it would be them."

"Why would he be way out here, though?" Niko asked curiously. "Why would *anyone* be way out here?"

"A fair question," Callum admitted. "Those who want to get lost go live in Alashadar. Those who want to be *forgotten* go live in the wilds of An-Terino."

Forgotten.

The word sounded so ominous, the way Callum growled it. Niko was well aware how the city turned her into nobody; she could only imagine what the Night would do to her.

Whatever. Hopefully they found this guy, conducted whatever business they needed with him, then returned back. She was already feeling guilty for disappearing on her friends — even if they were being ridiculous chums toward her. She especially didn't want to disappoint Anda, who'd done nothing wrong to deserve her abandonment.

"Did you want me to drive, Jack?" Callum asked, steering the conversation back on track. "We need to get going, whoever's driving."

"Niko and I got it," Jack replied. "I was getting sleepy, but the cold woke me up."

"Okay," Callum shrugged. "Holler if you need a replacement. Riiz and I could use some more sleep."

With that, they disappeared into the back once more, leaving Niko to sit up front with Jack as they resumed their journey.

Only six more hours to go…

The Rifts had become much narrower, and the valleys more twisted as they progressed further and further from the Twilight. The biggest telltale sign they were entering the real wilds, though, was the wind.

Howling, unrelenting wind.

She'd heard this weather existed out here, but didn't fully imagine it could be so savage. She thought it to be bad when they stopped for their bio break at that outcropping hours ago, but that was a breeze against a tornado compared to this. She hadn't even dared step outside during their last break, but she could feel the gale beating at their vehicle even through the thick doors, threatening to blow the damn thing over.

Her stomach twisted into knots when one particular gust lifted half the wheels completely off the ground, to which the uneven terrain offered them no favors. After that, Jack had slowed down considerably, taking care to keep their bearing straight and their wheels on the ground. The only downside was that their six-hour trip had now turned into eight. And counting…

"We should be coming up on it soon," said Jack.

He was right; they should be. Niko double checked the map, then leaned forward to peer out the windows.

"I don't see anything. But yeah, it should be just ahead. Like less than a kilometer. Shouldn't there be any lights? Any buildings?"

"I would think," Jack said. "It's so blazes dark out here. I can't see a damn thing."

It *was* dark. Whatever glow lay on the horizon behind them had now faded completely to black. There wasn't any fog, but the wind was so fierce that it had probably kicked up enough dust to blot the stars out completely.

Except that one bright one. The one her once-beautiful home orbited. But Arhanda was now a complete wasteland, one that probably made this place look like the gardens of Nevaly.

"Guys!" Jack called.

A few seconds later, both Callum and Riiz emerged from their slumber, squinting at the luster of cabin lights.

"We there?" Callum asked.

"We should be coming up on it, but there's nothing."

"I do not believe it will be an outdoor complex," Riiz stated. "Due to the conditions in this climate, the facility is likely to be constructed underground."

"Slow down," Callum directed. "Look for anything. Niko... may I?"

Niko stood up and allowed Callum to take her spot in the front passenger seat. He leaned forward and peered out the window as she had done, scanning from side to side, but there was nothing.

No buildings. No roads. Nothing.

They traversed for a few hundred yards past where the settlement was marked on the map, when suddenly, Riiz found it.

"I do believe I have sighted what it is we search for."

He was staring out one of the side windows, and once Jack aimed the floodlights in that direction, a small rectangular structure became visible against the side of some silvery rocks.

Was this the *settlement*? It seemed very anticlimactic if so. Niko had been half-expecting some city, a small version of Groundheim. But this... this was more reminiscent of nothing more than a bunker.

As Jack maneuvered closer to the garage, however, several figures peeked from around a side portal, all wearing those same poncho thingies that Callum had given her. One of them crouched down to fight against the wind, holding a hand up, signaling Jack to slow the vehicle.

He complied, and as soon as the craft had halted completely, Callum cracked open the door to greet the heralds. An icy blast swooped through the interior when he did, causing Niko to shield her face.

Blazes! She could never become accustomed to this level of cold...

"I'm Callum Sehs!" he shouted through the tempest. "I was directed here by Vicero Limon!"

"Welcome to An-Tun Village!" the man called back, nodding as if he was expecting them. "I am the one called Solor-Ven. I did receive a transmission from the one called Vicero Limon. We will open the bay doors momentarily and you may park your vessel in our docking bay."

"Thank you."

Solor-Ven and the others disappeared back inside, and a few moments later, the bay doors did indeed slide open. Jack steered the bulky craft inside, taking care not to hit the edges. After the vehicle was in the clear, the bay doors closed behind them with a resounding clunk of the locks.

CHAPTER SEVENTEEN

17

An-Tun Village

EVEN inside, it was colder than in Alashadar, but at least it was much, much warmer than the gusty air that was held at bay just on the other side of the gate. The place was definitely no Groundheim, but maybe there was a small settlement here after all...

Dim white lights lined a docking bay that was far more massive than Niko imagined lay buried here. Dozens of vehicles not unlike their own were parked in rows at the top, and further inside, people bustled about on walkways and mezzanines. On the opposite side of the chamber, a giant staircase ran down to an entryway that spidered off into many different hallways.

"I am the magistrate of An-Tun Village," Solor Ven said by way of greeting, "and these are my assistants, the ones called Viru-Mor and Raul Vess."

"I am the one called Riiz Alke-Tani." Riiz greeted him in turn, capitalizing on his An-Mara heritage to maintain friendly relations. "These are my companions — the one called Callum Sehs, who previously introduced himself, as well as the one called Jack Sehs, and the one called Niko Ryen."

"Very well met." Solor-Ven bowed respectfully, his posture rigid with An-Mara formality. "As I mentioned, the one called

Vicero Limon sent a transmission alerting us to your intended arrival. We expected you several hours ago."

"Niko's a slow driver," Jack teased, elbowing her in the side.

She returned the jab, rolling her eyes. "I did *not* drive."

A slight smirk tugged on the corner of Callum's mouth, but he didn't outright smile. Probably for the best, considering many of the people in this settlement appeared to be An-Mara. Suddenly, Niko wished she would've worn her Garments.

Not *everyone* was An-Mara, though. This Raul Vess guy looked like... well, she didn't exactly know what he looked like. Not An-Mara, and not Meridian. His freckles reminded her of the those ladies that she worked the fields with — Marial and Nuna.

Where did Anda say they were from? Ossion?

"Apologies," Callum offered. "My *son* was the one who drove slow. But we are unfamiliar with this terrain. We have never been this far into the Night before."

"It is of little consequence," Solor-Ven replied. "Although, I do regret I have a meeting that myself and the one called Viru-Mor are required to attend. The one called Raul Vess will show you to the guest quarters, which we have prepared for you in expectation of your arrival. I will send word in one hour and we may reconvene at that time."

"Thank you." Callum bowed, as did Riiz. Jack and Niko looked at each other before following suit, not to be outdone with etiquette.

They all watched as Solor-Ven and Viru-Mor turned around and glided away down the large stairway, disappearing into one of the halls at the bottom.

"Follow me," Raul Vess ordered gruffly.

Niko started, surprised at how much less friendly than Solor-Ven he seemed. She was half-expecting the quiet, sweet demeanor of Marial and Nuna.

As she followed, Niko nearly tripped on several occasions, caught staring at the unfamiliar surroundings rather than watching her steps on the uneven path.

"These are your quarters," said Raul, stopping at a small doorway cut roughly into the black stone. "You may explore as you like, but try not to get lost."

He grinned menacingly, then simply walked away.

"What's his deal?" Jack muttered after he was out of earshot.

None of the others reacted as they filed into their guest quarters.

The room was plain, but nice enough, considering they were kilometers and kilometers away from anything she knew as civilization. She was, however, dismayed that there was no washroom. What was she supposed to do?

"No washroom?" Jack asked, mirroring her own thoughts.

"They most likely utilize communal facilities," Riiz said.

"Eh," Jack said, collapsing into a chair. "I don't need to go that bad."

"I do," Niko admitted. She stood and headed for the door.

Jack sat up straight. "Need me to go with you?"

Niko rolled her eyes. "No, I don't need you to hold my hand while I do my business."

Jack laughed and clutched his chest, pretending what Niko said hurt him deeply. "Sheesh, I was just saying... In case you needed the company walking around this place."

"I'll be fine," Niko laughed back.

"Of course you will. But in the words of Raul Vess, don't get lost."

Niko rolled her eyes once again and walked back out into the hallway, hoping that the washroom wouldn't be too far.

Unfortunately, it was far. She'd been wandering through the tunnels for at least fifteen minutes without luck, until she happened upon a central communal area lined with a dining commons and other basic amenities, including a washroom.

Thank the Mara!

After she finished and found herself back outside, her gaze snagged on a tall An-Mara girl getting food at one of the stalls. Niko's eyes went wide as Bucon when she recognized who it was.

Blazes! Of all the people to run into here...

What was her name? Fellen-Sor?

Yes, that was it.

She was the An-Mara girl whose face had been plastered all over Machine Row a few weeks ago, while Niko stayed hidden like a groundbird in the brush. Because of her own cowardice, Fellen-

Sor had taken the blows from Shatter that were meant for her — the interrogations, the bruises, the humiliation, all of it.

Niko wanted nothing more than to hide her face, her gut twisted with shame. She knew she should go apologize.

But would Callum and Riiz approve?

Definitely not. And she *knew* what Kira-Tharn thought of the matter...

But Kira-Tharn wasn't here.

Without thinking, Niko edged toward Fellen-Sor.

"Hello," she croaked, looking up at her. Blazes, this girl was tall! How did Shatter ever confuse their identities??

Fellen-Sor turned around, a bruise still visible on her cheekbone, and her lip still displaying the signs of a healing cut. By the Mara, what did those brutes do to her?! She knew it was nothing compared to what happened to Anda, but still... mistreatment was mistreatment. A lump caught in Niko's throat, the guilt rising to the surface.

"I'm Niko Ryen," she introduced herself. "I'm not An-Mara, but I live in the An-Mara quarter. I'm only here in An-Tun Village on business trying to find someone. But I... I heard what those Shatter thugs did to you."

The girl nodded appreciatively. "I am the one called Fellen-Sor."

"I..." Niko started. "I just wanted to say I'm sorry. I'm sorry for what they did to you."

"It is of no consequence," the girl replied. "You do not need to apologize if you did not participate in the cause of an unfavorable outcome."

Oh, but she *did* participate. If only the girl knew... What would she say then?

Niko was slightly amused, though, at how Fellen-Sor's words seemed plucked straight from Kira-Tharn's mouth a lifetime ago.

"Are you from Aktun?" she asked.

The girl shook her head. "I was born here, on An-Terino."

"Oh," Niko replied. "You just sound exactly like a good friend of mine. Someone from Aktun."

"Many of those I live among hail from the world called Aktun. That is likely where my expressions are derived from."

Niko supposed that made sense. Although, living among the An-Mara these last few years hadn't done anything to change her own expressions, much to Kira-Tharn's dismay. Too many years of casual speech prevented her from picking up the proper, ridiculous patterns of the An-Mara.

"How long have you been here?" Niko asked. "In An-Tun Village?"

"I lived here for five years and three months when I was young," Fellen-Sor replied, "but I only arrived back here six days ago. I did not wish to remain in Alashadar any longer after my release."

"Understandable," Niko murmured. "Ever since I came to An-Terino, I've only ever been to Alashadar, other than while working in the Rifts. This is my first time into the Night. I didn't even know there were villages out here."

"There are not many."

"How do y'all survive?" Niko asked.

Fellen-Sor shrugged. "The same way anyone does here on An-Terino."

Not an insightful answer. "How do you get enough food and water?"

"We tap into the Rifts for water, which we also use to create our own power. And produce is smuggled here, primarily courtesy of the one called Kezane Pfase."

Niko perked up. So the guy was here.

The more she heard of him, the more remarkable he became: Child of the Nel-Mara candidate, ex-Valanse commander, traveler to the edge of the sector, keeper of Machine secrets, mysterious benefactor, and now produce smuggler, to boot...

"You have access to Rift water here?" Niko asked, ignoring the mention of Kezane's name. Best to keep it under wraps that it was *him* that she and her friends were here looking for. At least until they had their meeting with Solor-Ven...

"Yes," Fellen-Sor answered proudly. "We have created a diversion spike from the Great Reservoirs in the highlands."

Niko had heard of the Great Reservoirs before. Those provided all the water to Alashadar, if she wasn't mistaken.

"The EC's and Terion and all those big players don't notice?"

"I am uncertain." Fellen-Sor shrugged. "But I would be one to harbor doubts of that contingency. There has never been a raid out here thus far, and this village is decades old."

Niko thought it remarkable that this village existed out here unknown, siphoning water and resources from the greedy, overreaching hands of Alashadar for *decades*. Very impressive, and strangely satisfying.

"What do people do out here? Do y'all have jobs like in Alashadar?"

"Oh, yes. Multiple jobs. It is a difficult life out here, but simple. One that I find far more peaceful than that dreadful pit you call civilization."

Niko was officially intrigued. Maybe she could live out here for the rest of her life instead of languishing in shame as she scraped by in the city, trying to earn back the Terion she'd lost, one credit at a time. Even disregarding *that* situation, living in that city was like withering away little by little. One day, there would be nothing left of her or her soul.

"What do you do here?"

"I work in the water treatment rooms, as well as in sewage. Most individuals here in An-Tun Village undertake multiple specializations. And all residents must perform essential chores, menial as they may be."

Chores she could do, but working in sewage was one thing Niko would pass on. She'd been presented with a job in the sewers when she first arrived on An-Terino, but she declined *that* opportunity without second thought, even though the pay was substantial. Surely there were other jobs here?

"Very cool," Niko said. "I…"

"Along that topic," Fellen-Sor interrupted, "I am afraid I must report back to the water treatment room. There have been some… *anomalies* in the chemistry today, and I must assist to sort out the problem."

There was never an opportunity in the conversation for Niko to come clean about her role in what happened to Fellen-Sor, but at least she was able to talk to the girl.

"Ah, well, it was very nice to meet you, Fellen-Sor."

"And you, Niko Ryen. Perhaps I will see more of you?"

"I'm not sure how long we'll be here for, but perhaps."

"Then on that matter, I hope you find whomever it is you seek."

"Thank you." Niko said, bowing.

Fellen-Sor returned the bow, then walked away, her tall frame disappearing around a corner.

Blazes, she should've just told her the truth. Now Niko felt even more guilty, if that was possible. This girl had been so nice to her! Would she have been so forgiving, though, if she'd known the truth — that it was Niko who was responsible for her maltreatment?

Niko clicked her tongue in frustration. Maybe she would see Fellen-Sor again…

She would come clean then, if so. For now, she needed to get back to the others; enough time had been wasted as it was. She whirled around and tiptoed back from the direction she came, hoping that she remembered the way, suddenly recalling the parting words of Raul Vess.

───────────

After spending way too much time navigating the labyrinth that was An-Tun Village, Niko finally found the guest chambers where her friends waited.

'*Try not to get lost*', he'd said.

Hmph, Niko grunted. *Indeed.*

At least she had an excuse to explore the settlement, which was much bigger than she expected. Still not nearly big enough to be called a city, but way bigger than any of the Meridian stations she visited back on Arhanda. Way more cramped, though, with the rock squeezing many of the passageways narrow enough for only one person to pass. Someone who was claustrophobic may not enjoy this place.

"Blazes, girl!" Jack exclaimed when she finally walked in. "I thought we were gonna have to send out a search party."

"I thought I was gonna have to call for one!" Niko agreed. "This place is a maze."

"You find a washroom, at least?"

"Yeah. Why, did you decide you needed to go now?"

"Depends. How far was it?"

"I couldn't tell you," Niko laughed. "Maybe I took the long, long way. But probably four or five hundred meters, at least. Maybe closer to a k."

"A k?!" he exclaimed. "For the washroom?! I didn't even know this place was that big…"

"Tell me about it," she muttered. "This place is cool though. It's like a small city. Like a mini Groundheim."

"Wanna go explore, then?" Jack asked, his green eyes twinkling with mischief.

"Well, aren't we waiting to meet with that Solor-Ven guy?"

"Indeed we are," Callum spoke up, casting Jack a no-nonsense frown.

As if heralded by the conversation itself, a knock sounded at their door. Riiz sprang up to open it, and none other than Solor-Ven, Viru-Mor, and Raul Vess stood outside.

"May we enter?" Solor-Ven asked politely.

Riiz gestured them forward and in they all filed, gathering around a small table in the center of the room. After the door was closed, Solor-Ven spoke slowly.

"We are honored to welcome you to our abode," he began, "but unfortunately, the one you seek is not present. Nor has he been for some time."

"How long?" Callum asked. "Do you have any idea where we may possibly find him?"

"He is usually one to deliver shipments of supplies to us every two weeks, but it was one of his collaborators the past several occasions. We have not seen the one called Kezane Pfase in months."

Months... So did they waste their time coming out here, then?

Callum exhaled disappointedly through puffed cheeks.

"I will let the one called Viru-Mor elaborate," Solor-Ven said. "She is the one in our village most familiar with the one called Kezane Pfase."

Viru-Mor bowed her head formally, then announced, "Though he is not here currently, we do periodically receive communications from him. He is very engaged with his work at present."

"Do you have any inclination as to where?" Riiz asked.

"Under normal circumstances, he spends his time split between the city called Alashadar and a station much further into the Night," Viru-Mor said.

"Do you know where in Alashadar?" Callum asked.

"I do apologize," she said. "I am not familiar with the city called Alashadar, but I have heard there is a warehouse he operates in the district called Oldcity."

Callum tsked. "We've exhausted that option, unfortunately. He is no longer operating there, I'm afraid."

"Then I do believe your best option is to search for his laboratory deep into the Night," she responded.

"How far?" Callum narrowed his eyes.

"Quite far," she replied grimly. "It is for multiple reasons that he chooses to keep his work so remote."

"I can guess why..." Callum muttered.

"Have you been there?" Niko couldn't hold back from joining the conversation.

"I have," Viru-Mor said, eyeing her up and down. "It is a... *lengthy* trek... but I am confident that you will be hidden from any unwanted interference from the entities in the city."

"And you believe he's out there? Truly?" Niko asked.

"I... I cannot speak with perfect certainty," Viru-Mor admitted. "But I would say it is quite a likely contingency. It is the place he works on *whatever* it is he works on."

"*The Machine*," Jack whispered to Niko, but too loudly, for all heads shot in his direction.

"Yes," Viru-Mor confirmed. "That abomination. It is far too dangerous when undergoing experimentation and must be kept entirely isolated from any traces of civilization."

The pit in Niko's stomach dropped. Were they *actually* considering going near that thing??

"How far is this place exactly?" she asked nervously.

"We do not keep it on maps, per request from the one called Kezane Pfase. But I can tell you that it is a little over two thousand kilometers from here."

Niko's jaw hit the floor. There was no way she heard correctly. *Two thousand kilometers?!?* That would take days. *Weeks*, perhaps!

Her companions looked at each other sideways, suggesting that the others had the same internal reaction she did. And rightly so. Two thousand kilometers?! Into the Night?! It was already a hellstorm of icy fury out here, and they were only a couple hundred k's into it...

A sparkle shone in Jack's eyes, though. He was always up for an adventure, the fool he was. He probably thought this was the best news in all of the worlds. Niko was torn between half-admiration of his unbreakable spirit and half-loathing of his dumbchum bravado. If that man ever got himself into trouble, she'd... Well, she would wring his neck, that's what!

"That does sound like quite an extensive excursion," Riiz commented.

"It is," Solor-Ven agreed. "Which is why you must wait until we receive our next shipment of fuel. One of our associates is due back tomorrow with the resources."

"And you mean to let us have some?" Callum asked.

"We would, on the account that you provide a request on our behalf to the one called Kezane Pfase that he grace us with his presence. If you would relay the message that there is business that we would conduct with him, we would be indebted to you."

"Of course," Callum said, dipping his head respectfully. "We would be most grateful."

Did that mean he actually intended for them to go on this expedition? Niko shifted uncomfortably in her stance against the wall. There was no way...

"How long will this trip take?" she asked for clarification, hoping they'd give an answer more reasonable than the estimate she'd come up with for herself.

"From my recollection," Viru-Mor said, "it took six days to arrive the last time I sojourned there."

Of all the blazes. Looks like she would be disappearing from her job for longer than she had planned for. Much longer.

It was her own fault she was in this mess, though. It was her own fault she was in *all* of her messes. She chose to come along by her own free will, just the same as she chose to bet all her friends' Terion away. Maybe *she* was the dumbchum...

"It is a surprisingly smooth route," Viru-Mor continued. "Although there are some mountain ranges you must traverse. Before you leave, I shall provide you with thorough directions to successfully negotiate these barriers."

"Thank you," Callum acknowledged. "I do have to admit, I was not expecting such hospitality, nor the level of support you are willing to provide."

"You are most welcome." Solor-Ven inclined his head. "There is one other concession we might request, however. The one called Vicero Limon did mention that some of you lot were experienced in the way of machine tinkering?"

Callum nodded, glancing at Riiz.

"Very good," Solor-Ven continued. "We are currently burdened with a problem at the Great Reservoirs, which feed us our

215

water. The corporation called Shatter has recently installed automated allotment chambers that track the passage of all water. It seems that they have become suspicious of the discrepancies between what flows to Alashadar and what is harbored at the reservoirs. Since then, we have been unable to procure any water for fear of being discovered. Our question is… might there be a way to trick their readings at these chambers so An-Tun Village can remain undisturbed?"

Callum gestured to Riiz. "Any ideas?"

"I do believe there may be a possibility," Riiz mused. "I would need to access the system directly. In what manner of proximity do these Great Reservoirs exist?"

"The nearest is fifteen kilometers to the north, which is where we draw the water from," Solor-Ven responded.

"And we do not depart to continue our search for the one called Kezane until tomorrow?" Riiz asked.

"Correct. If the supplies arrive punctually."

"This would give us ample time to travel to these Great Reservoirs, would it not?"

"We could transport you there now, if you are willing."

Riiz looked around at his companions, taking silent note of the consensus. Callum returned a short, decisive nod; Niko and Jack simply met his gaze, wordless but willing.

Niko didn't have much of a say anyway, and honestly, the idea of sitting here stuck in this carved stone room until tomorrow held far less appeal than traveling to these Great Reservoirs.

"I cannot confirm it is entirely solvable, but we will attempt to help you with your problem," Riiz declared.

"Excellent." Solor-Ven clapped his hands once. "Would you require any time to recuperate before we venture forth?"

"We are recuperated," Callum said, answering for the entire group. "Lead the way."

———————

18

The Diversion Spike

NIKO'S party was first directed to An-Tun Village's water intake facilities, but after given a complete briefing of what to expect at the reservoirs, they were now on their way to the docking bay, and to the reservoirs beyond.

Everyone seemed a little exhausted by the monotony of the tutorial, but Niko appreciated the chance to see the village in its entirety. At one point, the underground streets widened enough for the group to pass through ten abreast. Much like in the An-Mara quarter of Alashadar, clotheslines were strung chaotically across the three or four stories that the residences were stacked upon.

Just like home, she thought.

Two children that couldn't have been older than ten were busy scrubbing clothes in a basin near a central well, and it was evident that the village was in a water crisis because they were continuing to recycle the now-brown water, grimy as it was.

Probably for the best that they were on their way to rig that machine program at the reservoirs. These people couldn't live like this!

The children barely looked up as the group passed by, completely engrossed in their chores. Niko wondered if they knew what was out there — a massive city and the civilizations beyond — or if they were as sheltered as she had been, ignorant to everything beyond what was in plain sight.

"You said around fifteen kilometers to the nearest reservoir," Callum said. "That should get us there within the hour, no?"

"The excursion will take longer than that," Solor-Ven replied. "The Great Reservoirs are situated in the highlands flanking our village, making the traveling slower."

"How high?" Callum asked.

"The water level of the nearest reservoir is eight hundred meters above our surface position, but the entry passage is at nine hundred fourteen meters above."

Well, that part was conveniently left out of the briefing...

Perhaps seeing Niko's concerned look, Solor-Ven added, "It is perfectly accessible by vehicle; it just takes some time to ascend."

Okay, doable, Niko thought, glad she'd be able to remain inside. At least they wouldn't have to scale mountains like Cryo and Ravenna back on Arhanda. Climbing in this Night weather didn't seem feasible in the slightest.

Callum, seemingly content with the situation, walked on ahead, side by side with Solor-Ven and his assistants.

"Can you actually do anything for that diversion spike?" Jack muttered under his breath to Riiz.

"Perhaps," Riiz responded with a shrug, his voice low. "Perhaps not. If it possesses the same electrical architecture as the intake facilities, then I do believe I can. And I do believe that you can be of assistance, Niko Ryen."

"Me?" Niko nearly laughed. "But I'm still brand new at the basics of it all."

"It will be a proper learning experience," he replied.

"What would I have to do?"

"That remains to be determined when we arrive. But the most likely scenario is that the system will be accessible through a terminal near the entrance. If my conjectures are corroborated, I will install suppressor hardware into the system. I would then need you to locate the associated wiring at this diversion spike they speak of and insert a T-bridge there."

Niko couldn't quite visualize what he was saying. She'd never even heard of a T-bridge before. How much did he think she blazes knew?!

"Show me when we get there," she mumbled.

He looked at her silently, then nodded, probably realizing she knew way less than he initially assumed.

"We will be boarding these two craft," Solor-Ven announced, gesturing to two vehicles that looked similar to the one she and her companions rode in on, gigantic wheels and all.

Callum didn't hesitate as he stepped inside the nearest one, along with Solor-Ven, Viru-Mor, and two workers whose names she didn't know. That left her, Jack, Riiz, Felln-Sor, and Raul Vess to take the other craft.

With a shrug, Jack grinned playfully at Niko. "Here we go again, I guess."

She managed to return a tight smile and followed him into the vehicle. Soon after, the docking bay door opened to the cold, dark wilds beyond, and they set off.

The drive was a strange kind of blind ascent. With their lights dimmed to near-darkness, the world outside dissolved into a black pane of glass, and Niko's own reflection was all she had for scenery. Her ears had popped a few minutes ago, the only indication that they were gaining in altitude. Now, though, the vehicle pitched and turned in repeating arcs, the kind of rhythm that was evidence of a steeper switchback climb.

"We are almost there," Raul announced from the driver's seat. "Be ready to head inside immediately. The weather up here is considerably... *less accommodating* than down in the lowlands."

Less accommodating?! How could the weather be any worse than outside An-Tun Village?!

"How cold are we talking?" she asked.

"Cold."

She narrowed her eyes. "*How* cold?"

"You don't want to know."

But she *did* want to know! Numbers! She needed numbers. It helped her put things into perspective.

"Don't worry about her," Jack said, nudging Raul on the

shoulder as he smiled back at her. "She's very particular."

That little… Ugh!! Why was Jack cozying up to that chum Raul at her expense? He probably thought he was being cute, but it was most definitely *not* cute. Not in front of strangers who she didn't particularly like…

Niko suddenly lurched forward, only halted from tumbling forward by the seatbelt that hung across her shoulder. What the blazes?!

"We are here," Raul said, smug as can be. "Stay low, and whatever you do, don't open your layers." He gave no further warning as he opened the door.

As he did, a swirling howl of unimaginable cold tore right through every layer Niko wore, a deep-seated pain cutting right down to the bone. The only thing this could be compared to was when she was literally almost sucked out to space back on the An-Mara space station above Arhanda.

She grabbed onto Jack's cloak as they all filed from the craft, fighting their way to a small doorway carved into the side of the mountain in front of them. The opening was barely twenty meters away, yet it felt impossibly far, each step a struggle against the hellish freeze.

After a few tense moments, everyone scrambled inside, and the door was pulled shut behind them with a reverberating slam.

"What the blazes?!" Niko cursed. "A little warning would've been nice!"

"I told you you didn't want to know how cold," Raul said, his eyes gleaming in amusement.

Ughh! Jerk.

"Welcome to the Southern Great Reservoir," Solor-Ven announced.

Niko wiped strands of errant hair out of her face, gathered her composure, then crept up to the edge of the precipice that Solor-Ven stood atop and looked out. Dim lights shimmered far below, and the presence of a dark mass was only given away by the slight ripples that disturbed an otherwise perfectly still surface.

How much water was actually in this place?! From first glance, it looked plenty enough to satisfy the thirst of the fifty million people in Alashadar… And this was only one reservoir out of four!

"The smallest of the four reservoirs," Solor-Ven continued, "but the oldest."

The *smallest*?!

"At the far end, the reservoir drains into the Rift canals and the water makes its way into the city. As discussed, our diversion spike is placed just in front of the meter there, so normally, the water does not get registered as missing. But also as discussed, there have been more meters installed in recent months and weeks, which is why we are here now, of course."

"Can you inform us of the location of the meters?" Riiz requested.

Solor-Ven nodded, beckoning for the group to follow. He strode over to the corner, disappearing out of line of sight. Niko didn't even hesitate, following the others after him, finding herself in a metallic stairwell that spiraled down.

And down.

And down.

And down...

Niko was beginning to think the thing had no end, but just as her legs began to feel like noodle broth, they finally exited onto flat ground. Thank the Mara!

"I believe this is the system you are looking for?" Solor-Ven asked Riiz, standing before a panel with the Terrovian Aquatics logo scrawled across its surface.

Riiz offered a nod of affirmation, then stepped over to it, carefully removing the fastenings that held it in place. Once he removed the panel and set it aside, Niko peered over his shoulder at what lay underneath. It didn't look different from any of the machines she'd ever seen Cryo or Kyler tinkering with, but then again, she knew next to nothing about the inner workings of all that stuff.

Riiz knelt down and pulled out a portable machine console, connecting a few wires to the exposed core before turning the thing on. He worked for a few minutes, then turned to Niko.

"Come see this," he instructed, pointing to a specific few lines of code she barely understood:

```
# Compute average water level of Southern Great Reservoir
readings = [sensor1, sensor2, sensor3, sensor4]
water_level_southern = sum(readings) / len(readings)

# Alert if water level is below threshold
```

allotted_water_level_southern = 54.22
if water_level_southern < allotted_water_level_southern:
    send_report("T1-T612", "Check status: Southern Great Reservoir")

"Ancient, primitive code, but one we are familiar with. This is what they are using to track inbound water levels. I shall write a quick script to mimic the inputs, then you will install the T-bridge at the location of the diversion spike, assuming that all four sensors are on this side of the spike."

"I don't even know what a T-bridge is," she confessed.

Riiz dug into his machine pack and pulled out a tiny piece of electronic equipment. Was this the T-bridge? It was not what she was expecting, though she supposed it did have the shape of a 'T'. She thought it would've been… bigger. Honestly, she didn't know what she was expecting, if she was expecting anything at all.

"The end of the T-bridge will transmit any fluctuations in the water levels, and the one I will install at this location will receive those transmissions. It will help keep the mimicked readings of the flow as consistent as possible, to avoid any suspicions on the end of Terrovian Aquatics or Shatter.

"Your task is to strip the wire casing like I have done here, then install the T-bridge like this." Riiz performed a series of demonstrations, then continued. "I will show you the script I have created when we have returned back to the An-Mara quarter."

Niko nodded, taking the T-bridge from him.

"And you are sure that this will not alert the authorities?" Solor-Ven asked.

"I believe that it will not," Riiz confirmed. "The transmission strength is very weak, diffuse within a matter of meters beyond the location of the diversion spike."

"Very well," Solor-Ven assented. "If you believe it is safe to proceed, then let us forge ahead with that contingency."

"I will accompany the one called Niko Ryen to the location of the diversion spike," Fellen-Sor offered.

"I'll go, also," Jack said.

Of course he would. Not that Niko was complaining — she rather enjoyed his company — but he had hardly left her side since returning with Callum the other day. He probably only felt guilty for being away for so many months.

As well he should.

Niko glanced over at him as he smiled at her, his shaggy blonde ringlets illuminated by the dim fragments of light. She supposed she could never be too angry at him or his maddeningly gentle soul.

"The rest of us should stay here," Raul advised. "The fewer people we have traipsing around in this place, the better."

"The one called Raul Vess has never been fond of this location," Viru-Mor said with a deadpan expression. Niko had come to know An-Mara humor over the years, and this was about as close to it as it got.

"For good reason," he snapped back. "Shatter has been showing its presence here more and more. I don't like that we're even out here at all."

"The one called Raul Vess makes a good point," Solor-Ven mediated. "Let us not expend too much time in this reservoir."

"I agree," Callum said. "I regret I'm not feeling... *great...* about this."

A sudden twist of unease knotted in Niko's stomach, but not from her own misgivings. She couldn't trust herself anymore, not fully. Her instincts had let her down in too great a way recently. Still, Callum's hesitation carried weight; the man was a trained Valanse in his previous life. She knew the tension in his voice was far from casual, and she knew better than to go against his judgments.

"We'll make it fast, then," Niko promised, turning to go.

Fellen-Sor was one step ahead, literally. She didn't even hesitate before briskly crossing the platform toward the reservoir. Niko and Jack nearly had to jog to keep up with Fellen-Sor and her broad strides.

The trio skirted the outsides of the great chamber, the water level only a meter below the edge. Soon, the room grew narrower and narrower, until finally, a small doorway presented itself at the furthest end. They passed through, then Fellen-Sor turned down a side staircase, stopping at a junction of wires at its base.

"I believe this is your target destination," she told Niko, pointing to the tangled mass of electronics.

Niko confusedly examined the exposed wires for a moment, then saw it.

Ah hah!

To her relief, it was just as Riiz had described. She cut the thing in half, then stripped the casing to its metallic base, intertwining the wires into the T-bridge.

Well, that wasn't so bad…

"That's it?" Jack asked.

"I guess so?" Niko shrugged, then turned to Fellen-Sor. "This is where the diversion spike is?"

She had maybe been expecting some pipes, or something. Anything. But there was nothing she could see that betrayed its existence.

"It is," Fellen-Sor responded.

"Well that was… anticlimactic," Jack quipped.

"I do not know what you were expecting, but I, for one, am glad that this operation is anticlimactic," Fellen-Sor drawled. Niko imagined that Fellen-Sor would've been rolling her eyes if the An-Mara expressed such emotions.

Niko let out a huff of agreement, then turned around to head back up the stairs, Callum's words ringing in her head as she did.

'*I'm not feeling… great… about this,*' he had said. The words were chilling enough to put some haste into her step, except…

She stopped.

"What is that?" she asked, pointing to a barely detectable glint in the upper corner of the room.

The color drained from Fellen-Sor's face as she studied what it was Niko spotted. "We must depart immediately."

"What is it?" Jack asked. Niko shifted over to let him get a closer look. "Blazes!" he shrieked.

"Yes," Fellen-Sor agreed.

"Who…" Jack started.

"It does not matter," Fellen-Sor cut him off, taking the stairs two steps at a time.

"The blazes it doesn't!" Jack shouted. "No one in the sector would ever dare surveil remotely. That is against…"

"Do your eyes deceive you?" Fellen-Sor snapped, interrupting him again. "I, for one, believe it would be prudent to trust them."

Jack glanced at Niko, who merely shrugged back as they labored to keep up with Fellen-Sor.

"She's right," Niko said. "What else would it be?"

Jack just shook his head, probably coming to the same conclusion that Niko and Fellen-Sor had.

"You're sure you've never seen that there before?" Niko called ahead to Fellen-Sor.

"I have only been here once, but I am certain it was not here the other day," she responded.

"Is it possible you just didn't notice it?" Jack asked.

Fellen-Sor paused long enough to turn around and shoot him a glare.

Enough said.

After wordlessly storming their way back to the others in a matter of minutes, Fellen-Sor nearly shouted to them once they were in earshot. "We must depart immediately!"

As in a portent, Niko's eyes were drawn to another corner, where the same glint of a video recording tool caught her attention.

She gasped, pointing.

Everyone turned to where she gestured, and curses broke out.

"The Sight..." someone whispered.

"We do need to depart immediately," Solor-Ven agreed. "Let us be on our way, now."

Riiz didn't question the order in the slightest, scrambling to pack his gear up quickly. And despite the protest from her legs, Niko followed the group as they hustled up the stairs at a blistering pace. Her only distraction came in the form of panic, where she was dismayed to spot several more surveillance recorders posted in discreet corners of the hallway.

Who was watching them?

From everything she'd learned, remote surveillance was deeply prohibited by culture and law. And of course, it wasn't just the Meridians that tabooed it — it went against the Time, as well.

Niko shivered, and not because of the frigid cold outside. Even when they arrived back among the relative warmth of An-Tun Village, a chill ran through her still.

Who was watching them? Had they seen them? Had they seen *her*?

CHAPTER NINETEEN
19
Requests

WRONGNESS. That's all Niko felt. Her mind raced and raced, her lip raw from being chewed in nervousness as she contemplated the one question that repeated over and over in her head:

Who was watching them?

The possibilities were unnerving, to say the least.

Of course, everyone around her being swept up in a frenzy didn't help matters. Callum and Riiz were calm enough, but they weren't the ones in charge out here. Solor-Ven, the supposed magistrate, ran off down one of the hallways the moment they returned. *Literally* ran. To where, Niko had no idea, but she thought a leader should show better poise than that.

His assistants scattered after him, and before too long, the entire village was tearing about, shock and alarm written on every face. Those surveillance cameras had rattled these people to the core...

It was their home after all, but Niko questioned the weight of their response. Maybe those cameras were always there? Maybe they weren't monitored automatically by whatever system was designed to watch over the place? Maybe they were only there as a precaution for theft?

Theft...

What An-Tun Village was doing *was* technically theft, Niko realized, righteous as their cause was.

She sighed, hoping it would all turn out to be a false alarm.

"Are we even gonna be able to leave to go search for that Kezane guy now that everyone is running around like a bunch of groundbirds?" Niko asked Jack.

"Dunno. My dad went off to go ask that exact question."

"I do believe they will send us on our way soon," Riiz said, pointing to a large drum of fuel next to their vehicle. "Otherwise, they would not have arranged such preparations for us."

Niko hadn't noticed that before. Maybe they really did intend to send them on their way. "Oh."

"For now, let us ask if we may be of any assistance to these villagers. It appears that they may need such support."

It was a proper gesture, one she should've thought to suggest herself. Ever since Niko had known him, Riiz was always one to help others in need. It was he who had been one of the few to save her sorry soul nearly five years ago on Arhanda. For that alone, she would forever admire the man.

"Good plan," Jack said, taking the initiative and hopping to action. He swiveled about, catching the attention of the nearest local rushing by. "Excuse me! Can we help with anything?"

The woman stared wide-eyed back at him before wordlessly shuffling on. Jack then offered his services to the next passerby. And the next. And the next. And the next…

After every single one of them denied his charity, Jack turned back to his friends, hunching his neck and spreading his arms wide as if to say, '*what the blazes?*'

"These people do live here alone without any interference from Alashadar," Riiz said. "They are proud and stubborn, but do not fault them if they reject outside help. The gesture alone is enough for them to appreciate."

"Well isn't that philosophical of you," Jack quipped.

Riiz tilted his head, staring back deadpan. "You know what I mean, Jack Sehs."

"I know, I was just kidding!" Jack raised his palms in surrender, conceding the point to Riiz as the group stood there idly, unable to help the villagers.

"So what now?" Niko asked.

"I believe it would be prudent to wait for the one called Callum

Sehs to return," Riiz said.

"Wasn't he trying to track down the magistrate?"

"Yeah," Jack responded.

"Well, he might be a while, then," she sighed, "since the magistrate sprinted across the entire blazes village as far as we know. Maybe we should go find him?"

"He told me to wait here," Jack said.

Niko adored Jack, but sometimes she was irked by how much he deferred to the will of his father. Sure, Callum was the closest thing to an authority figure they all had, but still… She wished Jack would do some of his own thinking for once.

"You wait here, then" Niko said, the words colder than she intended. "There's one thing I gotta do real quick."

Jack cocked his head to the side in question, as did Riiz. Maybe it was her disdain for Jack's incessant acquiescence to his father, but something rebellious sparked inside Niko. She wasn't going to sit here and wait around for Callum just because he said so.

"I promise, I'll be back in ten minutes."

"Niko, I don't think that's a good idea…"

Jack started to protest, but she was already skipping down the stairsteps into the heart of the village. She'd made up her mind a while ago that she would come clean to Fellen-Sor; she just hadn't found a good opportunity yet. Maybe there wasn't ever going to be a perfect opportunity — it wasn't clear if she'd ever come back here again, let alone see Fellen-Sor — so she should do it now before they left.

Where would the girl be, though?

Niko subconsciously wandered to the common area where she first encountered her in this place, but it was dead quiet. Empty. No Fellen-Sor. No anybody.

Idiot. Of course Fellen-Sor wouldn't be lounging about there. She and the rest of the villagers were probably busy dealing with whatever had them so spooked. Maybe at the water treatment rooms? Or the residential wing? She'd check anywhere, as long as she didn't have to hunt through the sewers.

To her great relief, she spotted Fellen-Sor stalking through the hallways not long after she left the common area. But upon seeing the An-Mara girl's face, doubt punched its way through to the surface, threatening to derail her mission of candor.

"Fellen-Sor!" Niko called, before she lost her nerve entirely.

"Fellen-Sor!"

The girl turned around, her solemn face a reflection of everyone else's in this damn place. "Yes?"

"I..." Niko started. She cleared her throat. "I wanted to tell you something."

"Make it quick. I am needed in many places, Niko Ryen."

Niko hemmed and hawed, her resolve slipping. *Blazes!*

"Niko Ryen?"

"Sorry! Yes, I needed to tell you something. You know that day not long ago?... Where you were taken by Shatter?... Well... that was... that was *me*."

Fellen-Sor stared blankly back at Niko.

Okay, she hates me, Niko decided, fighting against every instinct in her body to slink away. But against all odds, she held the woman's stare.

"I'm really sorry," Niko clarified, "the girl they were looking for — that was me. I was too afraid to say anything at the time."

After a wordless exchange of glances for longer than a few seconds, Fellen-Sor spoke up.

"You do not have anything to apologize for, Niko Ryen. I have told you before, you do not need to apologize if you did not participate in the cause of an unfavorable outcome."

"I know. But I did," Niko avowed, dipping her head in apology. "I did participate in the outcome."

"How so?" Fellen-Sor asked. "Were you part of the Shatter team that apprehended me? Were you one of the interrogators that beat me?"

"Obviously not, but..."

"Then you did not participate in that outcome. The Shatter guards, and the Shatter guards alone, had the power to abuse me or not. That had nothing to do with you. That had nothing to do with anyone else besides those men."

Blazes, why was the girl being so *nice* about this? Niko had prepared herself for every possible manner of hostility from this girl — *not* understanding and compassion!

Ugh!

"You say you have lived among the An-Mara for years now," Fellen-Sor continued, "but you seem to be ignoring one critical element of the Time — that we do not allow others to accept accolades for that which they did not earn."

Niko had heard that from Kira-Tharn before. Plenty of times. She just hadn't thought that Fellen-Sor would manipulate it around to absolve her of guilt in this matter. She hardly considered taking responsibility for something like this to be akin to '*accepting accolades*'.

Blazes, these An-Mara were absolutely infuriating sometimes!

Niko must've been standing there dumbfounded for too long, because Fellen-Sor continued.

"Harbor no guilt, Niko Ryen," she said. "I do not deign to concern myself with whom the organization called Shatter sought. I instead find solace to know they never found you. Their failure provides me with peace of mind."

Niko could still do nothing but stare at this girl. This girl who had taken a beating on her behalf, and still held no ill will toward her. She was a better person than Niko, that was for sure.

"Is that all you wish to have told me?" Fellen-Sor asked.

Niko nodded, finally finding words to express. "I just... I know you don't want an apology, but I *am* sorry that you had to endure that from them."

"If you truly seek repentance — which is *not* required — then put your energies toward disruption of the organization called Shatter. They are not good for this world."

"No," Niko agreed quietly. "They are not."

"Then that is my only request." Fellen-Sor bowed. "If that is all, Niko Ryen, I have many matters to attend to."

Niko nodded, returning her bow. "I hope to see you again, Fellen-Sor."

"Likewise." She offered one final nod before disappearing around the corner.

Niko, still reeling from the way the conversation *didn't* go, walked back to the docking bay in stunned silence, her heart ever so lighter. And as she reconnected with her friends, she promised herself that she would keep honesty at the forefront of all her dealings from now on. Even amid extreme anxiety, being truthful had been the best decision in a long time.

Even in the following days, Niko still thought about what Fellen-Sor had told her.

Do not feel guilty.

Take down Shatter.

Those were the essences of her request, more or less.

Niko would be all too happy if those thugs got everything they deserved, but as for how *she* would take them down, she hadn't a clue. Jack and Callum seemed much better suited to be the ones to carry out sabotage, being on the inside and all. Although, there was no way she'd compromise their position within Shatter — not when their cover was critical in helping them all get off this blazes planet. She'd think of something, though. She owed Fellen-Sor that much.

However, there were more pressing matters at hand — like navigating their way to this supposed laboratory deep into the middle of the Night. They'd been given fuel, good wishes, and a rough hand-drawn map to help them locate this place, but that was it. So much for the 'thorough directions' that Viru-Mor promised...

'Find the one called Kezane Pfase. We need him now more than ever.' That's what Solor-Ven's parting request to them was.

He and the rest of the people from An-Tun Village seemed terrified, perhaps of retribution for siphoning water from the reservoirs, or perhaps for merely existing outside the reach of Terion. Or the EC's. Or Shatter.

Whatever or whoever it was, the villagers found the threat to be palpable, and were desperate for Niko and the others to find their savior and return with his help.

From the way everyone talked about the guy, Niko wondered amusedly if Kezane was some sort of superhero or something.

Probably.

Or at least as close as any human could come to being one. She'd only ever heard him characterized as the embodiment of selfless heroism and righteous valor, sprinkled with a dash of god-like powers to boot.

Rational thought told her that he'd only end up to be far more ordinary than he was made out to be — in her experience, that's how every blown-up tale turned out — but still, he had to be *something* special. Even if she didn't trust Solor-Ven's word, she did know Callum to have a level head, and he thought Kezane to be the real deal.

The guy was elusive, though, that much was certain. Nobody ever seemed to know *exactly* where he was. They only knew someone who'd seen him recently, or knew of his previous abodes, and it was all secondhand information. If he hadn't yet been found by all these people that supposedly knew him, what made Callum and Riiz so confident that venturing into the middle of uncharted Night to search for him would be a good idea? It was just as likely that they'd become lost.

More likely, probably.

Niko pushed that thought to the back of her mind. She was with some capable people; they wouldn't let that happen. No way.

Right?

They'd now been driving for over two days, and the terrain stretched on and on in an unbroken monotony of rock and ash. Niko's eyes ached from scanning through the blackness for anything that might signal the mountain range the crude map promised.

But there was nothing. They should've detected peaks, or at least any hint of an elevation gain by now…

"I'm not seeing anything," Jack said, peering into the Night as if he could see anything at all beyond their vehicle's headlights.

"The altitude has remained constant?" Riiz asked, leaning over Niko's shoulder.

"Yes. And there haven't been any indications that we've crossed into any sort of range. I would expect it to look like the highlands by the reservoir the other day."

"Is it not possible that we are in a deep mountain pass within the range?" Riiz conjectured.

Jack shrugged. "I have no idea. The only way we'd find out is if we drive off the course they gave us to investigate. Which I don't think is a good idea…"

"No," Riiz hummed. "I would agree with that assessment."

"Doesn't this thing have any infrared sensors or anything on board?" Niko asked. Those might solve all their problems.

Jack shook his head.

What!?

"Nothing?!" she cried out disbelievingly. Why in all the worlds would they have ever set out into the Night *without* those?

"I'm afraid not," Callum said from the back. "In hindsight, that would have been a prudent investment."

Prudent investment!? she huffed to herself, trying hard to keep from showing her frustration. *She* could've told them that they would need infrared sensors before heading into the Night, and vehicular navigation wasn't even close to her forte! Jack being forgetful and airheaded, she could understand. But Callum? And Riiz? They should've known better...

"We have maintained the heading that they gave us. They said it would be a very flat journey, and we've passed the landmarks they told us about, so I think we're on course." Callum sounded like he was trying to convince himself more than anyone else.

"Yeah, everything except the damn mountain range," Jack muttered. "Tiny detail."

Callum shot him a disapproving look, and Jack turned his head down.

Niko really was starting to hate how subservient he was becoming. The Jack she knew was fierce and headstrong, not someone who succumbed to authority unquestioningly, even if that authority was his own father.

"Let me check the stars," Niko suggested, masking her annoyance.

"How?" Callum turned toward Niko, eyebrows furrowed in contemplation. "They never gave us any celestial angles."

"I know, but if this road is actually as straight as they said it would be, the stars will be in the same position."

"We don't even know where their position was before, though," Callum said.

"I do," she calmly replied.

Niko wished she didn't have to look at it, but that bright star that hung ever higher in the sky had been in the back of her mind for days now. She would know if their road was straight once she measured it.

"I'll have to go outside." If she was correct — which she knew she was — it would be too far out of range to be seen from their windows. "Just briefly."

"It's way too cold out there," Jack blurted out.

"It's for *one* minute." She didn't mean for her response to come across so sassy, but she thought it ridiculous to be coddled for little more than peeking her head outside.

Callum peered at her intently, his face giving the impression that he knew exactly which star she was talking about. "Okay, do it," he said. "Wear a mask, though. Jack is right, it's abominably cold out there."

Niko nodded, leaping up to throw some layers on, including a bulky mask she hadn't bothered to wear thus far. It was even more cumbersome than the Daylight masks, which was saying something. She wasn't sure she'd even be able to see any stars at all with the thing on.

"How do I look?" she joked to Jack, her arms comically fluffed out to the sides from all the puffy layers.

"Like an Antergian farmer in the winter."

Niko let out a sharp laugh. She *did* look like an Antergian farmer in the winter! Though none existed anymore, of course. That realization cut much of the amusement short.

"Don't drive off without me," she attempted to joke, opening the door and stepping onto the frozen, rocky surface beyond. Just as quickly, she slammed it closed behind her, careful not to let too much heat out.

She immediately crouched low, battling to keep her stance against the sweeping wind. If she thought the cold was oppressive before, this was next level.

'Cold' wasn't even an appropriate word; this was more like the complete absence of heat. Her breaths, even shielded with the mask, were hitched and restrained. It felt less like breathing air and more like a futile struggle to pull in something hollow and empty.

Tightening every muscle in her body for warmth, she stepped around the edge of the vehicle and looked into the darkness above. Her peripheral vision was obscured by the ungainliness of the mask, but as long as she looked straight forward, it was clear enough to see. She scoured the Night sky toward where she knew Arhanda's sol to be, and...

It was not there.

She squinted, scanning deeper.

Still, nothing.

This couldn't be right. Where was it?

She let her search drift further and further along the horizon, when at last, her eye was drawn to the bright object. However, it was several degrees to the right from where she expected.

Blazes!

They *were* off course. Way off course.

How had they not known? They passed landmarks! Like that one craggy rock formation that looked like the skyline of Alashadar.

Or those four pools of frozen water on their right side a few k's back. And then there was that other strange, smooth circular rock. They passed them — all of them! — just as Viru-Mor had told them they should.

But the stars never lied. Niko had learned the history of navigation before the days of the Arrival, back on her own planet. Even with limited technology, ancient captains used the positions of stars to calculate trajectories to astounding levels of accuracy *and* precision. If they could do it, then surely she should be able to do the same now.

But they'd been traveling for over two days, and they were nearly a thousand kilometers from An-Tun Village. Who knew how much of that had been completed in error.

Niko looked up one more time, praying she was mistaken, though she already knew the truth.

They were lost.

20

Lost

NIKO struggled to breathe, the inhospitable cold invading her lungs as panic started to edge in. She needed to get inside. Now.

The howling wind forced her to stay low as she scrambled over to the door, heaving it open against the gale, finally tumbling into the vehicle, exhausted as if she had just completed a Field match.

"We're off course," she croaked.

Jack pulled her in and helped her to her feet as the questions rang out from across the cabin.

"What do you mean off course?"

"Are you certain?"

"We passed the landmarks…"

Niko tugged her mask off, breathing in the welcome, machine-conditioned air. A minute ago, she would've complained that it was freezing inside the rover, but after only a few seconds in the deep Night air, it felt like a sauna.

"I… the star I was tracking… it's a few degrees to the right from where I saw it. We must've drifted left somewhere."

"Are you serious? Can't we go back to those pools of frozen water or something?" Jack suggested. "We passed those not too long ago, just like they told us. We can't be that far off."

Hmmm, Niko thought. Jack was right. This was strange — very strange. They shouldn't be off by as much as she'd recorded. They just shouldn't...

"I'm sorry if I messed up," he added with a wince. "I didn't even notice us start to drift."

He obviously felt guilty because *he* was the one driving. It wasn't his fault, though. Niko knew it wasn't; she'd been sitting right next to him the whole time! As far as she had observed, they continued in that same straight line the entire time, just like they were supposed to.

"Wait a second," Callum said, tentativeness creeping into his gravelly voice.

All eyes looked to him.

"Are you sure about where that sol was supposed to be?"

Niko pondered his hesitancy for one second, then it dawned on her.

Ohhhhhh...

Her eyes widened in recognition of her own mistake. "You're right..."

Callum nodded, affording her a tight grin. "I admit it is difficult to get used to thinking in An-Terino mechanics."

Though she should be happy that this might mean they weren't lost after all, she became embarrassed of the error — one in astronomy calculations, of all things. Unlike cold-weather travel accommodations, astronomy *was* supposed to be her forte.

"I'm so sorry," she breathed, her lungs still burning from the brief jaunt outside. "This fifty-day year keeps throwing me off."

She *knew* An-Terino had a fifty-day year to the hour — it was how she knew where Arhanda's sol was in the first place. So why did she forget now, all of a sudden?

It must've been the cold. Or the stress. The Mara knew she had plenty of either of those to deal with...

"As it does with me," Riiz commiserated.

"Wait, so when was the last time you saw the star?" Jack asked.

"That's what I'm trying to remember," Niko replied, fingers dragging through her hair. "I think it was... well, last time I saw it directly in front of our path was fifty-seven hours ago. I think." She would've once been shocked at her own ability to recall that detail, but all the time spent with Kira-Tharn had her noticing small things, particularly in regards to time, for whatever reason. It was an An-

Mara thing. "Yes, I'm pretty sure. Fifty-seven hours."

It was surprising that it had been that long. That moment when she looked up at that sol — the one whose light she once bathed in daily — only felt like an hour or two ago, not over *two days* ago!

"I'll be right back," she declared, suddenly leaping up, tugging her mask back on and refastening her jacket. Without much by way of warning, she flung the door open and jumped back out into the Night.

"What the bla…!" The muffled shout from Jack was cut off as she threw all of her body into sealing the door shut. Those dramatic babies could deal with a little cold. *She* was the one who had to brave the *real* chill.

Although… she supposed she had no right to call them dramatic when her lungs seized once again, her body convulsing as she fought to draw breath. How could *anybody* live out here?!

As quickly as she could, she staggered over to the front of the vehicle — which, in theory, was oriented in the straight direction toward their destination — and made a semicircle with her hands, raising them in front of her face like a visor. She aligned the heel of her palms level to the base of her eyes and overlaid her makeshift sextant onto the Night sky above.

Where is it? Where is it? Where is it? she asked herself, trying not to let her haste spoil the quality of her already ramshackle mode of measurement.

In answer, a flickering glimmer of light speckled through the swirling clouds, just beyond her second knuckle. She quickly made a mental note on that knuckle, then rushed back inside before the cold enveloped her mind completely.

Even though she experienced the same sensation only minutes earlier, the rush of heat upon her entry shocked her system. It wasn't unpleasant, but it crashed into her as if it had real force, a displacement wave with tangible mass behind it. Or maybe that was just Jack hauling her inside, dragging her along the floor as Callum slammed the door shut.

"Blazes, girl!" Jack cried, his curly hair amusingly ruffled from the blast of wind. "Give us more warning next time!"

"Sorry," Niko squeaked with a half-grin, tearing her mask off once again.

"What was that about?!"

"I was measuring where the star was." She then started to think out loud, muttering to herself as she went through some basic calculations. "Three sixty divided by fifty is a little over seven." She supposed she should be more exact, so she divided thirty-six by five, and was left with the remainder of one, which would add two-tenths to the seven. "Seven point two. So, seven point two degrees per day, or about a degree every three and a half hours. A little less, maybe twenty minutes."

She verbalized her process some more, continuing. "Actually, it's exactly twenty minutes. Seven point two times three is twenty-one point six, which is different from twenty-four by two point four. Two point four is exactly one-third of seven point two. So twenty minutes, out of sixty for the hour."

She really didn't need to be that specific, especially because the sextant measurement with her hands was so rudimentary and imprecise, but she came to the conclusion that the sky would move by one degree every three hours and twenty minutes.

A wayward piece of paper and writing utensil presented themselves by her feet, probably blown from the craft's dash when she opened the door to the tempest outside, and she scooped them up in one fluid motion. She placed her hands into that semicircle formation onto the paper, then drew three dots: one where her fingertips met to show zero degrees, one where the star shone just beyond her second knuckle, and one where the center of her hand-circle would be.

She traced a rather lumpy circle and divided it into equal sections — first into thirds, then each of those thirds into sixths, then into twelfths, then into twenty-fourths. It wasn't perfect, but she had a pretty good estimate of the star's position.

Since it was just beyond the first line she drew, that meant it was a little more than fifteen degrees, but not much more. Maybe seventeen or eighteen. Definitely no more than twenty, assuming her impromptu measurements were reasonably accurate.

She looked up proudly, showing the others her work. They only stared back at her blankly.

"Well?" she asked.

Still, blank stares and no responses. *For blazes' sakes.*

"Look," she explained, "this is about seventeen degrees, and fifty-seven hours divided by three point three hours per degree is a little over seventeen degrees!"

"Phwoosh, you've sure gotten good at your mental math ever

since you ditched your Ut..." Jack remarked, wide eyed in admiration.

Niko sighed in exasperation. She *never* needed her Ut for the easy math, and couldn't fathom why most people did — though she supposed she'd always been celebrated as quick with mental calculations when she was younger. It was ironic, then, that she bristled when it came to learning actual math.

"But I don't really know what that means, to be honest," Jack added with a wince. "Is seventeen degrees good or not?"

"Yes!" she exclaimed, half annoyed that he didn't follow. He was smart — really smart — but only when he wanted to be, it seemed. "It means we're on track. That we aren't off course after all."

"That is good news," Riiz said. "We would do well to continue on our way, if we are to connect to our destination in a reasonable interval of time."

Straight and to the point. Such a typical An-Mara response...

"Yes, that is great news," Callum agreed. "And Riiz is right. We need to be on our way. He and I will take the helm. You two have been driving for a while. Go ahead and get some rest."

Rest sounded nice, and Jack clearly thought so, too — he had disappeared to the back before she could even blink. Niko turned to follow, but was stopped short by a strong hand on her shoulder.

"Niko." Callum dipped his head in genuine respect. "Thank you."

She returned the nod, but let a satisfied smile spread across her face as soon as she turned around. Callum wasn't one to give his sincere respect lightly, so this was a moment for her. She was still smiling even after she retired to the rear car to take that much needed nap.

That nap was short lived, though, because a loud knock sounded from the door. For extra effect, Jack was standing over her, shaking her to consciousness.

"What?!" she snarled. What could possibly warrant this jarring awakening??

"Wake up!" he shouted.

"Blazes, Jack... I'm up."

How long had she even been asleep?? It couldn't have been very long... It didn't feel like it, at least.

"Your presence is required in the front." Riiz's voice snapped her into attention. "We would request further measurements of the stars to verify our bearing."

Blazes, againnn?...

She pulled herself to her feet, then dragged her way to the front. She'd only been half listening when Callum then explained that they had to turn the vehicle in all manner of directions in order to traverse that mountain range they'd been expecting.

So that range did exist after all.

"And so you see, we are a little... *disoriented...* at the moment."

Blazes... What would they have done if she hadn't decided to come along on this excursion of theirs?

She didn't have too much time to complain before she bundled back up, shoving the hood over her ears as she kicked the door open into the Night. As quickly as possible, she found the star, mentally traced it onto her improvised sextant, then hustled back into the vehicle before the cold knifed into her brain.

Once inside, she performed those same, basic calculations yet again, pointing them in the correct direction. After that, she was free to return to her nap, although it only felt like a couple minutes had gone by before she and Jack were summoned for their turn at driving duties.

———————

Days three, four, and five were more of the same.

They were lost.

They weren't lost.

They were lost.

They weren't lost.

The mountain ranges really messed with their travel, but each time they lost their bearing, they were able to determine the correct heading afterward, thanks to Niko's makeshift navigation method. Thankfully, the others were receptive to her teachings on how to do the calculations, so she wasn't awakened from her naps every few hours.

Seriously, what would they have done without her, though? They should all be thanking the Mara she'd decided to come along, for all their sakes. They were a bunch of fools, if you asked her.

She had once looked up to all of them as invincible — the people in *charge*, mentors who could do no wrong. She still *did* look up to them, to a degree, but she also saw another side to them: one where they were little more than men-children. She'd been right all those years ago — boys never grew up.

The days had since settled down. All four of them were now convinced they were on course, though none made mention of just how far into the wilds of An-Terino they actually were. The unspoken truth that hung over everyone was that if they became lost — well and truly lost — there would be no going back. The chances of any sort of salvation at that point would be near zero. They were on their own, desperate to find this lost laboratory in the dead of Night, their only guiding light coming from that blazes sol that Arhanda clung to.

It was ironic that the star whose presence evoked so much sorrow in her heart would be the very same that provided them with hope and direction now. But even that hope had its limits, as that star was sinking lower and lower to the horizon each day. If they were forced to return emptyhanded, its light might not be visible toward the end of such a trip.

And there were no other stars. None that Niko could see now, anyway...

No, Niko promised herself. They *would* find this place, and they *would* find Kezane. There was no alternative.

She yawned, propping herself up against a wall, not quite sleepy enough to fall into slumber, but tired nonetheless.

"Can't sleep?" Jack asked, his swaying figure obscured by the shadows.

"I slept a little earlier," she replied. "The bumps woke me up. And now I was just thinking about that lab we're supposed to find."

"I hear you," Jack whistled. "I don't understand how anyone can live out here. It's so dull."

"Yeah," Niko agreed, although she didn't think dull was exactly the right word to describe this place. Harsh, inhospitable, severe, unforgiving... but not dull.

They had been surrounded by nothing except pitch darkness this entire trip, but a few days ago, the sky cleared just long enough for the light of the galaxies to illuminate the horizon.

Towering volcanoes, sprawling mountain ranges, frozen ponds, and strange ice formations dotted the landscape as far as she could see. In that fleeting moment, a one-time phenomenon that hadn't occurred again, she was able to drink in the true natural splendor of this world.

She hadn't expected to admire it so. And yet now, every time she closed her eyes, she could still see the beautiful, alien wilds of An-Terino.

"You okay?" Jack asked out of nowhere, his voice soft with compassion.

"I don't know," she said. Normally she would've Cinto-coated it, but she knew better than to lie to Jack. "You?"

"I don't know." He rubbed his palms together, gaze fixed on the floor. "We need to get out of this place."

She knew he wasn't only talking about the Night... he was talking about this world. "Yeah."

"I..." he started. "We haven't made much progress the last few months. That's why we're looking for Kezane now. We were beating our heads into a wall working for Shatter, looking for a way where they could get us out of here. We needed a break."

Was he making an excuse for abandoning her all this time?? Niko didn't respond. What was she to say? That she was grateful that he left her to survive this hellhole all alone this past year?

"I hope we find him, though," he continued. "I really think he can..."

"What happened to us, Jack?" she interrupted bluntly. "Why did you leave me alone for so long? In this place, of all places? We were *best* friends. And I was hoping something more. And you just *left* me."

There it was. She said it.

Normally, her face would've turned bright pink at the admission, but she had no more energy left to waste in chasing shadows. She needed conclusions.

Jack looked down and sighed. "I... I'm sorry. I do care about

243

you."

"But…" she said flatly, knowing there was a '*but*' coming.

He looked up at her, flecks of green visible through the reflections in his eyes. "*But*, it's complicated."

"It's really not."

"I…" he started, his voice tight with frustration. "My dad *needed* me. After my mother died — and after he thought he lost me back on Arhanda — I couldn't leave him to work on his own. And family stuff aside, he can't do all this work without me."

"I'm sorry…" Niko offered, her voice dropping low. She really was sorry. "But *I* needed you also, Jack. I know we're not family, but I needed you. I needed a friend. And not blazes Kira-Tharn, who I have to walk on eggshells around at all hours of the day. Living among the An-Mara… do you know what it was like not being able to laugh or smile for months on end??"

Jack didn't respond. He must've been embarrassed, and as well he should be.

"I know how heavy the weight of family is," Niko continued. "I lost *all* of mine. All of them. Gone. Forever. And now, I need something else. I need *someone* else."

In years past, Niko might've let the waterworks flow at this point. But she supposed her humanity had been ripped away from her along with her home on Arhanda, for she hadn't shed one tear in nearly five years.

She only stared ahead, emotionless, as Jack got up to sit next to her, draping his arm around her shoulders. By the will of the Nel-Mara, if only he'd done that months ago — she had needed that for so long! But she wasn't about to let him know how much she did, because he was such a blazes chum for ditching her!

"I was an idiot," he confessed.

Yes. Yes, he was.

"I couldn't leave my dad," he continued, "but I should've brought you along, or pushed harder to stay. Maybe from now on, you can join us."

Blazes! That wasn't what she was asking! This man!… *Aghhh!!* She could've pulled her hair out.

"Don't get me wrong. I love your dad, but I don't want to spend all my waking hours with Callum blazes Sehs," she said dryly. "And I wish you would stand up to him every now and then."

Jack removed his arm from her shoulders and looked

questioningly at her. He almost looked… *hurt*.

"You don't like my dad?"

"Blazes, Jack!" Niko threw her hands up in frustration. "I literally just said I *love* your dad. I only meant that you let him boss you around *way* too much nowadays. You never did during those years with the Fleetnesses. So what's different now?"

"Nothing's different," he protested. "He just knows what to do in like… every situation."

"Like not having a backup plan to help navigate through the damn Night wilds?" she countered sharply.

"I… I… I don't know!"

"He's not this all-powerful Nel-Mara, Jack. He's not even like this Kezane guy we're trying to find. I think you need to realize that *you* are just as capable as your dad. You just need to believe in yourself more. You don't need someone else ordering you around. The Jack I know and love is more than capable of making his own decisions in life."

"You… you *love* me?"

"Of course I do," she replied, smacking him on the back of his head, trying to play it off as cool. This time, though, the blood did rush to her face. Thank the Mara it was dark in this rear car. "If you think we don't share some special bond, with everything we went through together, then you're the biggest idiot in the sector, Jack Sehs."

That characteristic smile that once had her dead to the worlds spread across his face, visible even through the shadows. Blazes was he beautiful… She would admit that much, even if she was still furious with him.

"Yeah, I know," he said. "I just… I've never heard you say it before."

His persistent grin was enough to melt tungsten, and when he reached out to grasp her hand with his, she withered entirely.

In all of the blazes…

"Well, I've most definitely never heard *you* say it to me," she said crossly, pulling her hand away and scooting just far enough away to face him, his prominent features highlighted by the faded yellow lights of the vehicle.

"Yes I have!" he protested.

She shook her head. "Never once."

"I…" he started, eyebrows knitting. "Really?"

She shook her head again.

"Well, you know that I do."

"Do I?"

He shifted uncomfortably, opening his mouth to say something. Niko smiled inwardly at seeing him squirm. She shouldn't be so cruel, but the least he could do was actually tell her he loved her.

"How would you *not* know?" he rebutted.

"Well, maybe because you never *told* me. Then you up and left me alone to fester on this Mara-forsaken hellhole of a world, toiling away in the Rifts and fields day in and day out, without so much as a clue to where you were or what you were doing…"

Jack winced. It was harsh, yes, but it was the truth.

"You know I had to go undercover," he protested.

"I know."

"Then why are you being so…? Ugh!"

She felt bad for pressing him so hard right now. He was such a gentle soul, but it wasn't enough to make her relent. "Being so what?"

"Being so… frustrating!"

Ohhh, that little… "*I* am being frustrating?!"

"Yes! I'm here now, aren't I? And all you're doing is guilt tripping me for the past, which I can't control."

"And what's gonna happen once we're done with this little excursion into the Night? Are you going back undercover into the depths of Alashadar? Are you gonna leave me for another six months? A year?"

"I… I don't know," he stammered. "But I do know that I'm here now, and you're wasting all our time together to sit and yell at me."

"So this is my fault now?"

"I didn't say that!"

"It's what you're thinking."

"It's not what I'm thinking! If you knew what I was thinking you wouldn't be yelling at me!"

"What are you thinking, then?"

"I'm thinking that you're my best friend, and that I… I…"

Niko held her breath, heart hammering, waiting for his words to level her to the ground.

A sharp crack split the air.

The vehicle heaved to the side, rocking back and forth with

savage fury, hurling her into the wall.

Niko braced herself with one arm, then wedged her legs against a heavy box that slid toward her perilously, metal screeching against the floor like a ravening monster.

There was no time. Her legs were but blacksquash vines against the weight of the crate. It was going to crush her…

She slammed her eyes shut, waiting for the impact.

After a few timeless seconds had passed, though, she managed to crack one of her eyes open.

Thank the Mara — no pain, no death. She was still alive!

Somehow, the box had miraculously skidded to a complete halt. But what the blazes even happened?! She wriggled free from her pinned position, eyes sweeping the darkness around her.

Jack looked just as bewildered, but he helped her to her feet as they both lumbered into the front car. Callum already had a sound enhancer blaring into the distance.

"CEASE FIRE! CEASE FIRE! WE ARE HERE ON THE WISHES OF AN-TUN VILLAGE!"

CHAPTER TWENTY-ONE

21

Abomination

ANOTHER sharp crack lashed at the windows, sending the vehicle spinning into a violent fit yet again. What the actual blazes was going on?!

"CEASE FIRE! WE ARE FRIENDS!" Callum's unanswered pleas continued to ring out through the darkness.

Cease fire?? Were they being *fired* upon?!

Niko froze, flashes of dire memories cycling through her brain…

An-Mara prisoners being executed in front of her.

A disorienting firefight in the Northern Mists of Nevaly.

A race through an orbital station with Ajane blazes Solase.

These were what surfaced now. She had no survival instincts then, and others paid the price because of it. If anyone died here because of her own inaction…

No. That would not happen. Not this time.

There was nothing to see, though. Only an endless expanse of blackness. Who could possibly be attacking them?! And why??

"They didn't warn us we'd be blazes fired upon!" Jack hissed.

Riiz spoke through the enhancer this time. "HOLD YOUR FIRE! WE WERE DISPATCHED TO THIS LOCATION BY THE

ONES CALLED SOLOR-VEN AND VIRU-MOR. WE CARRY A REQUEST FOR HELP ON THEIR BEHALF. PLEASE REFRAIN FROM FURTHER ATTACK."

That seemed to do the trick, for they were throttled by no further shelling. Yet, at least.

"Did they buy it?" Niko asked, her voice wavering from the adrenaline now pumping through her body.

"I don't know," Callum answered. "I would assume so."

"I do not believe they mean us any harm," Riiz stated. "This was a contingency we should have entertained. From the information that we have been made aware of, there are valuable assets to be protected out here. It can be reasonably maintained that they would go to certain lengths to keep their research free from outside influence."

"Okay, well, what now?" Jack asked. "Can we try to drive a little further? Will they let us?"

"Our wheels are shot," Callum reported, a grim set to his jaw. He pointed to the status bar on the dash. "Completely shredded."

Well, great. Just great.

"How do we get out of here then?" Niko gasped.

"I do believe we are at their mercy," Riiz remarked, his voice steady and restrained. How was the man so blazes calm right now?!

"That we are," Callum affirmed.

"So we just sit here and wait? For what? For how long? What if they just leave us stranded out here?" Niko couldn't help it; the questions poured out of her mouth like a fountain.

"We have made them aware of our intentions," Riiz replied. "If these are the ones who are protectors of that lost laboratory, then they are sure to make contact momentarily."

He seemed *way* too calm for just having been fired upon. As did Callum. Was this their plan all along? Just keep driving into the Night until they were blazes *attacked*? Niko was already beginning to think her companions were unnecessarily foolhardy. If this was actually their plan, then they were nothing but certifiable idiots, the lot of them.

She plopped into the nearest seat, not bothering to hide her great annoyance, massaging her temples with her fingers. Blazes, her head hurt... She still hadn't completely recovered from her likely concussion the other week.

She supposed things could've been worse, though — she could

have been crushed by that box or shot by those assailants. But still, they weren't in a wonderful predicament, and the others were acting like this was just any other day.

Agghhhhh...!! She could have screamed.

A booming voice echoed from outside. "STANDBY FOR BOARDING."

It was as if a phantom had delivered the instructions; only darkness awaited outside the windows. But soon, a soft jolt rocked the vehicle as a metallic clang resounded through the frame.

"HOW MANY PERSONS ABOARD?" the enhanced voice demanded, its sound now seeming to resonate from all directions at once.

"FOUR," Callum responded through their own enhancer.

"GOOD. DO NOT BE ARMED. SHOW YOURSELVES ENTIRELY UPON SAID BOARDING. PLEASE OPEN THE DOOR."

Jack obeyed first, pulling it open slowly, keeping his hands visible all the while. Beyond the threshold was a short tunnel, much like those of the airlocks on spacecraft she'd ridden. At the end of that tunnel, a man stood crouched on one side, a weapon pointed straight at Niko and her friends.

To her credit, she didn't flinch, though her gut instinct begged her to duck and cover.

A stray thought hit her. Was this Kezane?! Could it be? Had they actually found him?

Who else would it be?

The man seemed dangerous, like a cave viper waiting in the shadows, ready to strike at any moment. Much like Callum, Ajane, or Riiz, the guy clearly possessed military training. The way he crouched, the way he balanced. Niko just knew.

The shadowy figure surveyed all four occupants thoroughly, but after he determined they weren't a threat, he relaxed.

It had to be him.

The vaunted Kezane. The one they pursued across the stars. The one that would supposedly save them from the Machine. The one that would deliver An-Tun Village from whatever harm was coming to them.

But it was only one person that stood at the end of the bridge. One mortal human. That's all. It was strange, then, to think that this man carried so much mythical intrigue, so much legendary expectation.

"Callum Sehs?" The hooded figure removed his headgear, revealing the grizzled appearance of a man somewhere in his forties, his matted brown hair exactly what Niko would've expected from someone who lived way the blazes out here in the Night.

"Galen?!" Callum exclaimed, surprise etched onto every corner of his distinguished face. The two men stepped toward each other in a friendly manner, embracing forearms in Meridian fashion.

Niko became confused.

Galen? Not Kezane!?

How did Callum know this guy? And if this wasn't Kezane, then where the blazes was he?

"I was not expecting to see you here," Callum said, clapping the man on the shoulder. "It has been far too long…"

"Indeed it has been."

"How is it…" Callum started, clearly lost for words. "What are you doing out here?!"

"Nevermind any of that now. I will tell you everything once we get you to our base, but you should come with me now. The cold sets in rather quickly out here." He then turned toward the others, bowing in apology. "I am sorry about the… misidentification. We have been on edge of late. And I am sorry about the condition of your vehicle. We will make whatever repairs you need in due time."

Callum nodded to his companions, and they followed this Galen guy into his own craft, which was identical to those others in that An-Tun Village docking bay — only the interior was *way* colder than their vehicle had been.

"Forgive me, I should have introduced myself properly. I am Galen Anstraes. I know Callum from long ago, when we were both in service to the Meridian Empire." He turned toward his long lost acquaintance. "Though it seems that both our fortunes have reversed course, for better or worse."

"That they have," Callum replied, an austere smirk tracing the lines of his sharp face. "Galen, this is my son, Jack. And this is Riiz Alke-Tani, previously of the An-Mara, and Niko Ryen, of Arhanda. We are all in exodus from that place, and have now been stuck here, trying to seek a way off."

"I see. Well, An-Terino is not easy to find passage from, but there are ways. Perhaps we can be of assistance to each other?"

"How so?" Callum asked, tilting his head curiously to the side.

251

"Well, my team has some research that might be vital to the Empire, but we are in… less than good graces with them, as you may have heard. We were looking for a capable courier to deliver it into the right hands."

"It depends on what you need delivered," Callum responded hesitantly. "Some of my company is in a compromised position in the eyes of the Empire, as well. This situation with Shatter, and of the world Arhanda, has created some complications."

"Hmmm," Galen mused. "Well, for now, let's get to the base. Then we can decide what to do."

"We seek the one called Kezane Pfase," Riiz spoke up. "We were hopeful that you might have information on his whereabouts. Or perhaps he is with you now?"

Galen offered only a blank stare. "We will discuss it all when we get back."

"Very well," Riiz agreed, following as Galen sealed the door behind them all.

"How close did we get?" Callum asked, a hint of amusement crossing his face. "To your laboratory?"

"Not far off," Galen replied. "I'm impressed. And this was all from directions from those fools at An-Tun?"

"Sort of." Callum gestured toward Niko. "If not for her, though, we would have been driving in circles until we slowly froze to death."

Well, he said it; not her.

It wasn't untrue in the slightest, but she wasn't about to go boasting about it to others. She smiled inwardly, then nodded politely to Galen, who shot a questioning look to Callum.

"She tracked a star and kept us pointed straight along the plains out here, like they told us. What they conveniently forgot to mention was that the mountain ranges would turn us around and around… So thank the Mara for Niko."

"They just pointed you in a direction from An-Tun and you just set off? Without any infrared sensors?" Galen looked at them like they were the biggest idiots in all of the worlds. Which they might've been…

"Oh, please. I don't want to hear it," Callum responded with narrowed eyes. "We made it here, didn't we?"

Galen whistled. "You're lucky, then. We keep this place hidden for a reason. Maybe we need to take extra precautions, if you can find this place by the most simple of directions from An-Tun, then nothing else to go by but, quite literally, a lucky star..."

"What is this place, anyway?" Jack asked. "What is it you keep here?"

Niko was pleased that he was asserting himself into the conversation without his dad's permission. Maybe he actually listened to her?

Galen looked back and forth between the four of them. "Do you not know?"

No one responded for a moment, until Callum lowered his voice. "So the stories are real?"

"They are."

"And you have *it*? Here?"

"A small, incomplete piece of it, yes."

"What is it then, exactly?" Callum asked hesitantly, creasing his brows. If Niko didn't know better, it sounded like he didn't wish to truly know the answer.

"An abomination."

"As bad as we feared?"

"Oh no," Galen replied softly, a sinister chuckle highlighting his cynicism. "Worse. Far, far worse."

———

The entire ride back to the base, Niko couldn't shake those ominous words.

Worse. Far, far worse.

What did that even mean?

She knew Callum and Riiz — and so many others — were so adamant that this so called Machine was some extraordinary threat, but she never really thought too hard about the specifics of *why*. Or *how*. Maybe part of her didn't want to.

But also, she never truly learned just *what* the Machine even was.

Yeah, yeah, she knew the basics... that it was some artificial intelligence sweeping through the galaxy unchecked, supposedly consuming civilizations by mass. But who controlled it? And what was their endgame? For stalwarts like Callum and Riiz to be so petrified of the thing, it must be someone bad.

Worse than bad, Galen had said. '*Far, far worse.*'

Niko forced the thoughts away, as she usually did when it came to the Machine. Something to worry about another day.

"Wait, you haven't left at *all*?!" Jack exclaimed. "Not even *once*?!"

Niko herself wasn't sure she'd heard correctly. She'd only been half listening, but... did Galen say he hadn't left this deep Night facility in *three years*??

How??

She would've gone insane if that was her. As it was, she wasn't entirely sure she remained mentally stable after only *one* year in Alashadar... and that was the most comfortable place on the planet! Granted, the slums of Alashadar were no paradise, but they were a far cry nicer than the blazes Night. She'd only been out here in the wilds for a week, and she was already yearning to be back in the An-Mara quarter.

"None of us," Galen confirmed. "Kezane is the only one who goes about. Travel through the Night is a heavy burden, one that I am grateful he takes upon himself."

"Indeed," Callum replied. "So it's you and... who else is part of your team?"

"The others... I don't think you'd know them," Galen said. "They're a lot younger. Closer to Kezane's age. You will meet them in a minute, once we get inside."

"How many of you are there?" Niko asked, now back in the conversation after redirecting her focus away from thoughts of the Machine.

"Just three of us. Four with Kezane."

Four. Four people. Alone. For *three years*. As difficult as travel through the Night was, at least Kezane could go back and forth from the city. What a tragic existence for the rest of them. And to think she once lamented her own lonely misfortunes...

"Speaking of the man, do you truly have no word as to where he's gone?" Callum asked.

Galen shook his head. "I told you everything I know. I wish I knew more."

"You say that he is one to seek knowledge regarding the mechanics of the Machine; would it not be possible, then, that he is back at his previous laboratory in Oldcity?" Riiz asked.

Of everyone, Riiz was the one most intent on seeking Kezane. He had been for years. He must be utterly disappointed to learn that this entire journey to find the man had been in vain.

Well, not completely in vain, Niko supposed. They *did* find his laboratory *and* his team.

"From what Kezane told me, that place is gone. Ransacked. Destroyed. Shamefully typical Oldcity happenings, I'm afraid. I do not know how much material Kezane saved, other than what little he brought back here."

"If our chances at learning of ways to defeat the Machine were jeopardized by petty underworld wars…" Callum muttered, trailing off.

"Not to worry, we have most everything we need to study it here," Galen said. "Our main problem now is dealing with the scope of it all."

"What do you mean by that?" Callum asked, bracing himself as the craft lurched to a standstill.

The airlock, or whatever the gangway thing was called, hummed for a few seconds, then thudded as it made contact with what Niko assumed was the entrance to this hideaway that everyone had been making so much fuss about.

"Follow me and I'll tell you everything." Galen then turned and walked inside.

"These are my companions." Galen introduced two women, both several years older than Niko, but not old by any means. Perhaps around Kira-Tharn's age. "Michele Aragase and Noralie Mose."

"I'm Niko Ryen." She didn't wait for Callum or the others to introduce her this time. She was frankly tired of being an addendum to the conversations of others, after she played little to no role at all in the dealings at An-Tun Village. She wasn't a kid anymore. "This is Jack, and Callum, and Riiz."

"Well met," the women responded in tandem. They were spitting images of what she knew to be Meridians, with the dark hair and eyes, sharp features and all. They looked so alike that Niko thought they could've passed for sisters.

"From what I understand, Niko is the reason they even made it out here at all," Galen said, shooting a grin toward Callum. "Apparently, she used nothing more than a star and a makeshift sextant to find our location. Very resourceful, if I may say so."

"She is," Callum admitted. His tone was so neutral that Niko couldn't tell if he felt pride in her abilities, or shame over the lack of his own.

Niko inclined her head toward Galen, picking her chin up confidently. "So, it's only the three of you here?"

"It is," Noralie responded.

"Yes, since our fourth has been gone for quite some time," Michele added.

Riiz spoke up, clearly doing his very best to hide the bitter disappointment from his voice. "The individuals at An-Tun Village seemed exceptionally desperate for us to deliver word to the one called Kezane. They are rather worried they will be discovered by ones they do not wish to be discovered by."

"They've always been worried about that." Galen muttered. He wrinkled his eyebrows in thought. "But just how desperate do you mean?"

"*Desperate*." Callum emphasized the word, eyes widened for extra effect.

"Hmmm. Did they say what changed?"

"We were installing hardware at their diversion spike at one of the reservoirs," Niko explained. "Then we saw remote surveillance devices. They said those hadn't been there before."

"*Remote surveillance devices*? Are you certain?" Michele Aragase's words were uttered with a barely concealed tinge of disgust. She, Noralie, and Galen all exchanged glances that had surprise and alarm written all over. "Surely you are mistaken?"

"There is no mistake," Callum answered, shaking his head. "Which leads to another issue. I've been working undercover for decades, and I've seen a number of alarming trends. Not only surveillance by *Meridian* entities, but meddling and power grabs everywhere, all of which go completely against the heart and soul of our society. And I have *proof* that Shatter was behind interference on the world of Arhanda."

Galen whistled, his voice dropping to a low murmur. "I have

only heard whispers of what transpired there. But all the rest is what Kezane has feared for some time. He claims that is why we were sent on that suicide mission in the first place. He always maintained that Silvane wanted him out of the way for what he knew."

"That may very well be," Callum noted. "And I'm afraid that's not all. Shatter's presence is also increasing here on An-Terino. Considerably. And they aren't shy about revealing their Meridian connection."

"Yes, Kezane is well aware of that." Galen waved his hand, as if the matter were under control. "An unfortunate development, to be sure."

"For what reason the Empire could possibly have for wanting this place under its control, I have no idea," Noralie Mose muttered. "The planet is a hellhole."

Niko didn't disagree with that assessment.

"The cheap solar power generation in the Daylight is attractive," Callum suggested. "Shatter has been building a number of harvesting facilities out there, all attached to Lanthanide refineries."

"Yes," Galen partially agreed, "but I have a difficult time understanding how such rudimentary power generation offsets the energy of the batteries that allowed them to travel here in the first place."

"Well, you'd be depressed to learn that rational extrasolar policy is no longer a concern of theirs," Callum grumbled. He then peered at Galen, as if digging holes into his eyes. "How long has it been since you've been back?"

"Too long, I imagine."

"How long?"

Noralie answered. "Thirteen years."

"Plus some," Michele added.

"Well," Callum hummed. "I hate to bring the news to you, but much has changed in the years after your departure. I've only been nine years away, and even then, society has... shifted."

Galen, Noralie, and Michele all looked at each other sideways.

"Kezane surmised as much," Galen eventually said. "What has changed exactly?"

"Priorities. Tradition. The common good. Everything."

"So we're... what, exactly? Tying to colonize systems like this?"

"This and beyond."

Callum then looked at Riiz, sighing as he did. Riiz held his stare calmly, but after a second, the usually unflappable An-Mara let his stoic countenance drop.

"Do you mean to tell me, Callum Sehs, that the Meridians are intent on expanding their influence to the worlds of the An-Mara?" Riiz asked. "To *Aktun*?"

"I have reason to believe that's the long game," he answered, pursing his lips into a sympathetic half-smile for Riiz. "And the worst part is, the masses *want* it. Well and truly *want* it. I'm sorry to say there was an increasingly significant anti-An-Mara sentiment when last I was there."

The room was silent for a few moments, before Galen spoke up.

"I was hesitant to believe it myself, but this is what Kezane has alluded to for years. He hasn't been back to the Capital system, of course, but you are well aware of his foresight. He finds a way to *know* things."

Callum nodded. "Then you must be aware that it's optics and narratives gone to the extreme. The Waxing Crescent is more alive than I've ever seen in my lifetime, to be sure."

Niko didn't know what that had to do with anything. The only thing she knew about the Waxing Crescent was that it was the hand symbol everyone flashed to each other. All the kids on Arhanda who thought they were way cooler than they actually were, at least. Like blazes Riesen, and Brandon, and…

None of that mattered. What she *did* know was how proud the An-Mara were of their homeworld. If the Meridians encroached onto An-Mara territory, there would be blazes to pay. Nevermind that the Meridian Empire was far more powerful than the An-Mara, or so she'd been told.

"I've always thought that the Waxing Crescent can go to the Hole," Noralie chimed. "I refuse to believe the citizens would fall for such an extreme ruse."

"Well," Callum droned, "you better believe it. They're selling it well. Last I was there, way too many of the most popular socialites and dignitaries were waving the flag. It's a strange phenomenon. They were even talking about *mining* on Trevi Nali."

"Hah!" Michele crowed. "Mining? On *Trevi Nali*?!"

"A humorous thought, but I don't see that ever actually

happening," Galen said, as if willing it to be so.

"Trust me," Callum muttered, "I would normally say the same thing. But even nine years ago, it was as if our people were slowly losing the ability to think rationally. And judging from the increasing Meridian and Shatter presence here on An-Terino, I would bet all my Terion that the Waxing Crescent is now mainstream policy."

"Well." Galen slumped heavily into his chair. "That is not welcome news."

He sat pensively for a few seconds before shifting to a more productive tone.

"But there is nothing to be done about any of that now. Kezane has given us plenty of tasks to keep us occupied by... other concerns."

"Like the Machine?" Maybe it was blunt of Niko to say it outright, but she thought it ridiculous that people always spoke in hushed voices about the thing.

"Yes," Galen replied. "*That*."

"May we have the opportunity to see it?" Riiz asked. "I would inspect what sample you possess, if I would be permitted the occasion. And I would be very interested to learn of its technical mechanisms of function."

"You are so eager?"

"I'd be interested too," Jack said enthusiastically.

Of course he was, Niko thought, nearly rolling her eyes. Although, Niko had to admit she was slightly intrigued, also. After all, it would be a shame to come all the way out here for absolutely nothing. Maybe they could learn *something*, even if they didn't achieve their primary goal of locating the enigma that was Kezane.

"Very well," Galen said. "We can show you now, if you like?"

"You would accompany us at this very moment?" Riiz asked surprisedly.

"If it's your wish."

Riiz looked around at Niko and the others, who only offered him tentative shrugs.

"We would be most appreciative, then," he decided.

Galen nodded and slowly stood to his feet, gesturing for the whole party to follow him down a well-lit, spiraling hallway. A few side rooms peeked out from the hall on the way down, but no windows offered glimpses into any of them; only thick, blank concrete walls lined the edges. This place was more austere than the An-Mara Mainquarters she once visited.

And as she descended further and further, the pit of her stomach dropped without warning.

Coldbumps pocked her skin, those little, tiny hairs on her arms standing on end as… *something*… grew thick around her. Even her breath seemed to hitch as if she were plunged into the sea on a cold Green Coast morning. She resorted to rubbing her arms, closing her eyes, and grinding her teeth to rein in some of her misplaced anxiety.

Even still, her insides rose into her throat — not dissimilar to that feeling when she rode the railcoaster in the heart of NewCen last week — except this was no sensation of exhilaration.

This was *dread*.

What the blazes was going on?

She was probably only anxious because of everything she'd ever heard about this Machine — all those stories and the existential horror they evoked.

But… *No*.

This was her gut instinct, and she should listen to it. She'd just learned that valuable lesson last week, after losing all her friends' Terion credit on a whim devoid of any such instinct.

But could she really trust those feelings anymore? Couldn't this just be her imagination malfunctioning? That would be a much more plausible scenario…

The further down the hallway she spiraled, however, the greater her trepidation grew. It was as if a thousand voices were telling her to turn around, this descent into madness the farthest thing from a worthwhile endeavor. No, unfortunately, this gut feeling was not imagined.

Get away, get away, get away…

But she didn't listen. It would be fine; she was just being paranoid. Kezane and his cohorts surely had the matter under control…

The hallway corkscrewed down, and down, and down… until finally it leveled out, revealing a rounded concrete wall, and nothing else.

Niko looked around at her friends. Were they feeling the same anxiety that she was? Perhaps only Callum, whose jaw was set just a little tighter than normal.

Riiz looked calm as ever, and if Jack was feeling uneasy, he didn't show it; he was like an excited puppy dog going to the playpen. She wished she could carry his carefree demeanor through life. Things would be way more fun all the time.

But as it was, her own unease would not go away; instead it only continued to rise...

And rise...

And rise...

Wordlessly, Michele Aragase walked over to a panel on the side of the wall, one that escaped Niko's notice earlier. She tapped some sequence of code, and upon the press of a final button, the entire room upon which they stood turned like a carousel.

Niko steadied herself through the slow rotation, and when it finally jerked to a stop, she relaxed her posture. Though, 'relaxed' was probably not the word to describe what she was feeling...

Her thoughts raced in a million different directions, too scattered to focus on any one thing at all. The panic threatened to overtake her, overflowing from the precipice as once happened years ago, back in Amalkyne, on Arhanda. What in the worlds was happening?!

Please no... she begged. *Please not again...*

That experience had been awful... But even then, the anxiety had never been pressed so deeply inside her, its grip so all-encompassing. This was something different. Something more. Something primal.

What manner of abomination was this!? What in all the blazes could possibly manifest such complete dread so randomly?

Niko finally scraped enough concentration together to focus her eyes and actually see what was in front of her, and if she had to be honest, she was a little underwhelmed. She expected some sinister formation, something slithering or writhing or pulsating. Something *alive*.

Instead, what she observed was a small metallic chunk, barely more noteworthy than a common rock, sitting on top of a table with some sort of technical apparatus set up around it. If it had been on the ground in the dirt, she would've passed by without a second thought.

"Behold," Galen announced with dramatic flair, gesturing toward the rock. "The Machine."

This is what had everyone she knew spooked to the max?! *This* is what had her own stomach tying itself into knots?

"It looks... like nothing," Jack noted.

"It doesn't need to look like anything," Galen explained. "The damned thing is in a stable formation, ever resisting our own attempts at subjugating it."

"How do you control it?" Niko asked, curiosity taking over. If it was as she had learned, it was an artificial intelligence, a machine that could function like a human brain, only quicker and more ruthless, with thought processes rivaling advanced civilizations. Possibly *more* advanced, considering they all thought it to be some huge threat.

"This reinforced bunker, of course," Galen stated. "And in addition, we keep it atop a superconductor in temperatures near zero K, as you might expect."

Truthfully, she didn't know what to expect. Although, she supposed it made sense, from what she remembered of her lessons in physics from Riiz. At zero K, there would be practically no vibrations of particles or heat energy, so it would be functionally frozen, physically and chemically.

"Fortunately," he added, "we think it finds the effort to escape would not be a worthwhile use of resources. And since it has no access to any sufficient ionization energy, it is stuck with its current elemental makeup."

"Which is?" Callum asked.

"Primarily carbon alloys, some silicon, with very clever arrangements of heavier elements, particularly in the Lanthanides. That was the first thing Kezane analyzed when we isolated the thing."

"Do I even want to know how you managed to come by this?"

"Probably not." Galen let out a soft chuckle that didn't quite meet his eyes.

"Can we recreate any part of it to combat itself?"

"In theory, possibly. But the thing is, this is only the tiniest fraction of what the Machine as a whole possesses. Tinier than tiniest. Less than a grain of sand compared to all of the plains of An-

Terino combined.

"And with the amount of energy required to keep such a small sample confined... Replicating it for our benefit wouldn't be practical. Not in centuries. Not even in millennia. Tens of millennia, maybe. And if you are to believe Kezane, we only have a matter of years."

He briefly trailed off, before continuing in a lower voice.

"We *saw* it, Callum... We saw it in action. It killed everyone. Everyone besides us four." Galen looked down and shook his head. "That's how we even have this sample at all. It shot Kezane with... *something*. With itself, I suppose. It could have killed him, but it chose instead to inject itself into his flesh, keen to join us en-route back to civilization."

As if a chill coursed through the room, Niko and the others rubbed their arms subconsciously.

"So whatever this thing is, it has deeper plans. As I said before, the scope of it is the problem."

"Is there nothing to be done?" Niko asked.

"Oh believe me, we are trying," Galen defended. "We just have very little idea of what we're dealing with."

For the first time, Niko noticed how *tired* he actually looked. She felt guilty for not seeing it before. This man and his companions were on a crusade that probably drained the very essence of life from them. And they were doing it willingly, with no hope for glory or recognition, in the middle of the Night on some forgotten corner of the sector.

She suppressed the feeling of ever-persistent dread just long enough to acknowledge an ounce of admiration for these brave souls. They were better people than she was, that was for sure. Here she had some huge threat to the galaxy before her, and all she wanted to do was flee. Hide. Crawl back into her own bed and pretend life was normal again.

"Oh no! I didn't mean that you weren't," she backpedaled. "I just meant... there's gotta be another way, right?"

"To that end is where we devote our energies," Galen said. "And it's why I expect Kezane has been gone for some time. He has been trying a different angle. One of understanding this abomination's operational nature, and answers gleaned from tinkering into it."

"What sort of answers?"

"Anything. Everything. I am not certain, to be honest. Kezane knows infinitely more about this than any of us. Noralie, Michele, and I are really only qualified to run tasks that he has already set up." Galen narrowed his eyes. "Nor would we dare to do anything more. Confined or no, I do not trust this thing. Being this close to it every day makes my skin crawl."

She couldn't fault him for that, if he felt even a fraction of her own disturbance.

Suddenly, an idea sparked inside Niko.

"What about Kyler and Cryo?" she asked, turning toward her companions, then back to Galen. "We have friends that can take a look at the code this thing uses. Or create their own code to find answers within."

"I don't think that's how it works," Galen responded hesitantly. "It's not like our machines. It doesn't operate on lines and lines of code. This thing is sentient. It is more like a brain, with massive parallelism and adaptability."

"On the contrary," Riiz interjected, "with a proper application interface, anything can be reduced to lines of code. At the basic level, tasks and priorities can be organized. The ones that Niko spoke of — Kyler and Cryo — have been attempting to create such an interface for a project they call the Infinity Machine. They may be the perfect candidates to assist you with your project."

"Well, we can always use more help," Galen admitted. "But how well do you know these people you speak of?"

"They are with us," Callum stated. "We all traveled to An-Terino together, from the destroyed world of Arhanda. They live in Alashadar, in the Machine Row. And I believe Niko and Riiz may be on to something with them. They are the best tinkerers I know. Riiz here, in case you hadn't guessed, is also a tinkerer."

Galen cocked a single eyebrow in interest.

"I do know the basic ways of the machine tinkerers," Riiz said humbly, "but I concur with the one called Callum Sehs. The ones called Kyler Pierson and Cryo Siriar are significantly more proficient than myself at such practices."

"It sounds like we'd be fortunate to be graced with their presence. If we outfit your travel arrangements with enough fuel, would you be able to return with your friends? I know Kezane would be most grateful for the extra help. Assuming he decides to come back..." Galen trailed off.

"They are very busy with their own projects," Riiz said, "but we would certainly ask."

"Do you mean for us to leave so soon?" Jack asked. "We only just arrived after a week spent out in the Night."

Niko didn't disagree with him. She was sick and tired of sitting cooped up in that tiny, freezing vehicle for days on end, the only respites coming from bio breaks that were even more unpleasant than being inside.

"You can rest here for as long as you need, but it would be prudent for you to depart soon, if An-Tun is awaiting your return."

"Speaking of that matter," Callum said, "what response should we deliver? They were very keen on us returning with Kezane."

"We do not have the resources to deliver them any assistance at the moment, but tell them if Kezane shows up anytime soon, we will direct him to their aid. If I know them, that will serve to soothe their worries." Galen shook his head, then muttered nearly inaudibly, "Spineless wretches."

Noralie seemed to hear Galen's remark and defended the villagers. "Most of them have no say in the matter. And they are *trying*, what with the diversion spikes and everything."

"Yes, but what have they ever given us?" Michele asked. "Compared to what we do for them every single week…"

Suddenly, a screeching siren blared, red lights flashing through the hall. Niko nearly jumped onto the ceiling.

What the blazes!?

The Machine…? Was it escaping? *Could* it even escape?

Galen hissed what must've been a Meridian curse she didn't know, then shouted to Noralie and Michele.

"Check the console!"

Both of them did just that, the blood draining from their faces as they shouted their assessments back to Galen.

"Two craft approaching!"

"And airborne. They're moving way too quickly for ground vehicles!…"

So not the Machine.

Niko didn't know if that was good or bad, though. The relief she should've felt never materialized. Whoever was approaching, it didn't sound like a good thing. Galen let out that same curse from before, then brushed past Niko and her friends, not bothering to avoid nearly knocking her over.

"Who is it?" Callum demanded.

"I don't know," Galen replied, moving to the console where Noralie and Michele hovered. He performed a series of swipes, then let out another single-syllable curse she was unfamiliar with.

"They come from the direction of An-Tun," Michele informed him. "But it's none of them."

"Yes, I see that." Galen nodded, examining the screens.

"Are we compromised?!" Noralie asked urgently.

"I believe we have to be prepared for that possibility," he said grimly.

"Who is it?" Callum demanded again, even more firmly this time.

Blazes, the man was intimidating when he wanted to be. Jack must've inherited his mother's traits, because Niko couldn't imagine him being so scary in a million years.

"Shatter."

The word hit Niko like a Rift-borer to the chest. What the blazes was *Shatter* doing out here? There was no way they were tracked, was there?

"Is there any chance to hide?" Callum asked.

Galen shook his head. "Not entirely. We can seal off this lower level here, but they most definitely know the base is here already."

"Well, I can't allow them to see Jack and I out here. And we definitely can't be seen with *you*," Callum warned. "That would be a tricky situation, since we are undercover in their employ. This sort of fraternization is strictly prohibited."

"What do we do?" Jack asked, concern now affixed onto his voice, also.

"I have an idea," Galen said. "You stay down here and we seal you off on a timer. They won't know anything is down here, trust me. This wall will shield this room from any of their scans. I'll go and deal with them."

"I go with you, Anstraes," Michele said.

Noralie chimed in, as well. "As do I."

Galen hesitated, but eventually nodded. "Very well. I don't like the prospects of Shatter coming here, but I think we can redirect them. As long as they don't recognize us…"

Noralie and Michele both winced.

Just how likely was it that they'd be recognized? Niko figured that if they associated with this Kezane guy, it stood to reason that perhaps they were also famous back where they came from.

"Let *me* deal with them," she offered, the idea suddenly popping into her head. "If there's even a chance that all of you would be noticed, then let me and Riiz go up top."

"Out of the question," Callum said definitively.

"Callum's right," Galen added. "You do not know the inner workings of this base, and they will be sure to question you quite thoroughly."

She knew all too well just how *thorough* their questioning could be, after what happened to poor Fellen-Sor.

"Nor are they particularly known to treat An-Mara well. Let Galen deal with this one." Callum shook his head at Niko, letting her know that it was *not* up for debate.

"All of you stay here. It is for the best," Galen decreed. "And as much as I don't want to hasten farewells, we must seal you off now. They are nearly upon us."

"How long do we stay down here, though?!" Niko asked.

"The timer is set for two days. But hopefully we can convince them to be gone in a matter of minutes."

Two days!?

"And if you can't?" she asked skeptically.

"Then you wait two days."

"Niko." Callum said her name sternly, a grave expression carved onto his hard face. "Now is not the time to argue."

Oh, he did not *just speak to me like a kid...*

Niko fumed. That chum could talk down to Jack as much as Jack's heart would desire, but he would *not* order *her* around like she was some common child. If it weren't for her, he would be freezing his ass off, lost and defeated in the middle of the Night.

'Not the time to argue'... I'll show him arguing!...

"Trust me, it is best this way," Galen interrupted before she could say something snarky in retort. A dark smile crept over the man's face as he attempted to lighten the mood with a joke. "Unless you are squeamish about being locked in a room with the damned Machine."

The joke did not land in the slightest, because being locked in here with the blazes Machine sounded even worse than dealing with Shatter.

"Just please don't... *tamper* with it," he added, a more serious tone straining his voice this time. "Not in any way. We already have enough issues to deal with."

As frustrated as she was, he didn't have to tell her twice. She planned on staying as far away from that abomination as possible.

"We really must seal you off now," Galen announced again, more urgently this time. "The room is completely shielded from any radiation, so you'll be undetectable. But you also won't be able to send out any transmissions. If you don't hear from us before the unsealing, tread carefully. I would say find Kezane, but it seems he does not wish to be found at the moment. Fare well."

"Fare well," Callum replied, gripping forearms with Galen before the latter walked away, gliding up the spiraling hallway.

With that parting, the room rotated once more. This time, however, to Niko's eternal dread, they were on the other side of the stone wall when it finally clicked into place.

"So what do we do?" she asked disbelievingly. "Just sit and wait?"

Callum's voice was as unyielding as the stone around them. "Yes, we sit and wait."

CHAPTER TWENTY-TWO

22

Sit and Wait

NIKO could hear nothing, feel nothing, sense nothing, beyond the concrete wall that encased them all. They were well and truly sealed off, for better or worse.

Worse, probably, since the only other thing keeping them company in this blazes state of isolation was that amorphous piece of the damned Machine.

The Machine.

It was strange that something that elicited so many haunted whispers, so much existential dread, was something so unassuming. She had never really imagined what it looked like, but at the very least she anticipated something overtly formidable, whatever that might look like.

Yet this thing was just a... *rock*. Sitting on a table. There was nothing sinister about it at surface level.

But she knew it was more than that. *Felt* it was more than that. She hadn't honed these senses in years, of course, but she didn't need to. This thing emanated with power and... *wrongness*.

And she obviously wasn't misreading those feelings, as this *rock* was something Kezane and the others felt the need to spend inordinate amounts of energy to keep in thermal confinement.

"How do they have enough power out here to make something like this?" she asked Riiz, referring to the contraption that kept the Machine in suspension.

"I do not know," he responded. "I suspect that we may find the answer to that query if we investigate the facility further."

"How?" she asked. "We're stuck in here."

"Yes, but when the ones called Galen Anstraes, Noralie Mose, and Michele Aragase retrieve us, we can propose such an endeavor to them then."

"If they come back, they could just tell us themselves," Niko suggested dryly. "I doubt they want us snooping around this place."

Riiz paused. "I do suppose that would be the more reasonable approach."

"Are we really supposed to sit and wait here for two days?" Jack asked, returning to the group after unsuccessfully scouring the room for any options of escape.

"What's two more days on top of the week and a half we've been gone?" Niko let out a sharp breath through ballooned cheeks.

"We only have to wait that long if they aren't successful in dealing with Shatter out there," Callum said.

"I'm not hoping for a miracle," Niko grumbled.

Jack sighed. "Nor am I."

"What will Shatter do with them?" she asked, suddenly worried for their well-being.

"Well, for one," Callum replied, "they're going to be interrogated. If they don't get the answers they want right away, they'll probably transfer them to either the Frying Pan or their stronghold in Machine Row.

"Shatter will be curious as to how they're able to survive all the way out here. Like how they get enough power to be self-sufficient. And how they get their food and water," he continued. "They will also undoubtedly press them about An-Tun Village, if they haven't already wiped that place from the face of An-Terino…"

"Wait," Niko started. "You're serious?! They'd do that?"

Shatter was a bunch of worthless chums, that much was for sure. But there was no way they would actually wipe an entire village out, right? Surely that was against some sort of law or… something?

"If they were stealing from Shatter's resources, they would absolutely receive no mercy."

The pit in her stomach never entirely vanished, being in such close proximity with the Machine and all, but it somehow managed to get worse after thinking of what Shatter would do to the citizens of An-Tun Village. People like Fellen-Sor fled there to *get away* from that sort of treatment by Shatter and the EC's.

It was not right, but as Anda had told her, there truly was no justice on this planet.

The group of four now sat with their backs along the wall, staring down at the floor, trying not to think of the villagers' fate.

Niko's hands balled into fists. Why in the blazes couldn't she go anywhere without something going drastically wrong?!

It was one thing after another, an endless cycle of despair...

It started with her planet and home being destroyed. All of her family and most of her friends gone. Lost forever. Then, after she somehow managed to survive, she spent some of the prime years of her life cooped up on a damned spacecraft, only to wind up in a place even worse. Stuck, on An-Terino, laboring her life away. There was no freedom, no future — just work, work, and more work.

And just when she thought she may have found a way off the planet, fortune struck her down. Worse, the trust she had worked so hard to gain from her friends was shattered. There was no way they didn't hate her... and she wouldn't blame them for it.

Now, here she was, stuck in a bunker with three dumbchums, thousands of kilometers into the middle of the Night, staring down the throat of the damn Machine. The *Machine*!

Blazes!

This couldn't have been scripted any worse. Even if they managed to get out of here when the timer expired, it was likely that Shatter had whisked Galen, Noralie, and Michele away to some insidious manner of prison.

The Frying Pan. That's what Callum had called it. Jack mentioned that place, too, and it didn't sound great. A prison was bad enough, but a labor colony in the Daylight...

Niko's shudder was only masked by the simultaneous growling of her stomach. Blazes, did they even have any food with them? She was starving!

Jack seemed to know exactly what she was thinking, digging into his pocket and pulling out a protein snack, tossing it to her. Bless his heart.

"Thanks."

"Do we have any water?" Jack asked no one in particular.

"I don't." Niko grimaced, wasting no time to inhale the snack he gave her.

"Nor do I," Callum replied.

"We can survive easily for two days without any water," Riiz assured them. "We all hydrated not long ago."

Everyone nodded, but Niko suddenly wished she had more. She licked her lips, as if savoring every ounce of moisture.

Blazes! She shouldn't have just eaten that salty snack...

She looked up to the table where that Mara-forsaken rock sat suspended, and...

Was that... *water*?

She jerked her body upright, standing up to get a closer look.

Blazes! It *was* water. Tiny droplets of condensation clung to the exterior of the rock. Of course there could be condensation on such a cold object, but only if the ambient temperature was much higher. But the containment structure was encasing a superconductor at near zero K. If condensation was suddenly appearing now...

Did that mean there was a breach in the containment? Niko started to panic, looking top to bottom, side to side, for any leaks, but she found nothing. Nothing whatsoever had changed from before. What manner of monstrosity was this thing, then, in order to manipulate such effects?? Or was it her mind playing tricks on her?

"Is that..." Jack started.

"Get away!" Callum warned, rocketing upright and grabbing her by the wrist.

Oh, please... As if she were foolish enough to fall for an illusion...

"I know!" she snapped, yanking her wrist free. "I'm not stupid. I'm just looking."

"How is this possible?" Jack asked hoarsely. "Can it *hear* us?"

"I don't know," Niko said.

"They were right to keep this thing confined," Callum whispered, the color drained from his face.

"I do believe it harbors some form of self-preservation," Riiz suggested. "It must have conjectured that if it offers us that which we desire, maybe we would reciprocate."

"And what would *it* desire in return?" Niko asked.

No one responded.

A thousand thoughts whirred through Niko's mind, none of

them good. Finally, after a minute of silence passed, Callum spoke.

"We do not go near it. We do not even look at it. Ignore it completely. Everyone understand?"

Even Niko found herself nodding. She didn't care that Callum was being domineering. She understood.

"Good. Now I suggest we all relax. Our bodies will use far less energy if we do."

"Phwoosh," Jack exhaled. "That's easier said than done. Especially in front of this... *thing.*"

Niko agreed — her apprehension was burning a hole straight through her chest! How could she possibly *relax* right now?

"I find maintaining conversation is a good tool of distraction," Riiz offered.

"An An-Mara who wants conversation..." Jack hummed, his smile returning, if only a corner of it. "That *is* a good distraction!"

Niko would've laughed, but she was feeling far too subdued. The combination of hunger and anxiety — and guilt, she supposed, for letting Galen and the others take the fall with Shatter — all gnawed at her stomach. She wished she was back in those liquid suspension pods during the Fleetnesses, where she could choose how long to sleep for.

Two days, at least, she fantasized.

"I want to know if this thing can even move, though," Jack considered, glancing toward the table in the center of the chamber.

"Jack!" Callum growled. "Enough!"

"I'm just curious is all..."

"IGNORE IT!" Callum's gaze held no father's love, only daggers.

Jack looked down meekly. If he had a tail, it would've been between his legs. Callum was probably right, but...

For the love of the Mara, Jack, please grow a frame.

It was past time he treated himself like an adult in Callum's presence, not some small child who submitted to anything and everything. She hated to admit it, but he became less and less attractive every time he did this. She still loved him dearly, and she still *was* attracted to him, obviously, but...

She blew her breath out sharply, not caring if she drew stares.

"I, too, am curious about the inner workings of the Machine, Jack Sehs," Riiz commiserated, "but the one called Callum Sehs expresses reason. We do not know what manipulations this entity employs, so it is best we follow that advice and give it no attention at the present moment."

Jack, now beaten down, continued to look at the floor, only raising his eyebrows for a nod in response.

Blazes, why did the guy have such trouble standing up for himself?

It was an absolutely atrocious thought, but Niko wondered if Jack wouldn't have been better off if Callum had never joined them in the days before they left Arhanda. He would definitely have had more time to blossom and grow on his own.

Though, she knew the truth of the matter — had Callum not returned, Niko herself would've been killed in that An-Mara incursion upon Nevaly.

Furthermore, he provided much needed leadership and direction in the days after they lost Ajane. And she *did* feel comfortable with him around when things went awry, which happened all too often. The man was a necessary tyrant, she concluded.

Besides, Jack's passive submission wasn't on Callum; it was entirely on Jack. He had the choice to stand up for himself or not. She even *told* him as much! If he chose not to listen to her, then whatever. Not her problem.

"If no conversation is the preference, then that is satisfactory, as well," Riiz droned on, mostly to himself.

No one bothered to respond, not even Niko.

So they sat there in silence, minute after minute, hour after hour, waiting.

The two days had crawled by with no return from Galen and the others — and by the Mara, they went by slowly...

Niko discovered a whole new level of boredom, as if time was a different sensation entirely in this place. Conversation was rarely struck up, and if it was, it was never anything substantial. Which was ridiculous, if you asked her. These were supposed to be some of her closest companions and friends.

Their only real discussion was the brief speculation that it was Shatter who had been running that remote surveillance at the Southern Great Reservoir — and the implications involved because of their association to Meridian society.

Aside from that? Nothing. Smalltalk, if anything.

"How much longer?" Jack grumbled.

"Without the Uts, it's difficult to know exactly," answered Callum.

"Maybe the number whiz knows?" Jack asked, shooting Niko a smile. A flat smile, but a smile, nonetheless.

"I lost focus a long time ago." It was true; she tried to keep time as best she could, but without her timepiece — which she'd left back in the vehicle — any small distraction ruined her focus. If she had to guess, though, their forty-eight hours would be up soon.

She was honestly surprised it hadn't opened up already. It felt like they'd been sealed down here for an eternity! She tried taking a nap on a few occasions, but there was no position she could get comfortable in, no spot on the concrete floor suitable enough.

Maybe it was that... *thing*... in the room with them, but she couldn't take much more of this. She needed out.

"You have become restless in the recent hours, Jack Sehs," Riiz said. "I would venture that would indicate we do not have much longer to remain in here."

"I don't see how everyone else isn't restless, also," he muttered.

"I, indeed, am one that is keen to be removed from this chamber, also," Riiz agreed.

"You don't count," Jack said. "You An-Mara are always way too calm."

Niko snorted. "Have you met *the one called* Kira-Tharn?"

"I do agree, Niko Ryen. The one called Kira-Tharn is rather volatile." Riiz stood to stretch, his routine similar to the one Niko saw Kira-Tharn performing a couple weeks ago. "But I assure you, we all entertain the same feelings that you lot do."

Niko didn't know if she believed that. The An-Mara were *so* strange. Bless their hearts.

Although, not *all* their hearts...

"Why did the An-Mara destroy Arhanda?" Without thinking, the words tumbled from her lips.

Riiz paused, looking at Niko softly. "I do believe I have explained this to you, Niko Ryen."

275

"A little, yeah. But why the way they did? Why the entire planet?"

"It was not my decision," Riiz said defensively.

"I know that!" she snapped. "For blazes' sakes, Riiz, I know that. I know you tried to save us. I know you're our friend! I just want to know what happened. I've come to know the An-Mara to be an honor-bound people, not murderous chums. It never made sense to me why they actually destroyed my planet. My home. And please don't Cinto-coat it either."

Riiz sighed, one of the few times Niko had heard him do so. "As I have said, I do believe you already know of the reasons. The Heads of Knowledge on Aktun have been quite explicit in their fear of the Machine…"

"We shouldn't speak of this h…," Callum began to warn.

Niko cut him off quickly, holding up an outstretched hand; she would have none of his nonsense right now. "Callum. No."

Her words were powerful and cold, something she would be aghast of in a previous life. She was a new person, though. More confident, or perhaps she just didn't care what Callum thought about her anymore.

Riiz looked back and forth between them, but decided Niko's will won out, and continued.

"Decades ago, word began to circulate throughout the sector of the increased solar oddities in nearby systems, which could be attributed to nothing other than Machine activity. In the years following that revelation, faith and zealousness were mobilized in the intent to stymy the threat in any way possible. Your world was the nearest in the sector to the direction from where the Machine hails, a potential bulwark between the menace in the void and the worlds of the An-Mara. That is the reason for our influx to your planet in the years before Arhanda was destroyed.

"We came with the intent to evacuate your people, but when the Heads of Knowledge learned of the presence of the Child of the Nel-Mara, we were instructed to do everything in our power to extract him from your world. When it was learned that the Meridian delegation to Arhanda was a falsehood, a charade, it became difficult to convince the masses to evacuate.

"The most influential of the An-Mara voices were of the opinion that we needed to cleanse the world to prevent any knowledge, technology, or prophecies falling into the clutches of the

Machine. That necessity was paramount to any sum of goodwill bestowed upon your people. To that end, I disagreed, and in doing so, forsook my standing within the An-Mara."

Riiz looked Niko directly in the eyes. If any An-Mara could show any sign of sorrow, it was him.

"I would convey an apology on behalf of my people for the destruction of your world," he offered. "The An-Mara are not a conniving, malicious people — I do believe that you will find the Meridians to be far more so — but as remorseful as I remain, I do wonder if perhaps that destruction was necessary. I know you sense how malevolent this threat is."

His eyes flickered to the table, where a plain rock sat, no more hint of condensation visible on the thing.

A chill sent involuntary shivers down Niko's spine.

Malevolent. That was a good word for it.

"I know it's not your fault," she said quietly. "I've put that out of my mind long ago. I've put *all* of it out of my mind a long time ago."

"That is not necessarily the healthiest habit," he stated, looking at her sideways. "You were making significant progress in the ways of psychic potential with the one called Ajane Solase in the days before our exodus. Would it not be something you would consider resuming?"

Niko blinked.

No.

She wouldn't. She *couldn't.* It had been too long. And even if she could, all of that carried unwanted memories she would much rather leave forgotten in the dark depths of her subconscious. What was he thinking?!

"I..."

She attempted to compose her sentence, hoping she didn't stammer her way through it. But before she could, the room hummed, starting to turn. She almost yelped in surprise, but fortunately she'd been sitting down, so she wasn't knocked around too much by the motion.

Forty-eight hours.

All attention turned to the hallway, where gusting winds raged, leaving Niko and her friends enveloped in mind-numbing cold. Her lungs became constricted, taking in nothing but a whiff of overpowering smoke that whooshed through the room. Beyond, in the hallway, was only darkness.

"Blazes!" Jack yelled. "What the blazes?!"

"Can we shut it?!" Callum shouted.

"Please!" Niko demanded to no one in particular. The cold was too much, and they didn't have their layers with them. She instinctively reached for Jack and Callum, pulling both of them in to retain any heat she could.

"Let me attempt." Riiz darted into the hallway toward the console that Noralie and Michele accessed two days ago.

Many timeless moments passed when, by some miraculous feat of the Mara, the room rotated once more, turning them back into sealed position.

"What the blazes happened?" Jack yelled, after the room once again closed itself off from the elements beyond.

"I do believe the facility was entirely destroyed," Riz commented, much too calmly.

"How?" Niko asked. "We didn't hear anything!"

"Or feel anything," Jack added. "No explosions. Nothing."

"I suppose this chamber is very well sealed, indeed," Riiz said, shrugging, his expressions comically nonchalant.

"Thank the Mara for that," Niko exhaled, still trying to catch her breath. The cold continued to seep through every pore in her body, stabbing her with a thousand needles.

"So what do we do now?" Jack moaned.

To her dismay, there were no quick responses.

Eventually, Callum spoke up. "Riiz, do you think you could stay out there long enough to tinker with that console to... do anything?"

"I would be one to make such an attempt," he said hesitantly, "but I do believe closing the door was about the limit of our possibilities."

"There's nothing else in here," Callum said rather urgently. "I think we have to try."

"Wait!" Jack exclaimed. "Don't just go out there and tinker without a plan. We won't last long enough."

"We won't last long in here, either," Callum countered. "There's nothing in here, just us and that blazes abom..."

He cut his words short as he pointed to the table in the center of the room. Niko was still breathless and pumped on adrenaline, but what she saw made her blood run cold.

The Machine was no longer a rock, but it looked like an actual piece of machinery. Almost like some sort of network of circuits, something that she would see when a console was opened up.

It was giving them what they wanted: a way out.

"I'll be damned," Jack uttered. "Could we possibl…"

"Do *not* entertain that idea." Callum's words were sharp, but once again, Niko agreed with him.

"Jack, you can't possibly think you can mess with that thing," Niko said, leveling him with a no-nonsense glare. She sure hoped he didn't think he could. Otherwise Jack was the biggest idiot who ever lived.

"We don't exactly have a lot of options," he argued. "If we can't even go outside this room…"

"Do we even know what's out there?" Niko asked. "Can we try to get to one of the other rooms? Maybe those are sealed off? And maybe there's supplies, or food, or tools, or a console… Something? Anything?"

"We may attempt to examine our surroundings, but it appeared to me that the base was blasted to Oblivion," Riiz noted.

"It certainly did." Callum nodded, eyes wide in agreement. "I think we have to try, though."

"One problem," Jack said. "How do we even get this thing to open anyway, if the console was on the outside?"

Everyone looked around at each other. Blazes, he was right.

"Was there a timer when you resealed it?" Callum asked Riiz.

"I did not have time to arrange for one," Riiz said, sucking wind through his teeth. "I would convey an apology."

Callum muttered one of those curses Niko was unfamiliar with.

"Well, there's that," she whispered.

A minute passed while everyone caught their breath, looking around the room for anything that might help them. Anything except the Mara-damned Machine. Niko promised she would *not* let Jack, or anyone else, tinker with it. There had to be a reason why Kezane, of all people, sealed this thing in this secret location, so far from any traces of civilization, under extreme thermal confinement.

… which, Niko was reluctant to admit, didn't even seem to completely suppress the thing's functions. How was it able to transform?? Or produce *water*??

As long as it hasn't attacked us yet… she supposed. But the subterfuge was more than unnerving.

Finally, Riiz interrupted the silence. "You might not appreciate the suggestion, Niko Ryen, but along the topic from earlier... would it be a possibility for you to reach out to Cryo and Ravenna through dreams?"

No. Out of the question.

That's what she wanted to say, at least. As bad as their predicament was, she really, *really* didn't want to resort to that. Not thinking about any of that was the only thing that kept her sane these last several years. She couldn't dig up the past. She wouldn't.

"I... I don't know if I can."

"I do believe you continue to possess the capability. It perhaps might be our best option," he pleaded. "Potentially, it perhaps might be our only option."

"Riiz is right, Niko." Callum joined in before she had a chance to argue against the idea. "You should try. Even though I've been a Valanse for years, I was never on Ajane's level. Or yours. You could help us out a lot."

What?

Callum...? Never on her level...? She didn't think that to be true. He was a trained Valanse! And he always seemed to know what to do, and had those good instincts. Better instincts than hers, that was for sure.

Besides riding out into the blazes Night with no infrared sensors, she thought bitterly.

"I know how deeply those scars run," he continued, "which is why I've never asked until now."

"I..." How could she phrase this? She didn't think she could. And even if she could, it would be painful. She knew what she would find in her dreams. "I can't."

"Niko," Jack whispered, grabbing her hand tenderly with his own.

Against all her judgment, heat rushed to her face when he did. In all the blazes! This was not a moment to be all tingly! That blazes-accursed chum always found a way to get under every layer of her rational senses. She should be *mad* at Jack, not in *love* with him! But damn it all, she couldn't help how she felt.

"Niko, please," he mouthed, his words completely silent.

For blazes' sakes!

"Fine."

She hated Jack. She hated that he had a way to get her to do whatever he wanted, even when everything inside her protested. But she *did* love him, and she knew she had to sacrifice her own ill feelings for the good of the group. She couldn't just let them all sit down here and wither away.

But in all actuality, what did they expect her to do? Even *if* she managed to connect to Cryo and Ravenna — and that was a big *if* — what would *they* be able to do? Even well-stocked and with the proper means of travel, she and her companions barely even made it out here at all. How could Cryo and Ravenna be expected to randomly bring help on a whim? Besides, they would die of thirst long before any help arrived.

"So, that's a yes?" Callum's raised eyebrow left little room for Niko to dissent.

"Sure."

"I know how much it is to ask, but I regret that time is of the essence. Would you attempt it now?"

Blazes, they couldn't even give her five minutes?

"Whatever."

"Perfect," he said patiently. "What do you need from us?"

"Peace and quiet." She didn't mean to sound so grumpy, but she wasn't enthused about this. Not in the slightest. "I need to be asleep, which might be difficult considering this room is blazes uncomfortable. That, and the fact my heart is still beating a thousand pulses per minute…"

She didn't even bother mentioning the distraction of that *thing* lurking in the middle of the room.

"Okay, we'll leave you be," Callum said, seemingly unbothered by her attitude. "And Niko, thank you for doing this."

She nodded to him. She supposed she should try to maintain *some* sense of civility; she'd already been more rude than she would've liked.

"Did you want me with you?" Jack asked her quietly, after Callum and Riiz migrated to the other side of the room.

"No."

She didn't bother to offer him any consolation for the rejection as she lay down on the floor, turning away from him. The concrete dug into her bones, and her head tilted at an awkward angle as she rested it on her outstretched arm. Blazes this was uncomfortable…

She could sense Jack staring sadly at her back, but what did he expect from her? To cuddle up and take a sweet, innocent nap together? No, this was something that ratcheted at feelings buried deep, feelings she hadn't dared visit in five years. She didn't want anybody near her right now; she just wanted to face these demons alone, if she must face them at all.

She heard a long breath escape from behind her, then shuffling feet as Jack sulked off to join the others.

Whatever. She'd deal with him later.

She closed her eyes, but struggled to drift to sleep, her mind swirling too chaotically. Unfortunately, that damn Machine kept creeping into her thoughts, as did Shatter and all their nefarious plots.

This was useless. Cryo and Ravenna probably wouldn't even be asleep right now, anyway. It seemed that those two barely slept at all. She'd probably end up revisiting her nightmares for nothing...

She took a deep breath, gritting her teeth as she sought to separate those connections from everything else, the way Ajane had taught her to do long ago. It was an intentional process, but one that was surprisingly instinctual. Considering she hadn't done this in five years, she found the techniques fairly easy to remember.

Cryo.

Ravenna.

She breathed deeply, finding a rhythm, feeling a little more comfortable with each breath that passed. Maybe this would work, after all...

Cryo.

Ravenna.

Cryo.

Ravenna.

———

23

The Great Stadium at Sol City

SHE continued the monotony for a few more dreary seconds.

Cryo.

Ravenna.

Cryo.

Ravenna.

Maybe she was more sleepy than she thought...

Without realizing it, her intentions faded into unconsciousness, and it all came flooding back instantly. She knew the feeling as if it had only been hours since she last walked through her own dreams, not years.

This wasn't so bad.

She felt light and free soaring through a wispy nothingness, the ether that Ajane had only described so cryptically way back when. If Niko ever had to teach someone else how to do this someday, she would do a far better job than Ajane, she promised herself.

She chuckled — actually *chuckled* — at the thought. Blazes, that wasn't funny, was it? That latter thought sent her further into a spiral. What was so damn hilarious?!

It was as if she felt... *happy*. And that made her angry.

She clenched her fists, which only felt like sheets of soft felt.

What in all the worlds was even happening? Blazes, she was an emotional wreck!

She would've preferred to continue drifting into feelings of elation and mindless detachment, but she remembered she had a job to do. Other people were counting on her.

Yes, she remembered.

Jack. Callum. Riiz.

But what was it they wanted her to do, again?

It took some straining, but she refocused her thoughts in the way Ajane had taught her.

Cryo.

Ravenna.

Yes, that's right. She needed them.

But wait, what did she need them for?

Blazes. She really should've been practicing all this time...

She calmed her thoughts, pushing everything else out besides the task at hand, then suddenly remembered. She needed to reach out to Cryo and Ravenna.

For Jack. For Callum. For Riiz.

They were stuck. Stuck in a bunker. With some sort of... malevolence. Some sort of... darkness. A dark patch that ever filled the void around her.

Her reality shifted, and she suddenly stood on a pristine green field, the smell of grass seeping into her skin, the taste of sweat burning her eyes, the touch of night threading into her olfactory...

Her senses may have been jumbled, but she knew this place — this was the Great Stadium at Sol City. That meant...

Arhanda! It wasn't destroyed!

And yet it was. She knew that it was. But she was standing here now, and the stadium was exactly as she remembered, the one time she went there. Except she had gone during the day. This was...

Nighttime?

She looked up into the sky, gazing at the incredible heavens above. She'd forgotten how beautiful the sight was. Endless swirls of light wrapped around themselves, tendrils of glittering milk twisted with rich dustings of cinnamon, the galactic Dark Patch magnificently sprawled onto the tapestry beyond. Blue and white sparkles danced across the entirety of the dome above, as if brilliant diamonds were etched onto a wall of space and time. She reached upward to touch them all, but they were so, so far away, the fabric above immeasurably vast.

The place she lived now didn't have any of this. What was it called, again?

Oh, yeah. An-Terino. That place was a garbage dump of the highest order. That much, she remembered.

The mere thought of the place summoned red-brown clouds onto the horizon so thick, they began to blot out the stars one by one as they raced toward her. In the distance, a great city loomed, its dazzling lights only a mask for its dark underworld.

Alashadar.

She zoomed through its streets as if she were in a spacecraft, but she was in nothing more than her own skin, flying like a nightraptor on the hunt. Except there was no cold embrace of the skies around her, no wind that streaked across her face to make her eyes water. She smiled to herself as she sped through the streets of Machine Row, spotting her friends' place on a dimly lit corner.

She nearly let herself fall out of the sky, though, when she spotted a man who seemed familiar. What was his name?

Oh, yeah. Ce-Ellum, she remembered. She knew something was wrong about him. Something veiled in shadow. A dark truth he was hiding.

A tight knot of unease gripped her stomach as he watched her, leaning against a building with arms crossed, staring up at her with a slight smirk on his face.

Could he… could he *see* her right now?? How?! Or was she only dreaming?

Eugh!

Just in case, she sped away. That damn gangster made her skin crawl. She knew deep in her gut he was not the man who her friends thought he was, but the last thing she needed was to think about that dubious scoundrel right now.

At her will, she slingshotted back into the city like a streak of lightning. This time, the wind *did* whoosh past her face, and the cold air *did* squeeze the breath from her lungs. She paused atop a building, taking a break to catch her breath, when she spotted another acquaintance down in the marketplace below.

Anda!

The longer she stayed in this dream, the sharper her mind became, and the better she maintained control.

She watched her friend shopping, when suddenly, she turned

and looked up in Niko's direction.

Niko panicked. She liked Anda, but these people weren't supposed to be seeing her while she was an Observer.

That's what Ajane called it, right? An Observer? She knew she wasn't doing this correctly. What did she need to fix, though? Blazes, it was so difficult to remember…

She flew out of line of sight from Anda to refocus for a moment, then peeked her head around the corner again. This time, she maintained intention on her thoughts, but Anda was still there, peering directly at her.

This would not do, so she did what Ajane taught her and willed everything away.

By the grace of the Nel-Mara, it worked.

She was whisked back to the Great Stadium at Sol City, but something was different this time. It was… enclosed. Where she looked into the expanse of the cosmos only moments ago, she now instead saw the bounds of a dark, sturdy ceiling.

The stadium was also packed to the brim. More people than she'd ever seen in such a small space milled about, barely able to move. It made the streets of NewCen look like a wide open pasture by comparison.

She floated above the masses, but nobody paid her any attention. She was actually an Observer this time, thank the Mara.

Satisfied, she hovered across the stadium, studying each face to see if she knew anyone there. Of course, she didn't. It was almost all Islanders, their dark skin glimmering in the light, their golden hair flowing regally as they moved about.

She was moments from setting her feet back onto the ground when something from the corner of her eye caught her attention, leveling her focus to shambles.

Wha…

Her thoughts turned muddled, because in the foyer, she saw them.

Blurry vision threatened to blind her, her consciousness on the verge of dragging her from the dream. But she remained steadfast.

Dare she approach?

Her legs wobbled, even though she glided, frictionless in the dream, toward the entrance foyer.

It was he who saw her first, the man with the brown hair and a modest demeanor. The eye contact hit her with the force of a thousand sols as he turned toward her, a broad smile lighting up his entire aspect.

"Niko! We thought you weren't going to make it." He familiarly patted the top of her head, though her short hair only waved as if brushed by the wind.

Short hair!? What in the worlds? Since when did she cut it?

"Was I expected?" she asked.

"We've been waiting for you here! Your brothers are around with your mom somewhere. Though I have no idea where Riesen and Kate disappeared off to."

"I... missed you..." she croaked, as she threw her arms around her father's neck, settling her weight into his chest.

She knew she should have cried. She *would* have cried, but she supposed she was an entirely different person nowadays. One that didn't snivel like some witless child.

"I missed you too, kid."

She never thought she'd admit it, but right now, she didn't even mind being called 'kid'. She simply burrowed her face into his body, letting herself bask in the gentle embrace. After what felt like several minutes, she looked up.

"What's going on here?" she asked.

"I'm not sure," he replied. "They rounded up as many people into all the stadiums as they could. They said it's an emergency."

"Niko!" The shout came from across the foyer on the field side.

She scanned through the crowds and saw Keran and Mack rushing toward her. A huge grin spread across her face as she braced for impact. It never came though. It only felt as if fog was blasted into her. But they were there, nevertheless. They were... *real*.

"Where've you been, kid?!" Keran exclaimed. "We've been waiting for you forever!"

She playfully punched his shoulder, which only felt like petting soft snow on a winter Green Coast morning.

"Missed you, big brother. You too, Mack."

In typical fashion, her younger brother flopped onto the ground, playing with some blades of grass he had taken inside with him.

"Where's mom?" she asked.

Keran pointed toward the doors, and in walked that beautiful lady she had missed so dearly for years and years.

"Niko! By the heavens, we had no idea where you'd gone off to?! I've been worried sick!"

She swept over, exhaling into her mother's shoulder as she closed her eyes, returning the tight squeeze. Nothing had felt so satisfying in all her life. So complete. So blissful. She could linger here for eternity.

After many long moments, she reluctantly pulled herself from the cocoon of her mother's arms, sheepishly apologizing for her absence. "I'm so sorry! You wouldn't believe where I've been, even if I told you!"

The Ryen family laughed as they stood there, reunited at last. Mostly reunited, at least...

"Where're Kate and Riesen?" Niko asked.

"They weren't with you?" Her mother clicked her tongue. "I *told* Kate to look after you..."

"She was, but then she..." Niko trailed off. Why *did* Kate leave her? *When* did Kate leave her?

"Let's look around for them," her father suggested. "They have to be here somewhere. Riesen's so famous these days, we'd be able to spot his crowds from ten k's away!"

The family laughed again as they walked across the foyer, her father's arm draped over her shoulders.

Suddenly, horns sounded, the sirens blaring across the expanse of the great stadium.

Niko looked around confusedly, as did everyone around her. What was happening?

What started as droning murmurs quickly turned to panicked steps, the crowd moving as one, much like how a displacement wave would crash across an open beach. Hushed voices turned to louder ones, then those louder voices rose to shrieks, and finally, the shrieks turned to horrendous wails.

What the *blazes* was happening?!

Her father removed his arm from her shoulders as he cautiously stepped forward to investigate, peering upward for several seconds before turning toward the rest of his family, brown eyes wide in horror.

"What is it?" her mother asked.

He shook his head briskly. "I don't know. We need to get up to the top."

He grabbed Mack and Niko by the hands and strode away from the foyer, while her mother and Keran followed in tow.

Soon, however, the crowds turned from an orderly unit to a

chaotic mob, sprinting this direction and that, the shouts too jumbled to discern anything at all.

What the blazes! Why couldn't she just enjoy this reunion with her family??

And why, for the love of the Mara, was it getting so *hot*?!

In answer, Niko looked toward the ceiling, where the dark barrier now glowed with an orange hue.

Blazes, it *was* getting hot! She wasn't imagining it.

"Mom! What is this?! I wanna go somewhere else!" Mack cried, reaching his free hand toward her. The kid barely spoke, so Niko was worried to hear him utter syllables so clearly on that front alone.

"Let's go, Mack!" she urged.

They were stopped in their tracks, however, when not ten meters in front of them, a large support beam came crashing down, grotesquely crushing several poor souls beneath its weight. Niko and the rest of her family could only gape as they sidestepped the wreckage, but screams filled the air in all directions as the heat grew more and more unbearable.

Her absolute worst nightmare sprang to life, though, when from the foyer doors, a wall of glowing red lava sprang forth, burying fleeing denizens with merciless indifference.

This was how it ended.

This was how it all ended.

Niko froze, unable to do anything, think anything. This couldn't be happening.

Please, just let me be anywhere else. My family and me. Anywhere else.

She closed her eyes, willing it to be so, but to no avail.

"Niko!"

She heard the shout, but it didn't come from anyone around her.

"Niko!"

It sounded louder this time, like it was above her. Around her. *Within* her.

Where was it coming from?! And who in the blazes...

"Nikooo!"

Wait, she did know this voice. It was...

"NIKOOO!"

The lava was gone. The crowds were gone. Her family was gone. The heat had even dissipated, though she was still covered in sweat.

Sweat, and…

No, not sweat. Water.

She stood in the middle of a… reservoir? On An-Terino?

And there, before her, was Cryo.

———————

"We need to go back!" she shouted, pleading as she attempted to drag him along by the arm. They needed to get back. They needed to save them. "There's still time!"

"What do you mean?" he asked.

"They're in the stadium! It's holding, but barely. We need to be fast!"

"What stadium?"

"Sol City!"

He cocked his head in question.

"It's… the blazes destruction! It's the Engines! It's Arhanda!" she blurted out.

His eyes widened as he seemed to understand. But he shook his head. "It's over. You know it's over."

"It's…" she panted, still out of breath from racing across the field, dragging her little brother with her. "It's… over."

Devastated as she was, she knew the truth.

It *was* over.

"It's over," she repeated, her whispers hoarse with breathless-ness.

Wow. She'd lost her touch entirely. How did she get so lost in that dream? She knew that's all it was, yet she let herself be completely immersed. Swallowed whole. By a nightmare, no less. Ajane would've been disappointed in her for the lack of focus. The lack of intention. She needed to regroup. This lapse in concentration was surely to blame for summoning her worst and deepest fears.

She breathed deeply, each exhalation sending shuddering ripples down the waterline of the dark reservoir, which was dimly lit by some unseen light source.

"Are you okay?" Cryo asked, his concern earnest as he peered at Niko. His intelligent eyes always seemed one step ahead.

She shook her head, laughing.

Laughing...

How such a reaction was appropriate for this moment of ultimate sorrow, she had no clue. Maybe she was finally losing her sanity altogether. "I don't think I've been okay for a long time."

It was pure, unadulterated honesty. He looked at her grimly, then nodded his head, before pulling her into a tight embrace. She always thought the guy hated hugs, so that made the gesture even more genuine. Bless his heart.

She still had a job to do, but she had just relived the worst scene she could've possibly imagined, so she needed this hug. And it was strange — it felt *real*, not like the random sensory distortions typical in the dreams.

"We're in the dream, right?"

"Yes." He let out a soft, coaxing chuckle. "You seem out of sorts. You truly haven't done this in five years?"

"No."

"I don't blame you," he said. "But it's not so bad, as long as you always keep your intentions in the forefront."

He was right. She *should* have been doing this all along.

"Why didn't you force me to keep practicing?!"

He grinned, shrugging. "It wasn't my place to say so. You needed to take your own time to do things your own way. You're capable enough to decide what you do and don't do."

Cryo was the best. One of the things she loved most about him is that he always trusted her, even when she made the wrong choices.

"Do they hate me?" she asked.

"No, of course not," he replied, clearly understanding who she referred to. "They're worried about you. You didn't say anything before disappearing."

"Sorry," she managed to utter, a tight grimace set to her jaw.

"With Callum, Jack, and Riiz also gone, we figured you went with them. But you're gonna have to explain to Ven and Kira-Tharn why you left."

Niko's grimace widened. Imagining that prospect seemed nearly as bad as reliving the apocalypse.

"You wouldn't believe it, but Ven and Kira-Tharn were actually going around looking for you." Cryo shot her a knowing smirk. *"Together."*

Niko laughed. Ravenna and Kira-Tharn? *Together*? They were basically the same person, with the quick and fiery tempers, so she always found it weird those two hated each other. Well, not *hated* each other, but they definitely bristled in each other's company.

"Good luck dealing with them when you get back," he offered.

"I'll worry about that *if* we get back." She struck a more serious tone. "That's why I'm reaching out now. Thank the Mara you're here, because we ran into a bit of a... problem out in the Night."

"Oh?"

"We were looking for that one guy, Kezane, and we found his lab *wayyyyy* out there. But then Shatter showed up. We didn't find Kezane, but we met these people that worked with him, and they sealed us in this... room... to keep us hidden. That was two days ago. Shatter left now, but they destroyed the whole bunker. We're stuck in that room, and we can't go outside."

"You can't get out at all?"

Niko shook her head. "I don't even know how to describe it. It's *sooooo* cold. It's practically like space out there."

"Do you know where you are?"

"Kind of, but not exactly. We stopped at a village on the way out here. An-Tun Village, it's called. And this place is straight out from there."

"I've never heard of that place," he confessed. "I didn't even know there were villages out there at all."

"Yeah," Niko replied. "It's a long story. But, umm, if you follow the valley directly out from Machine Row, you should run into An-Tun Village after a couple hundred kilometers. I'm sorry, I don't know exactly how far."

"Hmmm, I don't know if that helps," he said regretfully. "Is there nothing else around the room you're stuck in? Anything at all?"

"I... I don't know. I think we need someone to come get us. There were landmarks along the way that I could try to describe, and I can show you what kind of vehicles they take. But if you come, make sure you bring infrared sensors, for the love of the Mara."

"Okay. You said a few hundred k's? That might be doable."

Niko sheepishly shook her head. "It's... it's a little bit further than that."

"How far?"

Niko gulped. "... a couple *thousand* k's."

Cryo tsked, pressing his lips tight. "I see. Wait here one second. Let me check with Ven and the others."

Without further warning, Cryo's image faded into the air, shimmering into nothing. Niko now stood alone in the reservoir hall, studying her surroundings. The place looked similar to the reservoir she visited with the villagers of An-Tun, but this one was different. Smaller and older, perhaps.

"Okay."

Niko jumped, whirling around to find Cryo standing there once more.

"Apparently there's an aqueduct that runs along an ancient Rift artery. It goes directly from Alashadar straight across to the very center of the Night side of An-Terino. Those highlands are where the first reservoirs were excavated during the days of the attempted terraforming of this planet."

Niko stood there, dumbfounded. "Wait, did you already talk to people?!"

"Yeah," he nodded, "and that's how I learned of this. I guess several stations were constructed along those aqueduct corridors, which is what I'm guessing the place you're trapped is. There might be a panel on the floor in that room you're in, and if there is, it could open an accessway to the aqueduct, if you're lucky. Let's hope that info is good."

Niko remained unmoving, staring back at Cryo. "How... *how* did you learn of this so quickly?"

"It didn't feel quick," he laughed. "But... it's kind of a long story. I'll tell you when you get back."

Blazes, she wanted to know now! But she also wanted to get out of the mess she was in.

"Okay. I'll give it a try. But if there is no panel, will you stay in the dream so I can reach you if needed."

"Of course," he promised. "Check it out, and if I don't hear back from you, I'll assume you found it."

"Thank you, Cryo," she enunciated, her sincerity coming straight from the heart.

"Good luck. Let's hope it works out. I *really* don't want to have to go find a vehicle to drive into the middle of the Night. I have to train for the Century, which is only in a few weeks."

"The Century?! Wait, so you're actually on the Tour?!"

"Yeah!" he laughed. "And I didn't do terribly on the race the other day."

"The Oldcity Blitz? What place?!"

"Tenth."

Niko's jaw hit the floor. "But you... you're *brand new*. How? How'd you do it?! How are you so *good*?!"

Cryo shrugged. His Mara-damned humility was annoying as blazes sometimes. "I had fun, and the team helped a lot."

The team.

He meant Vulture. Which she wasn't thrilled about, but she trusted his judgment. As long as he could be done with them after the Tour was over, she trusted him. Especially if he would garner a decent chunk of Terion to help get their group off this Mara-forsaken planet once and for all.

"Wow," she squeaked.

He nodded. "Ven isn't happy about it, though."

"She's never happy about anything," Niko muttered.

"Hah!" Cryo grunted. "Sometimes. But I do know that she cares. More than you know, she cares."

Niko sighed. "I guess."

She knew deep down that Ravenna *did* care, but it still didn't make her come across as any less cranky.

"Anyway, try the panel out, if you can find it. Let's hope for that," Cryo said, his image shimmering once more. "And if you need more help, I'll be waiting here."

"Bye, Cryo." Niko held up a hand in farewell, then watched as his image faded into thin air completely.

She now remained alone on the stone floor flanking the aqueduct, finally understanding why she stood where she did: she was meant to find this place in the waking world. What she didn't know was whose mind had guided her to this information — hers or Cryo's. But somehow, *somebody* knew what she needed.

She looked around once more, then allowed the aqueduct chamber to fade into the haze. Reality around her disappeared into that silky ether, its effervescence bathing her consciousness in silence. She willed herself back into the room where her body slumbered, hoping to the Mara that she would *not* end up in the Great Stadium at Sol City.

She blinked.

It was the room, thank the Mara, but...

Blazes!

Her elbows and hips felt as tender as... Well, as tender as if there was a concrete floor digging into them. Which there was.

Why couldn't there be a pillow or something lying around?! Blazes, one nap here made living in the An-Mara quarter feel like a pampering at some luxury palace.

"Niko?" Callum's gruff voice filled the stale air around her. "I know it's difficult to drift, but you really need to try to do this."

What? What was he on about?

"You sure you don't want my cloak and shirt for a pillow?" Jack asked.

"I'm awake now."

"Yeah, but we really need you to do this for us. It's kind of our only hope right now."

"No," she stated clearly. "I'm *awake*."

"I can see that."

What was their *deal*?!

She turned her nose up indignantly. "Then why're you acting like I didn't just dream for you guys?"

The others looked around at each other, confused.

"You already dreamt?" Callum's eyes narrowed in thought.

Niko spread her arms wide, giving them a no-nonsense shrug of affirmation. "Yes?"

"How?" Jack exclaimed. "You sat down, rolled over to your side, then popped up and started walking around just now."

"I don't know, but I *did* just dream," she stated matter-of-factly, looking around the room for the hidden panel Cryo spoke of. "Several dreams, actually."

Jack looked to his dad confusedly. "Does time flow differently in the dreams? Ajane never said anything about that."

He was right; Ajane *never* said anything about that, even to her. Niko knew Jack to be sensitive to the dreams, but he couldn't walk around lucidly like she could.

"Yeah, I don't know," she shrugged. "I've never really paid attention to time in the dreams before. It does feel weird sometimes, I guess."

"I..." Callum whispered to himself. "I've only heard stories. From long... Nevermind."

He looked up, digging deeply into Niko's eyes, as if searching for something he couldn't see outright. What was he talking about? What stories? Why was he being so *weird* about it?! It didn't exactly put her mind at ease.

Such a typical Meridian enigma… Whatever.

Niko tried her best to ignore him, instead focusing on searching the floor, making sure to stay well away from that damn piece of the Machine in the center of the room. She dragged her fingers across the concrete in sweeping circles, until she felt…

There.

A crack in the floor, too small to notice from afar. She traced her fingers along the edges, then pressed down.

"I'll be damned," Jack gasped, as a console panel emerged from an opening not much wider than two widths of her hand. "That's rad as blazes! How'd you know it was there?"

"I told you, I was able to reach out in the dreams. Cryo told me about a potential panel on the floor, and that it might be able to open an accessway to the aqueduct."

"The aqueduct?!" Jack exclaimed. "Here?"

Niko shrugged.

"Cryo said that?" Callum asked. "How would *he* know about any of it?"

"I don't know," Niko responded. "But I hope for the blazes' sakes that he was right. Riiz, you think you can tinker with this?"

"I do believe I have no choice but to attempt such an endeavor," he said.

"No, you do not," Niko said, grinning at him. He nodded to her in response, which may as well have been a smile for an An-Mara.

Riiz walked over, studied the newly appeared console for no more than ten seconds, and declared, "Oh. This, I do believe, is simple."

He performed a quick series of tinkering maneuvers, and with a soft click and a twist, a new breath of cold hissed into the room. Not the unbearable, agonizing cold from before. Just… cold. Once equilibrium settled, a hatch barely wide enough for a human body was revealed. As narrow as it was, it was strange they noticed no such cavity earlier.

"Phwooosh!" Jack howled.

Niko couldn't blame him for his exuberance, for her heart leaped with victory, as well. Were they actually making it out of here?!

"Wait," Callum commanded, holding an arm in front of Jack. "Let me check it out first."

Niko rolled her eyes. *Of course* he would feel the need to go first. He *had* to be the strong, brave protector for them all. Though, Niko was honestly glad she wouldn't have to be the one to go in first, irritated as she was to admit it.

Callum dropped down and disappeared from view, but not even a minute later, he reemerged. "It's the aqueduct. Let's go."

Niko smiled to herself, suddenly finding such admiration and awe for Cryo. He was right! How in the blazes was he even able to supply them with that information, though? She would make sure to ask him *everything* when they got back.

If they got back, she reminded herself grimly. The fact remained that they were still thousands of kilometers away from their destination, with no vehicles, no layers, and no food at their disposal. But for now, at least, they were able to be free of this Mara-forsaken bunker.

Niko and the others shuffled over to the hatch, but Jack paused, halting the group.

"What about that thing?" he asked, pointing to the sample of the Machine, still sitting innocently on the table.

"Leave it," Callum said flatly.

It looked so docile, so tempered. But Niko's psyche was still being thrashed by raw waves of anxiety in its presence. An abomination, Galen had called it, and rightfully so.

Niko, to her credit, pulled her eyes away, hopefully to never set sight upon the thing ever again.

"We never learned what the power source of its containment is," Riiz added, "but it appears to remain stable. I, for one, trust in the one called Kezane Pfase to maintain proper suppression. I suppose that is his responsibility and not ours."

Callum nodded. "Good riddance, if you ask me."

He then turned and disappeared down the hatch. Niko and the others didn't hesitate but two seconds before they followed suit.

PART THREE

Shattering the Underworld

CHAPTER TWENTY-FOUR

24

Out of the Frying Pan, Into the Fire

THE heat. The tedium. The oppression. The *Frying Pan.*

Bleakness was all too ubiquitous out here, and far too permeating to find any sort of comfort.

Through the shimmering scorch, Anda noticed a tall An-Mara girl struggling to carry impossibly heavy equipment from a Rift that was being excavated just beyond the edge of the yard, her protective equipment barely enough to shield against the unrelenting gaze of Bucon above.

The poor thing. How long would she last out here?

Anda turned her vision away, resuming her search. She peeked to the left and to the right, up and down… She scanned anywhere and everywhere in this Mara-forsaken death trap, because if Niko was in here somewhere…

Ugh. The thought was an unpleasant one.

There was no way her friend would be here, though, would she be? To imagine that girl stuck in a hellhole like this was intolerable, yet it made sense — rumors abounded that many residents of the An-Mara quarter had been rounded up and incarcerated here of late. Why else would she be missing for weeks on end?

Ever since Niko appeared to her in that dream, Anda couldn't get the image out of her head. It had been so, so odd. Like she was actually there…

Almost like…

A supposition pricked the back of Anda's mind.

There was no way the girl was a Valanse. Was there?

It was possible, but…

No, she didn't think so. Unless Niko was the best pretender in all of the worlds, there was no way that refreshingly innocent young thing was one of those pretentious meddlers.

But there was something strange about the manner of her specter. Something familiar. Something… *omniscient.*

Anda shelved those wandering thoughts as she looked across the yard, scanning one last time for signs of her lost friend. Unfortunately, she was forced to keep in tow with the rest of the group before anyone noticed her lingering. Unwanted attention was something she could do well without.

Her own woes were insignificant in comparison to what the prisoners suffered here, but seriously, how much longer would they parade around for? And why *was* she even part of this delegation in the first place?

Anda buried her annoyances, of course, holding her head high as the procession snaked through a hallway leading from the main yard into cooler climes. It was only when they passed through a double set of doors — a sort of airlock, she assumed — that the guide of their little tour unlatched the straps of his helmet, prompting everyone else in the party to do the same.

Finally!…

Removing the mask felt lovely. Welcome air rushed into her lungs, renewing her with a vigor that seemed to disappear by the minute out here.

It had been *so* long since she had to wear one of those accursed things — the last time was when she worked the Rifts, years ago — and she didn't miss it for one second.

Sweat was already pouring over every centimeter of her body, and she had only been outside in the yard for not more than a few minutes. She should consider herself blessed to only be along for a tour, though, and not imprisoned away indefinitely like these unfortunate wretches that languished in the Daylight heat out here, toiling away for whatever crimes they committed.

Shatter had really outdone themselves with this.

The Frying Pan, indeed.

Her face remained stoic, of course, but on the inside, Anda seethed at the cruelty of this place. No amount of power generation was worth... *slavery.*

Yes, that's what this was. Borderline slavery.

No, not borderline, she amended. This *was* slavery.

There was no other way to describe the conditions here. These prisoners were *forced* to dig Rifts in the Daylight... and high Daylight at that! This type of work was bad enough on the fringes of Twilight, but out here?... This was too much.

And as for the duration of their sentences...

Well, that was anyone's guess. Months? Years? Forever?

It was one thing to employ voluntary participants and pay them a handsome sum of Terion for such deadly working conditions, but it was another thing entirely to force people to labor like this, even if they were convicted criminals.

How was Shatter even able to get away with this? There was *no way* Meridian society could have fallen so far that they would think this was acceptable...

And everybody in the worlds knew Shatter *was* a Meridian entity, as much as they tried to hide the connection.

"If you follow me," instructed the guide, a middle aged man whose name evaded Anda, "we will be meeting with the administrators momentarily — namely our chief officer, newly arrived to the planet."

If Anda knew anything about Shatter, the addition of a new chief officer couldn't be a good thing for this world. Especially with the direction everything was headed...

The Cinto. The races. The riots. They were all distractions designed to hide Shatter's true intention of controlling the balance of powers here. And Terion must be playing along also, Anda conjectured, considering all the surveillance machines that were popping up all over their corner of the city.

The Terion Sight, she'd heard it called before.

Her suppositions were corroborated when they emerged into a large chamber, its atmosphere well machine-conditioned, very unlike that of the prisoners' quarters in the other building. On the far end of the room, atop a raised mezzanine overlooking the guests, both Shatter and Terion authorities stood side by side.

Anda, astute as she was, swung her gaze over the different

peoples assembled in the room, taking mental note of everyone in attendance. But it wasn't the people her eye was drawn to — it was the awesome sight through the large, tinted viewing wall holding the Daylight at bay. She'd never been this far from the Twilight before, and Bucon hung higher in the sky than she'd ever seen, easily observable through the carbon windows, its wide, orange breadth quite striking. She was never one to be easily impressed, but this was a sight to behold.

A whispering at her shoulder brought her back to the matter at hand.

"Why take us out there first?" Amon asked.

She shook her head. "I suspect we're about to find out."

As they waited below, murmurs droned from the other parties on the floor, the delegates from every large company in the city surely wondering the same thing. The EC's largely worked independently from each other, but they did organize a loose sort of coalition, mainly held together by the whims of Terion.

Now that Terion was put on a literal pedestal above them, Anda could only wonder what was at play here.

"Welcome," a deep voice boomed, its rich sonority enhanced through Ut technology.

The whispers hushed as everyone turned to regard an imposing man standing at the railing, surveying the mulling denizens below with imperious appraisal.

"Welcome all." The man's tone was pleasant enough on the surface, but threatening undertones were unmistakably veiled behind that façade. "Surely you are all wondering what you are doing here?"

Hums of assent filled the room, the countless representatives nodding mechanically.

"Not to worry, this is an important gathering, to be sure."

The man held up his hands to quiet the rising volume of the crowd below, as if what he had to say was the most important thing on this world.

Maybe it was.

"I am Chief Officer Andersane of Shatter Industries, and I've only just had the pleasure of arriving to this wonderful world. Together with Terion, it is our intent to complete development on this planet, bringing a new era of wealth and prosperity to all."

The crowd grew louder again, and Andersane looked annoyed

when they didn't quiet down immediately at his gesture.

"That's all good and fine, but what qualifies Shatter to be the ones to make the rules?!" a woman shouted. A representative from Gluoron Entertainment, Anda noted.

Another man from Terrovian Aquatics joined in. "Exactly! Shatter is only the newest player to show up here on An-Terino!"

"Yeah! Why Shatter?!"

"This is ridiculous!"

"Say what you need and send us on our way!"

More and more voices joined in the chorus of criticism, and as much as Anda disliked these corporations, they did have a point.

"ENOUGH!" Andersane slammed his hands down on the railing, thundering through increased enhancer volume after letting the objections rage on for only a few seconds. "Everyone here was given the *luxury* of an invitation to this conference. Complain all you want, but Shatter and Terion control all the resources necessary to exact control of this world. You are all here by our favor — by our goodwill — which we intend to extend to everyone."

The room went silent as previously unseen guards stepped forward from the perimeter of the assembly. Anda maintained outward calm, but her viscera crawled with unease. None of this felt right.

"There *will* be a new order here on An-Terino," Andersane continued firmly, "but it is far from an adverse situation for those who subscribe to it. Loyalty and good decision-making will be rewarded handsomely, which I know you will all take full advantage of."

Andersane then walked over to the other side of the mezzanine on which he stood, where he began to pull back thick curtains, revealing another wide window.

"And sedition and treason will be punished," he said with sinister calm. "This place has been lawless for far too long."

When the curtains finished opening, three posts were visible in the dusty yard, with what appeared to be three withered figures chained to them, completely baked in the unforgiving Daylight of Bucon.

Gasps and whispers surged throughout the room. Anda herself would've joined in, had she not schooled herself in composure over years and years.

"Did any of you know there was an entire society skulking in the Night?" Andersane asked the room. "One that siphoned off *your* resources. *Your* food. *Your* water. *Your* Terion. A society that would sooner fight and kill our people, rather than simply take their fair share."

The room was silent, except for the occasional gagging noises from some of those in attendance who were less tolerant to such grisly sights as decaying human flesh.

"You might say that I did you all a favor," he said. "Along with the fifty million honest folks barely scraping by for a living in Alashadar."

"Who are they?" a voice demanded. A familiar voice. "What were their crimes?"

Anda looked across, and...

Yes, she knew him, although it required a double take, since he still wore his mask. It was the man who called himself Ce-Ellum, representing that thinly veiled gang front, Vulture.

His presence had sent her running when she went to visit Niko's friends several weeks ago, but she supposed she didn't really care if he saw her now, in this environment. They all had bigger matters to worry about. He probably wouldn't even recognize her, anyway.

"These three extremists were conspiring to organize an uprising against all EC's, not only Shatter and Terion. They were caught stealing a considerable amount of water from the reservoirs, as well as supplying an active terrorist threat against our facilities with weapons and many vital resources, which have caused numerous deaths. As the ringleaders, they were due no less than execution. The remaining cell was disbanded, and those detained were sentenced to labor here for their crimes."

"What were their names?" Ce-Ellum asked again, tilting his head toward the three cooked husks beyond the window.

Andersane regarded Ce-Ellum judiciously. "Noralie Mose, Michele Aragase, and Galen Anstraes. Though I see how it matters little."

Ce-Ellum nodded politely at Andersane, looking bored as he returned to a side conversation with his Vulture cronies.

Naturally, Anda didn't recognize the names, and she supposed she wouldn't, considering they'd been hiding out in the Night. An-Terino was vast, and Alashadar was all she'd ever known.

Before she could reflect more on the unfortunate victims, a slow clap started near the back, from the Terrovian Aquatics delegation. Soon, more applause joined in, and before she knew it, most of the room had joined in ovation.

It was unbelievable. Absolutely disgusting. These prisoners were quite literally cooked alive in the Daylight, and people were *applauding*? Even if they were the worst criminals in the history of the sector, punishment like this was too harsh. Much too harsh.

And what was worse, Anda figured, was that Shatter could make these claims about the prisoners all they liked — about them being terrorists and inciters and extremists — but it was just as likely that these charges were made up entirely.

Corruption at its finest.

Why was everyone really here? For Shatter to show off what kind of power they possessed? To show what happened when the people disobeyed? If that was their true purpose, a mass demonstration back in Alashadar would be far easier and far more effective.

No, what they wanted here must be conducted behind closed doors, away from the public eye.

Distraction. That was the key to whatever was happening on this planet.

Eventually, the cheering died down, and only then did Andersane continue, looking ever so smug up on his platform. He addressed the man who instigated the ovation.

"An An-Mara with a sense of decency..." he quipped. "What is your name?"

"Armond-Dei," the man replied, his An-Mara accent riddled with other influences, as if he tried so hard to eliminate his heritage, something uncharacteristic of any An-Mara she'd ever met. He didn't even refer to himself as '*the one called* Armond-Dei'.

"Well, Armond-Dei," Andersane said, "I do so wish that all An-Mara would conduct themselves the way you do. With your shining character, you have a bright future in this new world."

Armond-Dei crossed an arm over his chest and knelt to Andersane.

Actually *knelt!*

Anda held no special reverence for the An-Mara beyond a general respect, but she found it shameful that one of them would be so obsequious as to *kneel* to this Meridian from Shatter.

"I regret that many of my people act with dishonor," Armond-Dei simpered. "And for those that were choosing extremism and violence against the peoples of An-Terino, I am glad they met the end they did."

"That manner of unpleasant business was regrettable," Andersane drawled in feigned sentiment, "and it is with no light heart that we make such decisions, but the greater good of An-Terino depends on our firm hand. I thank you for your understanding. I thank you *all* for your understanding."

More applause. More loathsome applause.

"Now, onto the matter at hand..." Andersane continued, quieting the praise with a swish of his hands. "The purpose of this summit is to mete out bids for energy and resource contracts. The Frying Pan alone is able to produce over a hundred Terawatt-hours of energy per year, and we have two more stations just like it in the works, complete with Lanthanide refineries. They should be completed within the year, if we are able to receive shipments as planned.

"We would like to make governance of An-Terino a group effort, with all of you helping to do your part. You will place bids, but with services as the currency, not Terion. In return, we would supply you with whatever energy you need to conduct your operations.

"Each delegation will be assigned an officer to liaise with, and we will come to an appropriate deal. You may take some time now to discuss among your own colleagues as to what your aims are — as well as with what services you are willing to provide exclusively to Shatter and Terion. We will reconvene in one hour."

With that, Andersane stepped down from his pulpit, and the room immediately broke out into raucous conversations. Even Anda's own delegation, ROTO, didn't wait but three seconds before turning to each other to discuss.

To her annoyance, she was excluded from their circle for the time being. She supposed she wasn't needed here after all; they only brought her along because she was the foremost expert on the technical processes of Cinto production, and therefore was indispensable to their business. But she was not and would never be involved with their business decisions.

"Is Terion exempt from this?" Amon whispered to her.

"It sure seems like it."

Indeed, the Terion 'delegation' only milled about up top, socializing with the Shatter dignitaries like they were the closest of friends.

"I don't like any of this," he voiced through gritted teeth, his lips not giving any hints of what he was saying.

"Nor do I," she responded. "Not at all. But this is not the place to discuss such things. Not when Shatter and Terion have both been increasing surveillance."

She said it as quietly as possible, hoping that the background bustle would be too great for any listening machines' algorithms to sort through.

Amon nodded in understanding, then turned toward their own delegation, who opened up their tight circle to let him in. They quickly shut it before Anda could work her way in, though.

Those *assholes*.

"Can I be of any assistance?" Anda asked, projecting her voice, doing her due diligence as a member of their delegation.

The ROTO lords turned and looked at her dismissively, only one bothering to shake his head in rejection.

So be it.

She held her chin high and sauntered to the side, refusing to let anyone see how much the exclusion bothered her. If she was stuck on the fringes, she could at least make good use of the time and eavesdrop on other EC's.

And it paid off — she learned quite a lot, including the tidbit she overheard from the Gluoron delegation. They asserted that the reason Shatter included Terion was because they needed their machine tinkerers and considerable influence over the economic infrastructure on An-Terino.

Did Shatter really have no tinkerers here, then?

Probably, she supposed. It was useful to know those fools lacked that sort of control without Terion's support. They would have everyone believe that they alone commanded the will of the planet, but Anda always knew that whoever controlled the machines controlled everything. Perhaps Shatter knew that, too.

She also picked up on the Marindise delegation whispering of the Terion Sight. Apparently, they had already been contracted to install the Sight in their halls, and the work was already complete. Anda figured that if the Marindise had the Sight, it stood to reason that the other powerful EC's in NewCen must also.

This new wave of remote surveillance was a real thing, and one that she couldn't believe was happening. It went against everything that the sector ever stood for, An-Mara and Meridian societies alike.

There was nothing she could do besides shake her head, though. This was merely a depressingly predictable circumstance, not a battle for her to wage.

And so the delegates worked, negotiating and squabbling while Anda remained on the perimeter the entire time. She was the only one in the whole room on her own — which was humiliating — but she took the slight in stride, of course, as she always had. She never expected to be brought along for the big decisions anyway.

She would've used the time to investigate the facility further for any signs of Niko, but doing so would draw more questions than she was willing to answer right now. It was clear as the Celean Sea that she must tread carefully in this place.

Besides, rescuing a prisoner in here was an effort that seemed futile. Even if Niko *was* inside, the prospects of reaching her were looking increasingly dim, especially since they had all just been shown that grim spectacle involving the three executed captives.

Foul, horrible business. One that Shatter would pay for. One day...

Apart from those poor souls, she'd only seen brief glimpses of prisoners from afar. She knew countless others still suffered in torment here, but they were surely concealed in the tunnels below, digging whatever Rifts that Shatter mandated. Inaccessible for someone like Anda, that much was certain.

This place was death, a merciless pit of fire and ash, one devoid of hope. The only reasonable thing left to do was implore the fates that her friend was somewhere else on this blasted world, far from the clutches of Shatter.

CHAPTER TWENTY-FIVE

25

The Wash

AN odd sensation swirled around her. Overhead. Underneath. To the sides. Everywhere, really. In this celestial form, Niko could sense the very exchanges of the fundamental particles of existence as she looked down upon the strange, ring-like structure below.

It encircled the star before her, which was a giant sphere of pure light, but not so bright that she couldn't rake in every photon. Every interaction. But that would mean…

Blazes, she was the size of a star! At least that big, if not larger yet.

Just how big was she?

Niko zoomed out from herself — yes, *zoomed out*.

Ah, this was better. Much better.

She now loomed high above both the star and the halo, while time had become an inconsequentiality. She knew the structure was far too small to see at this scale, yet she still knew the function of *everything* about it — every force interacting with every particle at every given nanosecond.

The thing below was a sort of particle collider, that much she knew. But for what?

Niko blinked.

Focus...

She was drifting again. It had always been a problem for her during her training, but without consistent practice over the last several years, the drifting was now more unpredictable. More addictive.

She paused to recollect her bearings. She had a job to do.

Focus!...

What was that job again?

Think, think, think...

Oh, right. She needed to find Cryo. She needed his help. *They* needed his help.

But where were they again?

Oh yeah, the Wash. That's what Callum called it. A fancy name for the sewers, that's all it was.

To her slight regret, she allowed her heavenly perch to transform into those very sewers, the damp, darkened corridors lit only by her own awareness. At least the stench remained absent...

Cryo.

She called his name with her thoughts, willing him to appear into her dream.

He was usually very present — punctual, too. Every time she reached out, he was there to answer, as if he slept at all hours of the clock, guiding her back to the realm of civilization. She still hadn't asked how he knew all those details so flawlessly...

Even with the directions, though, it was a hard journey, long and cold. A makeshift raft was their saving grace as they sailed along the underground currents for nearly two weeks, but they had no food and no extra layers. Even the water had turned rancid once they had entered the Wash.

But against her own misgivings, here they were, underneath the streets of Oldcity. At least that's where she thought they were.

The crudely cut caverns of the Rifts had now transformed into more finely cut stone, though the smell was pungent beyond all comprehension. Each of them had vomited several times so far. Even Callum.

"Hey, Niko."

Niko whirled around at the caress of her name, the dream providing an ethereal echo. Sure enough, Cryo's glimmering shape materialized before her.

"I think we made it. It looks just like you said," she told him.

"Sweet!"

"Yeah. But all the escapes are closed. Locked. Barred shut."

"All of them? There aren't any open?"

Niko shook her head. "We literally can't find any exits."

Cryo's hand flickered; he was clearly distracted. "Let me find out. Hold on."

He disappeared, but Niko was curious about the well-being of her friends, so she concentrated her thoughts on following Cryo to wherever it was he disappeared off to.

As Ajane had instructed her so long ago, she willed herself into Cryo's perspective, suddenly noticing that the Wash surrounded her no more. Rather, it was her friends' quarters in Machine Row.

She was getting better at this. She needed to keep from becoming distracted, though... Reining in her curiosity of her surroundings was the hard part. There were always temptations, whether it be space, or stadiums, or...

That, right there. Those were the thoughts she needed to avoid. That's how the drifting would always begin. Curiosity was risky here.

She focused her concentration upon her friends.

"Niko."

Cryo stood before her once more. He was with his companions, yet not with them at the same time. It was like he was on a different plane of communion. But how? He was with Niko, not with them.

Except...

In the corner, standing against a wall with arms folded, was a highly unsettling avatar of Ce-Ellum's consciousness, staring directly at Niko. Was he...?

Yes, he was definitely on this same plane that she and Cryo existed.

What the blazes?

"Niko."

"What?!" It came out snappier than intended.

Cryo's lambent aspect examined her for a second. "You okay?"

"Yes, sorry."

She looked back to where Ce-Ellum stood a second ago, but he was no longer there. In fact, his visage was across the room, only conversing with Ravenna and Kyler in the waking world.

What the blazes... Maybe she accidentally incorporated his awareness into her dream, her drifting thoughts superseding her mastery over the thing.

"I know where you need to go," Cryo said, calling her attention to him, and him alone.

"Oh?"

"Yeah. Do you mind if I try something new?"

"By all means," she responded. What did he have in mind?

He stepped forward, still flickering, still distracted.

"Reach out," he directed, holding an outstretched arm toward Niko in the darkness.

Darkness.

She looked around. There was no living space, no Machine Row, no Wash, no stars...

Where was she now?

"Trust me, you'll like this," he said, coaxing her back into focus.

She obeyed, and met his fingers with her own. They felt... *wavy*. Like her own long hair, or like fronds of seaweed off the Green Coast. But no sooner than she'd made contact, an image — or an awareness — flooded her psyche.

And suddenly, she knew.

She knew... *Everything*.

Cryo bowed his head, smiling as his image disappeared from her dream, and she was left alone, dumbfounded at the awesome feeling of it all.

Such *awareness*.

Such *omniscience*.

How did he...?

This was the most incredible thing she had *ever* experienced, besides when she first learned about the dreams in the first place. She would've pressed him with questions galore, but he was gone.

He *did* have other priorities, she supposed, what with the Tour and all. Still, she needed answers!

She bit off a short grunt of frustration, then retreated to her own waking world, the gnaw of an all-consuming pain returning with it.

———————————

"I told you already!" Niko insisted, her voice hoarse from the thirst. "It was more a map than anything he said."

"Like a Memory?" Jack croaked.

"Not even a Memory," she corrected. "It was like... pure knowledge."

Jack shook his head, his face gaunt with exhaustion. "The whole dream thing is so weird. I can only sense when you or my dad talk to me, but I can't *do* anything. I can't even *say* anything. I have no control. You guys are so lucky."

Niko shrugged. "Ajane used to say it was a gift to have any sensitivity at all. Even just being able to listen."

"Yeah, but it'd be rad as blazes to be able to interact, y'know."

Niko let out a slow breath. She knew if she were in his position, she'd want more, as well. As it was, she wished she knew more than she did. A lot more.

She wished Ajane were still here — she could've been learning this whole time, and things would be so much easier now. Still, she was already so improved from a few weeks ago when she reached out for the first time in years.

"You are certain that this is the location of our extraction?" Riiz scoured the walls of the Wash, pressing against a grating of bars so securely set that it would take some seriously heavy-duty tools to take it down.

"That, and did he also say *how* they'd get us out?" Callum added on.

"He didn't *say* anything," Niko repeated. "But yes, this is the spot. And yes, they will get us out. He's really busy with Trackripping stuff, but he assured me that help is on the way. We may have to wait, but they *will* come."

She *knew* it was true, but there was no way to properly convey that confidence to her companions. It was hard enough to wrap her own head around it, let alone explain it to others.

Callum exhaled through puffed cheeks. "So strange, this new manner of communication. I've heard that it had existed among the Praxeans — the more cerebral branch of the Valanses — but I wonder how *he* learned of it, without any instruction."

A fair question. And one she intended to ask next time she saw Cryo.

"Well," Jack hummed, "whoever's getting us out of here better hurry. My infection is getting worse, it's freezing as blazes, none of us has eaten in two weeks, and this Mara-forsaken smell is going to be the death of me!"

He wasn't wrong.

"Let me see your arm," Callum commanded.

Jack lifted his sleeve up, revealing a massive bruise, dark veins visible underneath, spidering outward from a small cut carelessly sustained while helping build the raft several weeks ago. It looked disgusting, especially knowing what putrid filth had seeped into the open wound. The mere thought of it sent Niko into another spiral of retching, though there was little to throw up at this point.

Nobody looked twice; all four of them were vomiting water — and only water — like clockwork, their emaciated frames containing nothing more substantial.

They needed out of this place. Like days ago.

And although the smell and hygiene were bad enough, it was the stomach pain that was next-level. *That* was something Niko hadn't been prepared for. She'd always known that starvation was a woe upon the poorest of Alashadar, but actually experiencing it firsthand — even just the beginning stages — was worse than she would've wished on her worst enemy. All she wanted to do was curl up into a little ball.

She wondered if they wouldn't have been better off staying in the blazes bunker, way out in the middle of the Night. Maybe they could've manipulated that piece of the Machine to do their bidding? Maybe they could've tinkered with it? Or maybe they should've just surrendered to Shatter…

She knew these fleeting thoughts were only desperate responses to her own pain, but focusing on anything besides her current anguish was a blessed distraction.

A wave of dizziness washed over her as she shifted to her other side. She shut her eyes against the persistent agony, supremely exhausted from the days upon days of suffering, wishing for someone, anyone, to bail them out of the Wash.

It wouldn't be long now, she told herself. Cryo would send help.

She didn't know how long she fell asleep for, but any respite from that ever-chewing hunger was a welcome one.

"Wake, Niko Ryen!"

She tried to open her eyes, but immediately squeezed them shut when she felt the urgency to vomit overtake every shred of her control once more. She gritted through the excruciating pain as she hurled up what little was left of her gut, too spent to even wipe her face of the sticky trail of bile.

A soft pat to her shoulder.

She looked up and squinted to see Riiz standing over her, an outstretched hand extended her way.

"You were correct, indeed, Niko Ryen," he said. "The ones called Kira-Tharn and Ravenna Night have come to lead us out."

Was this a dream?

She blinked once. Twice.

No, this was real. How long had she fallen asleep for?

She managed to drag her gaze around groggily, pulling the room into focus little by little: stone walls slick with slime, the low echo of dripping water in the background, and the reek of decay that clung to her nostrils. She rolled over to stand to her feet, but...

Blazes.

Her muscles were as noodly as blacksquash vines. She had zero control of her body, and the stomach pain was even worse than it had been before, if that was at all possible.

But wait... what did Riiz say?

Kira-Tharn? Ravenna? They were here?!

It was so difficult to think of anything through the unrelenting pain, but that's what Riiz had said. A vague memory of Cryo sending help danced on the edges of her mind. Is that what this was? Help?

She meant to look around to investigate, but it was just a fraction easier to deal with the pain through closed eyes, so that's what she did.

She may have even drifted back to sleep — who knew? — when the clanging of steel rang throughout the cavern. She could've sworn she heard familiar voices buzzing in the darkness, but didn't have the wherewithal to look.

Then weightlessness.

It was a surreal feeling as her body was hefted up by strong arms, while she let her own dangle to the sides, limp as her own hair.

It would've been nice to see which of her friends this shadowy savior was, but opening her eyes was beyond her powers at this point.

When she finally came to, Niko sat wrapped in a blanket in the corner of an eatery, the pressing warmth enveloping all of her. It couldn't be a dream, though, because the ridiculously sharp pain in her gut was ever-present and all-encompassing. She imagined it felt somewhat like what being stabbed felt like, as Ravenna had been all those years ago.

But maybe not. Maybe she was just being dramatic.

No, she decided, it wasn't dramatic at all. This *did* hurt, even though Kira-Tharn sat beside her, ladle in hand, scooping broth into her mouth.

Kira-Tharn!

Niko's head spun as she took in her surroundings, throwing her arms around her friend. Kira-Tharn stiffened instantly, more rigid than any iron deck she'd ever walked on.

To the blazes with An-Mara custom, Kira-Tharn would just have to deal. Niko was *happy* to see her friend. Happier than she'd been in a very, very long time.

After a few seconds, Niko released the hug, grinning sheepishly.

"Because of what you endured, Niko Ryen, I will allow that one lapse in judgment. But if you ever do that again, I vow to recycle you to Oblivion myself."

Sheesh, point taken.

"Thank you for coming," she breathed, moderating her tone to one more appropriate when conversing with an An-Mara, regardless that it was one of her closest friends.

Kira-Tharn nodded. "We will discuss the manner of your abandonment later, but for now, you must take care not to replenish your sustenance too rapidly."

Blazes! All Niko wanted to do was eat and eat and eat. But she knew of the dangers involved when starving people reacclimated to food too quickly.

"After you finish two more spoonfuls, that will be enough for this first refeeding."

Niko sipped the broth from the ladle. She'd only taken a few gulps, and was already starting to feel full, so she nodded, looking around at the others as they drank their own meals.

Against her pain, she turned to the other side. Out the window, the dark, dingy streets of Oldcity sprang to life.

So that's where they were.

People bustled by in droves, the swarms rivaling those of NewCen. But it was a shadier crowd, a more desperate, ruthless type of people. The hoods, the grim stares, the lack of connection. This was the place she'd always learned lawlessness reigned supreme. She hadn't ever been here before, wisely staying away from this part of Alashadar, but it was exactly as she'd imagined.

"Welcome back, Niko." Callum's gruff voice had never sounded so pleasant in her life.

The squeezing pain on her abdomen still racked every centimeter, but something felt lighter and easier, if only a little.

Relief was the word, she supposed.

"How long?" she asked. Blazes, her voice was scratchy...

"Three days since you last said anything. You were out cold since then, barely tossing and turning. Anymore dreams?"

Three days!? Holy blazes, it felt like twenty minutes... "No. None since he showed me that spot with the grating."

"Turns out that information was solid," Callum whistled. "And the timing couldn't have been closer. Another day, and we might have lost you. And Jack."

Blazes, how close to dying *was* she?...

She ran a hand through her damp hair, but it was stopped dead by a tangle of knots, soot, and grime.

Eughh! She needed a wash. Badly.

But Jack...

Jack!

Niko straightened in alarm as she looked to him, his face pale and slick with sweat. He lay on the ground, unconscious and shivering. Ignoring her own pain, she tensed up, trying to rise and rush over to him, before Kira-Tharn held her down with a firm hand.

"He'll be fine," Callum assured her. "I need to get him back to Shatter, though. They'll have the resources to fight the infection."

"Shatter?" she squeaked. "You're going back?"

"We must." Callum nodded, quieting his voice. "We will be fine. No one knows we were out there."

Niko was bitterly disappointed that they would be leaving again, but one glance at Jack and she knew it was for the best.

"When?" she asked.

"As soon as I can come up with an excuse for our absence," he replied. "And our... condition."

"I do not agree that you are strong enough to pursue such endeavors, Callum Sehs," Kira-Tharn warned, though Niko knew Callum's willfulness would probably override Kira-Tharn's own.

"I have no choice," Callum said flatly. "Look at him."

Blazes. He did look awful...

Unlike Ravenna, who was rather pretty even when she was near death, Jack looked like a shell of a human, thrashed to a pulp by the infection that riddled his body.

"Do it," Niko said. As if her permission was even needed for Callum to save his son...

"Where's the nearest Shatter station?" Ravenna asked.

Niko should've noticed her brooding across the table — her multicolored hair and violet eyes usually stood out. Maybe it was willful ignorance, because she did *not* want to face that woman. Not after what she pulled — first losing all of their Terion, then disappearing into the middle of the Night for nearly a month without saying a word, then almost *dying* on top of everything.

"Not far from here," Callum replied. "I can walk him there quickly."

Ravenna shot him a doubtful look. "You're weak," she said bluntly.

"Not so weak as to keep me from getting my son to safety."

Ravenna shrugged. "If you say so."

"We can be of assistance if you so wish for it, Callum Sehs," Riiz added. He looked rather feeble, himself, so Niko wasn't sure how much assistance he would be able to give.

"Jack and I have worked here in Oldcity for some time," Callum sighed. "I'm more than capable of operating in this district without help."

Stubborn fool.

Normally, Niko would've trusted his judgment one-hundred percent, but after he pulled that stunt of trailblazing out into the Night with no plan for navigation, she'd now come to second guess his decision-making skills.

The streets outside the tavern looked downright intimidating, but maybe he'd be fine. He was the only one of them familiar with this area, after all.

It seemed good enough for Ravenna, because she merely shrugged, turning back to the others. "We should all be on our way."

Niko wasn't quite sure if she was fit enough for travel, as merely sitting upright required great effort on her part. To test her capabilities, she leaned forward, putting extra weight on her feet. In response, her legs wobbled mightily, just as she figured.

Blazes.

"The condition of the one called Niko Ryen is not appropriate for travel," Kira-Tharn announced. The blazes woman probably *felt* her legs vibrating through the ground a meter away.

"Can you make it to the rail station?" Callum asked her.

"I... I can try."

"That would be a no," Ravenna said brusquely.

"Can someone carry her, then?" Callum implored. "I fear that outsiders are often... *unwelcome* in this part of the city. You would do best to leave this place quickly."

Oh, wonderful. More fear of this city was just what she needed right now...

"We can prop her between us," Ravenna suggested, gesturing toward Kira-Tharn. "It's no issue."

Blazes... walking along the Avenue in the worst part of town, propped between the two crankiest people she knew, sounded absolutely awful. Especially because *both* of them were sure to be irate with her. Still, it was amusing seeing these two ladies cooperating for once.

"Very well," Callum said. "I shall take my leave now."

He rose, masking his weakness well as he hefted Jack into his arms stolidly, stepping to leave.

"I'll be in touch soon to debrief," he added. "Tell Cryo and the others to expect me in a day or two. Three at most."

He better hold true to that, Niko demanded silently, hoping to the Mara that he wouldn't disappear for another year.

Ravenna nodded, then Callum swept out of the establishment, vanishing into the teeming crowds outside.

Niko, now alone with only Riiz Alke-Tani as a buffer between her and two angry women, stubbornly pushed herself to her feet before any of her companions could offer to help her. At the very least, she was *not* going to use Ravenna or Kira-Tharn as crutches. Absolutely not.

She took one step toward the exit. Then two. Then three.

Then she fell against the nearest table, splashing bowls of soup everywhere. The patrons cursed her angrily, threatening to do all manner violence toward her, but not before she was scooped up by her friends and whisked away.

———————————

The walk had most definitely been awkward. Niko was flanked by Kira-Tharn and Ravenna the entire time — she was too tired and too weak to walk on her own. Her impromptu experiment in the eatery proved that much.

The group received a few sideways stares as they all limped along, but only for their derelict appearance, not for the fact that two women were holding a completely incapacitated third woman upright, their male companion staggering on his own a few paces behind them.

Niko didn't know if she should be relieved or terrified that their display passed off as a normal activity here. Both, she guessed. Fortunately, nobody paid them too much mind, and they were able to traverse through the streets unobstructed.

Maybe what scared any potential muggers off was the fierce scowls of her two companions, both of whom delivered her a thorough tongue lashing. It hadn't been pleasant, but she'd been expecting it. Also, she was mostly focused on the considerable amount of discomfort she was in from the two weeks of malnutrition, so most of the scolding went in one ear and out the other.

When she wasn't concentrating on managing the pain or shutting out the admonishment, she was able to take in the ambience of Oldcity:

Independent entertainment shows that occasionally spilled from open café doors onto the streets.

Beggars crouched on nearly every corner, sunken eyes pleading with desperation.

The clashing tunes of countless impromptu musical groups scattered along the Avenue.

Sleazy fight clubs whose patrons occasionally took matters outside.

Dirty brothels patrolled by armed bouncers who tossed sketchy-looking revelers through the air onto the sidewalks.

Entire hotel complexes transformed into raging parties, glass shattering as objects were hurled from their windows.

And Cinto everywhere. So, *so* much Cinto.

Niko remembered what Anda had told her last month — about Shatter's plot to flood the population with distractions. If this walk to the rail station showed her anything, it was that their plan was working, and working well. These people had so much else on their minds *other* than the encroaching tyranny of Shatter.

Niko could see how easy it would be for them to take control of this place. The people wouldn't even care! As long as they got their Cinto fix, all was well.

Though, given the bleak state of Oldcity, maybe a little governance wouldn't be a bad thing. Thankfully, she hadn't witnessed any heinous crimes on her journey back, although Kira-Tharn made a point to recount exactly what went on in this city — whether as a cautionary tale or simply to antagonize her, Niko wasn't sure.

But she was already well aware of what went on here. For blazes' sakes, what happened to Anda in this district made her stomach pain seem laughable by contrast.

Anda...

Thinking of her friend brought her a fresh sort of anxiety. She knew she owed Anda the courtesy of an explanation for why she suddenly disappeared, but on the other hand, she couldn't tell the whole truth, for obvious reasons. Still, something made her feel like lying to her friend was the worst thing she could possibly do.

She took a deep breath, the pain spearing her sides as she did.

Only now, riding the rail from Oldcity to the central hub in Machine Row, did she manage to sit propped up on her own. Kira-Tharn and Ravenna had stopped talking to her at this point, so she was left alone with her thoughts. And her stomach pains, of course. Those were the new normal, and they made it *really* hard to think about anything else.

But she floated in thought, nevertheless. About what she'd tell Anda. About what she'd ask Cryo. About what she'd do to make up for her transgressions. About how she'd help regain the Terion she lost for her friends.

Niko released a long, slow breath.

Cryo's new stint on the Tour was nothing short of a miracle, but even still, a couple tenth place finishes wouldn't be enough to secure passage off world. She would certainly need to go back to the blacksquash fields. Although Kira-Tharn and Ravenna made it perfectly clear that she was *not* to return to work until she had completely recovered from her ordeal.

She would obey them, if only to avoid a firestorm. Those two, when their ire was compounded together, were the most fearsome duo she'd ever seen. It was definitely not worth provoking them any more than she already had.

Besides, she couldn't imagine plucking blacksquashes off the vines right now, stool or no. She couldn't even walk on her own! Blazes, she could barely talk...

A day off it would have to be.

And then she would return, and that's when she would tell Anda. Hopefully she'd be forgiven for abandoning the harvest team for all these weeks...

She would be, Niko decided. Anda was a gentle soul. Strangely intimidating in her own way, but a kind heart, nonetheless.

She let herself drift off to pleasant thoughts of friendship as the rail sped back to Machine Row, a momentary respite from the constant pain that settled in the pit of her stomach.

CHAPTER TWENTY-SIX

26

Blackouts

"**I** just want a shower," Niko lamented. "Is that too much to ask from these damned overlords?"

"I would also be one to enjoy such luxuries, but circumstances are what they are," Kira-Tharn stated matter-of-factly. "The situation regarding the water in our district has been thoroughly communicated."

Ughh. One would think that blazes woman didn't care about washing one bit. Or having access to actual drinking water...

"I don't care how well they communicate it," Niko went on. "It isn't right."

"You are to use the community well like every other citizen in the An-Mara quarter, not act like an entitled *Meridian*."

The way Kira-Tharn compared her to a Meridian with such contempt only magnified Niko's frustration. The heat rose in her temples, but she checked herself just in time, keeping her tongue at bay before she said something she regretted. Maybe Kira-Tharn was right. Maybe she *was* acting too uppity.

Kira-Tharn had no idea what she just had to endure, though. Weeks trapped on a tiny raft with three grown men, drifting down the Rifts in sub-freezing temperatures, nearly starving, spending days on end in the blazes-accursed Wash...

Not to mention the attack by Shatter — or coming face to face with the damn Machine...

She almost *died*, and Kira-Tharn was basically calling her a diva for wanting a simple shower.

"Maybe I shouldn't wash at all," Niko bemoaned. "Maybe you'd prefer I just smell like the Wash for the rest of my life?"

"You are being childish, Niko Ryen."

"Well, you're being unfair!"

Unfair? Blazes, she wished she couldn't hear herself. She *was* being childish.

Kira-Tharn released a weary breath. "The Time dictates that we do not experience matters through the perspective of fairness or unfairness. Those sentiments only lead to entitlement and resentment."

Kira-Tharn was right, but Niko wasn't in any mood for a philosophical lecture right now. Sure, her stomach was feeling much better, but she was still extremely exhausted, and irritability was her baseline emotion these last few days.

"I cannot do anything about the lack of warm water, but I do believe that I may be able to perform adjustments to the plumbing. That should improve the water pressure to this unit." Maro Del-Fiiz, in the attempt to mediate, offered the solution. Bless his heart.

"It's okay," Niko said. "Kira-Tharn's right. I need to just suck it up."

"What does that even mean, Niko Ryen?" Kira-Tharn asked condescendingly. *"Suck it up?"*

That pompous chum! Anytime Kira-Tharn became heated, she'd fling Niko's Arhandan slang back in her face, savoring every syllable like some victory. The blazes woman was going to be the death of her.

"Thank you, though, Maro," Niko said, completely ignoring Kira-Tharn's jab.

"Of course, Niko Ryen."

The man was good for Kira-Tharn, thoughtful and dedicated. During her time away, it seemed he'd become a more frequent visitor. As it was, during each of the last three mornings, he was over to make breakfast for all of them, though Niko's portions were still being rationed to allow her digestive tract to properly readjust to standard eating patterns. Three days recovered from near-death and she was *almost* back to normal.

'*Tomorrow*', Kira-Tharn had said. Tomorrow she might return to work.

Niko might've protested and tried to work anyway, but she knew deep down that Kira-Tharn kept her well-being in mind, frustrating as the woman was. Besides, she was more wrecked from her ordeal than she would've liked to admit.

Ordinarily, two weeks of starvation might not be fatal, but paired with the freezing conditions and the consumption of Wash water, it nearly had been. Taking an extra few days off from work to get healthy wasn't the end of the worlds.

I wonder how Jack's doing, she thought, her mind still on the topic of near-death. Was he alive? He'd been even closer to the brink than she had, and none of them had heard anything from Callum yet. The man said he'd reach out in three days maximum, and this was the third.

A knock on the door dragged Niko's attention away from her thoughts.

Kira-Tharn, still babying Niko to a degree, was quick to her feet. Niko half rolled her eyes, but she supposed she *did* appreciate the care that was given.

When Kira-Tharn opened the door wide, it was Riiz who stood outside, nodding to all three occupants. Like the proper An-Mara he was, he politely waited, making no move to barge in and make himself at home.

"How do you fare, Niko Ryen?" he asked.

"Feeling much better," she answered. "You?"

"Likewise."

"What brings you to our company this morning, Riiz Alke-Tani?" Maro Del-Fiiz asked.

Was that a hint of *tension* in his voice? Or was Niko only imagining it?

Riiz seemed to take no notice. "I would be one to pass along the message that the ones called Kira-Tharn and Niko Ryen are to join the ones called Cryo Siriar, Ravenna Night, Kyler Pierson, and Ce-Ellum in Machine Row."

"When?" Niko asked. "Now?"

Did they have some news? Maybe Callum and Jack??

"That is correct."

"They deign to assume they can just summon us at will," Kira-

327

Tharn muttered angrily, just loud enough for Niko hear. "I would have words with the one called Ravenna Night."

Oh, here we go, Niko groaned to herself.

Ever since those two had been forced to work together the other day, Kira-Tharn would not let her disdain for the woman go. However, Niko knew Kira-Tharn well enough to know that outward projection of animus was only a mask for what she assumed to be some sort of antiquated form of respect.

"I regret this meeting is one that is private," Riiz said, offering a genuinely apologetic look toward Maro.

Maro, though, only glared back at Riiz.

Niko was not imagining it; there was *definitely* tension in the air, if not barely concealed hostility.

"Yes, Riiz Alke-Tani, we will attend with you," Kira-Tharn accepted, glaring in turn back at Maro.

The glower caught Maro's eyes. He seemed to take the hint, as he meekly bowed his head and retreated from their quarters, leaving his unfinished biscuits on the countertop. Niko felt bad for the guy. He was only trying to spend more time with Kira-Tharn, even if the atmosphere became tense because of it.

"I would be one to convey an apology on his behalf," Kira-Tharn told Riiz, after Maro had left. "I do not know when this possessive behavior arose."

Riiz nodded. "No, it is I who would be the one to convey an apology. This is not an opportune time for such a liaison."

"It is beyond your control," Kira-Tharn said plainly, finishing the last vestiges of her meal. "Shall we be on our way now?"

She didn't wait for an answer, or two seconds for Niko to react, before marching for the door. She was certainly in no mood for idle chatter...

Niko inhaled two more gulps of the broth, then dumped the rest into the washbasin.

What a waste. As if she could afford to waste any food...

It didn't matter, though. If she didn't pack up and follow immediately, Kira-Tharn would've well-enough left without her, huffy as she was. At least Riiz was decent enough to wait, if only halfway.

Niko locked the door behind her, hustling after her friends on shaky legs, though a little less wobbly each day. She was so rushed in her flight, though, that she didn't even take the time to wonder why exactly they were being summoned to her friends' quarters in Machine Row, other than to hope Callum and Jack were there. She only followed, barely aware of anything more than putting one foot in front of the other.

What she did notice, though, was the lack of street lanterns as they made their way to the rail station, though the typical buzz of the An-Mara quarter continued to thrum around them.

"More blackouts?" she asked.

"There have been many," Kira-Tharn responded without breaking stride. "Our quarter is also mandated to remain in a temporary condition of brownout, though you may not have noticed in your state of near-constant sleepiness the last few days."

She said it as though Niko had a choice in the matter. As if her recovery was something that she was stretching out for maximum sympathy.

"When did this happen?" she asked, ignoring Kira-Tharn's dig.

"It occurred during the interval in which you two were out playing at becoming adventurers all across the planet."

Riiz wisely stayed silent while Kira-Tharn was so irritable. Niko knew better, also. Besides, she was far too tired to battle wits with the blazes woman right now.

"So they just cut our power?" Niko asked incredulously. "And expect us to pay the same fees?"

"If we do not pay, then we lose our lodgings."

Niko knew it was that simple, but it still didn't make it right…

"And who does this decree come from? Terion?"

"Yes. Actually, it does."

Of course it did.

"Can't we do anything? Can't anybody do anything about it? Like what if everyone in the An-Mara quarter just refused to pay, all at once?"

Kira-Tharn stopped dead in her tracks, turning on Niko, lowering her voice to barely more than a whisper.

"I will only explain it to you this once, Niko Ryen, since you have been gone," Kira-Tharn warned, her dark eyes locked onto Niko's like An-Terino was to Bucon. "There have been *changes* to the city in your absence. An-Mara are disappearing in large numbers, which does concern the lot of us. None that I have conversed with knows where they are being taken, but our plight likely involves connections to the organizations called Terion and

Shatter. Those entities are working cooperatively to install listening machines throughout the city, so I would suggest that you reserve your criticisms for private audiences only. That is all I will say on the matter."

Kira-Tharn then pulled her predatory gaze from Niko's eyes, then turned around and continued walking to the rail station at a brisk pace.

Enough said.

Dread washed over Niko once more. Not the same all-consuming fear she felt when she came face to face with that abominable piece of the Machine, but dread nonetheless. None of what Kira-Tharn said sat right with her.

She would've inquired further, but this wasn't the time or place. 'Private audiences only,' Kira-Tharn had said. But, blazes, she needed clarifications!

"Do you know anything about this?" she asked Riiz quietly.

He shrugged. "I did not know. But I do believe the one called Kira-Tharn in that we should not discuss such matters here and now."

Fair.

So she followed her friends to the station, stomach aching and legs wobbling, without saying anything else.

The Frying Pan. She'd heard of it before, but the name sounded comical. Nefarious, sure, but comical.

"So let me get this straight... you think *that's* where they've been taking all those An-Mara?" she asked.

"Do we need to spell it out in so many different ways?" Kyler snarked.

Niko did her best to ignore the bait. "Did they *do* anything to deserve it, though?"

"Is there such an action they would need to commit to deserve such a heinous consequence?" Kira-Tharn shot back.

"No, you're right," Niko acknowledged. Kira-Tharn *was* right — there was no reason in all of the worlds that would excuse what

Shatter was doing to the An-Mara. "What I meant was… is it random how they're picking the people up and sending them off?"

"It's the listening machines," Cryo said. "The surveillance algorithms. The Terion Sight. That's why it's *really* important you watch what you say."

"When did this even happen?!" Niko demanded. "We've only been gone for a couple weeks."

She'd been hearing more and more about such surveillance, but it seemed entirely different than before they left. More intense, and way more insidious.

Kyler let out a sharp, cruel laugh. "While you were out doing blazes knows what, we were busy dealing with trying to find an answer to all of this."

"Blazes knows what?!" Niko shouted, her hoarse voice cracking through the strain. "We almost died! And trying to find *your* Kezane! If I recall, *you* were going on and on and on about that guy not too long ago."

"Sheeeesh," he groaned innocently. "I was just saying, we've been really busy with this."

"I know what you were saying, Kyler," she snapped in frustration. "I just haven't seen this crackdown from Shatter and Terion, is all. Callum did talk a little about their plans, rising surveillance and all, but I didn't think they'd implement stuff here in the city so *quickly*."

"Turns out it wasn't so quickly," Cryo said. "It's been in the works for a long while, and somehow, we didn't pick up on any of it. Terion's tinkerers are good. Better than we thought, for sure."

"And speaking of," Kyler continued, "their new system is already online. We were hoping to use the transition to hack in, but it happened so quietly."

"Do you know any of the tinkerers at Terion, Kyler Pierson?" Riiz asked. "Is there any insight we have on this new system?"

"I know *of* them," he said, "but only in the cyber world — not in the real world. T2, T8, T9, T11, T12, T21… Those are the main ones I come across, but there are actually hundreds of them working on their systems. And no. Not much insight, unfortunately."

"*Hundreds*?" Niko squeaked.

"Did I speak something other than Common?"

Niko made a face at him. The petulant ass.

Cryo took over, mediating the quarrel that always seemed to

spark up between her and Kyler. "This new system… we can't crack it. Not with what we've got. We need way more time, more people, more resources… All of it. For now, we're relegated to finding more traditional methods of getting the Terion we need."

Well, that wasn't the news she wanted to hear.

"What about your work on the Infinity Machine?" she asked. "You were saying those Infinity algorithms would be able to crack any of the Terion machines quickly?"

"We've run into severe problems with that," Ce-Ellum conceded. Blazes, she'd forgotten that guy was even in the room. "It needs way more development time, and we also need some materials that don't exist here. At least, not anywhere we'd have access to."

"Yep," Cryo agreed. "It's looking like something that we aren't gonna be able to complete. Shame, because it was pretty fun working on it."

"If only we had somewhere with an infinite power source and massive amounts of space…" Kyler trailed off.

"A particle collider would be nice," Cryo muttered.

A particle collider… And lots of space…

Niko suddenly remembered her dream and that ring-like structure around that star. Obviously a fantasy, but an interesting thought.

"What about one that's in space? One that orbits a star?" she conjectured.

Kyler stared at her for a split second before bursting out in derisive laughter.

"Space?!" he howled, doubled over for the extra effect. "Are you daft?!"

Even Ravenna rolled her eyes and let out a loud sigh of annoyance, as did Kira-Tharn. She shouldn't have said anything; she should've known they'd only make fun of her.

"It was just a… thought," she said quietly, embarrassed to all blazes. "Forget I said anything."

"Space!…" Kyler continued to laugh. "That's a good one!…"

Niko bowed her head to the floor in shame, but from the corner of her eye, she could see Ce-Ellum studying her intently, far from joining in Kyler's ridicule.

"Why do you say space?" he asked slowly.

"Nevermind," she answered, still more than aware of Kyler's scornful gaze. "Just forget it."

"I'm being serious," Ce-Ellum pressed.

Though she appreciated that he didn't appear to be mocking her, the way he looked at her with intense contemplation filled Niko with unease. She already knew he was an agent of Alashadar's underworld, but this stare unnerved her. There was something about his eyes, his posture, that told her she did *not* want to mess with him. It was exactly what one would expect from some Oldcity enforcer, and she could only hope her friends would pick up on it before it was too late.

Niko tightened her jaw. She tried to warn them...

The tension that hung thick between them must've been so obvious that even Kyler paused in his fit of scorn, eyes darting quickly between Ce-Ellum and Niko.

"Wait, you're serious?" he asked unbelievingly, still out of breath from laughing at Niko.

"What did you have in mind, Niko?" Ce-Ellum repeated.

Blazes, the man's stare was intense!

"I just... I think I've seen an image of a particle collider in space somewhere, orbiting closely to a star," she answered, if for no other reason than to be rid of his poring gaze.

Ce-Ellum remained quiet, looking at her for a few more moments before pulling his eyes away. Was she supposed to say something else.

"It's an interesting idea, and there are such structures that exist," he finally responded. "But unfortunately, we don't possess the resources to construct anything remotely similar."

"Hmph, that goes without saying," Kyler grunted.

An awkward silence ensued. Kyler probably felt shut down by Ce-Ellum's acknowledgement of Niko's suggestion, and no one else bothered to strike up new conversation.

Before anyone could break the ice, the lights completely shut off. Darkness swallowed the room for a split second, then flickered back to life with a hum, albeit more dimly.

Of course her friends would have a backup generator... Maybe they could help build one for her and Kira-Tharn?

"Blazes," Ravenna cursed. "Again?"

"This has been an occurrence very common in the An-Mara quarter," Riiz said, shrugging.

"No offense, but the An-Mara quarter has always had frequent power outages," said Ce-Ellum. "This past year has actually been the most stable I've ever seen."

Kira-Tharn glared at him, as if she took offense. Niko felt a sense of ownership over the An-Mara quarter, also, but she held no illusions — it wasn't the nicest place to live, and it didn't surprise her in the least that it was always a place hit hard with blackouts.

"The An-Mara quarter, I could see," Ravenna dismissed with a toss of her hair. "But Machine Row...?"

Ce-Ellum shrugged. "Anytime there's variability in output, they will make sure Terion's system is fed first. And since it uses a *vast* amount of power compared to their old system, that's where all power is diverted. Terion *is* Machine Row, at least in their eyes. Nothing else matters to them, and all lines lead to that vision."

"Yeah, and now the outages are everywhere," Cryo added. "Oldcity's getting hit pretty hard with them, as well."

"Yep," Ce-Ellum agreed. "And speaking of Oldcity, Cryo and I need to get back to the Vulture works. We still have much race preparation to complete."

Vulture...

Niko found it both amusing and disturbing that Ce-Ellum didn't even try to hide his association with that crime front anymore. She only hoped that Cryo wasn't being pulled in too deep, especially after her own slog through the streets of Oldcity showed her just what that sort of life looked like. It wasn't a place she would want any of her friends to spend their time.

"Yeah, we best be on our way," Cryo said. "Race is in two days."

"Good luck," Niko offered. "If I don't see you before."

"Thanks," he replied, returning a quick side hug. "Maybe tomorrow. But if not, then after the race. And Niko, I'm glad you made it back okay."

She forced a crooked smile. "Me too."

Kira-Tharn, Riiz, and Kyler also gave their farewells, in case none of them saw him before the race. Ravenna, though, only offered him a wordless exchange, a glare that said all it needed to. She had made it plenty clear that she did *not* approve of his association with Trackripping. Or Vulture.

Both, actually.

A couple minutes after Cryo and Ce-Ellum left, Niko became desperate for an excuse to leave. Besides Riiz, Cryo was the only buffer between her and the ire of her friends, but now that he was gone, things were… tense.

Between Ravenna and Kira-Tharn's passive aggressive digs and Kyler's unfiltered rudeness, she had to get out of there. She was about to just get up and leave without explanation when a knock sounded at the door.

Kyler leapt up to answer, and in walked Jack and Callum.

Niko's eyes widened in relief.

Jack! He was not dead!

Niko sprang to her feet, unsteady as she was, and threw her arms around his neck, thanking the Mara that he was alright.

"Easy," he whispered, weakly returning the embrace.

Blazes, he sounded terrible! Even worse than herself!

"You okay?" she fussed.

"I've felt better," he replied honestly. "But I'm not gonna die at least. I heard you weren't doing so well, either?"

"I'm fine," she lied. "But I've been worrying this whole time. We had zero word from you guys!"

She gave Callum a pointed glance with those last few words.

"We had to get him into Shatter right away," Callum explained. "But they took over his care with minimal questions. It turns out, all we had to do was blame the An-Mara and they bought it."

Kira-Tharn muttered something under her breath too quiet for Niko to hear. She probably wouldn't have wanted to hear, anyway.

"It is quite dark outside," Callum remarked, redirecting any angst away from him. "I didn't think the Row would be suffering the blackouts like the rest of the city."

"We were just talking about that," Kyler commiserated. "Terion is using all the power for their new system. They've rerouted all power lines away from the outlying areas."

"It is already online?" Callum asked, surprise lining his hardened face.

Kyler nodded. "Oh yeah."

"Wow, that was fast. You weren't able to hack the old one in

335

time, I assume?"

"Nope," Kyler responded, wincing.

He looked like he took Callum's innocuous question more personally than he'd ever taken any insult in his life. Maybe Niko would use that as fodder for the next time Kyler made her feel like blazes...

"Shame," Callum said. "Well, we came to brief you all on the Kezane situation, as well as that of the Machine, if Riiz and Niko haven't told you anything."

"The Machine?!" Kyler blurted out. "As in *the* Machine?"

"I take it that means you two haven't updated our friends here?" Callum asked Riiz and Niko.

Niko shook her head. "We didn't get around to that yet."

"Since you are present now, Callum Sehs," Riiz said, "I believe you would be the one to deliver that assessment."

"Wait, wait, wait," Kyler interrupted. "Can we go back to the part about *the Machine*?"

"Is Cryo here?" Callum asked, ignoring Kyler's request. "I think he'd want to hear what we have to say."

"Hellooo. The *Machine*?!"

Niko was enjoying the sight of Kyler squirming while everyone ignored his pleas.

"Cryo just left. Fill us in, and we'll relay it to him," Ravenna said tightly, extending the spectacle. Niko thought Kyler was about ready to explode with the suspense.

"Very well."

So Callum did, to Kyler's great relief, going over every detail much more thoroughly than Niko would have. Except for the part where *she* had to save their sorry asses on multiple occasions with her navigation techniques. That omission sightly irked her, but at least he did make mention to thank her for reaching out in the dreams.

She meant to ask Cryo about all that tonight — about how he was able to know the inner workings of the An-Terino aqueduct system, and about how he was able to project all that information through a single touch — but she didn't get a good opportunity.

Now he was gone, the Mara be damned. She'd have to make a point to ask him after the race.

Everyone's appreciation for Niko's willingness to reach out via the dreams did little to soothe Ravenna's distrust of her judgment, though. Before Niko left for the night, Ravenna made a show in asking when she would return to work to earn back the Terion *she* had lost for everybody.

'Tomorrow', Niko had responded curtly.

Ravenna only snorted in response, making some comment she didn't quite catch.

Niko knew she messed up, but Ravenna just *wouldn't* let it go. It made her not even want to go over to her friends' place anymore. All the relief and happiness she felt at seeing Jack alive had fleeted when Ravenna turned on her, and she was left to dwell on less content feelings as she journeyed back to the An-Mara quarter with Riiz and Kira-Tharn along darkened streets.

She hissed the worst curses she knew at the blackouts, but she and the others knew those weren't the primary source of her frustration.

CHAPTER TWENTY-SEVEN

27

The Contract

THE low angle solrays at the blacksquash fields were a welcome reprieve from those she'd been forced to suffer the other day. The brutal thrashing of Bucon wasn't even the worst of the experience, however. Not by a long shot.

Shatter was far worse.

Or more precisely, the fact that every single one of the EC's cowed to them wholly and completely, giving them anything and everything they wanted.

Or that farce of an execution...

Anda couldn't help but wonder if those three hapless souls were indeed innocent at the end of it all — merely political pawns caught in the wrong place at the wrong time. It was certainly a stirring for reflection.

She steeled her countenance and mindlessly lobbed another blacksquash into her bin.

All of that Shatter business was something to worry about later. Or not at all. Something for someone else to worry about, surely. What could she possibly do? She was only one person, and held absolutely no sway on this world.

But if not her, then who?...

"Well, isn't that something."

Anda looked up, startled at the utterings of the woman next to her, unsure of the meaning.

"Yes, Nuna?" she asked.

"Our friend has not worked with us for weeks, but she once again graces us with her presence. What an occasion!"

What was the woman on about?

Nuna caught Anda's obvious confusion, so she gestured across the fields to a lone figure striding toward the offices.

Oh, good. Maybe they were finally hiring a replacement to round out their team number to ten.

It was about time. Harvesting the work of ten people with only nine had become tiresome over the last month, to say the least.

She took one last glance at whoever it was heading toward the offices before turning back to her work. But something familiar caught her eye. Something about the way that person moved...

She spared a second look, narrowing her vision.

Was that actually...?

Anda peered closer, annoyed at the lack of depth perception from only having one eye. She would never admit it was a crutch, to herself or anyone else, but it did make discerning faces from afar rather difficult.

By the will of the Nel-Mara! Was that *Niko*?!

She wiped the sweat from her face and squinted.

It *was* her!

And neither dead *nor* incarcerated in that blasted inferno they called the Frying Pan.

———————

Niko's gaze caught Anda's simultaneously. Part of her was hoping she wouldn't have to face her friend right now, if only so she didn't have to explain why the blazes she disappeared when she did. Or where she was currently headed...

But she was also happy for the reunion, her heart leaping with joy at the sight of the friend she hadn't seen in a month.

To her gratitude, there was no hint of resentment in the light blue of Anda's eye, only a look of what Niko thought to be relief, which was a welcome change after dealing with the chafing reactions of Kira-Tharn and Ravenna.

She gave her friend a heartfelt hug atop the familiar dirt mounds on which the blacksquash rows were planted, comforted when Anda returned it with equal enthusiasm.

"It is good to see you, Niko Ryen," Anda greeted her with a smile, or what looked like one, through the poor woman's jagged scar tissue.

"You too! I'm *sooo* sorry I never sent word! I… had to leave… on short notice."

"It is quite alright," Anda assured her.

Blazes, thank the Mara the girl was being so nice about it. She didn't think she could take another verbal thrashing. Though, the fussy look on her friend's face was uncharacteristic. Had Anda been *worried* about her all this time?

"I missed you," Niko said earnestly.

"As did I," Anda replied. "You've been well?"

"Ummm…" Niko hesitated. "I've been okay."

A flash of worry flickered across Anda's face, before it was schooled back into serenity.

"I mean, I'm fine now," Niko clarified. "I just… we had to go out into the Night for a short while."

Niko nearly laughed at her own stretching of the truth. '*Into the Night for a short while*' was putting it lightly…

But… should she have even volunteered that information at all?

She supposed it was fine, because even though she hadn't known Anda for very long, she *had* grown to value the girl as a trusted confidant, a friend who she felt comfortable sharing deep secrets with. After all, Anda had shared her own.

"The Night?" Anda sounded surprised. "You've been out in the *Night* this entire time?"

"Niko! Welcome back!" two familiar voices called from across the fields.

Niko whirled her head around. "Marial! Nuna! I missed you!"

"And we have missed you, young lady," Nuna chimed. "Have you come to complete our team once more? We would be blessed to have your energy among us."

"I… I need to talk to ROTO," Niko said, eking the words out

through a grimace.

"I'm sure they will take you back without hesitation." Marial smiled warmly. "Our team is still missing one worker."

"If you need a good word, let Anda accompany you," Nuna suggested. "We can more than manage the harvesting while you two are gone for a few minutes."

Anda seemed ready to protest, but she was interrupted by Marial before even saying anything.

"Yes, Nuna, what an idea. Anda, why don't you go with her?"

Anda was silent for a moment, then nodded in agreement. Niko grasped hands with both ladies in crisscross fashion the Ossion way, then gestured for Anda to lead the way to the offices, which she did.

"Excuse me?" Anda didn't know if she heard correctly. The girl intended to enter into a *contract*? Of *servitude*?! She had better be jesting...

"Before you yell at me, hear me out," Niko pleaded. "You know how badly I screwed over my friends with the betting. I *need* the Terion to make it up."

Anda didn't know what that phrase meant — 'screwed over'. It was surely Arhandan slang, and probably meant the same thing as 'betrayed' or 'wronged', based on the context.

"You are in this predicament *because* of the betting," Anda stated. "And your response is to suggest *more* of it?"

"This isn't betting!" Niko protested. "I told you about the contract they provided! It's just a one-time th..."

"This is absolutely betting." Anda cut Niko off, leveling her a very serious stare. As serious as she could muster, and she hoped it accomplished what she intended. "Except instead of betting Terion, you're betting your life."

"It's not like that!"

"It *is* like that. That's all it is."

For being so smart, this girl was acting quite obtusely.

"Did you already forget my story about how I got these scars? About how I was almost killed?" Anda continued, exasperation starting to show.

"I can't keep living like this," Niko sighed. "I have to get out of here, Anda. I can't take this place anymore."

"I know, but... That is the primary reason why you *can't* go ahead with this." Anda softened her tone. "Please."

"I... I have to." Niko lowered her pleas to a whisper. "I'm just asking for your support."

"I do so wish to support you, I really do. But you don't know these companies like I do. The contract wording will be so lengthy, and there are sure to be all sorts of loopholes they can and will use to exploit your service. They will lock you in, and then you'll never get out." She paused for extra effect. "Like me."

Niko let out a long breath. "Then I will demand to their faces that there are no such loopholes to keep me any longer than a one-time deal. They have to respect that."

"In theory."

"And I will read every line of the contract if I have to."

"You would be the biggest fool on An-Terino if you didn't."

"I promise to. Just please let me do this, Anda."

Anda regarded Niko closely for a few moments. The girl was being *extremely* pushy right now; she hadn't seen her like this before. Something must have happened during her trip out into the Night, but she'd let Niko talk about it when she was ready.

"The timing is not the best," Anda said flatly. "Things are really unstable right now."

"If what you're talking about has anything to do with Terion's new system, or the surveillance that they're rigging everywhere, my friends are all aware of that," she said.

"I'm talking about..."

Anda paused, debating on how much to tell Niko.

In the end, she decided it was best to tell of everything that happened during her summons to the Frying Pan, and what was at stake.

Niko's jaw may as well have been on the floor.

She knew about Shatter trying to seize control of An-Terino, but... *slavery*? Here?

Her thoughts drifted to Galen, Noralie, and Michele. They had been taken by Shatter... Would *they* have been sent to the Frying Pan? Or what about the people of An-Tun Village? None of them had been seen or heard from since.

And judging from all she'd been told, this injustice would not be uncharacteristic of Shatter. Not by any stretch. And if those chums were now taking slaves and executing prisoners...

Niko worried at the prospect. She knew those people, had come to respect them. People like Fellen-Sor, who had just been trying to make a better life for herself. People like Galen, Noralie, and Michele, who had devoted their lives to stymy the Machine. Even people like Solor-Ven, Viru-Mor, or Raul Vess, who gave up a more comfortable lifestyle in the city to lead others to a simpler life of freedom.

It was terrible to imagine these people suffering in such a manner, yet one question even more worrisome lingered:

How widespread were these listening machines?

Since she had shared her own misgivings about Shatter out loud, could *she* be taken and hauled away into the Daylight?? A chill ran through her at the thought of being forced to work in those conditions. The Rifts were bad enough, but deep Daylight...?

"So you see," Anda finished, "that is why I am so adamant that you do not sell yourself into indentured servitude."

She wasn't keen on Anda lecturing her on this matter, but she *needed* this work. She *needed* the Terion.

"This *isn't* indentured servitude!" she objected.

"It absolutely is," Anda retorted. "That's what the servitude is. It's a contract into service for a specified amount of time. Which is exactly what you are agreeing to."

"Yeah, but it's a *one-time* deal," Niko argued. "One evening of first-class catering service, and that's it."

"As far as you're aware of." Anda wasn't letting this go. "These EC's are not to be trusted. Besides, I just told you about all the bids they put into Shatter, and that's why it's even worse than normal to be making deals with them now."

"How many times do you want me to say I'll be careful?!"

"You know what I want you to say — that you won't do this at all."

Blazes, she didn't expect this big a fight from Anda. She'd read the contract that was advertised, and it didn't seem nearly as bad as Anda was making it out to be. It was literally just one evening of serving food to elites. Not gangsters. Not their minions. Elites.

"Well, I'm doing this, and as much as I respect you, Anda, my decision is final." She knew that this was something she had to do. Anda would never understand the debt she owed her friends.

"Very well."

'Very well?' That was it? That's all she had to say this whole time? That her decision was final, then Anda wouldn't argue further?

"But Niko Ryen, if you do this, then I do it with you."

Ohhh, no she would not...

Niko tightened her jaw. There was no way in the blazes she would let Anda sign up with her.

She shook her head vehemently. "This is my burden, not yours."

"That it may be, but I refuse to let my friend sign herself into such a situation with no backup."

"Anda..."

The woman held up her hand, silencing any further arguments. "If your decision is final, then so is mine."

Blazes. She hadn't been anticipating this.

"Please just let me do th..."

"You refuse to listen to my reason — and my experience — that such contracts are nefarious by design. Even if you sign your Terion badge to the contract, who do you expect will be there to enforce the terms? No, I will be going with you on this."

"Anda, please..."

"My decision is final," Anda repeated, stealing Niko's own words. Even through her slight frame, the blazes woman looked so imposing, almost haughty, and arguing with her seemed pointless.

"Whatever," Niko grumbled.

If Anda was satisfied at the submission, she didn't show it, as if winning a battle of wits was an ordinary occurrence. "Do you have any friends also accompanying us?" she asked.

"Umm... I hadn't asked."

"Then I will be recruiting Amon to join us, also."

Of all the blazes... Amon also?!

As happy as she was to see her friend, Niko really wished she could've avoided crossing paths with Anda on her way to the ROTO offices to accept this contract.

"Anda, just pl..."

"I do not wish to be a thorn on your conscience, I really don't," Anda interrupted again. "But I *know* this world, Niko Ryen. Believe me when I say I know it. The presence of Amon and myself is non-negotiable. It's for your own relative safety. Better than going alone, that much is certain."

"Fine."

"Let us be on our way, then," Anda said, emotionless as she marched toward the offices with Niko in tow.

———————————

CHAPTER TWENTY-EIGHT

28

Tough Conversations

NIKO was frustrated beyond words.

Anda hadn't been condescending like Kira-Tharn or Ravenna, but she was being blazes ridiculous in her own right. Why couldn't *anyone* trust her to make decisions on her own?! Sure, she'd made some bad ones recently, but that didn't mean she needed her hand held at every corner of the city.

The reunion with her friend was *not* how she'd have wanted it to go. She meant to go into ROTO, sign the contract — which was for a blazes *one-time* deal — then leave. Maybe even work the fields after.

But instead, she stormed off immediately after signing the damned thing, barely able to meet Anda's eyes. That had been the guilt setting in, since the blazes woman had refused to back down from joining the contract with her.

Maybe there was some way to sneak into the city and fulfill the job without Anda...

Probably not, since they signed an actual binding contract, stamped with their Terion badges and all. And of course, Anda had dragged Amon into the contract also, just like she said she would.

He hadn't been able to sign onto the service detail, though; instead, he was recruited as security reinforcement outside the suite. Either way, he did *not* seem pleased about the situation one bit, and laid into Anda for it.

Hard.

Anda barely defended herself; she only raised her chin in this ridiculous manner and turned on her heel to the offices, forcing both Niko and Amon to hurry after her. She never once mentioned it was Niko's idea, and when Niko tried to confess, Anda shut her down, insisting it had been her decision alone. What she said wasn't exactly untrue, the way she manipulated her words, but she seemed determined to take full responsibility herself.

Blazes! Just remembering that whole interaction had Niko balling her hands into sweaty fists.

"Are you certain you are feeling healthy?" Kira-Tharn asked.

Niko took a deep breath. She needed to cool down already; she'd been home for hours now.

"I'm fine."

"You do not appear as though you are one that is in satisfactory condition to be working just yet."

"What an astute assessment, Kira-Tharn."

Blazes, she was feeling feisty right now. Where was this resolve when Anda insisted on butting into the contract, dragging Amon along as well?

"I only serve to ensure your well being, Niko Ryen."

Niko's shoulders slumped as she exhaled. "I know. I'm sorry. I just... nevermind."

"What is it you wished to verbalize?"

"Nothing. Nevermind."

"You did not have *nothing* in your thoughts, Niko Ryen."

Blazes, could the woman just drop it? Niko searched for something to shift the conversation. She was *not* about to tell Kira-Tharn of that contract she signed herself into for tomorrow. If Anda's reaction to it was bad, then she *really* wouldn't like Kira-Tharn's...

"I'm fine," Niko lied. "But I did need to talk to you. Both of you."

Maro Del-Fiiz, who'd become a near-permanent fixture in their quarters, had been trying to lie low, appearing *very* interested in sifting nutrient mix into bowls of soup. However, his eyebrows perked up at Niko's address.

"What is it you needed to speak to the both of us about?" Kira-Tharn asked, arms now crossed over her chest.

Hmm. How was she going to phrase this without Kira-Tharn getting all huffy?

"It's about the Rifts. You can't be working there anym..." Niko started.

"We have been over this many a time, Niko Ryen," Kira-Tharn interrupted. "We are required to work in the Rifts to meet the demands for the increasing living costs."

"You have to choose something else," Niko spat out.

"I will not brandish words with you further on this matter."

Ugh, this was going to be more difficult than Niko hoped. So much for diplomacy...

"That's too bad, because I'm serious this time. What I heard fr..."

"The matter is closed, Niko Ryen."

"It is *NOT* closed," Niko snapped. "Can you listen to what I have to say without interrupting me like some petulant little child?"

Kira-Tharn didn't respond, but Niko could practically see tendrils of wispy smoke billowing out of Kira-Tharn's flaring nostrils. Oh, she was *pissed* to be spoken to like that, to be likened to a *child*. Maybe Niko should've been calling her out like this all along. Whatever did the trick in shutting her up long enough to get sentences out...

"Anyway, it was about all the companies, and deals they made with Shatter," Niko continued. Kira-Tharn let her speak, for the moment at least. "That girl I work with — Anda — she told me there was this secret deal Shatter forced all the companies into."

"Which companies?" Kira-Tharn asked. "And what deal?"

"All of them. And if you'll let me finish, I'll tell you."

Kira-Tharn leaned back against the wall, arms still crossed, no doubt taken aback by Niko's newfound boldness.

"What I was going to say was that they forced *all* the companies to meet in this prison way out in the Daylight called the Frying Pan, then they threatened everyone and made them basically swear allegiance to Shatter. The EC's are required to provide whatever Shatter wants, but then in return, Shatter will supply them with energy."

"And how would the organization called Shatter have the

ability to enforce such terms?" Kira-Tharn asked. "I do know them to maintain a modicum of power out here, but... *all* the companies? I do not believe they hold that amount of authority."

"They do," Niko responded flatly. "They've been working with Terion, which we kind of already know. Anda said Shatter provides the forces and energy, and Terion provides the infrastructure and machine tinkerers. And all the rest of the companies, no matter how powerful they are, are at the mercy of what Shatter and Terion can provide together."

"I do still find it difficult to believe that these two corporations can bend all the others to their will."

"Well, you better believe it," Niko said.

Blazes, she was doing a poor job of explaining it. She wished Anda were here to tell them; it was way more believable when she said it...

"Shatter has all the power," she continued, doing her best to recreate the account. "They've been importing batteries or something here, and then building extra power plants and refineries. And to run those facilities, they're taking prisoners and forcing them to work. That's where so many An-Mara are disappearing off to. And I *know* you know that's true — you were the one who shushed me the other day because of all the listening machines and everything. If they don't like what you say, then they arrest you and send you to the Frying Pan."

Both Kira-Tharn and Maro glanced at each other. No doubt the tidbit about An-Mara disappearing off the streets struck a nerve. It was one thing to be arrested, but it was another thing entirely to be shipped off to the Frying Pan without a trace...

"But the main thing I was getting at... was that Terrovian Aquatics, where *both* of you work, made a deal providing Shatter with labor to send to the Frying Pan. So you wouldn't even have to do anything wrong to be sent out there... You'll become a *slave*, and for nothing more than working for the wrong company. Anda heard it with her own ears. And that's why you can never go back to work at the Rifts."

"Would that not be a gross exaggeration on the matter, Niko Ryen?" Kira-Tharn asked. "The organization called Terrovian Aquatics is operating just like they always have."

Blazes! Could the woman, for once in her life, trust what Niko had to say?? Niko fumed, cheeks reddening.

"I do believe the one called Niko Ryen speaks with a degree of reason." Maro Del-Fiiz spoke up on her behalf, although he said it meekly so as not to incur the wrath of Kira-Tharn. "What I have seen and heard in the offices of Terrovian Aquatics may substantiate such claims."

Kira-Tharn glared at him. "And you never thought to speak to me about this matter, Maro Del-Fiiz?"

He winced at the assault. "It was a matter I was unsure of, until Niko Ryen revealed the information she did. To which I am most grateful."

"Of course. I don't mean to stress either of you out, but you can't go in anymore. We *know* Shatter, and I trust Anda completely when she told me of what she saw at the Frying Pan."

Niko trembled on the inside recalling the specifics of what Anda had told her.

"An-Mara, slaving away, under Shatter's complete control. They were even *executing* disobedient prisoners. Anda saw the bodies with her own eyes. And the EC's and all the other companies… they just went along with it. They'll do whatever benefits them the most, *not* what benefits their workers."

Finally, for once in this conversation, Kira-Tharn didn't have a quick retort. Nor did Maro. They sat there, looking at each other, then at Niko, then at the floor, obviously unsure of their commitment to Terrovian.

Good. Let them be unsure.

"Just promise me that you'll never go back into the Rifts," Niko implored. "Come work with me in the fields instead."

"Even if what you say is to be factual, what makes you think that ROTO will not demand the same from its workers?" Kira-Tharn asked.

"Anda told me their deal involved Cinto production," Niko replied. "That and more produce being sent to Shatter's facilities. There was nothing about labor in their deal. Terrovian Aquatics was the only EC that had that."

Kira-Tharn frowned, knitting her eyebrows as she chewed her lip. Was she actually considering her proposal? Niko had hoped she would, but she'd also been prepared for a combative Kira-Tharn, especially after the damn woman kept interrupting her. Maro on the other hand…

She had counted on him to be her tool of reason, which is why she was disappointed when he expressed his reluctance to heed her pleas.

"I regret that I cannot abandon my new post at Terrovian Aquatics," he announced. "I have been newly appointed as assistant foreman, after the one called Armond-Dei was promoted to an administrative position within the organization."

"You have to stay away," Niko pushed. "I think even assistant foremen aren't exempt from being hauled into the Daylight."

Maro shook his head. "I was given this new position upon my honor to maintain long-term commitment to their company. I must abide by my honor."

The blazes An-Mara and their damned honor!

Niko clamped her teeth tight. "And what about you, Kira-Tharn?"

Kira-Tharn remained quiet for a few short moments, her eyes flitting between Niko and Maro. Eventually, she spoke. "I am inclined to believe you, Niko Ryen. What you say does carry merit, and I would be one to hesitate before working for Terrovian Aquatics after being confronted with the information you have revealed. My concern remains, however, that the fields of ROTO will not pay as well as the Rifts of Terrovian Aquatics."

"I've already told you *so* many times," Niko replied, doing her best to not show her exasperation, "it doesn't pay that much worse. As long as we're both working, we'll make enough."

"I will consider what you have said."

Well. She supposed it was better than nothing. And at least Kira-Tharn wasn't being a stubborn, pig-headed chum about it. Not completely.

"And you, Maro?" Niko asked. "Will you at least *consider* it, like Kira-Tharn?"

"I will," he promised.

Niko got the feeling that his pledge to consider was only meant as fodder to appease her.

"For the current hour, however, let us eat our meal," Maro said. "We can discuss the matter of Terrovian Aquatics later."

"Fine," Niko sighed. At least it wasn't an outright 'no', but she got the impression that his damned *honor* was going to be a significant impediment to rational thought.

Whatever. She was hungry and irritable, and these thoughts could be tucked away for a few minutes while she ate. Her stomach hadn't been aching in over a day, and she might even be able to have half a meal by now.

So she pulled up a chair to the table, let Maro serve her, and dug in.

———————

After dinner, they never talked more about the situation with Shatter and Terrovian, of course. Kira-Tharn and Maro disappeared into their room, leaving Niko alone to stew over whether or not they'd listen to her.

Now it was late, and Maro had finally just left their quarters moments ago. Kira-Tharn never emerged from her room, so Niko assumed she'd retired for the night, as would happen more often than not. If the woman ignored her warnings and got herself shipped off to the Frying Pan, she would throttle the blazes lady herself for being such a foolish dumbchum.

And if Maro didn't heed her words… well, then both she *and* Kira-Tharn would throttle him.

Niko had seen the way Kira-Tharn acted around Maro. The way she looked at him. The way she glowed in his presence. The woman was in love; that much was obvious, even if she would never admit to such feelings. Maro could *not* risk being taken by Shatter. Not for Kira-Tharn's sake.

A sudden thought popped into Niko's head.

She leapt to action, sprinting out the door as she chased the disappearing figure of a man around the corner of some dilapidated buildings that had entirely too many floors stacked atop each other.

When Niko rounded the corner, she found herself in the midst of a busy street full of dozens of An-Mara ambling about. It was hard to tell which one was Maro, especially with the streets darkened from the continued blackouts.

"Maro Del-Fiiz!" she called after him, ignoring the stares of everyone around her. "Maro!"

One man stopped and turned around more slowly than the others, the hint of a wince imprinted onto his tanned face. "What is it, Niko Ryen?"

"Sorry to hunt you down!" she panted, jogging up to him.

Blazes, her body had been so decimated by the recovery from her near-starvation that she couldn't even run four blocks without becoming completely winded.

"It is nothing to convey an apology for," he assured her.

Niko nodded, catching her breath. "I just… I wanted to try to convince you… *really* convince you. Please don't go into the Rifts tomorrow. I wasn't kidding about any of what I said earlier. And I believe my source one-hundred percent."

"I… I do believe you," he hesitated, eyes darting left and right. He was probably concerned about the listening machines, and rightly so.

But to the blazes with the listening machines — she needed him to understand…

"Then please don't go in! For Kira-Tharn's sake, please don't go in."

"Like I said earlier, Niko Ryen, I was only awarded this appointment to assistant foreman after swearing upon my honor that I would remain committed to the Terrovian Aquatics mission."

"Forget them!" Niko cried out. "What about your honor when it comes to your commitment to Kira-Tharn?"

"My commitment to the one called Kira-Tharn does not carry bonds to my honor in the same manner."

"Like the blazes it doesn't!"

Maro turned his eyes down and sighed. "You may live among us, but you are still very unfamiliar with the ways of the An-Mara. With the ways of the Time."

Niko took a second to craft a response to avoid exploding on the man.

"Sure," she began, "I might not know every single thing about your culture, but I do know Kira-Tharn, and I know that if *you* get taken away to the Mara-forsaken Frying Pan, or worse, her heart will be broken."

"An An-Mara does not suffer a 'broken heart', as you call it. Our social and familial ties are not what are considered traditional in Meridian society."

She knew that was nonsense. Complete and utter nonsense. She knew Kira-Tharn, and she knew very well that her heart *would* be broken.

"Just… just please don't go in. Please find something else,"

Niko pleaded. "I care very much about Kira-Tharn, even if she is the most stubborn, ridiculous woman I've ever met, and I know it would crush her if you were to be taken. And besides, *I* consider you a friend also, and *I* would be upset if you were taken."

"I do consider you a friend, as well, Niko Ryen. And I do not intend on being taken anywhere. The organization called Terrovian Aquatics assured me that my services as assistant foreman are to be of great importance to the health of their current Rift operations."

Maybe he was right. Maybe Shatter wouldn't take him. Maybe he would be too important here. Maybe, maybe, maybe.

Too many maybes.

"And I do understand your warnings to be very serious," he added. "I assure you, I do understand. I will take great care with the paths that I choose going forward."

"You better," was all Niko responded with. "For Kira-Tharn's sake, you better."

Niko then turned around and stormed off, leaving Maro standing alone on the dimly lit corner. Hopefully her exit, which she imagined would make even the crankiest of An-Mara proud, delivered the effect she intended. The man needed to understand that if he were taken, it would affect more than just him. Niko couldn't bear to think of Kira-Tharn with a broken heart. The woman was already touchy enough without one…

But as Niko trudged back to her quarters, she wasn't quite confident that Maro would make the right decision.

CHAPTER TWENTY-NINE

29

Twilight Elegance

NIKO slept in. Glorious, uninterrupted sleep that she hadn't experienced in far too long.

When she finally dragged herself out of bed, she emerged to find Kira-Tharn puttering about the kitchen, fixing some sort of meal for herself. That would mean...

"So you listened."

"I did, Niko Ryen, but do not gloat over your coercion."

The small gleam of a smirk stayed well hidden behind the corner of Niko's mouth. A little bit of internal gloating was in order, because this was perhaps the first time she'd ever convinced Kira-Tharn to do anything. Anything this consequential, at least.

"I'm glad you listened," she said. "I was not exaggerating about *any* of that last night."

"I did not expect so, which is why I shall accompany you to the agricultural fields of ROTO today."

Niko was ecstatic that Kira-Tharn was serious about switching to the fields, but there was one small problem.

"About that..." Niko hesitated. Blazes, how was she going to tell Kira-Tharn about the contract? "I'm not going into the fields today. They have work for me in the city, instead."

Not a lie. Just not the whole truth, either.

Kira-Tharn merely shrugged. "Very well. Would you care to accompany me to the fields for an introduction, at minimum?"

Niko supposed she technically *did* have the time to do it, but she also doubted her standing within ROTO carried any weight. Not anymore. Not after she disappeared for nearly a month without saying a word. The people at the ROTO offices hadn't been friendly with her yesterday, that was for sure.

"I didn't plan on going to the fields at all today," she replied, shaking her head, feigning apology. "I have to go straight into the city."

Niko felt bad for leaving Kira-Tharn on her own, but she had more than enough on her mind today. Not only was she stressing about her contract with Anda and Amon, but there was also Cryo's race to think about...

The Century was the biggest race of the year, and if he did well enough, he would earn a huge cut of Terion for the group. Perhaps over five million, if he replicated his success from the Oldcity Blitz a few weeks ago.

That thought brought her hope, but it was tempered with another source of stress — the very real dangers involved in actually competing. She shuddered at the image of Jon Wilhe's bloody body being dragged off the course. Trackripping was *dangerous*; there was no denying that.

"That is unfortunate," Kira-Tharn said. "If you cannot accompany me, do you have any information to make my chances at hire more favorable?"

"They'll take you," Niko assured her. "One-hundred percent. When I went in the other day, they were shorthanded."

"And you are certain that ROTO will not pawn its laborers off to the whims of Shatter?"

A fair question, although she already answered it several times over last night.

"As far as I know, no," Niko responded. "Anda seems content to work there, so I'd trust them."

"Will your friend be there to work alongside me?" Kira-Tharn asked.

Niko shook her head. "No, she's working with me in the city today."

"Very well."

"Sorry..." Niko started.

"Niko Ryen, you know better than to apologize if you did n..."

"Yeah, yeah..." Niko threw the ceiling a grimace of exasperation. "You tell me that every time. I'm only saying I wish I could be there with you on your first day."

"It is no hardship. I shall manage adequately on my own."

"I agree," Niko said. "And I do think you'll like this job much better than the Rifts. It's strangely fun. Almost therapeutic."

"If you say so."

"Trust me. You'll like it. You just twist and snap the blacksquashes from the vine, then toss them into your bin."

As Niko described it, fun wasn't exactly the word that came to mind. But it was enjoyable in its own sort of way. Or maybe that was because the only alternative she'd known was toiling away in the blazes Rifts.

"Also, take my stool," she offered. "It makes all the difference in the worlds."

"I do not find a necessity for such pitiful supports. I am more than capable of funct..."

"Kira-Tharn, just take the damn thing."

Kira-Tharn let out an inflated huff, but to Niko's relief, accepted the object when Niko rolled it to her.

"Do you leave soon?" Niko asked.

"I do think it would be prudent for me to arrive before 09:00, so I shall leave momentarily."

Niko nodded. "Good idea."

Kira-Tharn finished eating whatever that monstrosity she called breakfast was —some slimy yellowish mass wrapped around a conglomeration of chopped blacksquashes and pebblegrains — then gathered her belongings and headed for the door.

"Fare well, Niko Ryen. I do hope you will join me in the fields on the morrow, after you so eloquently pressured me to switch professions."

The way she made it sound, Niko did her a great disservice. A resigned breath escaped Niko's lips as her roommate turned to leave.

"Oh yeah, Kira-Tharn..."

"Yes, Niko Ryen?"

"Any chance Maro Del-Fiiz is switching to the fields today also?" Niko asked. She really hoped he took what she told him last night to heart. "Or at least not going back to the Rifts?"

Kira-Tharn did not say a word. She only turned around, the glint of fiery scorn flashing in her dark eyes, as she slammed the door shut behind her.

Well, that answers that...

———————

The hazy streets of Machine Row transitioned into the neon incandescence of NewCen as the trio rode the rail into the city. Most people would say they felt safer moving further and further from Oldcity, but Anda knew that there was little difference between the two opposite ends of Alashadar. The only real distinction was that here in NewCen, those shameless criminal kingpins put on quite the charade when they stepped into the big EC venues. They would appear as upstanding, law-abiding citizens on the sprawling casino floors, but behind closed doors...

Anda gritted her jaw.

Behind closed doors was exactly where they were headed now, and she could only hope that the contract played out how it read. She made absolute certain there was no ambiguous print that could be manipulated into nefarious intent, and it was not until she felt one-hundred percent satisfied that she allowed Niko to sign it with her Terion badge.

She probably could have pressed the girl to abandon the notion altogether, but that would only serve to drive a wedge in their relationship. For years, Amon had been her only companion, and she rather enjoyed finally having a female friend. And after she'd been certain that her new friend was gone forever in the depths of the Frying Pan, Anda swore to herself that she wouldn't let her go after she'd seemingly returned from the dead.

Maybe because of that, she was not keen on Niko's insistence that they take this contract. This endeavor did not rank highly on the risk versus reward scale: the hundred thousand Terion they were getting was a meager sum for the amount of risk involved.

"I've never been inside," Niko commented, drawing her gaze up from the streets.

"Twilight Elegance?" Anda assumed that's what she meant.

"Yeah."

Anda shrugged. "It's as you'd expect from the fanciest place in the city."

"Even fancier than the Skytower?"

Anda nodded. "Skytower Palace isn't really that nice. It's the view that people pay for. Twilight Elegance is far more *elegant*, as the name might suggest."

Elegant, but still far from her tastes.

"Have you guys spent a lot of time in NewCen?" Niko asked.

"No," Amon replied. "We try to stay away. As far as I see it, NewCen is only a Terion trap. The EC's always win."

Anda nodded in agreement. She had been growing increasingly frustrated with Amon over the years, annoyed at his clinginess, but she had to admit that he was absolutely correct there.

She wished she could ease her feelings toward him. After all, she should be eternally grateful he agreed to come with her and Niko today. Two slightly built women on their own in the depths of the Alashadar underworld... That would be a formula for trouble.

Nothing would make her feel entirely content about being here in any capacity, but having Amon along with them made her feel orders of magnitude more comfortable, even if he was to be posted outside the suite.

And of course, she would also be forever indebted to him for saving her life years ago... But all of that that did little to soothe over the waves of annoyance and distaste whenever she had to spend time with him. Which was practically all the time. Thank the Mara he *at least* stopped pressing her to live with him.

"That's what my friends always say," Niko commented, referring to the EC's rigging of the games.

"They are right to say it," Amon responded. "I've been around this cesspool long enough to know it to be true."

"How long have you been here?" Niko asked him, tilting her head to the side. "Where are you from?"

Wow, thought Anda. *The girl is bold again, today.*

She didn't learn of Amon's past for months, even when she was cooped up alongside him day and night during her recovery.

"Family moved here from Samarind when I was six."

"I've never heard of that place," Niko said quietly.

"Samarind?? You've never heard of Samarind??" It was

obviously difficult for him to hide his disbelief, but of course he didn't know of Niko's origins on that forbidden world of Arhanda.

Niko shook her head, looking to Anda. "Should I have?"

"It's a world in the Capital system," she clarified.

"Yeah," Amon added sarcastically, "only the most populous in the entire sector. By about a trillion…"

"Oh." Niko's face reddened.

Anda knew the girl had an excuse for her ignorance, but if she put herself in Niko's place, she knew it must feel embarrassing.

"So you moved here when you were six? How old are you now?" Niko asked, quickly hiding any hint of humiliation.

Anda did her best to stifle the chuckle that threatened to escape. She knew that Amon *hated* to admit his age. This conversation was entertaining, indeed.

"I have passed Sol One forty-one times."

"Amon here is an old gun," Anda teased, capitalizing on Niko's initiation of the topic. She appreciated any chance she got to highlight the age gap between them. Maybe at some point, he'd stop lusting after her.

"Not that old…" he argued.

"I wouldn't have guessed over thirty-five," Niko said, surely fluffing his ego.

"Thank you," he beamed. "And where are you from?"

"She's from a Meridian system," Anda intervened. She knew her friend would be thankful if she didn't have to answer any sensitive questions herself. "But not the Capital system."

"Yeah," Niko agreed. "One of the other systems."

It seemed good enough for Amon, for he simply turned and casually looked out the window. "Oh, we're already here."

Indeed, the train slowed down to a stop, and all three of them filed out onto a busy platform raised high above the bustling street below. There was so much buzz, so much hoopla about the Trackripping race today, that it was difficult to move about. Anda didn't bother herself with any of that nonsense, but apparently it was the biggest event of the year, so it was no surprise that Alashadar seemed even more alive today.

In front of them loomed the monumental black doors to Twilight Elegance, but before they took three steps toward their destination, Niko called out to someone.

"Ravenna?! What're you doing here?"

"Getting ready for that Mara-forsaken race is what," the girl replied gruffly. She couldn't have been more than a few years older than Anda herself, and by the Mara she was striking...

Violet eyes, multicolored hair, athletic-looking as a tiger... these people from Arhanda certainly had some unique genes, if this was one of Niko's homeworld friends as Anda suspected.

"Oh yeah, Ravenna, this is my friend Anda!" Niko introduced her eagerly. "Anda, this is Ravenna, one of my friends from home."

So it was one of her homeworld friends. She gave this Ravenna girl a full, respectful nod of the head, which was returned with only the smallest of inclinations.

"Oh yeah, and this is Amon," Niko sheepishly added, forgetting about him. Anda laughed inside because she knew that Amon didn't take kindly to being left out. "Amon, Ravenna."

"Pleasure," Ravenna said briskly, before turning back to Niko. "What're *you* doing here? Shouldn't you be at work?"

"Oh, well, about that..." Niko hesitated, probably panicking for an excuse to be here. Anda couldn't imagine that Niko's friends would approve of this contract. "ROTO sent us into the city for work today."

Not an outright lie, Anda supposed, but positively not the whole truth.

"Are you watching the race from here?" Niko asked Ravenna.

"I'm trying not to watch it at all," Ravenna growled. "But Ce-Ellum asked me to meet someone from Cryo's *Vulture* crew here."

"I can't believe Cryo agreed to work with Vulture," Niko said casually, hoping to score some points with Ravenna.

"Wait, you two know Cryo?" Amon asked. "Cryo Siriar?"

Anda didn't know the significance of the name, but she also didn't follow Trackripping one lick. She did know the name Ce-Ellum, though... and she did know the name Vulture...

"Yes...?" Ravenna side-eyed him.

"Wow," Amon buzzed. "What an acquaintance to have. They say he might be the next big thing in Trackripping."

"Hah!" Ravenna clacked. "Not if I have anything to say about it..."

This must certainly be one of Niko's short-tempered friends that she was telling her about. She had two, though, if Anda remembered correctly. The other one had an An-Mara name. She forgot what it was.

"Well, when you two are watching from the chief officer's suite, maybe you can mention you know Cryo Siriar for extra Terion tips."

Amon said it in good nature, but Anda was adept enough at reading people to catch the glint of fire that flashed across Ravenna's eyes.

"The *chief officer's* suite?!" Ravenna demanded. "What are you really doing here, Niko?"

"We... We're..." Niko stammered.

"And do *not* think to lie to me," Ravenna challenged. "Not after everything you've already pulled."

Blazes, Niko thought. Why did Amon have to say anything at all?!

"We're just catering for ROTO is all," Niko defended herself. "It's a one-time deal that pays a hundred thousand Terion. You were the one who told me to make back the Terion we lost."

"That *you* lost," Ravenna corrected. "And I did *not* mean like this. Do you know how dangerous this is? Do *any* of you know how dangerous this is? It's a blazes swampwasp's nest in there, and I don't care if they give you all the Terion on An-Terino, this was the stupidest place you could've come to."

Ravenna now turned on Anda and Amon, glaring unblinkingly at them. What was her *deal*?! Niko thought she saw Amon flinch, and she couldn't blame him; Ravenna was a force. Anda however, held the stare, her one eye softly regarding Ravenna, calmly as ever. Anda was also a force, Niko knew.

"I agree with you, Ravenna," Anda conceded, "which is why I asked for Amon to be conscripted into this service, as well. He has a background in security with ROTO and will be watching over us."

"It doesn't matter what kind of background he has, this place is *dangerous*."

"I don't disagree," Anda repeated. "I am not happy to be here myself, but ROTO already signed our contracts, so we have little choice in the matter."

Ravenna clicked her tongue, clearly upset. "And how long does the contract specify the catering service to last? I hope you at least determined a termination hour?"

"Yes, yes, of course," Anda waved her hand dismissively. "It is only for the duration of the race."

"And how can you be sure that the *patrons* will adhere to that?"

"I assure you," Anda said, "these are all concerns that I share. That is why I demanded Amon come along. He will be posted just outside our door, and after the race, he knows to be vigilant on our behalf."

"And do you know anything about this chief officer?" asked Ravenna, her eyes narrowing in scrutiny.

"I met him last week," Anda admitted. "I'm sorry to say, I do not like him one bit. But again, we have little say in the matter at this point. The only thing we can do now is keep as low a profile as possible, and be done with our service."

"I don't like it," Ravenna muttered.

"Nor do I!" Anda commiserated. "If it would make you feel better, you can come along with us. We may be able to smuggle you in under the guise of being another server?"

"I can't come with you. I'm needed elsewhere." Ravenna looked intensely conflicted, as if she were fighting some unseen battle within. "But you can be damn sure that I will be holding your hand wherever you go from now on, Niko."

Wonderful.

"While you are away, I will be watching over Niko closely," Anda promised.

"Niko better be returned unharmed." The threat was plain and unfiltered.

Blazes, she wished Ravenna would trust her. And if not her, she should at least trust Anda.

"She will be," Anda confirmed.

Ravenna nodded. "I'll hold you to that. I'm needed at the Vulture suite in here, but you can be *sure* we'll talk later, Niko."

She then stormed off across the platform, disappearing down a flight of stairs that led to another entrance to the building.

Blazes.

That did not go well at all. The only saving grace was that Anda was one patient woman. Niko would've given up immediately if she had tried to go toe to toe with Ravenna, as she'd done on many occasions before. But Anda didn't appear flustered one bit. Not even one strand of her thinning, orange hair was out of place. She simply had an answer for every one of Ravenna's concerns, and presented her points with measured composure.

"Well, your friend is… spirited," Amon quipped, grinning at Niko.

"Pfft," she exhaled. "If you thought that was rough, you should see her in a bad mood…"

Amon laughed, but Anda said, completely deadpan, "I like her."

Niko recoiled in surprise, narrowing her eyebrows. She would've expected Anda to hate the girl. "She was just rude as blazes to you…"

Anda shrugged. "She was protective over her friend. A good quality, to be sure."

"Yeah, and it's super annoying. I make one wrong move and then she's lording it over me."

"I think you're actually quite lucky to have someone like that watching over you. Even if it does seem annoying."

Niko thought it was more irritating than lucky, but whatever.

"Which is why I'm glad our friend over here was able to come along," Anda said, playfully patting Amon on the shoulder. "Shall we, though?"

Anda then gestured toward the opulent glass entrance to Twilight Elegance, to which Niko nodded. The trio walked through the massive doorway, then were funneled into a dark lobby where eight armed guards stood at the far end. This place *was* exclusive, if the entryway was this well guarded. Niko couldn't describe it, but even the sounds and smells of this place were exactly as she'd have guessed from what it looked like on the outside.

Elegant was the first word that came to mind, go figure.

"Welcome to Twilight Elegance," the shortest of the guards greeted, once they reached the end. "Names and business?"

"Anda Len, Amon Valerun, and Niko Ryen," Anda answered. "Here to report for a ROTO catering service contract."

The guard paused, staring into space, no doubt cycling through order databases on his Ut.

"Terion badges, please," he commanded.

Niko and the others handed them over, and the guard scanned them, each clicking with a chime when they checked out.

Good thing they didn't take Ravenna along, Niko realized. There's no way they would've been able to smuggle her into this place...

"You are to report to the Shatter executive suite," the guard announced. "Follow the veranda to the left, then when you see the main elevators, travel to the forty-third floor. Your Terion badges have been granted access. From there, exit left down the hallway and the suite will be at the end. Before you enter, you may change into the uniforms in the room just across the hall. The guards there can direct you, should you require their assistance."

"Thank you," Anda said, sweeping past the checkpoint gracefully, while Niko and Amon followed in tow.

"Not you," the guard ordered, pressing a hand against Amon's chest. "You are needed on another level, per the orders of the contract I received."

A pang of worry shot through Niko like a bolt of lightning. Amon was supposed to be with them! That had been the plan, had it not?

Anda and Amon shared a confused glance, then Anda spoke to the guard. "Are you certain? We signed our contracts together."

"My logs are showing that Amon Valerun from ROTO is to report to the thirty-ninth level for security detail. That is your name, is it not?"

Amon nodded.

"Then you will report to the thirty-ninth level using the service elevator, just beyond the main lift foyer," the guard directed. "And it would be unwise to deviate from those instructions. I do not have to remind you we are completely updated with the Terion Sight here at Twilight Elegance."

Niko looked concernedly at the others, but Anda merely shrugged, thanking the guard again, before moving off onto the veranda overlooking the massive interior of the venue.

Black and magenta undertones were sifted into the modern architecture seamlessly, the soft tunes of a strange melancholy musical arrangement echoing across the expanse, its haunting melody brushing against Niko's very soul. In the background, the elites of Alashadar glided about, their extravagant dresswear setting them apart from the common folk in every way. Niko would've been dumbstruck with awe at this hidden world within, if she didn't get the feeling that she was walking into...

What was it Ravenna called it? A swampwasp's nest?

It was a good comparison to how Niko felt right now as she careened against her will toward the elevators at the midpoint of the veranda.

Niko had read the contract... read *Amon's* contract. This change shouldn't have been possible. Only now was she beginning to understand everyone's aversion to her taking of this deal.

"Well, I suppose this is where we part ways," Amon grimaced as they approached the elevators. "I'm sorry I can't be of more use to you both."

"It will be fine," Anda said.

Niko thought she only said that for her sake. But hopefully it *would* be fine.

"I'm sure it will be." Amon nodded to them as they stepped into the elevator car, an impossibly luxurious capsule with spotless black mirrors on all sides. "We'll catch up after. See you two on the other side."

The elevator doors closed, and up they went.

———————

CHAPTER THIRTY

30

The Century

"**ABSOLUTELY** not!" Niko whispered, her eyes as wide as Providence. "There's *NO* way you'd ever catch me *dead in the Night* in that!"

The girl was still simmering, and rightfully so. Anda had been half-expecting attire of that sort to be part of the deal, but when Niko took one look at what they were expected to wear, she refused. Anda was all too happy to join in the refusal.

'We are happy to serve in what we wear currently, or otherwise there will be no service at all,' Niko had demanded of the guards posted outside the suite. Naturally, they seemed unhappy about the ultimatum, but to Anda's surprise, they weren't refused entry.

It was hard to suppress a grin. Not only was she was proud of Niko for standing her ground with such confidence, but the girl was so offended that it was endearingly amusing.

Now inside the suite, Anda supposed the situation might not be as bad as she'd feared. None of the patrons they served appeared to notice the lack of... *uniforms* they donned. The only thing they seemed to care about was if their drinks were full, their Cinto was stocked, and the hors d'oeuvre trays were cycled. That, and what was on the massive screens that lined the walls of the lavish room.

The suite looked ridiculous, like something out of a painting. Too-fancy, reddish curtains billowed like thin, wispy clouds as they hung from the ceiling by threads, surrounding gaudy monstrosities of lounge divans like royal bedroom curtains. The giant pillows on top of them were completely unnecessary and only added to the farce, comfortable as they might have been. The walls, black and sleek, served as mirrors, just like throughout the rest of this whole caricature of a palace.

Anda could sense the awe emanating from Niko, but she was far from impressed herself. She never really liked this place, deluxe as it was. Something was just… *off*… about its whole aura. But that went for all of NewCen, as far as Anda was concerned.

The dignitaries in the suite clearly did not share her own sentiments — their excitement only rose and rose, even as some in the room attempted to hush each other.

"Here we go!"

"Quiet!"

"It's about to start!"

However, there was anything but quiet as last minute bets flurried throughout the room.

"Fifty million Terion says that Delmatic wins by more than two hundred meters!"

"I'll take that bet! Double says he wins in a photo finish!"

"I'll throw down twenty million Terion against someone's five million — if anyone wants to take Delmatic as losing. Any takers?!"

"I'll take it! And five million more says it's Cryo Siriar who beats him!"

Clearly dazed up on the Cinto, the obnoxious elites of An-Terino continued their insufferable swaggering until someone entered the room and turned up the volume of the screens.

"There he is!" someone shouted. "We were beginning to think you weren't coming!"

"I was held up with business," the man apologized.

Anda knew him — the deep, booming voice of Andersane, chief officer of Shatter on An-Terino, was unmistakable. She wasn't comfortable in the slightest being in the same room with him again, but there was nothing to be done about her situation now.

Lay low, provide the service, and be done with the contract. That was all. Although, laying low might prove to be more difficult, because Niko...

What in the worlds was she doing??

The girl was frozen, mouth quite literally agape, staring at the chief officer who just entered. If Anda had to compare her expression to anything, it might have been the look of someone who found themselves face to face with the Machine!...

Anda nudged her friend in the arm, and Niko's tray rattled.

By the Mara! She was lucky she didn't spill the damned thing all over the floor.

"Niko!" she hissed.

"Sorry," Niko blushed, scurrying over to fill drinks along the path.

What was the girl so spooked about?! She herself didn't particularly like Andersane — hated the guy, even, for what he had done at the Frying Pan — but Niko's fright was something more. Something deeper.

Anda bit short a curse, then filled the Cinto dispenser. How did these fools already go through the thing? They were going to be dead asleep before the race even started if they kept at it...

Moments later, when Anda and Niko both returned to the service station around the corner, Anda wheeled on her friend.

"Niko! What in the worlds, girl?! We're trying *not* to draw attention to us."

"I'm sorry! It's just... it's..." Niko trailed off, her voice shaky.

"It's okay. If you don't want to talk about it now, that's fine. But by the grace of the Nel-Mara, keep it together!"

"It's that man. Andersane. I know him."

Anda peered at Niko thoughtfully. She *knew* him?

"From Arhanda," Niko continued. "He was the Magistrate there. I heard some Shatter guards talking about him coming here a while ago, but I didn't think I'd ever run into him."

"Will he recognize you?" Anda blurted out.

"I... I don't know. I don't think so. No. I was pretty unremarkable." Niko gasped a halfhearted laugh.

Well, okay then. But even if she wasn't recognized, Anda still worried about her friend's reactions. If she couldn't school her features, this contract could get messy very quickly.

But she supposed she should have some sympathy for the girl. From what little Anda knew of the man, she couldn't shake the suspicion that if he'd been involved on Niko's planet, he may have played a part in its destruction. She'd heard enough rumors that pitted it upon the An-Mara, but this man... he was no good.

"Are you going to be okay?"

Niko nodded. "I'm sorry. It just... surprised me is all."

Anda placed a firm hand on Niko's shoulder, offering her what solidarity she could. "Okay, let's get back out there. No drawing attention to ourselves, remember."

Niko nodded again, darting around the corner with another tray of hors d'oeuvres. Anda sucked in a deep breath. She hoped to all ends that her friend would keep her wits about her. She felt bad Niko had to relive that part of her past, but for both their sakes, they needed to blend in.

Serve, and be done with this contract. It was as simple as that.

When she finally emerged back into the suite, she found Niko gliding around virtually unseen, passing around snacks to hungry patrons with efficient indifference.

Good. It seemed the girl had calmed down.

Even better, Niko had just served Andersane himself, and it appeared he didn't recognize her at all.

The pompous oaf, she thought dryly. Although, she was hardly complaining. A complete lack of recognition of Niko was the best scenario she could hope for.

It also helped that the only thing the guests seemed to care about was the Trackripping broadcast, where two squabbling announcers were loudly debating the merits of all the competitors.

"Yes Turnslinger," the woman announcer squawked, "but I really think his performance may have been a fluke last month. He's so new to the Tour, and with virtually no Trackripping experience at all, I think it may be too difficult to recreate that effort."

"I have to disagree with you there, Tivane," the man screeched back. "I have seen Rippers for years and years now, and I'm telling you, Cryo has real talent. It was not a fluke."

So they were talking about Cryo. Niko's friend.

"Fluke or not, I think we can both agree that Vulture is really cementing their status as a major competitor in the world of Trackripping. Their sponsorship of Jon Wilhe, and now Cryo Siriar, has been wildly popular."

"I absolutely can agree with that. And I think we might see their popularity skyrocket even further after the race tonight."

"We will just have to see!" the woman, Tivane, announced.

"That we will," the man replied. "In just a few moments, actually. The racers are all lined up now, and I say it every race, but this is where the nerves really start to become exposed. The Rippers try to remain focused, but sometimes this waiting period starts to eat at some of them."

"Yes, Turnslinger, and this is a perfect moment to deliver our special message on behalf of our friends at Shatter and Terion. Ever since the dreadful NewCen Circuit Riots last month, where one-hundred thirty-seven innocent fans, workers, and peacekeepers lost their lives, a monumental planet-wide effort has been undertaken to improve An-Terino. We here at the Trackripping Syndicate wholeheartedly support everything that's being done to make our world a better place.

"Never before in An-Terino's history has there been such an effort to clean up the streets of Alashadar. Criminals are finally being prosecuted and removed to where they belong, and crime has dropped an astounding seventy-five percent over the last month! Those wretched slums on the outskirts of the city have been a haven for the worst criminals for far too long. Now, brave and honorable men and women are involved in cleanups that are underway.

"Coming straight from Machine Row — the undisputed beating heart of Alashadar — Terion's noble and watchful presence, along with Shatter's determined grace, will rid this planet of all wrongdoing, allowing for more peace, more leisure, and more Trackripping!"

Whooping cheers resounded.

The thinly veiled spattering of propaganda made Anda furious — how were the people so damn gullible??

"Aaaaamen, Tivane!" the other broadcaster proclaimed. Turnslinger, Anda figured his name to be. "Amen."

"Girl!" The word was shouted at her, again.

She bowed her head in apology, then rushed over to refill one of the patron's Cinto-wine glasses.

"Go easy on her," another man chided after she walked away. "Did you see her ear? She probably can't hear a thing…"

"Indeed. Why did they even send us someone so ugly?" another man complained.

Anda cursed herself. How had she let her attention drift so far into that blasted broadcast? She didn't care if they thought she was ugly, or stupid, or slow. She only cared that they noticed her at all…

She hurried around the corner, refilled the pitcher of Cinto-wine, and returned to the suite, resuming her rounds. By now, though, most people ignored her. The race had started, and the elites in the room had become little more than commonplace Trackripping enthusiasts, each of them hollering for this racer and that with boisterous exuberance.

Anda let her eye drift to the screens again, which were mainly focused on a fancy green and black kart. As she watched, she made certain to remain attentive to any guests that needed refills.

"As you can see, Delmatic's team learned from Vulture," Turnslinger announced. "He really upgraded his impulse drive this time, so nobody has any clear advantage over him."

"Oh yes, Turnslinger, and that doesn't bode well for any rivals. Even at a disadvantage, he still found ways to win every single race this season, so far."

"Absolutely, Tivane. He has a chance to cement his legacy once and for all tonight. If he wins, he will be the first Ripper to ever complete an entire Tour with nothing but first place finishes."

"For any listeners out there who do not know, Delmatic currently shares that record for the most first place finishes during a season, which is ten. And he shares that record with none other than our very own Steven 'Turnslinger' Osinroler!"

"That is true, Tivane! I am honored to still hold that record, but I think he might take this one from me today."

The two broadcasters wheezed insufferably fake laughs before they returned to their ridiculous analysis. Anda found herself more interested in the actual race going on, though, especially when the broadcast flashed to on-board views from the karts. She had to admit, Trackripping looked thrilling!

She only removed her eye from the kart point-of-views when the portrait of a familiar figure was plastered onto the screens. She'd seen him before; it was that same handsome man outside of Niko's friends' abode in Machine Row.

So *that* must be Cryo.

She glanced across the room at Niko, who chewed nervously on her lip as she watched the race. It was a dangerous sport, after all, so she didn't blame her friend. She heard there was a fatality on one of the races only a few weeks ago, and then another one a few weeks before that. Considering there were only twenty-four racers on the Tour, those weren't exactly odds that screamed safety.

"Cinto-wine!" a woman called, the lone woman patron in this entire room…

Anda hurried and filled her glass, then returned to watching the race as she feigned vigilance over the needs of the guests.

No sooner had she refilled the woman's Cinto-wine when she heard another call, this time for hors d'oeuvres. She looked across to Niko, who held the hors d'oeuvre tray, but her friend didn't react.

Anda knew she was completely invested in the race — probably more than any of the patrons here — so she glided over, scooped the tray out of her hands, and delivered the requested snacks herself.

Niko mouthed a silent '*sorry*', before snapping her nervous eyes back to the broadcast.

———————

Niko felt bad for making Anda do everything, bless her heart. But by the Mara, she was *dying* inside.

Cryo already had not one, not two, but *three* close calls. It was as if that chum Delmatic was intentionally trying to knock him out of the race. Seriously, what issues could Delmatic possibly have with him?

The track was straight here, with only a couple rises and dips. Of course, there was that sharp turnaround at the far end of the course by the Estates, but the Rippers were long past that. Still, she wouldn't feel comfortable until Cryo crossed the finish line unharmed.

Niko, now more in touch with her senses than she had been a month ago, didn't exactly have *bad* feelings per se — not like she had when she was in a room with the blazes Machine — but she felt something… *impending*. Something… *inevitable*. Not necessarily anything bad, but definitely something major.

That weird speech Tivane gave at the start of the broadcast surely didn't ease her feelings. The fact that the majority of the common people seemed to cheer for what Shatter and Terion were doing made her angry. But she couldn't react in any way. Not in front of that man. Not in front of *Andersane*.

373

At least he didn't notice her, thank the Mara, but seeing him in the flesh threatened to shatter the hardened exterior she forged for herself these past five years. If he was alive, could that mean her family possibly escaped Arhanda also? Would that dream of the stadium being swallowed by the lava flow turn out to be a false memory after all? Should she introduce herself and ask him? Surely he would remember Riesen...

She knew deep down that she should *absolutely not* ask any of this, but she longed to know the truth of what happened. Instead, she only allowed a silent exhalation to herself, all the while schooling her face into complete stoicism, much like she noted Anda to do frequently.

"Would you look at that, Turnslinger?!" Tivane's voice shouted through the enhancers in the suite. "Astine Rivers is really making a push on Delmatic!"

"Yes, Tivane. She isn't letting him get away with this one easily. And we would expect no less for the finale to this year's Tour. So much is on the line! And not only for Delmatic and his legacy, but for Rivers' own standings. If she's able to take second or higher tonight, she will cement third place overall on the Tour."

"That would be huge for her, Turnslinger, it really would be. She already came into the Tour this year with a top ten seeding, but this would be unprecedented!"

"Absolutely, Tivane. And I know you don't agree with me on this one, but we still can't count Cryo Siriar out just yet. I think the only reason he drifted back a few spots was to test Delmatic's resolve. For whatever reason, Delmatic seemed to have it out for him."

"There's got to be some underworld drama between his team and Vulture," Tivane laughed. "He had it out for Jon Wilhe in almost every race we watched, also. We all remember what he did to poor Wilhe's wreckage back on Excavation Run."

The way those announcers laughed over that scene — actually *laughed* — left Niko seething to the core.

"For Siriar's sake, hopefully that doesn't happen to him."

The announcers laughed some more.

"You know, Tivane, in all seriousness, I actually think Cryo is Ripping a smart race. He's still within striking distance, but he's out of range of whatever dirty tactics Delmatic is employing. He's really only a few kart lengths back."

"That is true, Turnslinger. But a few kart lengths behind Delmatic, of all Rippers, might as well be race over."

"Only time can tell, and we shall find out soon! The leaders just passed down into the Machine Row tunnel from Oldcity, and will be emerging onto the glorious streets of NewCen in only a few minutes. From there, they have a sprint to the finish line underneath the Skytower Palace."

"Now Turnslinger," Tivane purred, "ever since Cryo Siriar went on the pre-race show last week, I know a lot of our fans are now rooting for him, especially our female fans."

Niko's anger rose when Tivane giggled like a child. How annoying could this grown woman be?

"He's become a fan favorite, that's for certain. I think everyone could sense the chemistry between him and Astine Rivers on that show, and I think many fans are rooting for them to become a team that takes down Delmatic."

"And a team outside of Trackripping." Tivane winked at the camera, nudging Turnslinger's elbow with her own.

"Yes," Turnslinger laughed. "I have heard those rumors. Wouldn't that make for a great story?"

Niko was disgusted with how they were talking about Cryo like he was some good to be bought and sold at one of the trading hubs. She was in utter denial that her modest friend, who she'd known almost her entire life, was a Trackripping superstar today. A household name in Alashadar. He always seemed to *hate* this kind of attention, so she wondered what he made of it all.

She owed him big — they all owed him big — if he was doing this all for some Terion to get them off this damned planet.

"OOOOOOOOOOHHHH!" The announcers and patrons alike shouted as one.

The blood froze in Niko's veins, the air sucked from her lungs. *What just happened??*

"And there goes Wenno Daks!"

As Tivane called out the name, the unfolding crash was highlighted on the screens. Debris, and lots of it, rained down across the track, sending the Rippers scattering around the hazard. Luckily, Cryo was mere meters ahead of him, and avoided it altogether.

"Yes, very unfortunate for Daks," Turnslinger agreed. "It looked to me like he tried to pass Relm on the right, then got cut off and caught the corner of his bumper on an edge. Fortunately, it looks as if he's unhurt."

"His body looks unhurt, but his ego… that's another case."

Tivane and Turnslinger laughed some more, the worthless chums.

Seriously, who thought it would be a good idea to pick these two to be the face of the Trackripping Syndicate??

Niko, hiding her annoyance, gulped a deep breath of relief.

"Yes, and such an unlucky finish to his Tour. He was as high as second potion on the standings earlier this season, but a series of poor finishes, and now this crash, have doomed him from even finishing top six."

"Very sad for him, Turnslinger, but he does have next year to look forward to. If he can fix the little things, he will have a very bright future ahead of him. And speaking of standings, Turnslinger, let's see where we're at if the places hold as they are."

"Well, obviously Delmatic has the Tour victory already wrapped up. But if Astine Rivers holds onto second position, she will finish in third place, bumping Marl Vikers to fourth. Morland Relm would then take the second position if his current third place holds. It's all a bit too premature, I think. Cryo being in this mix won't change his own standing in the Tour much, but it can shuffle things up quite a bit for everyone else."

"Yes, Turnslinger, and it can mess up *a lot* of bets, that's for certain. That's where he's glad he has Vulture watching his back, because there could be a lot of angry folks out there."

"Yes, and he not only has Vulture, but the good people at Shatter and Terion have tightened up security considerably. I think all the Rippers are quite safe."

"Very true, Turnslinger. Very true. All of us, Rippers and common citizens alike, owe Shatter quite a lot."

"That we do, Tivane. They are nothing short of heroes."

"Now it looks like the Rippers are coming up and out of the tunnel soon! After that, it's a five-kilometer straightaway to the finish!"

"Yes, Tivane! This is where things will heat up. You can already see Rivers starting to push onto Delmatic's bumper a little. And then behind her, Relm and Vikers are also getting into position. And behind them, Siriar looks like he is biding his time."

Would Cryo be punching into the top five tonight?! How much Terion would he even be getting from that?! Possibly upwards of ten million...

Niko only dared to hope.

"There's not much time left, though. I think he may have waited too long to make his move."

"Don't speak too soon Tivane! See that little positioning tactic he used just now, swinging to the left? He sees Vikers trying to pass Relm on the right. I guarantee you he's waiting for Vikers to make his move, and when Relm moves to cut Vikers off, he'll pass them both. Just you watch..."

"OOOOOOOOHHHH!" the roar echoed throughout the suite, the fools yelling and shouting as the Rippers neared ever closer to the finish line.

"Wow!" Tivane squealed. "You called it! I suppose you aren't a two-time Tour champion for nothing!"

"Thank you, Tivane," Turnslinger laughed. "But I could see that move he was making. It was the little swing to the left at the precise moment when Relm was focused on Vikers. He may be new, but Cryo Rips as if he were a twenty-year veteran."

"And now we have a race to the finish! Rivers is pushing Delmatic to the brink, with Cryo creeping up on both of them, Relm and Vikers right behind him!"

"This is coming down to the centimeter. Mark my words, Tivane! Anything can happen, and any of these five are in position to win it."

"Delmatic's legacy on the line, a fifty-million Terion bonus on the line, pride and bragging rights for an entire year on the line — it all comes down to this moment!"

The raucous bedlam of the patrons in the suite threatened to drown out even the screeching tones of Turnslinger and Tivane, but Andersane turned the volume up.

"One kilometer to go!"

Niko watched silently as the five karts in the lead sped toward that final line underneath Skytower Palace, the glitzy high point of Alashadar towering iconically in the distance.

She was plunged into flashbacks of the last time when she watched a Trackripping finish, to that moment when her Ripper had been barreling toward the finish line and...

No.

She couldn't do this. Not again. Not when it was her friend's life on the line. It took everything she had to keep her eyes open.

Please be safe. Please be safe. Please be safe.

"Here it is, Tivane! The move I was telling you about. Look at Rivers moving up on Delmatic. Cryo is doing it again! It's almost identical to his move against Relm and Vikers!"

"I see it, Turnslinger! I see it! Can he actually pull it off, though? There's not much track left…"

"And there she goes! Rivers is making her move! Delmatic sees her, and he's cutting her off! But oh! There comes Cryo around the left!!" Turnslinger's voice squealed in a blaring crescendo, the screens in the suite vibrating with unrestrained fury. "He's going to do it, Tivane! He's going to do it!!"

Niko held her breath as the shouting raged on around her. In that timeless moment, Cryo's grey kart edged closer and closer to the front as Delmatic swerved to cut off Astine Rivers. Delmatic probably realized his mistake, but it was too late. When he swerved back to cut Cryo off, he was already behind. Cryo then moved to box him against the wall, allowing Rivers to shoot the gap.

All three karts crossed the finish line less than a fraction of a second apart.

———————

Against her better judgment, Anda had been glued to the screen. She still didn't know what happened, though — there was no way to know over the frantic shrieks of everyone around her.

Who were the three racers at the front that crossed first? Better yet, who won outright?

She strained to hear something, anything, through the enhancers. But she couldn't discern the broadcast from the incessant chanting in the room.

Anda stepped closer to the screen to get a better look.

Why she was so invested, she had no clue. It was no secret that being a Trackripping fan was an addictive pastime, but she didn't think herself to be susceptible to such trivialities. No matter, it *was* still captivating. She would admit that much.

The cameras all seemed to pan over to two karts in particular: a flashy pink and white kart, and a plain, grey kart. All attention was focused on them, so one of those two must be the victor.

Anda was shocked then, when it was Niko's friend Cryo who got out of that ugly grey kart. The female racer from the pink and white kart strode over to him, gave him a friendly embrace, then both of them locked hands in victory as they faced the crowd, raising arms to the sky.

She looked over to Niko, who was eagerly clasping her own hands in front of her and rocking back and forth. Anda imagined the girl was trying oh-so-very-hard not to burst out into celebration.

She was happy for her friend, but she knew it was only a momentary distraction, for they were still locked into servitude in this damn suite by that infernal contract. She could only hope to the Mara things would die down, and that all the guests would leave soon.

To her chagrin, however, things were far from dying down. Anda resumed her service, delivering unreasonable amounts of Cinto-wine to all the guests, as they demanded more and more and more. Their shouts grew louder by the second, some looking rather smug at their victories, others holding their heads and drowning their sorrows in their drinks. Some were taunting the others, and some were gathered in circles that leaped up and down, arms draped over each other in jubilance.

Childish. Yes, that's the word Anda would choose to describe this spectacle.

Things only quieted down when gasps rang throughout the room.

Anda was not comforted when all heads swiveled toward the screen, where a man wearing a ridiculous costume pulled himself out of a green and black kart and stormed over to where Niko's friend Cryo celebrated, advancing on him with a long knife in hand.

31

A Vulnerable Woman

TIME stopped for Niko.

Cryo. Cryo. Cryo. Cyro!

She urgently reached for him, but that's not how it worked. They both needed to be asleep.

She pleaded anyway. *TURN AROUND!*

By some miracle, he did. And just in time to jump away from the swing of that sinister-looking blade.

Niko watched helplessly as Cryo stood before Delmatic, unarmed against an assailant with a massive dagger.

Tivane and Turnslinger continued to announce, but nothing they said registered to Niko. She was locked into a bubble, one where nothing existed. No time. No sound. No feeling. Only every movement of Cryo's.

Delmatic's mouth tilted into a nasty sneer as he leaped forward at Cryo again, this time slicing and stabbing, but Cryo effortlessly sidestepped the assault. He deflected Delmatic's thrust to the side, threw an impossibly quick punch to his jaw, then seized upon that short moment of daze to grab ahold of his arm, flipping him onto the ground.

Cryo then landed hard over the top of Delmatic, throwing quick blows to his face and throat in rapid succession until the hand that held the knife went limp. Cryo kicked the knife across the track, then backed away as armed guards rushed in to secure the scene.

Niko's jaw dropped open.

Did her eyes deceive her? Did Cryo just beat the ever-living pulp out of Delmatic??

The stunned silence in the suite suddenly transformed into deafening cheers that erupted throughout the room.

"What the...!"

"Delmatic just got rocked!"

"What a phony!"

"We should have put bets on the fight!"

Laughing, cheering, and jeering filled the chamber, everyone obviously shocked at the outrageous turn of events at the climax of the Trackripping event. Even the Syndicate announcers were in a frenzy.

"Can you believe that just happened on live broadcast?!" Tivane exclaimed.

"I am beyond words," Turnslinger replied shaking his head in bewilderment.

"Well, all I can say is that I am a doubter of Cryo's no longer. The man is a legend in my eyes. And where one legend is born, another is snuffed out completely," Tivane said, as the cameras panned across to Delmatic's motionless body.

"It's unbelievable to think he'd do something so foolish. A very disappointing note to end such an illustrious career on, Tivane," Turnslinger agreed.

"Very disappointing, indeed. I don't see how Delmatic will *ever* be allowed back on the Tour after that stunt."

"No, Tivane, I don't imagine he would be. He'll be lucky to retain his Tour title from this year. He pushed the boundaries for so long, and eventually the boundaries pushed back."

"And in the form of the most unlikely of Rippers. Let's hear it for Cryo Siriar, everyone!"

Niko could hear the thunderous background roar from the broadcast. Like her brother had been long ago, her friend was now well and truly a celebrity.

"And don't forget about Astine Rivers," Tivane added. "She is now the first new champion in eighteen races! Ten from this year and eight from last year. Delmatic held a stranglehold on first place for so long, and her win was well deserved."

"Very well deserved indeed, Tivane. She has been a staple among the top Rippers this year, and I believe this win cemented her a second place standing at the end of the Tour. And I absolutely love to see her sharing her victory celebrations with Cryo Siriar. He had the race won, but he sacrificed that first place finish to box out Delmatic, allowing Rivers to sneak by."

The drone cameras zoomed out from Cryo and Astine's celebration, and skimmed over to Delmatic, lying there vanquished on the ground. She'd never seen such a pathetic loser in her life. She remembered how the arrogant ass had treated Jon Wilhe after the races, and felt nothing but gladness as the chum lay there while Syndicate authorities dragged his unconscious body away.

"Now, Turnslinger, onto more pleasant business. We at the Trackripping Syndicate are proud to bring you an exclusive post-race interview with none other than the victorious champion herself, ASTIIIIIINE RIVERSSSSSSSS!"

Tivane strutted over, gave the new victor a hug, then hauled her onto a raised interview booth.

"Many congratulations, Astine! We have been following your progression closely this season, and it couldn't have capped off more magnificently. Tell us, what was going through your mind in those last meters of the race."

"Thank you, Tivane! Thank you, Turnslinger!" she chimed. "I suppose in those last few seconds, I wasn't thinking anything. It was pure instinct and reaction. I made that move to get around Delmatic, he cut me off, and then suddenly he veered out of the way. Then I saw Cryo cut him off into the side, and I hit the impulse drive, praying there was enough track left to speed ahead."

"That there was, Astine! That there was. Now tell us, when you made that move, did you realize what Cryo was doing?"

"I didn't realize until the very end. Until after we all crossed the line together. I was fairly sure Cryo was going to win, so it surprised me when I looked up at the results."

"Have you seen the replay yet?" Turnslinger asked.

Astine widened her eyes and shook her head vigorously, straight brown hair falling out of her bun. "No I haven't. May I?!"

Turnslinger laughed. "Let's pull it up, Tivane. Are we able to do that?"

"Yes, let's watch the replay!" Tivane echoed, signaling instructions to her media team.

All screens suddenly lit up with the replay cinematic, and Niko saw exactly what happened in slow motion. It was just as she had described it. Astine tried to pass Delmatic, but he moved to cut her off. Cryo used that move to speed ahead of both of them. When Delmatic realized what had happened, he tried to cut Cryo off, but was too far behind. Cryo then made a move to box him out, rather than hitting his impulse drive for the win. That little move to screw with Delmatic cost him the win, but it also immortalized him as the track hero.

"Ooohhh!" Astine cooed, once she finished watching the karts all cross the line. "Yeah, I knew Cryo should have won that."

"Well, *you* are the victor, and nothing diminishes what an incredible race you had," Tivane offered.

"Thank you! But can we get Cryo up here?" Astine asked. "I think he deserves credit also. Without him, Delmatic would have won again."

"I think we can fit one more!" Tivane clucked. "Let's bring him up!"

Both broadcasters turned around, and a few moments later, the Syndicate team hauled Cryo up into the booth with the other three.

"Congratulations on your second place finish!" Turnslinger congratulated him. "And only on your second ever Tour race. Very impressive performance, if I do say so myself."

"Thanks," Cryo said politely.

Blazes, the poor guy looks so uncomfortable, Niko thought amusedly.

"Now Turnslinger can accost me all he wants, but I'll be the first to admit that I wasn't a believer in you, Cryo," Tivane said. "But now I am! By the Mara, now I am."

Turnslinger and Tivane laughed, and Cryo only offered a tight-lipped smile in return. Oh, this was entertaining watching him squirm up there. Niko nearly grinned.

"Now that move, Cryo — the one you made on Relm, and then again on Delmatic — where did you learn that?" Turnslinger asked.

Cryo shrugged. "I don't know, it just felt right in the moment."

"Well it certainly was brilliant," Tivane gushed.

Did she just... *bat her eyelashes* at Cryo?

"He is a brilliant guy." Astine shot Cryo a wide, beaming smile.

"Working with him these last few weeks has been a wonderful experience, and this race couldn't have turned out any more magical if it had been scripted."

Astine reached over and placed her hand over Cryo's. Tivane, not to be outdone, reached out and tenderly rested her arm around his neck. Cryo only stared ahead, but Niko knew he bristled underneath those patient eyes.

Are they serious? Niko scoffed. She suddenly felt possessive over her friend, and she didn't approve of these fake, *fake* women hitting on him.

"Now, Astine, what do you plan on doing with your fifty-million Terion bonus?" Tivane asked.

"Well, since you asked, I plan on giving Cryo twelve and a half million! I think we deserve even amounts. That victory is half his, at least. Thirty-seven and a half, and thirty-seven and a half."

Niko felt as if her heart stopped.

Twelve and a half million Terion?!... On top of the twenty-five million Terion bonus for taking second place?!... That would be enough for her and all her friends to leave this place!

Forever!

She supposed she could be patient with Astine Rivers if she was willing to donate to their cause in such a generous manner...

Niko wanted to leap, to cheer, to dance, and it took every ounce of self-control to steel her nerves in front of all these patrons she was supposed to be serving.

"And you, Cryo?" Tivane asked. "What do you plan on doing with your Terion? I'm sure there are plenty of young ladies who would *love* for you to take them out to Twilight Elegance for one of their famed gala shows."

Niko's good mood fluctuated to sour once more. That blazes lady needed to shut it. *No one* was going to objectify her friend, especially on planet-wide broadcast, no less...

"I don't know yet," he replied. "I'm not a big spender."

"Well," Tivane laughed, "get used to spending big. There are going to be celebrations and parties aplenty in the next few days. Both of you are the biggest stars on An-Terino right now, and you deserve to enjoy your spoils!"

Cryo returned another trite smile, then stepped off the interview booth after he and Astine Rivers were dismissed.

Niko tuned the rest of the broadcast show out, which mostly

dealt with betting results, final Tour standings, and other Trackripping logistics. She didn't have to worry about that anymore, since she was forbidden from *ever* betting again, under no uncertain terms. Nor would she need to, now that Cryo had earned them a way off.

Her heart felt like it was beating a hundred pulses per second. They were leaving this place! And very soon, if everything panned out the way it should.

The whole thing was surreal. She blinked, just to be sure she wasn't dreaming.

"Congratulations to everyone who had the gall to wage Terion against Delmatic," Andersane's voice thundered from across the suite.

Niko nearly squealed from the startle. She had forgotten he was even there. There was no chance he'd know Cryo's name, would he?

Probably not. It had been five years since Arhanda, and Cryo wasn't even all that famous there. Not like Riesen.

"Everyone who lost, which was most of you, pay up!" Andersane charged. "And servers, let's get one more round of Cinto-wine for everyone."

Niko jumped to action, collecting one of the pitchers from Anda before threading through the room, filling glasses to the brim. As she did, that feeling of... *inevitability*... returned. It never really left, she supposed, but she'd been so distracted by the race that she was able to ignore it entirely.

A sudden regret sprang forth, the triumph from seconds ago now spoiled by a storm of self-reproach.

Why? she scolded herself. *Whyyy did I take this contract?*

She suddenly felt very foolish. She didn't need to be here at all. She didn't need to earn Terion for her friends anymore — Cryo had done it.

He'd earned enough.

Enough to escape An-Terino once and for all.

But here she was. Trapped. In a room full of intoxicated sycophants and powermongers.

Blazes, what could go wrong? she thought wryly to herself.

Maybe she and Anda could sneak out now. After all, the race was over. Didn't their contract specify the end of the race as their termination hour? Or was it the end of the Syndicate broadcast show? Or were they truly in here until Andersane cleared them to leave?

Niko released a silent sigh.

It might be worth a try to make their exit now, but would the guards outside even let them leave? When she retreated around the corner to refill their jugs of Cinto-wine, she approached Anda to ask her just that.

"Are we done, yet?"

"We're done when they say we're done," Anda replied, her expression neutral.

"I… I just… I realize I don't even need to be here. I don't need the Terion anymore. Can't we just leave now?"

It was a bold admission, one Anda must've hated her for. Niko dragged her into this mess, and now she told her they didn't even need to be here… But she didn't care what Anda thought of her right now, so long as they'd just leave.

Yet Anda showed no emotion. "We're done when they say we're done," she repeated.

Ughhhh… fine. So they were stuck here, then.

Niko filled her jug once more and walked back into the room, topping off glasses as she scurried from patron to patron.

"Alright." Andersane's voice rumbled across the chamber, catching everyone's attention. "I apologize, but some business with Shatter just came up. I must leave to Machine Row momentarily, and I'm afraid I must remove you all from this suite."

Music to Niko's ears. The sooner everyone left, the sooner she could get the blazes out of here. Then, just maybe, she could make plans with her friends to get off An-Terino for good.

Groans and grumbles sounded from the patrons, though they all thanked Andersane as they filed out one by one.

"You are all welcome to stay at Twilight Elegance and indulge in the fineries. The game floor, the shows, the spas — they are all yours to enjoy for the evening."

Niko didn't care if that invitation was extended to her or not; she would be leaving this place as soon as she could.

And she did just that, hurriedly following the last remaining guests toward the exit after she and Anda collected all the glasses.

"Not you two."

Niko froze in her tracks. Was he talking to *them*? She looked sideways at Anda, who closed her eye and took a deep breath in resignation.

"You two stay."

Niko looked back and found him glaring directly at the both of them. Panic raced through her veins as she wondered if he did indeed recognize her. What would she say?? Would that mean he knew Cryo also?

The door closed as the last of the patrons left the suite. Only she and Anda remained, left alone with this blazes man in this blazes swampwasp's nest. Her blood curdled as involuntary memories surged from long ago — from that one time when Andersane, calm as the doldrums, shot those three unarmed An-Mara right in front of her.

"I believe you two did not fulfill your end of the contract," he said menacingly.

"We did as it specified, to our knowledge," Anda replied diplomatically.

"I'm looking right here," he said, "and it says there will be two servers from ROTO in uniform to serve food and wine, keep the Cinto dispensers stocked, and clean glasses and trays after the conclusion of the event."

"Did we not perform those duties to your satisfaction?" Anda asked.

"You did," Andersane said calmly. "But I fail to see two servers in uniform."

The uniforms? Niko thought incredulously. That's what he was complaining about??

"We were not given any such uniforms," Anda said plainly.

"You were," he countered, tossing two tiny pieces of cloth toward them, the ones that had made Niko recoil the first time she saw them.

"We were anticipating something more substantial for a uniform," Anda replied. "We searched the changing room, but we didn't find anything. We thought we were missing something."

"You were not. You may change into them now."

He couldn't be serious. Why in all the worlds would it matter now?

Anda stared at him appraisingly for a few moments.

"Very well," she said. "And then our contract is fulfilled?"

Anda must have decided it wasn't worth it to resist his authoritative will. Niko, on the other hand, would not be caught *dead* wearing that... *thing*. She felt embarrassed just looking at it.

"Why does it matter now?" she challenged. "The event is over."

"It is in your contract, and since you failed to adhere to such a binding agreement, you are now to entertain the guests of Twilight Elegance as recompense."

"No." Niko would fight this. "That is completely against the contract!"

"Since you are so eager for insolence, I will personally escort you to your posts in the main room. You may change right here, right now. And if you fail to agree, then you are on grounds to be arrested."

And sent to the Frying Pan. That was the threat that needed no words.

Anda glared sideways at Niko. She should've just shut up. She should've just put the damn thing on in the changing room at the beginning and been done with it. Now they'd attracted attention, and the worst kind, at that.

Maybe they could run? Maybe they could make it out before he caught them? If they rushed the door together...

No.

Andersane's powerful frame suggested otherwise. He would be more than a match for the two of them.

Maybe there was some trick. Some loophole in the contract. Some way out of this.

Think, think, think...

Suddenly, she remembered what Ravenna had told her, several years ago, in the aftermath of Andersane's execution of those unarmed An-Mara.

'*Men will always underestimate a vulnerable woman.*' That's what she had said.

But there was no way out. Niko couldn't think of one quickly enough, at least. So she grabbed the damn outfit and turned to walk to the changing rooms.

"No," Andersane thundered. "Right here. Right now."

"What do you mean righ..."

"I mean right here and right now. Or else all your liberties are forfeit to Shatter. You've already proven you are not to be trusted." A malicious smirk climbed the sides of his harsh face. "You have ten seconds to comply."

Was this what her anxiety was hinting at the last few hours? Niko always knew this man was bad, but *this*...

This…

She became angry, furious beyond words. How could Riesen *ever* serve a man like this?? This was disgusting, repulsive beyond all comprehension. He was the worst of the worst, the vilest of all humans. Niko wanted him to die. To end.

She had to get out of this, somehow. She had to. She could *not* go through with this. She *would* not. They made *absolute* sure their contracts did not include *anything* like this!

But Anda, completely stoic at this point, took a deep breath and started to remove her shoes, when suddenly the door burst open.

Before Andersane had a chance to fully turn around, he roared in pain. Niko jumped back in surprise, unable to process what was happening.

It was too quick for her. Too quick for Andersane even, for he had no defenses. None that prevailed, anyway.

It was over in a matter of seconds. The bellows turned to gargles as the man collapsed to the ground, but even then, the assailant, a blurred whirlwind of wrath and fury, did not stop.

Niko didn't even have a chance to react. Not even a chance to process fear. She only stood there, mouth agape, unbelieving at what her eyes told her.

Ravenna.

Standing there, knife in hand, covered in blood.

CHAPTER THIRTY-TWO

32

Worlds Within

RAVENNA was death incarnate, a savage huntress devoid of emotion or remorse. Yet she was also something else entirely — something tantamount to a soulless husk of a human.

"We leave now," she intoned, her eyes distant and cold.

Niko could only gawk. She couldn't move, couldn't respond, couldn't process. She could barely breathe, for blazes' sakes.

"Niko!" Ravenna barked.

"How did... what..."

"Will you snap her out of it?" Ravenna demanded of Anda.

Anda nodded curtly, turning toward Niko and affectionately touching her arm. "Niko, she's right. We must leave. Now."

"Sorry," Niko apologized, a sense of renewed vigor suddenly flowing through her. "I'm here."

"Let's go, then!" Ravenna growled.

Niko and Anda made to follow, sidestepping the now deceased Andersane's bloody mess of a body.

By the Mara... What had Ravenna done?

Niko averted her eyes from the heaping pile of flesh that had been her nemesis only seconds ago, looking up as Ravenna whirled back through the doors, disappearing around the corner.

Niko was about to shout and warn her about the guards, but when they stepped out of the suite, Niko saw the full scope of what Ravenna had done.

Six guards.

Dead, just like Andersane.

Slumped, shredded, and lifeless, as if they stood no chance.

Who was this girl that was with her??

She knew Ravenna always had a vicious streak to her, but this was something more. It was like she didn't even know this person.

How the blazes did Ravenna even get here though? Had she followed them inside after they talked to her earlier? Unlikely, considering the stacked security at the entrance... But if not then, how?

Something to worry about another time. The more pressing issue was how they'd escape now. Were they being monitored? Was the alarm already sounded?

Probably, since the one guard had mentioned that Twilight Elegance was already outfitted with the Terion Sight...

Blazes, how were they going to get out of here?!

The three women dashed along the hallway to the elevator, and just before Niko reached to use her Terion badge to signal the elevator down, Ravenna shouted at her to stop.

"It won't work! Your contract wasn't fulfilled," she said. "Let me do it."

How would she even know that?? She hadn't seen their contracts. Niko made sure not to divulge *any* specifics when they spoke earlier.

Ravenna instead pulled out a bloody Terion badge and pressed it against the elevator controls, and to Niko's relief, it flashed green.

"We need to go to the thirty-ninth floor," Anda said.

"Like the blazes we do," Ravenna replied. "We're leaving."

Anda squared on her. "My friend is there, and I cannot leave him. Not after what you pulled."

"After what *I* pulled? You mean how I saved your sorry hides?"

Anda paused, sighing. "That didn't come off as intended, I'm sorry. I do appreciate what you did, I really do. But you must understand that I cannot leave Amon here to suffer whatever consequences would come his way."

Ravenna regarded Anda respectfully, probably impressed that

this tiny girl had the gall to face her down after she just witnessed such savagery.

"Then you are free to go get him, but Niko and I are leaving."

"I go where Anda goes," Niko resolved.

"Niko, I will not say it agai…"

"No, Ravenna," she insisted, calm but firm. "I go where Anda goes. You can either come with us, or flee on your own."

For a few moments, Ravenna looked like she could've fired lasers from her eyes, but to Niko's wonder, she acquiesced.

"Fine. But we leave *right* after."

"Thank you," Anda whispered earnestly.

The elevator doors closed, and they descended a few floors to level thirty-nine. The ethereal music in the background was in stark contrast to the sight of their bloody desperation in the mirror.

Blazes… Niko thought to herself. This was insane. This was blazes insane. There was *no way* they were getting out of here without attracting attention.

Sure enough, when they exited the lift, gasps rippled from all directions as they swept through a crowd of the Alashadar elite. Ravenna was a sight to behold, and not in a good way, dripping with streaks of dark red. She should've remained in the elevator, but it didn't matter — it would be a miracle if they hadn't already been spotted by the Sight.

"Excuse me," Anda asked one of the guests, "did you see any security around?! We need help!"

A good ruse, Niko thought.

The woman clutched at her ornate emerald necklace, eyes wide with fright, and pointed them down a hallway to the right.

"Thank you!" Anda bowed, a feigned waver set to her voice.

Niko and the others hurried in that direction, but halted not halfway down when a guard stepped into their line of sight.

"Stop!" he commanded, upon seeing them from the other side of the hall. He then turned to his colleague. "I have them!"

Both guards removed sidearms from their holsters and raised them cautiously in their direction. Niko flinched, but Anda continued on, unfazed by the threat.

"Thank the Mara!" she shouted. "There were these women back there, killing everyone! Our friend here is gravely wounded. You must help!"

The men appeared confused, hesitating for the slightest of

seconds. Then, they both twitched, dropping to the ground as Amon appeared from around the corner, decked out with full body armor and a sidearm of his own in hand, the barrel still hot.

———————

"Amon, we need to leave now," Anda pressed, quiet but urgent.

There would be time to explain later, but for now, they needed to get out of here. Fast.

"Let's go, then" he said.

His eyes widened ever so slightly at the gruesome sight of Ravenna, but he merely nodded at her, wordlessly requesting that she lead the way.

Ravenna stooped down to pluck the deceased guards' weapons from the floor, tossing one to Anda before continuing toward the elevators they had just come from.

Anda noticed Niko glaring at Ravenna. She supposed Niko was upset that Anda was given the weapon instead of her, but she was surely more proficient with it than Niko would have been. Even with no depth perception anymore...

That glare could well have also been because Niko was upset — and rightfully so — at Ravenna's stunt, which undoubtedly put them all in grave danger.

Still, Anda was relieved Andersane met his end when he did. She shouldn't feel glad about anyone being slaughtered in such fashion, but she was. She vowed that the man would pay someday, after what she observed at the Frying Pan, but she had no inclination that day would be today. The timing also couldn't have been more impeccable, as she and Niko were in some serious trouble.

It was strange Ravenna came when she did, though... There was something at play that Anda didn't quite understand just yet.

No matter, there was time to think about that later. For now, they needed to find a way out of this blasted building, since they were likely being tracked by the Sight.

Nobody stopped them in their flight, thank the Mara, and when they arrived at the elevator, Ravenna used another badge she pulled from her pocket, then ordered the elevator to descend to level twenty-six.

Level twenty-six... What was on that level, again?

She'd been here twice before, but she didn't know the place well enough to remember what was on each floor. So she followed Ravenna out after they exited onto level twenty-six, imploring the Nel-Mara to keep them from being apprehended.

Without a word, Ravenna stormed over to a side corridor, then down another hallway, unfazed by the disorienting effect of the mirrors. She was efficient as a machine, cold and calculating in her flight to the exit. The woman knew *exactly* where she was going.

The twisted hallways stretched on, endless and dark, but eventually, an opening appeared in the distance.

Yes, that's right!

She knew there was something special about level twenty-six. Just ahead lay the sky bridge between Twilight Elegance and BlueWorld, where the dark tones of black and magenta would fade into bathing lights of blue and silver.

There was no security checkpoint leading into BlueWorld; access to this floor *was* the safeguard itself, granted only by a special badge. Ravenna clearly had this assassination planned out well — the fact that she had access to this floor proved that.

So the group rushed across the walkway, still drawing stares from everyone around, thanks to Ravenna's blood-stained visage. At the midway point on the bridge, Anda looked down, where only a translucent layer of carbon-sheet separated them from the darkened streets of Alashadar a hundred meters below.

Those who suffered from a fear of heights would not prefer a stroll along this bridge, but such precariousness never bothered Anda. She rather enjoyed the view. Except right now, there was not much enjoyment to be had, for there were far more dire matters transpiring.

The group paced after Ravenna, following her over to a massive escalator, one that stretched far into the distance above. The group strode up as if they were stairs, pushing past people lounging on the rails, earning groans, grumbles, and even curses in their direction. After riding the thing up for perhaps a hundred meters, Ravenna leaped over the side without warning, landing on a platform only about a meter below. The others didn't hesitate to follow, lest the escalator take them up to a height that would make for a more perilous jump.

Anda stifled a grunt as her ankles buckled on the landing, but she ignored the pain, only focused on matching Ravenna's blistering pace.

Now on this new level, it was more of the same: stares, gasps and hurled insults from the thousands of people that had assembled into a crowd. Where was Ravenna leading them??

They were attracting far too much attention, but upon second thought, Anda supposed it mattered little. She knew that ever since they left that suite back in Twilight Elegance, they were no doubt being tracked by Terion's algorithms, so no amount of discretion was going to hide them at this point. The only thing to do was continue to follow Ravenna forward.

So they all did, trailing her onto a long, curving ramp enclosed by an ultraviolet blacklight tunnel, which made all their clothes look so strange. Especially Ravenna, who was coated with those dark slashes of blood that shimmered with iridescence under the light.

After finally making their way to the top, they emerged onto a sort of catwalk, and Anda looked down to see exactly what the crowd was amassed for.

A show. A great show.

It was one of those giant entertainment concerts, where acrobats, musicians, actors, and effects teams cooperated as one, all of their talents intertwined into one grand performance. She had seen one of these before — not in BlueWorld, but at the Marindise — and she had to admit it was rather intriguing. Not quite to the level of those great Triumphares she had attended as a child, but still very entertaining, nonetheless. She might have stayed to watch, had she not been fleeing for her life.

As it was, it seemed that the show was nearing the finale anyway. The music, from what Anda could hear, had been steadily building along a crescendo, the instruments expertly woven into the surge. She couldn't quite tell who the composer was, but she thought she heard certain elements of some of her favorites here on An-Terino.

Marian Filorine, perhaps? Or Ricka Geshalatan?

It mattered little. There was no time to sit and analyze.

As the music plateaued, a giant blue animal that resembled a dolphin was projected onto the mists in the gaping central cavity of this monstrous building, which was like an entire world within, one completely different from Twilight Elegance. And one different yet from every other EC in NewCen.

Anda supposed these worlds within provided them with the means to hide, but they also provided the means to become trapped. Escaping to the streets of Alashadar seemed a monumental impossibility, if that's where they even intended to go.

Anda believed Ravenna had a plan, the way every turn and every hallway was met with intention, but part of her subconscious was beginning to harbor the first kernels of doubt, if only because they had slowed down from the pace she had set thus far.

Doubt was the death of the way forward, though, or so she'd been told so many times growing up. It seemed highly relevant now, and she tried hard to cast those feelings of doubt aside. But they surfaced once more when she looked to the distance ahead.

How she saw them first, with her missing eye, Anda didn't know. But she did.

Two armed guards, walking directly toward the group.

Niko saw them next.

"Blazes!" she squeaked.

The girl uttered that word more than any other in the Common vocabulary, but she supposed it was called for in a situation like this.

Anda wasn't sure if the guards saw them, but it wasn't worth taking any chances. "Ravenna."

Ravenna nodded. "Other way."

She turned the group around, this time opting to head down a spiraling causeway, crowded for certain, but not so crowded that they couldn't move quickly.

Amon saw them first this time.

"More company," he growled.

Another patrol, heading toward them from the other direction. This was no coincidence; security personnel were on to them.

The agents hadn't made a move to rush them yet, but Anda knew the only reason they hadn't was because there were *so* many people around. Even the EC's wouldn't risk mass panic. That would be bad for profits.

"Keep going," Ravenna hissed. "But faster."

She and the others accelerated into a brisk walk, and when the crowds thinned further, the guards broke into a gallop.

That's when Ravenna uncorked the flood. "Run!"

Anda did just that, trying her best to avoid collisions on the spiraling ramp, all the while resisting the instinct to turn around and look back. She didn't know how much space separated the group from the guards, but it couldn't have been more than fifty meters.

Poetically, the extravagant BlueWorld entertainment show had now reached its climax, the caress of the horns overlaid onto the wail of the strings, with the faint prickle of machine synthesizers in the background. Anda would have very much enjoyed this show in any other circumstance.

Instead, she was too busy sucking wind, desperately clinging to the rest of the group in their flight down the spiral. She was the slowest in the group, by far, which she was ashamed to admit. Before, she imagined she might have been about as fast as Niko.

Not even close, it turned out; the girl was astonishingly nimble on her feet.

They had almost reached the bottom of the ramp when Anda spotted an armed intercept ahead, weapons pointed straight at them.

They were trapped.

Ravenna saw them, too, and somersaulted behind a barrier, staying low to avoid any fire. She then pulled out her own sidearm and fired into the patrol behind them at the top of the spiral causeway, buying the group precious seconds.

Amon, seeing her objective, provided suppression fire against the intercept ahead, clearing a path toward a small, round hallway beyond.

"Go!" Ravenna ordered, her command blended with the shrieks of fleeing citizens.

Niko, of all people, didn't hesitate one second and dragged Anda by her sleeve to the corner where Ravenna gestured. Anda didn't have much time to appreciate this new tunnel, which turned out was an impressive tube surrounded by an aquarium, complete with hundreds of rays, sharks, and fish that circled overhead and below.

Instead, she could only look on helplessly to where Ravenna and Amon were now pinned down.

"Anda!" Niko yelled. "Help them, or give me the gun!"

The gun. How had she forgotten?

She could scold herself later, but now was a time for action, so she pulled it out, made sure it was loaded, and crept out behind the corner. The security intercept was almost upon Ravenna, so she aimed carefully, and discharged several times right into the middle of the pack.

One went down immediately, and the others scattered to find cover. Ravenna used the distraction to dart into the tunnel, skidding to a halt as she arrived, panting heavily. Then, both Anda and Ravenna turned toward the corner where Amon was trapped.

To Anda's horror, more security forces flooded the causeway. She desperately fired the remaining bullets into the guards nearest Amon, not hitting any, but providing him a split second of respite to join them.

He used that moment to dart out, but immediately stumbled to his knees, twitching as he became riddled with bullets.

No.

Please no.

She was about to run out to haul him to safety, but Ravenna grabbed hold of her, restraining her effortlessly with one hand. By the will of the Nel-Mara, the woman was strong...

"Amon!" she called out. "Amon!!"

No response.

Please no.

She peeked out once more to call his name again, but was forced back immediately. They were about to be set upon. There was no way out.

"Blazes!" Niko shouted. "Where do we go?!"

"Stay here!" Ravenna commanded. "Do not move."

"We're fodder if we remain," Anda told her. "They're almost upon us. We need to surrender. We're dead if we don't. And Amon needs help."

It was a tough decision to make, because Anda knew what surrender meant.

It meant the Frying Pan. It meant slavery. Or worse... it meant execution.

But if they didn't surrender, they were dead for certain. And besides, there was only one chance to help Amon, if he was still alive.

Amon, no...

He couldn't be dead. She still owed him her life.

"Ravenna?!" Niko yelled again. "Where do we go?!"

"Blazes, Niko!" Ravenna snapped. "Wait here!"

"What do you mean wait here?!" she hissed back. "They're on us NOW!"

As if an answer presented itself out of thin air, a previously unseen door opened up and a man stepped out.

Anda's breath caught, nearly discharging her weapon into him. But she recognized the man, barely in time to keep from firing.

What is he *doing here!?*

Her instincts screamed that she shouldn't be here. Not in his presence. Not yet. But those instincts were overridden by the necessity to get away from these EC security agents.

"What the blazes?!" Niko shrieked. "What is *he...*"

Ravenna ignored her, providing a round of suppression fire before turning to the man who called himself Ce-Ellum. "We could have used you several minutes ago..."

"I'm sorry," he said. "There was no path to clear the Sight machines, so I had to improvise. I got to the spot as soon as I could."

"It's okay, Ravenna said. "Let's go. Now."

"Amon..." Anda started.

"He's gone, Anda!" Ravenna snapped coldly. "We need to leave *now.*"

She knew it was true, but she owed Amon. She owed him everything. She couldn't leave him. Not like this. Even if he wasn't dead — which he probably was — he would be arrested and shipped off to the Frying Pan after being nursed to health, forced to labor for the rest of his life.

She bowed her head, offering him a silent apology, then turned to follow the others through the service staircase that spiraled down through the aquarium. This was the only rational option, and there was no room for doubt.

Doubt was the death of the way forward.

Before they left, though, Ce-Ellum turned to Ravenna.

"Is it done?" he asked quietly.

"It's done."

"Good." Ce-Ellum nodded grimly. "Follow me."

_____

CHAPTER THIRTY-THREE

33

The Weight of Life

FOR many tense hours now, Niko half-expected to be set upon by security forces at any moment. She jumped at every small noise — every drip of the water, every echo through the pipes, every cough from her companions. However, the moment of her doom never arrived, by whatever stroke of luck.

Maybe what Ce-Ellum had said was true — that he and Kyler disabled the surveillance devices, enough to blind the EC's temporarily to allow their escape. In any case, it was likely the service staircase they fled down was one of the last places searched, and by the time their pursuers scoured every exit, they were long gone.

It wouldn't set them back indefinitely, though; they still had to hurry.

Niko was exhausted, still not completely recovered from her brush with death last week. Ravenna also suffered from the exertion, her lungs still not recovered from her even closer brush with death five years ago. She'd probably never return back to normal, if she hadn't by now.

"How much further?" Ravenna wheezed.

"About four or five more kilometers," Ce-Ellum responded. "Almost out."

Four or five kilometers?! That was considered '*almost out*'? Blazes...

"Now I know how you feel, Niko," Ravenna empathized.

"Trust me," she said, "this is way easier today. Try doing this while you're freezing cold with no gear, haven't eaten in two weeks, and the only thing you've drank is this sewage."

It was the truth. Today was a day spa pampering compared to that blazes outing.

"Why would you drink the sewage?" Anda asked.

Her friend attempted the humor, probably to distract herself from the misery of leaving Amon behind. It seemed to work, because it was the first Niko had heard Ravenna laugh in a long, long while. She could've otherwise sworn the girl was becoming An-Mara.

Niko rolled her eyes at Anda.

"How far do you think we've gone already?" she asked no one in particular.

"Around thirty or forty k's," Ce-Ellum responded indifferently.

How the man was seemingly unbothered by the stench of this place, Niko had no clue. It probably had to do with his association with the damn underworld in Oldcity, where the stink seemed to permeate into everyday life there.

She still didn't trust the man, not by a long shot, but she *was* grateful for his help in escaping from BlueWorld. The one question that remained, though, was how in the worlds he and Ravenna even knew to rescue them in the first place...

One minute, she and Anda were in the hottest of water, on the verge of being trapped into who knew what manner of servitude. But then the next instant, Ravenna had arrived out of nowhere, quite literally murdering Andersane and whisking them off to safety. Then, to make matters even more strange, Ce-Ellum also arrived out of nowhere, seemingly in cahoots with Ravenna.

Niko would demand the truth about it, but later. Now was not the time. If Ravenna hadn't said anything about the suite yet, then Niko certainly wouldn't be the first to bring any tough conversations up.

Along the same lines, she hadn't dared try to defend her own actions to Ravenna. She knew it was foolish to sign that contract.

Beyond foolish. People had warned her, yet she did it anyway. She'd done many rash things in the last several weeks, but this had perhaps been the worst. She deserved a tongue-lashing of the highest order for such a dumbchum stunt. But maybe the reason Ravenna hadn't reprimanded her about it yet was because she may've felt even more guilty than Niko, after hacking and slicing a man to death.

Blazes...

Niko may have been glad that the bastard was dead, but part of her felt sick thinking about his feeble, desperate attempts at stopping his attacker. It was awful. All of it, awful. And the worst part was knowing that it was her *friend* who had done it.

Niko shuddered, the gag reflex triggering her to vomit once more.

At least she wasn't the lone sufferer... Everyone except for Ce-Ellum was retching up their bowels in these Mara-forsaken sewers.

"I would be happy to never visit the Wash again," Anda muttered, comforting Niko, patting her on the back as she finished throwing up.

"When we get out of here, you won't have to," Ce-Ellum said.

It was strange... Anda said that she knew Ce-Ellum, but he gave no indication of that acquaintance. He didn't give her any greetings, didn't ask how she was doing, didn't look twice at her. He even *introduced* himself to Anda back when they first entered the Wash...

The arrogant chum had probably forgotten he even knew her, so wrapped up in underworld business that a lowly blacksquash harvester was beneath his attentions.

Niko supposed she would steer the conversation in a positive manner before she said something rude.

"So Ravenna, I take it you haven't spoken with Cryo yet?" she asked, wiping her face clean from the bile and vomit that trickled down her chin.

"No."

"Oh. What about Kyler?"

"No."

"Does *anyone* even know we're here?" Niko asked.

"Yes. Everyone," Ravenna responded. "Cryo's the only one who doesn't."

"Everyone?"

"Kyler, Callum, Jack, Riiz, Kira-Tharn..."

Great. Kira-Tharn. How was she going to explain all of this to *that* blazes woman?...

"Oh. Well, did you all see how much Terion Cryo got?"

"I heard. Which is why we're leaving now. Callum and Jack already arranged for passage offworld."

"Really?!" Niko blurted out, unable to contain her excitement, even in the misery of the Wash. "Like actually leaving?"

"Yes."

"When?!"

"Today."

Niko was speechless.

It was happening?

It was *actually* happening?

And today?!

She had imagined this moment for so long — for the better part of a year, actually. She pictured it to be a moment of ecstasy — jubilant, triumphant. But now that her salvation was imminent, she only felt... tired.

So, so tired.

Tired, and hungry, and cold. Not starving and freezing, like she had been the last time she was in the Wash, but...

Anda clapped her on the back of the shoulder, grinning through her marred flesh. "You get to leave."

A mirthful glow radiated from Anda, one only Niko could see. Her friend looked genuinely happy for her.

"As do you, Anda," Ravenna said. "You can't remain here. Not after what happened. And for what you did for Niko..." she paused, trailing off. "Thank you. We will purchase your passage."

Anda appeared stunned for words. At first, it looked like she was about to speak, but she refrained.

Niko's heart became a little lighter. A little more hopeful. Was she actually considering going with them?! Niko supposed Ravenna was right. She *had* to go with them. She couldn't stay here. She was surely wanted by Shatter, just as much as the rest of them.

"None of us can stay." Ce-Ellum's expression was dark, brimming with conviction.

Blazes. Did that mean *he* was going with them also?

She'd just been so excited at the thought of Anda leaving with them, but now, learning that Ce-Ellum would be one of her traveling companions...

The thought did not sit well with her. Not at all. Something about that man did not add up. He was hiding something. Something deep. She knew it in her gut, and she never did convince her friends of her suspicions.

"How did you guys know to save us?" The question escaped Niko's lips before she could contain it. "And how did you know exactly when and where?"

Ravenna let out a labored breath. "Not now, Niko."

"Yes, now. I'm not leaving anywhere with anyone until you tell me."

Niko stopped in her tracks for extra effect. Hopefully Ravenna wouldn't murder her for her boldness...

"You want to know the truth?" Ravenna challenged.

Niko nodded, holding her stare.

"Alright then," Ravenna spat. "It was luck. I wasn't there to save you at all."

Wow. Harsh.

"Don't get me wrong," she continued. "I was glad I was able to, but that's not the reason why I was there."

Niko blinked, unable to follow. "Then why?"

"I was there to exact justice upon a vile, filthy waste of human breath for all the sins he committed. Which go way beyond what you know about, Niko. *Wayyy* beyond.

"And when you said you were providing catering service to the chief officer's suite, I knew you'd be there. Because of that, I had to speed up the timetable, because I *knew* you were getting into a situation you couldn't handle.

"So you can blame me for our current predicament all you like, but if I didn't have to save your sorry ass, it would've been clean and fast and no one would've known who it was. We wouldn't be in these sewers, we wouldn't have to flee, we wouldn't be wanted fugitives. Amon would even still be okay."

Ouch. The accusation hit deep, because Niko knew it to be true. It *was* her fault. It was *always* her fault.

"I... I wasn't blaming you," she said to Ravenna softly. "I... I just..." She drew a shaky breath. "Thank you for saving us."

Ravenna glared at her, though the harsh lines of her eyebrows softened just a tiny bit as she imperceptibly bowed her head.

And Amon...

Ravenna was right... Amon *would* still be okay if not for her.

How could she possibly make it right with Anda? There were no words that would ever do proper justice. Anda hadn't asked to be part of this, and now she had to flee the planet because of a decision Niko made. She could only guess what was going through the woman's mind right now.

"I'm sorry," she mouthed, barely above a whisper. It's all she could offer. "I'm sorry for everything."

But Anda placed her hand on her shoulder again, the touch soothing to her very spirit. The weight of the guilt was almost unbearable, but at the same time, the touch filled her with solidarity and resolve. Somehow, she knew Anda didn't blame her.

In this moment, Niko vowed that this friendship was one she would never give up. Ever.

Amon…

Anda couldn't stop thinking about him. She knew she should harbor such deep feelings of love and connection toward the man who saved her life years ago — had saved her life again today, she supposed — but all she felt was guilt.

A guilt that deep down, she only felt a huge weight lifted, now that he was gone.

She never comprehended how heavy that weight was before, but she felt its absence now. This sense of relief was an awful realization, but she knew better than to deceive herself. Long ago, she vowed she would never hide her true feelings on any matter. Not from herself.

She must stop dwelling on it, though. There were urgent concerns at hand, and they still weren't in the clear. At least, that's what Ravenna had been saying this entire time. Now, hours and hours later — Anda wasn't sure how many, exactly — they had arrived back to Machine Row.

Machine Row.

The beating heart of the beast. The center of Shatter's brute power and Terion's cold, mechanical operations. How Niko's friends ever managed to make their home in this corner of the city was beyond her.

As it was, they each had to slink to the hideout separately, wearing disguises and altering their gaits to avoid detection by the Terion Sight. Remote observation machines were now set up on every corner, and after what had happened with Andersane, security was fortified to the maximum.

It seemed to work, though, because none of them had been stopped, thank the Mara. Even still, the atmosphere was tense, to put it lightly. Everyone seemed tired. Irritable, argumentative, and tired.

Anda herself was drained to zero from the series of events she endured:

After escaping BlueWorld through that aquarium stairwell, she and the others descended thousands of steps into the subground levels, only then accessing their real challenge — the Wash — which was another world within Alashadar entirely. Traversing forty twisted kilometers of that wretched stench was enough to turn her stomach several times over. Niko had described it to her the other day, but she didn't realize just how bad it was until she lived it and breathed it herself.

Finally, after many arduous hours, they emerged into Oldcity through some gate Niko somehow remembered from instinct, upon where they paid desperate vagrants to swap clothes in order to trick any surveillance machines.

This was the first time she'd been back to Oldcity since... well, since she nearly died years ago. The sights, the sounds, the smells of this place... all of them brought back such dreadful memories of hopelessness and pain. She became intensely aware of the stares of the passersby around her, each of them poring holes into her soul with every manner of depravity. The denizens in this corner of the city were so desperate, so hollow.

Anda shivered. Would this place *ever* be healed? *Could* it ever be healed?

Not her problem anymore, she supposed. She was leaving. And for good, the Mara willing.

The slog through this place had stirred up such awful ghosts of the past, but she did well to keep them to herself. However, her steeled exterior almost melted when she learned that instead of returning via the trains, they'd have to walk another thirty k's back to Machine Row.

Of course, Anda knew better than to risk taking the rail, for the stations were patrolled to the brim with Shatter forces. Ordinarily, Anda wouldn't mind the physical activity — she might even relish in it — but she had no energy left. None at all.

Whatever was required for her liberation, though, she would do it without complaint.

So she walked. And walked. And walked. And walked...

It was an eternity in her fatigue, but eventually, the group neared the viper's pit that was Machine Row. It was here they decided to split up, each schooling themselves on changing their own manner of gait for safe measure.

And *finally*, when Anda knocked on the door and was admitted by this Kyler guy, she nearly collapsed into his arms, too exhausted to even care about the stink she dragged in from the Wash. She had no strength left. Even after she was given a hot meal, her legs continued to wobble beneath her. If only she could sit down for a little while longer...

'Blazes, girl!' were the first words Kyler had uttered. Niko had told her stories of how frustratingly quarrelsome the guy could be, but his expressions were so similar to Niko's, and that familiarity gave her comfort. Also, she rather enjoyed his humor at first impression. She would let time tell if he was as bad as Niko had described.

Ce-Ellum was the next to make it back, followed shortly by Ravenna. Anda became slightly worried when Niko never showed up, her mind going to the worst places, as it had when she was searching for the girl in the damn Frying Pan. However, Niko came stumbling in about two hours after Ravenna, claiming that she didn't want anything to appear amiss about this residence. It was probably a good ruse, Anda supposed. Necessary, even.

And now that they were finally assembled, the group discussed their next steps. Much to her relief, it appeared they were not jesting in the slightest about leaving this place.

Anda knew she didn't have any option to stay. There was nothing here for her anyway — now that Amon was gone — and that finality somehow eased the prospects of leaving. She even felt relaxed about it.

Though, she didn't like that they intended on going to the Capital system. That served her with no small amount of stress.

The one time she did speak up during the whole discussion was when she vocalized her reservations about their An-Mara

407

companions traveling to the Capital system. From everything she had been hearing, and judging from Shatter's conduct here, the Capital system might not be the safest of places for them.

Niko had only jokingly responded that it was Riiz and Kira-Tharn's turn to masquerade as Meridians, but Anda knew that would be easier said than done. Any Meridian with half a brain would be able to pick up on their An-Mara heritage within three seconds of talking to them. At least they would have several years to practice, she supposed.

"*You* may not respect the Time, Niko Ryen," Kira-Tharn accused her, "but *I* will always carry such respect. You cannot expect me to forego my ways, even to save my own life."

"Blazes, Kira-Tharn!" Niko shot back. "For the thousandth time, I don't expect you to forego your respect of the Time! All I'm saying is we need to have a plan, so you aren't blazes persecuted. You heard what everyone says about the anti-An-Mara attitudes going on there."

"I would prefer if such advice came from someone less brash in their own personal decisions."

Kira-Tharn's dig got to Niko. Anda could tell it did, from the way she inflated her lungs, ready to unleash a firestorm of ripostes. Maybe she should try to diffuse the tension before Niko enflamed it...

"I have spent much time with Niko in the recent weeks," Anda interjected, "and I agree with you, Kira-Tharn. Niko *is* brash." She shot her friend a small grimace, hoping she'd take it as a peace offering. "But she also makes decisions when others don't. She isn't one to sit around and be inactive. She makes things happen. More than almost anyone I've met, she isn't afraid to make things happen. It's not fair to blame her for that ROTO contract. I had the power to stop her from doing it, and instead I went along with it. If you want to blame anyone — if *any* of you want to blame anyone — blame me. Blame me alone and be done with it, so that we may move on."

Kira-Tharn and everyone else sat staring at Anda, but they didn't argue further.

Good. That was her intent for speaking out.

After several seconds of silence reigned over the table, Callum Sehs spoke, changing the subject.

"The thing I forgot to add about the travel arrangements," he said, "is that everyone will be serving as deckhands on the vessel."

"Deckhands?!" Kyler blurted out. "What does that mean?"

"Is that word too big for you, Kyler?" Niko chided. The girl sure was feisty with him.

He made a face at her, then continued to look inquisitively toward Callum.

"It's exactly as it sounds," Callum clarified. "Everyone will be helping run the ship."

"They said separate jobs would be assigned at the beginning," Jack added. "They were especially interested if we had any engineers."

Anda supposed she knew enough about the engineering on those ships, but she wasn't about to volunteer. She'd rather do menial physical labor, like cleaning. Something to keep her hands and feet from becoming too idle.

"I'd rather just be along for the ride," Kyler muttered. "You'd think forty million Terion would get us that much…"

"We finally get off this dump, and all you can do is complain?" Ravenna leveled him an unamused stare.

"I'm not complaining! I'd just rather enjoy myself for once, after working myself to death for the last year…"

"No, you didn't," Cryo said softly. "Niko worked herself to death. Kira-Tharn worked herself to death. Anda worked herself to death. You lived a nice comfortable life compared to them. All of us did."

Kyler shut up after that, perhaps realizing the magnitude of his own imprudence. Maybe Niko was right about him; he was quite the pigheaded clown, indeed. Though, there was something refreshing about him. Something wholesome. Yes, Anda decided, she rather liked the guy.

"Anyway," Callum resumed, "when we report to the Dockyards, they'll be asking what your skills are."

"How're we supposed to know what our skills are?" Niko asked. "We've never worked a ship. Not as deckhands. Everything was automated on our way over here from Arhanda, and everything else was taken care of by the An-Mara crew."

"Just your personal skills. Like for instance, you're good at astronomy, math, physical fitness… that kind of thing. That's what you could answer with. Not necessarily your experience in operating a ship," he explained.

"Niko, good at math?" Kyler sneered. He was about to say

something more, but immediately stopped when he detected the glare from Cryo beside him.

"I know the one called Niko Ryen to be exceptionally gifted in the ways of mathematics," Riiz said.

"I would agree with that," Jack chipped in. "She's a blazes genius."

Some of the others nodded in agreement.

Interesting. Anda knew the girl was smart, but she didn't know she was genius level smart. She looked over at Niko, who gushed at the praise, though she appeared to be trying to hide it.

"And after you submit your list of skills," Callum continued, "you will be assigned a job, like we said."

"When are we to make our departure?" Kira-Tharn asked.

"At 16:10," Jack replied.

"And just how do you propose we get to the Dockyards under the watchful eyes of Shatter and Terion?" Ravenna asked.

A fair question, to be sure.

"The same way you traveled here from Oldcity."

Anda would have grumbled, but Niko did it for her. She was so exhausted! They all had to be, and now they had to travel over ten more kilometers to the Dockyards, by themselves, disguised in filthy clothing, faking unfamiliar stride patterns once again...

Wonderful.

"Shatter and Terion can go to blazes," Niko said. "I hope to never see them ever again."

The others grunted in agreement.

"You won't. And I agree. We are fortunate to be leaving when we are," Callum announced. "Machine Row is on the last vestiges of existence. The whole Row is turning from a livable city into one giant Shatter complex, probably within a few weeks."

"What's that supposed to mean?" Kyler blurted.

"They will be knocking down all of these homes, clearing the way for Lanthanide refineries. It has always been Shatter's plan."

Well, that was news...

"And you only thought to tell us now?" Kyler demanded.

"It was not information worth making you stress."

"Yeah, but what would've happened if Cryo didn't score all that Terion?" he pressed. "What would've happened if we weren't able to leave now? When would you have told us?! Where would we have gone?!"

"Your other friends have lodging outside the Row," Callum shrugged.

"You would have had all four of us trying to fit into *their* quarters?" Kyler asked incredulously, pointing at Niko, Kira-Tharn, and Riiz.

"It doesn't matter," Cryo said, diffusing the rising quarrel. "We're off now, and there's no use fighting over what-ifs."

Anda agreed with him. There was no point in arguing over this. They were leaving now, so they would never have to deal with the aftermath of a transformed Machine Row. But goodness, these people bickered so much. If this discussion was any indication, she was in for a *lonnng* trip to the Capital system.

"Where did you learn of this information, Callum Sehs?" Riiz asked.

"After we returned from the Night, we were asked to debrief in a high-profile meeting, where the plans for Shatter's expansion on this planet were laid bare. They don't care about being clandestine anymore. To them, it's a done deal. The planet is already theirs in their eyes."

"Yeah, they control a straight-line Rift connection that runs from the Night, all the way through Machine Row and to the Daylight Rifts, and then finally out to the Frying Pan and their other two facilities they're building," Jack added. "And that line is the lifeblood of this planet. They literally control everything. If you want to live here, then you'll do Shatter's bidding."

"And if you don't want to live here…" Callum finished. "Well, there's no way to leave. Unless you have a way smuggle yourself off, like us."

"Where do they expect millions of people to relocate to?" Niko asked, her face scrunched up in disbelief. "If the people knew this, wouldn't they rise up?"

"Did you see the race?" Cryo sat forward. "The people *love* Shatter. They *love* Terion. It doesn't matter whether its convenience based, or just from pure blindness from all the Cinto — they *love* them all the same. Shatter already has the planet under their control, and there's nothing to be done to change it. Not right now at least."

A cynical take, but it was absolutely true. Anda was surprised at how astute these people were. For being from a backwater, isolated world that was destroyed by manipulators playing a larger game, these people were smart, resourceful, and surprisingly quick to learn of how things worked in the sector.

"Yep," Ravenna agreed. "You can't change the minds of fifty million people. This planet is not ours to worry about any longer, which is why we must leave now."

Niko opened her mouth, but she stopped short from protesting. The girl *had* to know that there was nothing to be done. Surely there was nothing keeping her here.

The way she looked at Ravenna, though… Anda could sense the wistful sadness in that look.

Granted, the woman's efficiency and savagery with which she dispatched Andersane was formidable, but there was something more to it. Something deeper. Anda knew she wasn't some unhinged killer. There must have been some sort of history between those two. Anda only knew of Andersane's role in the Frying Pan, but Ravenna had claimed to Niko there were many, many sins the man committed, more than Niko knew. Maybe someday she would ask Niko of the tale, but that day was most certainly not today.

"Speaking of leaving now," Kyler said, "shouldn't we be… y'know… leaving? Like now? Since we have to walk separately, and in blazes disguises…"

"Yes," Callum said. "And I regret there is no time to sort out personal belongings at your living quarters, but you aren't to be taking anything with you, anyway."

That was unfortunate. Anda had amassed a collection of literature over the years here, and space travel could be oh-so-dull. Especially an interstellar trip like this was to be…

"There is one last order of business before we depart to the shipyards," Callum added carefully, clearing his throat. "Because of the current political climate here, I regret I cannot travel with you. Nor can Jack. We must stay behind to maintain our cover within Shatter. We can cause enough disruption from within to throw them off your scent for a small time. Enough for you to enter the Greater Accelerations, at which point you will be out of reach."

Anda looked to Niko. She had a small inkling of what the girl felt for Jack. The way she looked at him now… she knew.

Steeled features were the only thing visible on the surface, but Anda knew a storm roiled inside her friend. The poor girl. She could *not* catch a break.

In defense of her friend, part of her became angry at Jack. Why couldn't Callum stay behind by himself? Why must Jack also stay?

It wasn't fair to the girl. Not fair at all.

"You must be joking," Ravenna said flatly. "We finally find a way off, and you don't take it?"

"I think we could *all* be gone before they realize we're on that ship," Cryo added. "I think you'd be safe to go with us."

"No." Callum ended the discussion sternly. "It is not safe. Not without intervention. It has to be this way. Trust me. Once things here have cooled down, Jack and I will find passage off. You have our word. We still have plenty enough Terion saved up, let alone our connections within Shatter."

The room was shocked silent for few seconds, people no doubt searching for solutions that would allow Callum and Jack to stay with the group, but it was Riiz Alke-Tani who spoke out.

"If that must be the way of such matters, then I, for one, will regret our parting, Callum and Jack Sehs," he said.

"We will miss you, too." Callum gripped forearms with Riiz in Meridian fashion.

Strange. Anda had never seen an An-Mara deign to perform such a Meridian ritual. These people must really share a tight bond.

"We will miss you all." Callum's vision raked over every single one of his companions, his eyes widening ever-so-slightly as it finally settled on Ce-Ellum, who stood against a wall at the far end of the room, arms crossed casually. "But I assure you, all will be well."

"Welcome to the bleakness," the transit clerk said. Over and over and over, to each new hopeless person arriving on this desolate world.

It wasn't untrue, Niko now knew, but it was such an unhelpful introduction. She supposed it was a humorous sort of quirk to the planet, but maybe if they shifted their tone to a more hopeful one, people would have more to fight for, rather than just being a bunch of witless groundbirds content with submitting to the will of Shatter.

She pulled her vision from the flock of people waiting at the arrivals over to a wide open runway, where a pockmarked white shuttle sat awaiting their departure.

Ravenna muttered something unintelligible under her breath.

Niko only stared into the distance, knowing that if she acknowledged her friend, resentfulness might seep to the surface. She understood why Ravenna did it — or at least could learn to understand it, given time — but that didn't stop her from seething at the fact that had she not killed Andersane, they might not be in this situation where Jack had to leave.

But it wasn't Ravenna's fault. It was Jack's.

She didn't know what possessed her to initiate the conversation with him. She was *so* angry. Beyond angry, actually.

Sad — which was a thousand times worse.

And maybe that's the reason why she felt the need to talk to him now. That, and the realization that this was the end. Maybe not the end in the *forever* sense... But even under the best-case scenario, she wouldn't see him for several years.

Several. Years.

At least.

Gusts whipped Niko's hair into her face from all directions, the air thundering with the relentless roar of engines around her. It was so loud and windy, but she needed to have this conversation. For her own sanity, she needed it.

"I..." Jack started. "I know you must hate me."

Niko shook her head. "You know that I *love* you, Jack. Am I pissed at you? Absolutely. Could I punch you in the face? Sure. But if you don't know anything else, know that I care about you."

He laughed. "Well, please don't punch me in the face."

"You deserve it." Her face didn't show a flicker of amusement.

"I know," he sighed.

"So what? You stay here and battle the forces of evil from within? Then what? They just let you go and you join back up with us in the Capital system?"

"Something like that," he muttered.

"Why, though? Why must *you* do it? Why can't you let your dad do it? You belong with *us*."

"I belong with my dad, too," he countered. "We've already talked about this. Besides, there needs to be two of us to pull off what he plans."

"What *he* plans? What about what *you* plan?"

"This plan was both of ours, actually. And it involves

sabotaging Shatter equipment out in the wilds to keep them distracted. I stay undercover within their ranks, and he does the dirty work. If we planned accordingly, this could keep them from finishing construction on those new labor camps for years."

A noble plan, she had to admit. But by the blazes, why did *he* have to be the one to do it? There were fifty million other people that could take his place...

She wanted to curse every noble bone in his damned body.

"And then once it seems like our efforts run out of steam, I promise we will find passage to the Capital system. Besides, we still need to think of something to do about the Machine. And find Kezane. He's out there, Niko. Somewhere. And he needs us."

"And to what end will you search? It just seems like it's one thing after another out here. Once you complete one task, another will always pop up. That's how things are. When will you decide enough is enough and leave?"

"I promise that's all we have to do. Throw Shatter off your trail, deal with the Machine, find Kezane. We will only be apart for a couple of years."

Niko shook her head. "These are the prime years of our lives, Jack. And we've already spent too many of them either wasting away in space or rotting to death on this Mara-forsaken hellhole of a planet."

Jack let out a forlorn breath. "Please don't try to change my mind on this. I already feel bad enough. You know I do."

As well he should, the blazes man! *Uggghhhh!!*

Breathe, Niko. Breathe. It was all she could do to not scream. The red in the periphery of her vision thankfully subsided, if just a little.

"I know," she murmured. "And I don't mean to. I just... I don't know what I want."

"Come here," he said, looking deeply into her eyes.

Her breath caught.

Blazes, she hated herself for being so susceptible to his pretty face. His strong jaw, his blonde ringlets, his clever smile.

She stepped forward, perhaps daring to expect a kiss, but... no. Of course not.

It was a hug.

She shouldn't complain — the hug was nice, and the Mara knew she needed one — but...

"I promise I'll see you again," he said. "And time will go by faster than you think."

A big promise, and one that was beside the point.

"I'll hold you to it."

He released the hug, offering her his sweetest smile, then stepped back. "You need to go."

She did need to go. Her shuttle was about ready to start the boarding process, and as much as she wanted to stay here with Jack, she was *not* about to spend one more minute on An-Terino that she didn't have to. If the shuttle left without her...

But still, to drag herself away from Jack in this moment was more painful than anything she'd ever done.

"I... I'm gonna miss you," she said, offering him one last, longing look.

"Me too." He smiled once more at her, clearly expecting that this wouldn't be the last time they'd see each other.

It had better not be.

Her hand was still up in farewell when he turned around and headed into the bustling crowds of the customs offices.

And as Niko watched Jack disappear into the concourse beyond, something cracked inside her. Not her soul. Not her will to survive. Not the dream of a better life. But something else. Something that tethered her to a weight. The weight of... life?

Yeah, she supposed. The weight of life was the best way to describe it.

It was something she ran from for so long, but now that she snapped that tether, she felt free to embrace that weight, even though her heart was being ripped in half once again. It was a sign of her humanity, which was something she worried had left her entirely.

But it hadn't.

Against the hazy, fluorescent radiance of Machine Row, two streaks glistened on her cheeks just below her eyes.

For the first time in five years, Niko let the tears flow.

———————

CHAPTER THIRTY-FOUR

34

Deckhands

WAS *it worth it?* Ce-Ellum wondered.

He looked around at his fellow traveling companions as they waited to board the craft. They made for an odd bunch, and he wasn't sure that the crew exactly bought their charade as 'deckhands', but he supposed no one would truly care. Not with the amount of Terion they made from the deal. As long as everyone pulled their weight, none of the crew would make a fuss.

Hopefully no one on board recognized him, though. He'd given the authorities at Terion and Shatter — among others, including all those underworld goons — plenty of reason to hunt for his head. Navigating his way through Machine Row had always been nerve-wracking, but moving through the Dockyards and actually boarding a ship bound for the Capital system was ill-advised on another level entirely.

His biggest regret, however, was failing his friends, and now leaving their memory behind. Years of trials and tribulations had bonded them closely; now they were gone, little more than dust on the An-Terino winds. He had been too late to make a difference, and worse, had to take it all with stoic indifference. He had no time to mourn them, for there was so much to do.

And then there was all of his work he was forced to leave behind, of course. He'd made significant progress over the last few years, especially with all the resources of Vulture at his disposal. At least it wouldn't be a complete reset, though, since he fortunately had some of the greatest minds he'd ever met traveling with him. Still, it was still a lot to give up.

Lines and lines and lines of code that they'd need to repeat. And then more lines and lines and lines on top of that. And then more lines and lines and lines on top of *that*. It was a lot to make up for, and they weren't exactly blessed with time...

Though, he supposed Kyler's revolutionary approach to the whole thing would make it easier to recover that lost work by orders of magnitude.

Kyler was truly one of a kind, as was Cryo. For his entire life up to now, Ce-Ellum could only dare to hope that the rediscovery of the Infinity Machine would someday be a possibility, but working with these two anchored those hopes in reality.

Their languages... Their algorithms... Their methods of parallelism... These people had a way of thinking that was unlike anything he'd ever seen before.

But even Kyler and Cryo aside, Ravenna and Riiz's skills would also come in quite handy, for every extra pair of hands mattered.

And then there was Niko.

Oh, Niko. An impulsive hothead, sure, but one oozing of untapped potential, a genius of undeniable proportions. She would most certainly be indispensable in this crusade. She only yet needed to finish learning of the tinkering languages, and then she would be ascendant made flesh.

He wasn't expecting it at first — his attention had been focused on the rumors of another exceptional prodigy hiding somewhere out here in recent years — but it was this group's remarkable collective intellect that stole his devotion now. It might just be exactly what he was looking for this whole time. These individuals were the most intriguing bunch he'd ever met in his entire life, and they'd just happened to land right in front of him.

Which is why, in the end, he decided to travel with them.

Speaking of Niko, the girl walked toward him now, the last one in their group to get in line to board the shuttle. She had been speaking with Jack outside, but now she simply strode over to the others with an unreadable expression, hints of red lining the edges of her eyes.

She scowled at Ce-Ellum when they shared a brief glance, then stormed off to wait for the seating bay doors to open. He supposed that she was rightly upset that Jack wouldn't be making the journey with them, if relationship drama was what the glower was all about...

Ce-Ellum suppressed a grin. He wasn't ever offended, but he got the feeling she never really liked him, for whatever reason. She always gave him such resentful stares, such skeptical squints. And always had, ever since she met him. One would think he was some sort of supervillain, the way she looked at him.

Oh, well, he chuckled to himself.

He supposed it was probably good survival instinct on her part to never trust strangers implicitly. Besides, he had no shortage of time to win her over on this voyage. Three years would be plenty adequate. And maybe, just *maybe*, she would one day learn that *he* was the one to supply Cryo with the information that delivered her from the middle of the Night via the reservoir system.

Ce-Ellum offered himself a small, inward smile at that revelation he kept hidden.

A few moments after Niko fumed by, he turned to meander over to where the rest of the group stood, annoyed anew when his leg began to ache. Those phantom pains seemed to sprout up whenever he went too long without calibrating the prosthetic.

Unfortunately for him, those calibration programs were also left behind with all the rest of his work. Everyone had to pack up and leave with almost zero warning, thanks to his and Ravenna's stunt from earlier. It could have gone much smoother than it did, but truthfully, his only regret was that he wasn't the one to stare the man down at the very end.

Before Andersane came to this planet, he never really knew him personally, but he did know he was one of Silvane's unquestioning henchmen, and that alone earned Ravenna his approval for what she did to the man. Not to mention all the nefarious ill the chum caused in the recent weeks. He should be above such personal retribution, but...

Whatever.

In any case, the phantom pains of his leg were of no

consequence; they were a small price to pay for getting out of here. He'd have plenty of time to recreate the calibration programs in the coming days, anyway. For the time being, he would just have to deal with the discomfort, which was nothing he hadn't done many times over the last few years.

He willfully shoved the aches out of his mind and stalked over to the others, standing beside Niko and Anda as they all waited for the doors to open. He was happy that those two, in particular, were finally getting out of this place. They had suffered so much; it was only fitting that they were among the ones to escape such a bleak doom as remaining on An-Terino. At least there was *some* justice left in the sector.

Ce-Ellum offered both of them a reassuring smile when a strange feeling pricked the back of his mind. It wasn't the overwhelming flood he normally would have felt, but rather a soft, trickling stream that seeped through, one droplet at a time. Although it was only the slightest of senses, it was one that he had learned to trust long ago.

He quieted his mind, reaching inward as he scoured the room for the source, and was ultimately confused when his gaze instinctively settled on Anda.

Strange...

It was as if she was a light in the dark, a most brilliant signal, a beacon drawing moths to a lantern. Without being conspicuous, he studied her intently from the corner of his eyes. What was this all about?

Before he thought too long about it, the answer to his unspoken query hit him as hard as an Alashadar train.

No.

It couldn't *be*...

In the case that his senses were going haywire, he reached inward again, narrowing the scope of his mind and concentrating all awareness upon her, unbothered that she now openly stared back at him. Could it actually be...?

There was only silence. Until it clicked.

Of all the blazes!

It *was* her! How did he not notice before?? He'd seen the girl around for *weeks* now! And she'd seen him! All this time cooped up on this blazes-accursed Hole of a planet must have dulled his talents to the point of ineptitude. How embarrassing.

Ashamed as he was, though, he had no doubts. His entire consciousness' worth of focus told him that this *was* her, even though he hadn't seen her since she was a little girl — the very same one who he'd instructed in the ways of the Valanses in a previous life. No doubt that was the reason she'd avoided his subconscious attempts at Intrusion for so long.

And she was so... *old*... now. All grown up.

As he peered at her marred face, Ce-Ellum realized he wasn't sure he wanted to know what awful things had transpired that brought her to An-Terino, or why she was unrecognizably disfigured. He regarded her with a hint of sadness in his eyes, but she simply lifted her chin and held his stare confidently, as if she knew his intended pity and wanted none of it.

Comprehending his mistake, he wiped away any trace of the projected sympathy, allowing himself an introspective smile as he remembered how she'd never been one to accept charity from anyone.

When last he knew her, she was a precocious little thing, an impossibly young prodigy who *demanded* he taught her everything: Valanse techniques, politics, and advanced engineering, all in the most rigorous fashion. And to think she was little more than a *child* when he did...

What a wonder she had been.

And still was, he presumed, if she was here now, alive and mostly well. She glared back at him proudly, the look being one that he was well-accustomed to. Yes, this was the same girl, indeed.

What should he even say, though?

His mind flailed around for something. Anything. What was there to even *begin* to say?

Did he need to explain his desertion? Should he ask about Meliane? Should he tell her of his plans? Ce-Ellum struggled to think of any one thing on the spot, but he had to say *something* — their staring contest was getting awkward. Even Niko was looking back and forth curiously at the both of them now...

Blazes, he nearly muttered, becoming both amused and annoyed at how these contagious Arhandan curses were rubbing off on him so thoroughly. *What to say...*

Well, at this point, he might as well just let the truth come out. There was no point in keeping his identity — or hers — from these people any longer. As Providence would have it, they were all in this together, companions bound on a journey that could very well shape the fate of the entire galaxy.

"Your Highness," he finally managed to utter, bowing deeply in reverence toward Logan... Anda... whatever she wanted to be called.

Her one eye acknowledged him knowingly.

"Kezane."

————————

APPENDIX

GLOSSARY OF CHARACTERS
(in alphabetical order)

Ajane Solase (uh-JAYN soh-LAYZ): Meridian who traveled to Arhanda in the years after the Arrival

Alin (uh-LINN): Meridian Valanse

Anda Len (ANN-duh LENN): young adult that works in the blacksquash fields on An-Terino; known for her disfiguring scars and confident poise

Andersane (ANN-durr-sayn): Magistrate of the Meridians on Arhanda; chief officer of Shatter on An-Terino; known for his booming voice and intimidating nature

Armond-Dei (ARR-mund-DAY): a foreman of excavation operations within the Rifts of Terrovian Aquatics on An-Terino

Astine Rivers (AST-een): well known professional Trackripper on An-Terino

Bayors (BAY-ers): member of the Imperial Aegis assigned to Logan

Brandon Jenaei (JEH-nye): young adult from Arhanda; thought by Niko to have been killed in the destruction of Arhanda; best friends with Niko's brother Riesen

Callum Sehs (CAL-lum SEIS): Meridian who traveled to Arhanda with Ajane Solase in the years after the Arrival; now living on An-Terino; Jack Sehs' father

Cryo Siriar (CRY-oh SEAR-ee-arr): young adult from the Green Coast on Arhanda; now living on An-Terino; known for being calm, cool, and collected; close friends with Niko

Delmatic (dell-MAT-ick): well known professional Trackripper on An-Terino; multiple-time defending champion; known for his cocky demeanor and flamboyant antics

Dingo Walalam (DEEN-go WALL-uh-lam): well known professional Trackripper on An-Terino

Fellen-Sor (FELL-inn SOAR): tall, young An-Mara adult living on An-Terino

Galen Anstraes (ANN-strayss): First Officer in the Meridian Contingent; worked with Kezane aboard the *Duskletter*; now works with Kezane at a base in the Night zone on An-Terino

Glace Castore (GLAYSS cast-ORR): Meridian Valanse

Ingan Ostreodase (EEN-gunn OSS-tree-oh-DAYZ): Princess Imperial of the Meridian Empire; eldest sister to Morgan and Logan; heir apparent to the Meridian throne

Jack Sehs (SEIS): young adult from Arhanda; now living on An-Terino; known for being light-hearted and jovial; one of Niko's best friends

Jame Ryen (JAYM RYE-inn): adopted father of Niko; thought by Niko to have been killed during the destruction of Arhanda

Jon Wilhe (JONN WILL-ee): well known professional Trackripper on An-Terino

Kate Ryen (RYE-inn): Niko's sister, two years older than her; known for being an empath; thought by Niko to have been killed during the destruction of Arhanda

Keran Ryen (KEER-inn RYE-inn): Niko's eldest brother; thought by Niko to have been killed in the destruction of Arhanda

Kezane Pfase (kuh-ZAYN FAYZ): Meridian Valanse commander; notable for being the most powerful Valanse in an age; thought by many to be hiding somewhere on An-Terino

Kira-Tharn (KEER-uh-THARN): An-Mara from Aktun; one of Niko's closest friends and roommates on An-Terino; notable for her no-nonsense attitude

Kyler Pierson: young adult from the Green Coast on Arhnada; notable for his exceptional machine tinkering skills and argumentative attitude; close friends with Niko

Logan Ostreodase (OSS-tree-oh-DAYZ): Princess Imperial of the Meridian Empire; youngest sister to Ingan and Morgan

Mack Ryen (RYE-inn): Niko's younger brother; thought by Niko to have been killed in the destruction of Arhanda

Marial (MARE-ee-uhl): elderly worker in the blacksquash fields on An-Terino; thought by Niko to be from the Ossion system

Marian Filorine (FILL-orr-EEN): musical composer on An-Terino

Marius Silvane (sill-VAYN): Meridian Valanse commander; serves as head of the Tricouncil

Marl Vikers (VEE-kers): well known professional Trackripper on An-Terino

Maro Del-Fiiz (MARR-oh dell-FEEZ): An-Mara worker in the Rifts of An-Terino; friends with Kira-Tharn

Max Elsireon (el-SEAR-ee-onn): professional Trackripper on An-Terino

Meliane (MELL-ee-enn): someone of import to Anda and Ce-Ellum

Mera Darline (MEER-uh DARR-leen): prolific vendor in Alashadar

Michele Aragase (mish-ELL ARE-uh-gayz): Second Officer in the Meridian Contingent; worked with Kezane aboard the *Duskletter*; now works with Kezane at a base in the Night zone on An-Terino

Morgan Ostreodase (OSS-tree-oh-DAYZ): Princess Imperial of the Meridian Empire; middle sister between Ingan and Logan

Morland Relm (MORE-lind REALM): well known professional Trackripper on An-Terino

Nicodaren Amibar (NEE-koh-dare-rin A-mih-barr): called 'Daren' by his friends from the Green Coast, not to be confused with 'Niko' Ryen; known for being exceptionally quiet; thought by Niko to be living on Aktun

Niko Ryen (NEE-koh RYE-inn): young adult from the Green Coast on Arhanda; now living on An-Terino; primary protagonist

Noralie Mose (NOR-ruh-lee MOHZ): Flight Deck Engineer in the Meridian Contingent; worked with Kezane aboard the *Duskletter*; now works with Kezane at a base in the Night zone on An-Terino

Nuna (NOO-nuh): elderly worker in the blacksquash fields on An-Terino; thought by Niko to be from the Ossion system

Paul Lorise (lorr-REESE): prolific nutrient vendor in Alahsadar

Ramen Ostreodase (RAW-men OSS-tree-oh-DAYZ): Emperor of the Meridian Empire

Raul Vess: assistant to Magistrate Solor-Ven in An-Tun Village on An-Terino; thought by Niko to be from the Ossion system

Ravenna Night (ruh-VEN-nuh): young adult from the Green Coast on Arhanda; now living on An-Terino; notable for her naturally multicolored hair, purple eyes, and fiery temperament; close friends with Niko

Ricka Geshalatan (RICK-uh GESH-uh-luh-than): musical composer on An-Terino

Riesen Ryen (REE-sinn RYE-inn): young adult from the Green Coast of Arhanda; Niko's brother, one year older than her; thought by Niko to have been killed in the destruction of Arhanda; notable for being of exceptional skill in multiple areas

Riiz Alke-Tani (REEZ al-keh-TAW-nee): An-Mara now living on An-Terino; close friends with Niko; notable for his friendly nature uncharacteristic of most An-Mara

Solor-Ven (SOLE-orr-VENN): An-Mara magistrate of An-Tun Village on An-Terino

Steven 'Turnslinger' Osinroler (OH-sinn-ROLL-err): popular Trackripping personality for the Trackripping Syndicate; previous Tour champion

Tivane Fry (tih-VAYN): lead Trackripping announcer for the Trackripping Syndicate

Trienne Ryen (tree-ENN RYE-inn): mother of Niko; thought by Niko to have been killed in the destruction of Arhanda

Verane Anstrile (veer-AYN ANN-style): Public Forum luminary; Meridian elite

Vicero Limon (VISS-err-oh lee-MOAN): contact of Callum Sehs that helped connect him with the populations that lived in the wilds of An-Terino

Viru-Mor (VEER-ooh-MOAR): An-Mara assistant to Magistrate Solor-Ven in An-Tun Village

Wenno Daks (WENN-oh DACKS): well known profession Trackripper on An-Terino

GLOSSARY OF TERMS AND PLACES
(in alphabetical order)

Aktun (ock-TOON): homeworld of the An-Mara

Alashadar (AL-uh-shuh-DARR): great city on An-Terino with a population of over fifty million

Alashadar Unlimited: giant entertainment mall located in the NewCen district

Amalkyne (AHM-all-KYNE): coastal resort city on Arhanda; known for hot, desert climate

An-Mara (ANN-MARR-uh): civilization that shares the Local Sector with the Meridians; split from the Meridians shortly after the disappearance of the Nel-Mara; seen by the Meridians as zealots clinging to a long-gone past

Anterg Territory (ANN-turg): the territory encompassing the lands on the north and east sides of North Continent on Arhanda; known for its harsh, wintery climate

An-Terino (ANN-tear-EE-no): planet home to a mix of peoples; tidally locked to the star Bucon; an incomplete terraforming project of the Nel-Mara

Arhanda (arr-AWN-duh): planet in the Local Sector; homeworld of Niko Ryen and her friends; destroyed by massive outgassing from the Engines five years before the events of *Machine Row*

Avenue, the: the main thoroughfare in Alashadar; runs parallel to the Terminator

Avion Flavor: a high-end poultry restaurant in the Alashadar Unlimited mall

BlueWorld: giant entertainment complex in NewCen; known for its blue and silver lights, as well as its aquariums that are woven throughout

Bucon (BYOO-conn): the star at the center of the An-Terino system; M-type main sequence star

Capital System: star system at the heart of the Meridian Empire; includes planets such as Mareia, Trevi Nali, Samarind, and Jeheddon, as well as the star Providence

Celean Sea (SELL-ee-enn): body of water in between the Islands and North Continent on Arhanda; named after a body of water on Trevi Nali

Child of the Nel-Mara (NELL-MARR-uh): in the Prophecy of the Stewards, purported to be the child of Beriph Nel-Arana, the last Nel-Mara

Cinto (SEEN-toh): luxury herb grown on An-Terino; used as a tasteful spice in small quantities and an opulent psychedelic drug in larger quantities

Dawn of Civilization: described in the Legends as the epoch in which the ancestors of the Nel-Mara first emerged as an intelligent civilization

Daylight: half of An-Terino always facing toward Bucon; characterized by hot, inhospitable temperatures

Droneripping: popular sport on An-Terino in which competitors remotely control airborne drones that race through obstacle courses

Duskletter: Meridian long-range vessel; sent on a mission to the *Marina* under the command of Kezane Pfase

Earth: according to the Legends, homeworld of the Nel-Mara

Engines: the terraforming engines on each of the planets; constructed long ago during the days of the Nel-Mara; An-Terino, as an incomplete terraforming project, only contains one functioning Engine

Entertainment Corporations: also referred to as EC's; large corporations that dominate the economy on An-Terino

Equatorial Territory: Territory on Arhanda; characterized by tropical climate and dense, mountainous rainforest

Field: a team sport where the objective is to score goals, allowing for both kicking and throwing of the ball; a favorite pastime of Niko and her friends form Arhanda

Fleetness: the An-Mara term for the maximum acceleration during space travel, allowing ships to reach great speeds; also called the Greater Acceleration by the Meridians

Galactic Dark Patch: a large part of the galactic disk that appears abnormally dark due to increased debris and dust obscuring the light

Garments: the traditional dress of the An-Mara; there are several variations depending on occasion

Gluoron Entertainment (GLOOR-onn): gaudy entertainment giant in Alashadar

Greater Acceleration: the Meridian term for the maximum acceleration during space travel, allowing ships to reach great speeds; also called the Fleetness by the An-Mara

Green Coast: town in northwestern North Territory on Arhanda; home to Niko and her friends

Groundheim: large city on Arhanda; known for its extensive tunnels and caverns

Harvesters, the: largest manmade structures of the Meridian Empire; arc-like projects based in close proximity to a star that are used for multiple modes of energy generation

Heads of Knowledge: An-Mara judiciary; rigorous mental conditioning program to become a Head of Knowledge

Hole, the: Meridian slang term for the black hole in the center of the galaxy

Imperial Aegis: branch of the Meridian military that serves the imperial family; not subordinate to the Valanses

Intrusion: technique by which Valanses can read people's thoughts or intentions

Islands Territory: Territory on Arhanda; notable for its striking citizens, who boast dark skin and flowing golden hair

Lamperian Colonies: a collective of Meridian colonies in the Lamperian triple star system

Legends, the: literature detailing the history of the Nel-Mara

Leviathan: the massive water treatment and energy generation project on Mareia

Local Sector: the collective of inhabited worlds within the local star cluster at the edge of the Galactic Prime Meridian; includes the Meridian and An-Mara civilizations, as well as neutral systems such as An-Terino or Arhanda

Machine: any piece of technology that can perform tasks for humans; see 'Machine, the' regarding the purported artificial intelligence threat

Machine, the: according to the Legends, an alleged artificial intelligence that is sweeping through the galaxy

Mainquarters: the base of operations for the An-Mara on Arhanda; located in Groundheim

Mara (MARR-uh): all the people and places of the Nel-Mara civilization prior to the disappearance of the Nel-Mara

Mareia (muh-RAY-uh): waterworld in the Capital system; primary source of usable water in the Meridian Empire

Marina: one of millions of Nel-Mara vessels whose objective after the Scuttling was to aimlessly transmit signals to stall the spread of the Machine

Marindise, the (MARE-inn-DEESE): a prominent, upscale entertainment venue in NewCen

Meridian Empire: the governing entity of the majority of the systems in the Local Sector, including the Capital system, the Ossion system, and the Lamperian colonies

Minedyne: organization set up by the Meridians on Arhanda to focus on materials acquisitions for their empire

Nel-Mara (NELL-MARR-uh): mythical beings of the past that possessed technologies far beyond those of any current civilizations in the Local Sector; according to the Legends, descendants of humans from Earth

Nevaly (NEH-vull-ee): capital city of North Territory; known for old-style stone architecture, lush gardens, and the famed Northern Mists of Nevaly

Night: half of An-Terino always facing away from Bucon; characterized by freezing, inhospitable temperatures

Oblivion: An-Mara term for the warping of space-time beyond the event horizon of a black hole

Observer: in the dreams, one not interacting with anyone is considered an Observer

Ossion (OSS-ee-onn): most populated planet in the Ossion system

Ossion System (OSS-ee-onn): major system in the Meridian Empire; culture whose history is characterized by now-banned religions; major inhabited worlds are Ossion and Proteia

Podsuits: the full-suits that are worn in liquid suspension pods to regulate metabolism

Praxeans (PRAX-ee-inns): a branch of the Valanse Arcaneum that specializes in developing psychic intellect

Prophecy of the Stewards: the word spread primarily by the An-Mara about the return of the Nel-Mara through a human child

Proteia (pro-TAY-uh): waterworld in the Ossion system; settled planet, but also used as a source of usable water for the Meridian Empire

Providence: the name of the star in the Capital system; G-type main sequence star

Recycling: An-Mara penalty system characterized by progressive demotions

Rifts, the: narrow, excavated quarries that run perpendicular to Alashadar and the Terminator; primarily used for resource transportation and climate regulation

Ripper: a Trackripping competitor

ROTO: stands for Rural Operations and Trade Ordinance; one of the major drivers of agriculture and industry on An-Terino

Scuttling, the: the moment when the Nel-Mara vanished 60,000 years ago; no trace was left of certain technologies, such as galactic-scale travel and machines that were able to process near infinite amounts of information

Shatter Industries: industrial organization with Meridian ties that has now began encroaching upon An-Terino

Shell: a feature on ships during periods of high-speed travel that is used to protect against micrometeoroid impacts; upon such an impact, the angular momentum of the rapidly spinning outer shell of particles acts as an external dampener

Skytower Palace: tallest building in Alashadar; narrow tripod, topped out with a giant rotating disc

Sol City: capital city of the Islands Territory and the largest city on Arhanda

Sol One: the name of the star that the mythical world of Earth orbited long ago; the measurement of Earth's year is still used as a standard year among all societies in the Local Sector

Standard Gravity Level (SGL): the Meridian term for simulated gravity by linear acceleration

Stewards: the remnant searching for the Child of the Nel-Mara

Switching of the Decks: at the midway point of journeys through space, linear acceleration is reversed and all tables, furnishings, etc. are switched to the ceilings; all floors are in such ships are constructed in a mirrored and minimalistic manner to conveniently accommodate the Switches

Tel-Mara (TELL-MARR-uh): the people presided over by the Nel-Mara before the time of the Scuttling

Terion: the unit of currency on An-Terino; also, the corporation that manages the currency

Terion Sight: the surveillance system used by Terion to assist Shatter in exacting control over the citizens of An-Terino

Terminator, the: the thin band of Twilight separating Night from Day

Terrovian Aquatics: major industrial company on An-Terino that controls much of the water flow into Alashadar; they control and operate excavation on most of the Rifts on the planet

Time, the: a set of values and traditions observed by the An-Mara; refers to the time that will be spent awaiting the return of the Nel-Mara

Trackripping: a popular kart-racing sport on An-Terino

Trevi Nali (TRE-vee NAH-lee): capital of the Meridian Empire

Tricouncil: the three heads of the Meridian Valanse Arcaneum

Twilight: the thin band separating the Night from Day; also called the Terminator

Twilight Elegance: prominent, high-end entertainment venue in NewCen

Universal Common: the standardized language that both Meridians and An-Mara use

Ut (YOOT): short for 'Utility Machine'; small device that performs many functions; features an implant that allows users to exert minor thought processes over certain utilities

Valanse (vuh-LANCE): an elite officer in the Meridian Empire that specializes in mental conditioning to perform extrasensory abilities

Valanse Arcaneum (vuh-LANSE arr-CAY-nee-umm): the headquarters of the Valanses on Trevi Nali; also used as the name for the Valanse organization as a whole

Venting: when Engines are activated on a planet in order to regulate atmospheric conditions

Vulture: a smaller entertainment company that is known for being a front for one of the most notorious gangs on Alashadar; sponsor of Trackripper Jon Wilhe

Wash, the: the sewer system in Alashadar

Waxing Crescent: the symbol of the Meridian Empire; displayed as a hand gesture with the thumb and forefinger forming a "C" in the shape of the Meridian Crescent, with the other three fingers tucked into a ball to signify the star Providence

TRACKRIPPING TOUR OF AN-TERINO

The Trackripping Syndicate is the umbrella organization that owns all the tracks and broadcasting rights for the Trackripping Tour. Each year, the Trackripping Syndicate hosts the twelve races that the Tour is comprised of. There are seven qualifying races throughout the year that are held in the Alashadar Unlimited Speedway. At the end of this qualifying period, the twenty-four Rippers with the fastest time-trial results are invited to the Trackripping Tour.

Alashadar Unlimited Speedway
- The track and stadium are set in a sub-ground arena underneath the famed Alashadar Unlimited mall.
- Two-kilometer circuit, with half-kilometer alternating sections of straightaway and turn.
- On the Tour, Rippers will complete twelve laps.

The Dockyards
- A track that runs under and around the Dockyards of Machine Row, the airport that harbors sky traffic going to and from orbit.
- Characterized by wide tunnels and sharp, ninety-degree turns. Eight-kilometer loop.
- Rippers complete six laps.

The Ashfield Jamboree
- This track is set in the outskirts of Alashadar in a wide open ashfield.
- One of the faster tracks on the Tour, the Jamboree is characterized by long, flat straightaways and wide, banked turns.
- The most notable feature is a vertical loop, which Rippers must navigate within appropriate speeds to maintain traction. This feature is one of the most feared elements on the Tour.
- Twelve-kilometer loop. Rippers complete three laps.

Middletown Mania
- A figure-eight circuit that traverses Middletown.
- Half the course is open to the air; the other half runs through a long tunnel. Five-and-a-half-kilometer loop.
- Rippers complete six laps.

The Belly
- A track that runs in and out of an active volcano on the outskirts of Alashadar. This track has the distinction of requiring the highest maintenance costs on the Tour.
- Characterized by rock obstacles, blind corners, tight tunnels, sweeping turns, grand vistas, and long straightaways. Considered by many Rippers to be the most balanced race on the Tour.
- Seventeen-kilometer loop. Rippers complete three laps.

Spiral Sprint
- Set on the outskirts of NewCen, this race is four octuple-helices of ascending and descending spirals, two up and two down.
- Characterized by the continuous banked turns of the helices, the only straightaways coming from the dashes between the towers.
- Four-kilometer loop. Rippers complete four laps.

The Wash
- This track runs through converted Wash sewers. Considered the tightest, slowest race on the Tour, with most of the race only wide enough for two karts to fit side by side.
- Characterized by tight turns and narrow track, aside from the long finish line straightaway.
- Two-kilometer loop. Rippers complete twelve laps.

The Highlands Challenge
- Set on the slopes of a mountain range on the outskirts of Alashadar, this track is considered the most dangerous one on the Tour, statistically speaking.
- Characterized by hairpin turns with no guardrails, Rippers are at risk from falling from great heights.

- Fifteen-kilometer loop with a total of over one thousand meters of elevation gain.
- Rippers complete three laps.

NewCen Circuit
- Set in the heart of NewCen, this track winds its way through the major ECs. This is the track that draws the greatest crowds outside of the Century.
- Characterized by long straightaways followed immediately by sharp, low-visibility turns.
- Ten-kilometer loop. Rippers complete six laps.

Excavation Run
- The newest track on the Tour, Excavation Run is built along an old Rift system. This is the only track on the Tour in the Daylight.
- Characterized by blind turns, Rift mining equipment obstacles, and a long sweeping turn exposed to the Daylight. Considered a very technical race with the amount of tight, blind turns.
- Four-kilometer loop. Rippers complete six laps.

Oldcity Blitz
- Track that winds its way through downtown Oldcity, then around through the surrounding slums.
- Not a very technical race, but this Track is notorious for the interference of spectators.
- Eighteen-kilometer out and back. Rippers complete three laps.

The Century
- The final race of the season brings Rippers from one end of Alashadar to the other, and back. This is the most spectated event on An-Terino.
- Characterized by long straightaways. Not considered a very technical race, but it is the longest one on the Tour.
- One-hundred-kilometer loop. Rippers complete one lap.

Tour standings are calculated by multiplying the points earned on a particular course by the weight that course carries.

Place	Points	Place	Points	Place	Points
1	45	9	21	17	8
2	42	10	20	18	7
3	39	11	19	19	5
4	36	12	18	20	4
5	33	13	12	21	3
6	30	14	11	22	2
7	23	15	10	23	1
8	22	16	9	24	0

- Alashadar Unlimited Speedway (1.0)
- The Dockyards (1.0)
- The Ashfield Jamboree (1.3)
- Middletown Mania (1.0)
- The Belly (1.9)
- Spiral Dash (1.0)
- The Wash (1.0)
- The Highlands Challenge (1.5)
- NewCen Circuit (1.9)
- Excavation Run (1.8)
- Oldcity Blitz (1.8)
- The Century (2.0)

For instance, if a Ripper places first on the Alashadar Unlimited Speedway, they will get the 45 points from that first place finish multiplied by the 1.0 weight that course carries. So they would get 45 points. However, if they take first on the Century, they would get the 45 points multiplied by the 2.0 weight that course carries, so they would get 90 points.

A LOOK AT TRACKRIPPING KARTS

Impulse Drive

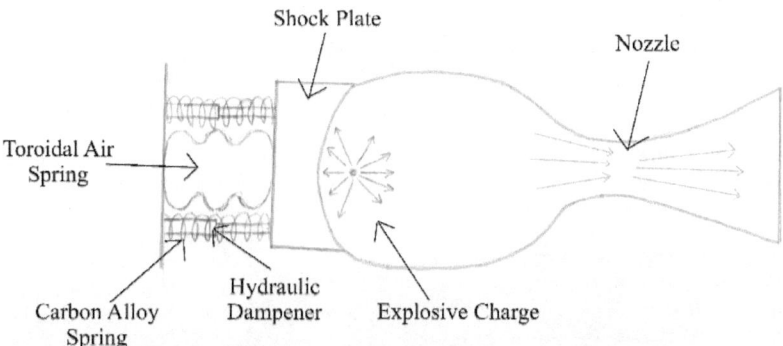

On straightaways, Trackripping karts utilize a variety of propulsion methods to achieve maximum velocities quickly. A relative newcomer to Trackripping, Vulture has pioneered the impulse drive, which uses a mild explosion whose shockwave creates an external force that acts upon a shock plate. The plate pushes forward against the springs, which extends the time that the force acts upon the body of the kart. The acceleration involved is still intense, but the impulse drive makes it manageable for the Ripper.

The springs, which are a combination of air springs and carbon alloy springs, are outfitted with hydraulic dampeners to allow energy stored in the springs to escape as heat.

Similar to a rocket, the gasses from the explosion are funneled and ejected out the back through a nozzle designed to take advantage of the increase in pressure differences, creating more thrust force.

Wing Technology

Rippers lift flaps on top of their wing to provide a small amount of lift to their kart on straightaways, reducing friction. When they approach turns, they activate the flaps underneath the wing, increasing the downforce and keeping the car locked to the track on tight turns.

Energy Systems

Each kart uses energy efficiency systems to minimize fuel waste. In most karts, the heat energy lost in inefficient processes is used to power mini steam turbines. As with everything on An-Terino, the processes are unregulated, and have led to accidents. In addition, the pressurized exhaust from most karts is also used to spin a turbine, allowing the karts to retain more power.

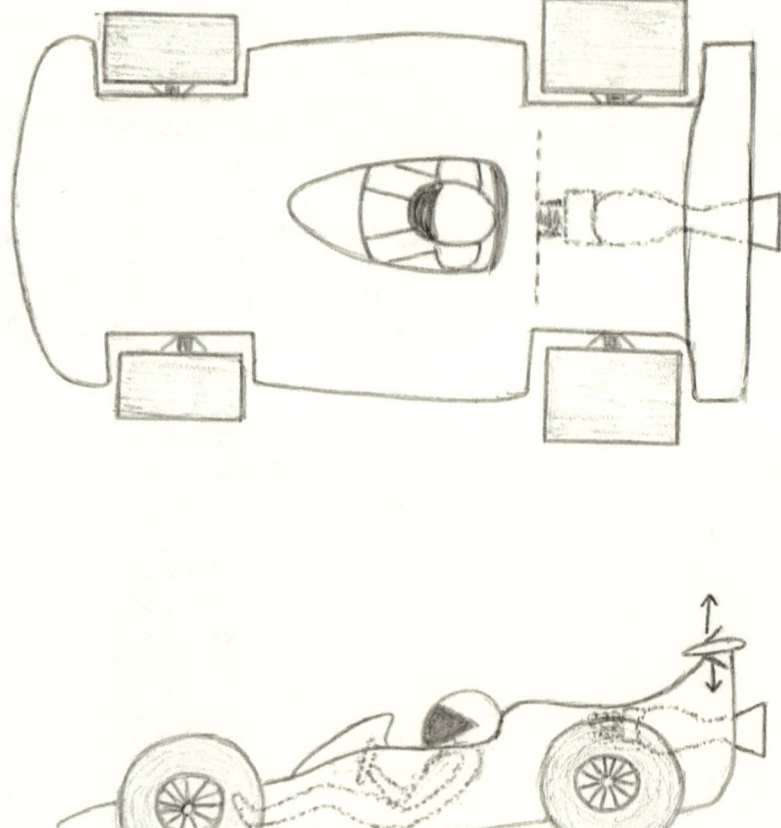

ACKNOWLEDGEMENTS & AUTHOR'S NOTES

First and foremost, thank you to all the readers out there! I hope you enjoyed reading this book as much as I did writing it. If you did, it would greatly improve the exposure of the series if you left a review on Amazon and Goodreads.

I'd like to express a huge thank you to my family for everything over the years, not to mention the unconditional support in this undertaking. I wouldn't be where I am without you! I'd also like to give a big thanks to Natalie, who has been nothing but patient as I bounce ideas off her 24/7.

Thank you to everyone else who helped in one way or another — providing feedback or even simple words of encouragement. Your support means everything to me.

This book is dedicated to both my grandfathers, who were old school science fiction enthusiasts. I wouldn't have the love myself if not for my heritage. This book is also dedicated to Courtney, who was my earliest confidant when beginning work on this series. She believed in the journey of Niko and gave me the inspiration to go ahead in telling it.

If you are interested in this series and would like to become an ARC reader for future installments, feel free to reach out or follow:

cjyee.books@gmail.com
instagram.com/cjyee.books

READ ON FOR A PREVIEW OF

THE FIRST TWO CHAPTERS:

BOOK THREE IN THE MERIDIAN SERIES

1

Preview

"**SHOULD** we do it again?" Rush Fils' voice dripped with mischief. Pure, unbridled mischief, along with a hint of juvenile enthusiasm. What were they — nine years old again?

Riesen Ryen shook his head, smirking at his friend through the dim blacklight. "We probably want to make a good impression this time."

Indeed, if the doors opened and half his crew were found lying maimed on the ground because they wanted to play around like a bunch of uppity youth, he would surely lose the privilege he'd been afforded lately. Although, it was tempting; it had been wildly fun when they did it during the Switching of the Decks, the midway point of the voyage.

... *No!* he snapped at himself. They were adults. And they should behave like it. He really shouldn't entertain this idea any longer. Besides, they'd had enough fun anyway.

Riesen had been anticipating a dull week of travel, but instead, the journey felt like a Solstice holiday trip. The liveliness of such a thin skeleton crew was something he hadn't expected. It was one of those rare moments that made him feel like a carefree youth again.

"Aww c'mon," Rush persisted. "One more time…"

"We're lucky no one got hurt last time," Riesen said, closing the debate.

Ordinarily, a stunt that foolhardy would be reprimanded thoroughly, but nobody needed to know about it. One of the perks of being the ranking Valanse on this mission. Still, they shouldn't push their luck.

He really needed to start acting like a leader. It was hard not to smile, though. How did commanders ever manage to do it?

Riesen barely restrained himself at the memory of Rush Fils rallying the entire crew to attempt the Switching of the Decks free from their seatstraps. The man had everyone hooting and hollering as if it were a Salutatade festival instead of a standard travel procedure. He could still feel the thrill of shifting from Standard Gravity Levels to weightlessness, then that tense pause when everyone hung suspended in the air, waiting for the exact moment when the ship's thrusters fired in reverse. Most had played it safe, hovering near the floor. But not him. He'd been floating near the top when SGL resumed on the opposite deck.

How his entire crew managed to escape with zero injuries when the floor snapped up to greet them was a mystery. Not everybody was as athletic and coordinated as he was…

Like one of those snow leopards in the polar reaches of Trevi Nali, he managed to land nimbly on his feet, even against the tangle of seats across the way. Not so with Rush Fils, though — he'd landed hard on his backside beside him. Now the oaf wanted to do it *again*? Idiot…

"Last time, I promise" Rush entreated. "We might never get the chance again!"

"No." Did all commanders have this much pushback from their subordinates? "Our contact is meeting us right outside the airlock. As soon as we clamp on, we're outta this thing and onto our mission."

"Pfft, fine." Rush turned to the others sitting in the equilibrium seating. "Just let it be known that *I* wasn't the one who bailed out."

"You're completely strapped in right now…" Riesen taunted, narrowing his eyes playfully at Rush. "Seems to me like you're all talk."

"Listen to Ryen, Fils," a voice growled from behind them. First Officer Vineson Morey was one of the pilots, and aside from Riesen, he was the commanding officer on this ship. "We let you do it the one time during the Switching, and once is enough."

Rush saluted the man without a word of protest, Crescent to chest and everything.

Riesen became a little irritated that Morey was able to command such unquestioned respect, when he himself had to spar with his crew like they were his schoolyard mates. Even if they *were* his longtime friends, they still needed to honor the chain of command.

To be fair, though, this was their first mission of import together. It was designated as a training mission, but it was one unaccompanied by a superior Valanse commander, their final trial in a grueling five-year program at the Arcaneum.

The directives: meet their contact, investigate the purported An-Mara activity out here, mingle with the locals to get a read on the sentiment, and report their analyses. It was a loose mission, which Riesen figured was the essence of their test. Hopefully it would prove to be simple and straightforward.

It was a little disconcerting that they'd be walking among An-Mara and their sympathizers, though. He hoped to never meet another An-Mara again in his life, unless it was in the effort to rid the sector of them forever. Silvane himself hinted to Riesen that their efforts on this mission were for that explicit purpose, so he supposed he'd just have to endure their presence a little longer for the greater goal.

"Wait, so who all's been here before, again?" Rush asked.

"Wasn't that all we talked about on the way over?" Eagane Melase was not amused at Rush's antics. Hadn't been for years.

"All *you* talked about, maybe…" Rush shot back.

Eagane sighed, long and slow. "Me, Jeriane, and Idys. How do you *not* remember this?"

He had a point… how *did* Rush not remember this? Riesen specifically recalled him being part of the discussion when they were talking about this exact thing. Though, he knew Rush liked to dismiss people just to stir things up, so he was probably only feigning ignorance.

"He was too busy nursing his hindside after the Switching," Riesen chipped.

"Truth!" Idys Claron burst into laughter, wiping away black ringlets from her face. She always did that when she looked at Rush.

"You landed *hard*!"

"That *had* to have hurt," Morey added, wincing.

"Did you ever sit in the pods afterward, like I suggested?" Idys fussed.

"Yeah, I heard those are good for that kind of recovery," Jeriane ribbed. "Gotta keep the hind nice and firm."

Even through the dark, it was evident that Idys rolled her eyes at him, her smile never dipping from the corners of her mouth. "But seriously, Fils, you okay?"

"Oh, I'm fine!" Rush responded coolly. "I'm not some delicate flower. Gonna take more than that to scratch me."

By the Mara, he was cocky... but truth be told, Riesen appreciated that kind of confidence in his company.

"Well, something rattled your brain," Idys chided. "We were specifically talking about how you, Ryen, and Ferrugan were the only ones who hadn't been anywhere in the Capital system besides Trevi Nali or Samarind. You seriously don't remember that?"

"Ohhhhhh, I think I remember now..."

Of course he did. He was just playing for a reaction this whole time.

"Well, then, you remember that once we get there, we don't have time to waste on sightseeing," Eagane lectured. "Or did you forget that you are a newly ordained Valanse of the Meridian Empire?"

Riesen appreciated Eagane's no-nonsense attitude. Of course, he also appreciated the humor and lightheartedness that everyone else in the party seemed to favor, but sometimes, he just needed an anchor to keep everyone grounded. Eagane was that weight.

Whispers cut through the darkness around him. No doubt the others found the banter between Rush and Eagane to be supremely entertaining.

"All the more reason to do what we want," Rush countered, his swagger oozing through the dark.

Eagane huffed loudly. A rule follower, through and through.

"But in all seriousness, I'm looking forward to getting back to civilization," Rush remarked.

Riesen nodded in agreement. Even though the trip had been fun, the extra five days to Jeheddon from what he was used to on his trips to Samarind was one of those things that had him wishing they could just rediscover Nel-Mara teleportation already.

"I don't know if this place qualifies as civilization," muttered Eagane.

"Ryen and Fils wouldn't know any better," Jeriane quipped.

Some of the others snickered in amusement.

"Now, now," he continued. "Be understanding, it's not they're fault they're just some backwater refugees."

Riesen laughed with Jeriane and the others, shrugging it off with a light heart, but inside he wished they would shut up already. It was funny at the beginning, but he'd been hassled about his Arhandan heritage for *the entire* five years at the Valanse Arcaneum. So annoying.

"You're right. I don't know any better — I've been way too busy with your sister."

"Oooohhhoo!" Rush bayed. "Gottem!"

Howling laughter tore through the equilibrium seating, far too loud for a ship with only sixteen people aboard. Everyone was either doubled over or pointing fingers at Jeriane — everyone except Vineson Morey, who looked nothing short of exasperated from dealing with this cadre of Valanses who acted like they were fifteen years old. Riesen supposed he was part of the problem, but whatever. No harm ever came from joking around.

"Good one, Ryen," Jeriane acknowledged after the clamor died down. His perfect white teeth were illuminated like fangs when he grinned through the blacklight.

"Better not let her Highness hear that." Idys smirked at Riesen.

Blazes, she was right. He probably shouldn't have said that, even if it wasn't true — which it wasn't. The last thing he needed was Morgan on his case for something stupid...

"Oh, don't you worry, that's the first thing I'm mentioning in my mission debrief," Jeriane teased. "I can see it right now — the next big Meridian scandal: Princess Imperial spurned by the Child of the Nel-Mara over Jeriane Elade's sister."

"Oh, don't you start that back up..." Riesen groaned. He hadn't heard the words '*Child of the Nel-Mara*' uttered in some time. Talk about annoying...

"Hah! Better get used to it if we're going into an An-Mara-friendly zone," Idys chimed. "They're all about that nonsense out here."

"Yeah, they are," Morey interjected. "Which is why you all should temper your comedy. I've enjoyed my time on this trip, but I can't believe the Arcaneum is ordaining *twelve* jokers with this mission…"

Morey was right. They needed to get serious; they were only moments from docking. But he could've been a little more respectful, considering Riesen technically outranked him.

"We should listen to Morey — he has more experience than any of us. Let's shape up, starting now," Riesen commanded. He didn't completely concede to the man, however — he offered a playful grin to his companions to let them know he was still on their side.

The others grumbled their assents, though he could still hear some chuckles though the dark.

"Seriously, though" Rush said, "is this place as bad as they say?"

"It's not that bad," Idys replied. "I mean compared to Trevi Nali, obviously. But it's not any worse than Samarind, to be honest. A little darker, perhaps."

"I'd say it's worse," Eagane grunted. "A lot worse."

"Well you grew up on Trevi Nali," Jeriane retorted. "Anything that's not *that* is like a garbage dump to you."

More chuckles.

"And you're not from Trevi Nali?" Eagane shot back.

"I never said I didn't think the place is a dump." Jeriane grinned back, holding his nose high in the air the way Trevi Nali natives did.

"Arrogant chums," Rush commented under his breath.

"You're one to talk, Fils," Morey snorted, as Rush flashed a wide smile to the others.

"Right?" Eagane agreed. "I'll never understand how their planet ever produced some of the most egotistical people I know."

"Hey now!" Riesen protested. "Don't lump me into that!"

Silence. Then laughs.

What the blazes? They didn't think he was conceited, *did they*?

Riesen laughed along with everyone, as he would never be the end of any joke, but this bothered him. He didn't think he was arrogant at all. Confident, self-assured, assertive… sure. But cocky?!… He *knew* he wasn't cocky.

Whatever.

His mind was taken off the matter as he glanced out the window, to where the biggest space station he'd ever laid eyes on dominated the entire view. As far as the Capital system space stations went, Port Jeheddon was second only to Port Saries in sheer volume. Unlike the numerous smaller ports that were perched in their orbits above Trevi Nali and Samarind, only one served the entire Jeheddon system, so it made sense that it was built on such a massive scale.

Several minutes passed in weightlessness as they drifted to their destination, the ring so large that it ballooned out of sight once they got close enough. All the while, the crew continued lobbing hilarious insults at each other, despite Riesen's command to pipe down. It wasn't worth shutting them down at this point. A happy crew was worth far more than a pissed off one. That's what the Valanse commanders always said.

"Woahhh!" Jeriane shouted, exaggerating disorientation as the ship's docking maneuvers suddenly engaged. Their weight was pressed into the floor once more, before they were released just as quickly, sending their stomachs into their throats. "Morey, what the Hole?! What'd you program this thing to do?!"

Jeriane may have been jesting, but the docking process *was* wobblier than normal. The alternating positive forces and airtime moments felt like those railcoasters back on Trevi Nali. Every time the force would shift, shrieks and 'woah's' rang out across the deck to tease Morey, since he was the primary pilot.

Riesen could see him shaking his head through the docking process, though he thought there was a small hint of a smile on the edge of his jaw.

Finally, after about a minute of the wild ride, the ship reverberated with a thud, signaling the docking had completed. A wave of cheers and laughter swept throughout the equilibrium deck.

"We made it!"

"We aren't dead!"

"Wait, we didn't crash?!"

"Good thing we didn't ride that one out of our seats like Fils wanted!"

"Are you so certain we didn't?! It sure felt like we did!"

The Valanses gave Morey no breaks, egging each other on with each successive roast. Eagane, however, was less than amused.

"That could've been smoother," he muttered.

"Don't act like it's my fault," Morey defended. "That's how this place always is."

"Suuuure it is," Jeriane tormented him.

"Oh, don't give me that. You've been here before — you know they don't have the proper machine power to update the trajectories continuously."

"That's for sure," Eagane breathed. "This place is nothing but a low society stain on the Capital system."

"Even Daness?" Rush asked. "I've heard that place is nice."

"You heard wrong," Eagane said.

Jeriane just laughed as he unfastened his seatstraps, putting on a mock show of dizziness as he staggered to his feet.

"Like I said…" Eagane drawled. "Welcome to Jeheddon."

As much as they complained about this place, though, an atmosphere of excitement hung thick in the air. It was their first mission on their own as full-fledged Valanses, and everyone felt it. The eleven others in Riesen's team sprang up, slinging their packs over their shoulders while they clustered eagerly at the airlock doors.

After only a few seconds, the doors hissed open and Riesen's gaze pierced across to the other side of the airlock tunnel. Lounging against the wall on the other side, amidst the backdrop of a bustling space station, was a man.

The hairs bristled on the back of Riesen's neck.

The man was *An-Mara*.

———————————

2

Preview

WAS this a joke? Was their contact really an *An-Mara*?

The disgust welled up in Riesen's throat. All those memories of his homeworld, his family, his friends... They all came crashing down at once, slamming into him with the force of a thousand sols.

"Welcome to Port Jeheddon," the man said. "I am the one called Ala Maza-Thon."

Riesen appraised him coldly, not bothering to hold his arm out in the typical Meridian greeting. The man probably wouldn't accept anyway, being An-Mara and all.

"Riesen Ryen," he responded.

"Well met. I am here to liaise under the direction of the one called Feryl Atain. He bade me deliver information to you lot."

"Why is Atain dealing with the likes of the An-Mara?" Idys blurted out to no one in particular. Riesen had the same question, as surely they all did.

"I am of the An-Mara no longer," Ala Maza-Thon clarified, his gaze calm. "I only seek to balance previous transgressions on behalf of that people."

"By doing what, exactly?" Riesen demanded.

"By delivering information, to start." Ala's eyes darted between Riesen and his eleven companions, none of which seemed enthused to deal with this man — this An-Mara *defector*, apparently.

"Fine, then. Out with it."

If Riesen's frigid tone bothered him, Ala didn't show it. "In my experience residing among the Jeheddon system, I find the primary hotbed of An-Mara sympathizers to exist on Daness. True, it is generally an upscale Meridian world, but you will find it has become rotted from the inside out with An-Mara sympathy."

"And what of the actual An-Mara?" Riesen asked. "Where're they?"

"I do not believe there are any who exist out here..."

"*You* exist out here," Riesen interrupted, his tongue sharp.

Ala stared back at Riesen for a moment before continuing. "Let me rephrase... I do not believe there are *many* who exist out here. And if there are, it is in extremely small numbers, such that they have not coalesced into a faction."

Good news.

"Let's say that's true," Riesen probed. "We go to Daness... then look for what, exactly?"

"That is for you to decide," Ala sighed. "If what I knew was so valuable to the one called Feryl Atain, there would be no necessity for your mission."

"Watch your tone," Riesen warned. "If that is truly all you know, then there is not much necessity for *you*."

The veiled hint of disposing of the man was harsh, Riesen realized. He should temper himself, for the sake of their mission.

He drew a cleansing breath, continuing on more tactfully. "Isn't there *anything* you can give us? Hints of who to look for? Cities to visit? Locales within those cities to devote our efforts?"

"I regret that I am unable to provide names of specific culprits, for there are none. This movement of An-Mara sympathy does not begin with one person, but is rather a living entity in itself, woven seamlessly among the people." Ala paused. "However, I would suggest you familiarize yourself with the Kotoroan district in Emyriss, capital city on Daness. That is the place where knowledge may be traded, if there is any to be had."

"Kotoroa?" Eagane recoiled. "You would send us there?!"

Riesen held up a hand, silencing Eagane.

"He means to send us into a trap!" Eagane protested. "Everyone knows that Kotoro…"

"We are *Valanses*, Melase," Riesen snapped, clenching his jaw tight. "We go where we please. There is nowhere in the Capital system, nor anywhere else in the sector, that is off-limits to us."

Eagane Melase knew better… What had gotten into the man? Valanses bickering with each other like Ossion schoolchildren was completely unacceptable, as was shirking from duties. This was *not* who they were. If anyone else saw such a display of indecision and weakness, it could hamstring their entire effort. Besides, what could be so bad about this Kotoroan district that they couldn't handle?

The others shifted their weight uncomfortably, still carrying their packs, half of them still standing in the airlock.

To his credit, Eagane comprehended his error and clamped his mouth shut.

"Thank you for the information," Riesen said to Ala, pretending Eagane's outburst never happened. "We will start at Kotoroa."

Ala bowed. "I am content to deliver su…"

"That is all." Riesen cut him off, turning to stride past Ala imperiously, before the man caught him by the elbow.

What in the blazes-accursed Hole…

Who did this man — this *An-Mara chum* — think he was?! How *dare* he touch a Valanse of the Meridian Empire…

Riesen slowly glanced at his elbow without tilting his head a single centimeter. The man let go at the unspoken threat, but not before pulling in close to Riesen.

"I do sense some hostility towards myself, Riesen Ryen," Ala whispered. "While I do not blame you for your reluctance to engage with the An-Mara, it is my hope that you will understand that I am no longer one of them. I may speak and dress as such, but on no occasion will I ever be party to their genocide again. For what the An-Mara did to your people, I have splintered from the Time and do not follow its ways any longer. I hold no allegiance, no respect, no love for the An-Mara."

Riesen stared him down for several long seconds, before nodding ever-so-slightly in acknowledgement. He would never trust another An-Mara for the rest of his life — that much was certain — but at least the man *said* all the right things.

If he wasn't lying…

Which he probably was, considering that's all those blazes

chums were known for. Seriously, how could Atain keep a man like this in his employ?!

"We will investigate this lead," he said, "if you can call it that. If it turns out to be fruitful, you have my appreciation."

Ala bowed to Riesen, sidestepping to allow the procession of young Valanses to pass into the station beyond.

———————

Riesen's senses were on heightened alert in this unfamiliar environment. This place didn't even feel like a space station. The wheel of Port Jeheddon was so enormous that it gave the impression of standing on flat ground.

He drifted his gaze across the concourse, allowing the setting to wash over him. At a transit kiosk to his left, a young couple begged a stubborn clerk to let them pass; behind them, two unruly youths chased a smaller boy down a corridor; and from a corner stall at the food court came the warm, greasy smell of a fried dish.

Still, nothing truly shook his mind free from his dealings with the blazes An-Mara just minutes ago, even as his eye caught the bulbous, striped body of Jeheddon looming through the windows in the distance, suspended against the blackness of space like some sort of magnificent painting.

"Riesen, you *know* the Empire doesn't provide the numbers to deal with disputes in the Jeheddon system anymore," Idys challenged, now that they were out of earshot of others. "Not since the mines have been depleted. It's not the safe haven that you might be expecting."

"Maybe we can change that. You don't need numbers to exact control; you only need a handful of Valanses to show their presence, to show the Empire's commitment. If the people here see a team of Valanses mingling with the people, keeping streets safe, the whole system will shape up, and quickly. You'll see."

"Maybe." Idys and the others shared skeptical glances.

"Just walk around like we belong here, and we will." That was the best advice he could offer. After all, that's what Feryl Atain had told him many times during his years of training. "Everyone go get some food or something. Practice fitting in. Meet back here in twenty minutes."

"I still don't think it's a good idea to be romping around Kotoroa," Eagane said, fidgeting with the straps on his pack. "I've heard stories of t..."

"You've been there yourself?" Riesen pressed.

"I've been to Emyriss several times..." he replied.

"To Kotoroa, specifically?"

Eagane went silent for a few seconds, before sucking in a deep breath. "No. But it's somewh..."

"Then you don't have any leverage against my decision," Riesen decided. "No disrespect intended, but *I* have been given command of these decisions. Don't get me wrong, they're decisions I mean to include everyone in, but *not* so long as there will be pushback against following the *one lead* that we have."

"I just don't trust a word that An-Mara pile of filth says," Eagane said. "He called Daness an *'upscale Meridian world'*."

Jeriane barked a laugh. "Indeed. That might have been the most ridiculous part of his whole spiel."

Idys joined him in derision. "I can't *believe* they expect us to follow the word of an An-Mara..."

"An An-Mara traitor, no less," Rush chimed in. "If there was anything worse than an An-Mara, that would be it."

Idys laughed. "That would be it," she echoed.

The other Valanses added their assessments of Ala, none of them friendly. Riesen agreed with everyone, but the conversation was being steered in an unproductive manner.

"Of everyone here, I would say I have the most against the An-Mara," Riesen claimed. "But two things... One — I am inclined to believe the man about Kotoroa. Don't ask me why; it's just a feeling I have. And two — we really have no choice but to follow. It's the *only* lead we have."

A murmur of uncertainty passed through the group, but no one voiced outright objection, until Eagane stepped forward, opening his mouth to say something.

"Riesen is right." It wasn't Eagane who had spoken, though — it was Molly Ferrugan. She was normally a woman of few words, but when she did speak, her words carried weight. "We follow the lead."

Riesen had always been a little wary around her. Not

intimidated, just… wary. She was dreadfully serious at all times, but was an undeniably promising Sentinel. Over their years in training, she had pushed his own limits to the brink on several occasions. Of course, he never lost to her in any manner of competition, but he would admit that she was one of his main challengers.

After she had said her piece, she shoved by without making eye contact, her red hair falling to the side, only kept out of her face by the signature black headband of the Valanses.

For blazes' sakes, he told her to *not* wear anything that gave them away as Valanses… He had told all of them! Though, he wasn't about ready to come to conflict with her over a damn headband, especially not when she took his side just now.

"Oh, so everyone will listen to the Ossion woman, but not to reason?" Eagane muttered to himself. He gave Riesen no chance to respond before whirling off to find food himself.

Riesen filled his lungs with a retort, but decided to let it go. He didn't need to explain himself. They were going to follow the lead and that was his final decision.

"Twenty minutes," Riesen repeated, gesturing to the rest of his team. "Meet back here."

Everyone scurried off, half nodding to him, half staring into the distance with downturned faces.

"Care for the company?" Rush asked after everyone else had left.

Riesen shook his head. "I need to find a damn washroom. But I'll be back. We can talk then."

"Sure thing." Rush then clicked his heels and headed over toward the cluster of food stalls, Idys chasing after him.

Riesen chuckled. Those two always pretended that they weren't a thing, but everyone knew better — their on again, off again involvement had been going on for the better part of five years. Riesen couldn't care less, though, so long as it didn't interfere with their mission.

He breathed deeply through his nose, then set about on a stroll to clear his head. He didn't really need to use the washroom; he just needed some time to think. And to acquaint himself with the happenings around Jeheddon, if this was where the next several weeks of his life would be spent.

He turned to the right, but too sharply, for a wave of dizziness hit him.

Strange.

That never happened on the other stations, or at least not as bad. Maybe it was the discrepancy between what his eyes told him versus what his body felt. The corridor *appeared* to be flat, with only the smallest hint of an incline, yet SGL was simulated by rotation, just like any other station, so that spin-induced force was still very much at play. At least on those other stations, he expected that feeling. Here, the illusion caught him off guard.

He was fine, though. He clenched his jaw, steadied himself, then sauntered down the hallway into the next big room, eavesdropping on conversations as he made his way further into the station.

Against a wall near him, a couple argued about what time their shuttle to Ausur was departing. Nearby, another family was playing a game of Providence Six. To their left, a group of young men looked to be competing at a drinking game, downing their liquor with reckless abandon. Next to them were two elderly ladies staring into space, probably too engaged in their Uts to notice anything else. All up and down the hall, it was more of the same — and nothing that he wouldn't see at any other station he'd ever been to. Even the dress of the people was the same.

The only major difference was that there were *so* many people on this station! Tens of thousands, at least. He couldn't believe this planet had *this* much traffic. He'd always learned that Jeheddon was a dying outpost, more or less. What was once a center of bustling industry was now relegated to second-class residential provinces, after the moons had been depleted of their valuable ores.

Riesen wove his way throughout the crowds, indistinguishable from the other travelers as he wore nothing that gave himself away as a Valanse. For good measure, he pulled his hood on. His unusual golden hair was wildly out of place here, a telltale sign that he was not from around these orbits. Not from anywhere in the Capital system, even. He supposed no one would really care — these people all had lives of their own that were far more important than worrying about the color of strangers' hair — but it was best to be cautious.

He passed into room after room, until he felt a tug on the threads of his mind. He nearly stopped at his own surprise, but forced his steps into automated cadence, focusing his attention the way he'd been instructed the last few years.

He likened the tug to a stream of music, one that would ring louder as he tracked it to the source. He followed it under a low-hanging metallic archway, then around a marketplace bend, where his eyes were instantly drawn to two women who stood in a shadowy alcove off to the side.

What could possibly be th...

His internal alarms sounded when he realized just who these people were.

An-Mara.

And meeting *together.* What was *this* all about?

He nearly spat in disgust over the fact that he had to share air with these people. How could they get away with destroying an entire planet without any semblance of justice? The Meridians on Trevi Nali had always promised him that they would answer for what they'd done, but nothing substantial had yet come to fruition.

At least there were influential figures like Silvane and Morgan, among others, committed to his cause. Societal opinion was turning, and for the better. Maybe one day soon, the Emperor would actually do something decisive about the An-Mara problem. Riesen needed their entire civilization gone once and for all, and that day couldn't come soon enough.

The women stopped talking and looked in his direction.

Without being conspicuous, he stumbled his way into an empty seat not four paces away, then started rifling through some items in his pack, pretending to count belongings for his upcoming journey, or whatever. That should be an activity commonplace in this travel hub, right?

The ruse seemed to work, because the two An-Mara chums carried on their discussion once he appeared to be just another preoccupied traveler.

"As I had indicated," one of the women whispered, "this is not the appropriate time for a reunion of such scale. You must respect the wishes of the Conclave."

Everything about them — their voices, their accents, their slow and proper speech — it all grated on his soul like Lanthanide deposits being crushed through a grinder. The way they thought themselves so superior, the way they acted so righteous, like everyone else was in the wrong... He hated it.

He hated *them* for what they did to his homeworld. But really, their annoying existence was the only justification he needed for such disdain.

The Conclave, though…

What was this about? This was the first he'd heard of it.

"I do agree with that assessment, Vin-Turon, but I also believe that we have waited long enough."

Riesen paused.

I know that voice… he thought. Where did he recognize it from?

It was probably nothing. He honestly could've heard it anywhere, he admitted; he'd had the misfortune of meeting many An-Mara over the years. Besides, the woman was cloaked, so he wouldn't know if he'd seen her before. It mattered little anyway; they were all the same to him — self-important, murderous, good-for-nothing chums.

"The duration of *your* waiting is not of our principal concern," the woman asserted. Vin-Turon, he supposed her name was.

"If the Conclave had any sense, you should be," the other woman — the familiar one — replied indignantly.

Riesen bit the insides of his lip in revulsion. The haughty, *haughty* tone of these women were enough to drive him insane, but he remained calm and cool, inspecting his luggage as if he were just another ordinary wayfarer, seeking passage to whichever destination he claimed.

"You do *not* get to make that assertion," Vin-Turon hissed. "Not you. Not after all these years."

The cloaked woman shrugged. "Make that judgment at your own expense. There may never again come a time when the Conclave has a chance to recruit so many capable individuals to its mission." The woman lowered her voice, realizing that there were others in earshot. "I dare not make mention of who is in our company. Not here. But these individuals I speak of… they are *exceptional*. And willing to take up the cause. And there are many others who would rally to our interests, if such a campaign were initiated."

Riesen's gut twisted in on itself, attempting to squeeze the air from his lungs. It was all he could do to maintain stoicism.

This was wrong. This was all wrong.

Ala had led him to believe that…. what was it he said? That there were no An-Mara in sufficient numbers to form a '*faction*'? This whole Conclave business sounded very much like a faction. One that needed to be put down.

Vin-Turon leaned in closer to the woman with the familiar

voice. "The rumors are true then?"

The cloaked woman only nodded in return, causing Vin-Turon to reel back and exhale.

"Begone, then," she commanded. "Return to Ausur. I shall inform the Conclave of your requests, but do not deign to expect a response for several days. You may be contacted by another agent beforehand, but perhaps not. We shall see. I fear this system is becoming... monitored. Too many watchful eyes, too many listening ears."

Riesen didn't dare look up, but he knew the woman's gaze passed straight over him. If she suspected anything, however, she gave no sign of it.

"I would convey gratitude for your relay," the woman with the familiar voice said, bowing in that repulsive An-Mara fashion. "Fare well until we meet again, Vin-Turon."

Vin-Turon nodded. "Fare well, Kira-Tharn."

ABOUT THE AUTHOR

C. J. Yee was born, raised, and currently resides in Santa Barbara County, California. Yee has a degree in the earth sciences, but has many interests, with special passions for astronomy, history, and anything to do with the natural world.

Reach out or follow Yee at:

cjyee.books@gmail.com
instagram.com/cjyee.books